He s   r, that   aroused him.

he stood in the doorway of his room. "Maggie?" he said softly.

"I'm looking for a nice Southern gentleman named Jackson," she said, her voice slightly husky.

That would be me," he replied, his chest suddenly tight with anticipation.

"I thought you might be interested in a night with a woman who isn't looking for anything more than this night and this night only."

"Maggie…" He said her name with hesitation. Man, he wanted her. He thought he might even need her. But he knew things she didn't know, things that would forever stand between them and make any future impossible.

SCENE OF THE CRIME: RETURN TO MYSTIC LAKE

BY
CARLA CASSIDY

Published in Great Britain 2014
by Mills & Boon, an imprint of Harlequin (UK) Limited,
Eton House, 18-24 Paradise Road, Richmond, Surrey, TW9 1SR

© 2014 Carla Bracale

ISBN: 978 0 263 91358 3

46-0514

Harlequin (UK) Limited's policy is to use papers that are natural, renewable and recyclable products and made from wood grown in sustainable forests. The logging and manufacturing processes conform to the legal environmental regulations of the country of origin.

Printed and bound in Spain
by Blackprint CPI, Barcelona

New York Times bestselling author **Carla Cassidy** is an award-winning author who has written more than fifty novels for Mills & Boon. In 1995, she won Best Silhouette Romance from *RT Book Reviews* for *Anything for Danny*. In 1998, she also won a Career Achievement Award for Best Innovative Series from *RT Book Reviews*.

Carla believes the only thing better than curling up with a good book to read is sitting down at the computer with a good story to write. She's looking forward to writing many more books and bringing hours of pleasure to readers.

Chapter One

Jackson Revannaugh knew he was in the land of Oz when the jet touched down in the middle of a patch-work of farmers' fields. Nowhere near the Kansas City International Airport did he see any signs of a city.

It was already after 7:00 p.m. and he was eager to get off the plane. The flight from Baton Rouge had been over three hours long, and not only had a baby cried the entire trip, but the kid behind him had seemed to find great amusement in kicking the back of Jackson's seat at regular intervals.

Jackson was working up to a stellar foul mood. Too little sleep in the past couple weeks, a long ride in cramped quarters and a bag of pretzels as his only food for the past eight hours or so had made Jackson a cranky man.

Thankfully, it took him only minutes to deplane. From the overhead bin he grabbed the large duffel bag that held everything he would need for the duration of his stay in Kansas City, Missouri. He then headed down the walkway toward the terminal entrance.

Just ahead of him were double doors that led outside the building. As he exited, Jackson realized that the humid mid-July heat of the Midwest had nothing on

Bachelor Moon, Louisiana, where he'd spent the past several weeks of his life working on the case of a missing man, his wife and his seven-year-old stepdaughter.

He'd been yanked from that case before they'd had any answers and sent directly here to work on something similar. He stepped to the edge of the curb and fought the exhaustion that, over the past month, had settled on his shoulders like a heavy weight.

He'd been told a car would pick him up to take him to the small town of Mystic Lake, a thirty-minute drive from Kansas City. But he hadn't been told specifically what kind of a car to look for.

What he'd like right about now was a big, juicy steak, a tall glass of bourbon, a ride to the nearest posh hotel for fluffy bath towels, a king-size bed and about twelve hours of uninterrupted sleep.

Instead he stepped to the curb with a frown and the knowledge that it was probably going to be a long night and he wasn't at the top of his game.

He had been given no details about whatever crime had taken place here; he knew only that he was to work with a partner from the Kansas City FBI field office.

Now if he could just find his ride, he could, sooner rather than later, solve the crime and be on his way back out of town and home to his luxury apartment in Baton Rouge.

He stepped back from the curb as a large blue bus pulled to the curb and belched a whoosh of hot exhaust. The doors swung open and for a brief moment Jackson wondered if he was supposed to get on the bus, but that didn't make any sense.

When he'd spoken briefly on the phone earlier to Director Daniel Forbes of the Kansas City field office, he'd told Jackson to stand on the curb outside the luggage area of Terminal A and a car would be waiting.

He remained standing, tamping down an edge of new irritation. Where was the car? His plane had been right on time.

When the bus finally pulled away, a black sedan slid next to the curb. A petite woman with shoulder-length strawberry-blond curls and eyes the green of a Louisiana swamp opened the driver door and stood.

If there was one thing that could transform Jackson from a grouch to a gentleman, it was the sight of an attractive woman. God, he loved women.

"Agent Revannaugh?" she asked.

"That would be me," he replied. He opened the back door and tossed his duffel bag onto the seat and then got into the passenger seat.

She got back behind the steering wheel, bringing with her the scent of honeysuckle and spice. Clad in a pair of tight black slacks and a short-sleeved white blouse that hugged her breasts and emphasized a slender waist, she was definitely a hum of pleasure in Jackson's overworked brain.

As she swept her hair behind one ear, he noted what appeared to be a nice-sized emerald earring. Emeralds were a good choice for her, with her green eyes.

"Well, I feel my mood lifting already," he said as she pulled away from the curb and into the traffic lane that would take them away from the airport terminal. "Darlin', I wasn't expecting my driver to be such a gorgeous piece of eye candy. What a nice welcome to Kansas City." As usual when Jackson worked his charm, his Southern accent grew thicker and more distinct.

She slid him a quick, cool glance and then focused back on the road. "You just assume I'm nothing but your driver because I'm a woman? Hmm, not only a silly flirt, but a chauvinist, as well," she replied. "I haven't had a chance to introduce myself yet. I'm Special Agent Marjorie Clinton, lead investigator on this case. You'll be working with me and you'll quickly discover I'm not anyone's 'darlin.'"

Jackson sat up straighter in his chair, seeking a mental shovel to get out of the hole he'd already dug for himself. "I'm not a chauvinist," he finally said. "I was told a driver would pick me up—I just assumed you were my driver and nothing more. And you might not be anyone's darlin', but you're definitely a fine piece of eye candy."

He watched her slender, ringless fingers tighten on the steering wheel and realized he'd just made the hole a little bigger. "Since it appears we're going to be partners, perhaps it would be nice if we start all over again. Hello, I'm Special Agent Jackson Revannaugh."

Once again those lush green eyes slid in his direction and then back to the road. "We're about twenty minutes from Mystic Lake, a small town on the outskirts of Kansas City. I suggest we use that twenty minutes with me filling you in on things rather than pretending to play nice together. How much do you know about the case?"

"Virtually nothing," Jackson admitted. She might look like a hot piece of work, but there was nothing hot in the cool disdain in her eyes when she glanced at him. *Focus on the work and then get the heck out of Dodge,* he thought.

"I was pulled off a case I was working in Bachelor

Moon, Louisiana, and instantly dispatched here with no details other than the fact that this case appears to have some similarity to the one I was working."

"Missing persons?" She turned off a four-lane highway and onto a two-lane that appeared to take them farther away from civilization.

"Three people seemingly disappeared into thin air at some point during an evening. Evidence of an interrupted late-night snack was on the table, but the two adults and one child have yet to be found. Me and a couple of my partners were on the case for several weeks and we found no clues, no real leads to follow."

He took the opportunity to study her. Faint freckles, evident in the fading light of day, smattered the bridge of her nose. He had a feeling she wasn't a woman who smiled often, although he knew instinctively that a smile would light up her face, warm her features into something even more beautiful.

"We have two missing persons, but unfortunately we don't have a specific time line as to when exactly they went missing. The couple, Amberly Caldwell and her husband, Cole, were newlyweds, and were transitioning between Cole's house in Mystic Lake and Amberly's home in Kansas City."

She stopped talking and slowed to make a right-hand turn, and then continued. "Amberly has a son, Max. The boy had spent the weekend with his father, John Merriweather. The arrangement was that Amberly would pick up Max from school yesterday afternoon. When she didn't show up, John got worried and drove to Cole's place."

"But they weren't there."

Marjorie gave a curt nod of her head. "Both of their

cars were in the driveway, but he couldn't rouse them. Unfortunately, the deputy who had been called out made the determination that it would be best to give it twenty-four hours before officially doing anything."

"He didn't do a well-check?" Jackson asked in surprise. A well-check would have required an officer to get inside the house to make certain the occupants were okay.

"Small police force, underzealous officers and two people who aren't old or sick." Her voice once again held a faint touch of derision. "It was only late this afternoon that an officer finally broke into the front door and discovered that things weren't right inside. That's when my director got a phone call from Roger Black, Mystic Lake's number one deputy. Apparently our director knew what was going on in Louisiana, and that's when you were dispatched here."

"I've heard there's nothing better than Kansas City steaks, and my first impression of the women of the city is definitely a positive one." He couldn't help himself. Part of the way he prepared himself, part of his process in approaching a crime, was to small talk, to attempt to get on the good side of whoever he'd be working with during the course of an investigation.

Marjorie shot him a baleful look. Apparently she didn't have a good side, he thought, as he sighed and stared out the passenger window, where the landscape was so different from what he was accustomed to.

Here there were stately oaks and leafy maples, stretches of fields with cornstalks reaching high. There were no graceful magnolia trees or cypresses with Spanish moss hanging like ghostly spiderwebs.

Jackson had never been out of Louisiana before.

Kansas City would have to work hard to match the beauty and charm of his home state.

Speaking of charm, he turned his head to look at Marjorie. "Have you already been to the scene?"

"I came from there to pick you up," she replied. "We've just done a cursory walk-through of the house. The crime scene unit hasn't touched it. Nobody else has been inside except me and a couple of the Mystic Lake deputies. We were waiting for the hotshot from Louisiana to officially begin."

"And that would be me," he replied easily. "So, what did the initial walk-through tell you?"

"I'd rather you draw your own conclusions by seeing it first. I can tell you this—the doors were all locked and there is no sign of forced entry anywhere."

"Tell me more about the potential victims. Who they are and what they do." A victim rundown was usually as helpful as an official profile of the potential perpetrator.

"Cole Caldwell, thirty-six years old. He and Amberly married less than two months ago. She's thirty-one, has a seven-year-old son and is a beautiful Native American woman. Apparently the two of them had been spending weekends packing up Caldwell's place and getting his house ready to put on the market, as they'd decided to live full-time in Amberly's home in Kansas City."

Her voice was pleasant, but her tone was all business. "Amberly shares custody of Max with her ex-husband, who lives down the block from her house. They had an arrangement that worked well for everyone involved."

"You never told me what each of them does for a living," Jackson asked.

"Cole Caldwell is the sheriff of Mystic Lake." She turned into the driveway of an attractive ranch house where several other Mystic Lake patrol cars were parked. She pulled up next to the curb, cut the engine and then turned to face Jackson.

For the first time a hint of emotion darkened her green eyes. "Amberly works with me. She is one of the brightest FBI profilers in the area."

Jackson's stomach gave an unpleasant lurch. "That's odd. The case I was investigating in Bachelor Moon involved a man named Sam Connelly, a retired FBI profiler from the Kansas City office."

MARJORIE HAD BEEN SICK from the moment she'd realized that one of the missing persons was Amberly. Although the two women hadn't been superclose friends and had never worked a case together, they'd been friendly. Everyone in the office was on edge due to this new development.

She was grateful to get out of the car, where the scent of Jackson Revannaugh's cologne had been far too pleasant. It whispered of bold maleness and an exotic spiciness that could be intoxicating if allowed.

She didn't like him. She knew his type…the hotshot Southern charmer who never met a woman he wouldn't take advantage of, who skated through life on a lazy smile and smooth style.

Oh, yes, she knew his type intimately, and she wasn't about to fall prey to his questionable charisma. All she wanted was for the two of them to work as hard as possible to get Amberly and Cole back where they belonged.

Deputy Fred Morsi stood at the door as sentry. "Nobody has been inside since you left," he said to Marjorie, as if assuring her he'd done his job properly.

He was one of the first locals Marjorie had met when she'd arrived on scene, and he'd instantly impressed her with his earnest face and professional attitude.

Marjorie nodded and grabbed a pair of booties from a box sitting on the front porch. As she pulled them on over her black sneakers, she noticed Jackson doing the same over his expensive-looking leather shoes. He grabbed a pair of latex gloves, his easy smile gone and his mouth set in a grim line instead.

So, there was another side to the hot Mr. Southern Charm, she thought. She frowned as she realized she'd just thought of Jackson Revannaugh as hot.

Of course, she was certain most women would find him a hunk, with his slightly long, slightly curly black hair and blue eyes, with chiseled features and a mouth that looked soft and pliable. She stifled a yelp as the latex of her glove snapped her wrist.

"Shall we?" she said to the tall, broad-shouldered man who was her temporary partner. She gestured to the closed front door.

"After you, darlin'," he replied, and then winced. "I didn't mean that…. Force of habit."

The front door opened into a small formal living room. The only pieces of furniture were a couple of end tables and a stack of large boxes. Jackson stopped just inside the door behind Marjorie.

His dark blue eyes narrowed and he lifted his

head, like a wild animal sniffing the air for prey. "No evidence that anything happened in this room?"

"Nothing," she replied. The small formal living room opened into a large great-room/kitchen area. Here was the evidence that something unusual had taken place.

She followed Jackson's gaze as it traveled around the room, taking in the oversize pillows on the floor in front of a coffee table that held two half-empty wineglasses and a platter of hardened, too-yellow cheddar cheese, crackers, and grapes starting to wither and emanate a slightly spoiled scent.

Jackson picked up one of the long-stem glasses and sniffed the contents. "Fruity... I smell a touch of cherry and plum and a faint dash of damp leather. Pinot noir would be my guess." He set the glass back on the table as Marjorie stared at him in astonishment.

"There's a bottle of pinot noir open on the kitchen counter," she replied in surprise.

Jackson nodded. "Like a good Southern gentleman, I know my wines, although I definitely prefer a good glass of bourbon or brandy, and preferably with a lovely lady by my side."

"But, of course," she replied dryly.

He frowned at the coffee table. "So, it appears our two missing souls were seated here sharing what appears to be cocktail time together."

"And something happened to interrupt their intimate little party," Marjorie said.

"So it seems." Jackson turned away from the coffee table and his gaze swept around the room. "No sign of a struggle. What have we here?" Nearly hidden at the edge of one of the pillows was a small black purse.

bedroom and she hurried after him. He walked back into the great room and stared at the coffee table and the oversize pillows. "On the surface things look very similar to what I was working on in Bachelor Moon, but it would be a mistake for us to leap to any conclusions this early in the investigation."

"I can take you to Amberly's place now. I have a couple of officers sitting on it so that nothing is disturbed."

Together they stepped outside, where they both removed their booties and gloves. "I'll be honest with you—at the moment what I need is a good meal, a strong drink and a soft bed," Jackson said.

"But we still need to go to Amberly's," Marjorie protested.

"That can wait until morning," Jackson said. "Whatever happened to Sheriff Caldwell and his wife happened here, not at the house in Kansas City. We've got a lot of work ahead of us."

"Exactly," Marjorie replied. "And we need to work through the night if that's what it takes to get to the bottom of this."

"It's going to take more than a single night to get to the bottom of this," Jackson said as he headed for her car.

She hurried after him, irritated by his lack of work ethic. She didn't know how they solved crime in Louisiana, but they sure as heck didn't do it in Kansas City by eating a good steak and finding a soft bed.

"But you know how important the first forty-eight hours are right after a crime," she said as they got into her car.

"I know, but as far as I can figure, we've already

He opened it and pulled out a cell phone, a wallet and a tube of lipstick.

Marjorie's heart tumbled a little lower in her chest as she watched him open up the slender wallet. Inside was Amberly's identification, thirty-two dollars and two credit cards.

"If somebody came in here to confront the two, it wasn't anybody with robbery on their mind," he said, his voice that low Southern drawl that Marjorie found both irritating and evocatively inviting at the same time.

He placed the items back in the purse. "We'll take that phone to your techies at the bureau and see if they can find anything useful. Maybe somebody called and the two of them rushed out of here on an emergency."

"Amberly would have let John know," Marjorie replied with conviction.

He walked from the coffee table toward the kitchen area, his footsteps surprisingly heavy for a man who appeared so physically fit and agile.

She followed him into the kitchen, where she knew he would find nothing suspicious, nothing that might indicate what exactly had happened to Cole and Amberly.

She leaned a slender hip against the cabinet and watched as he checked the back door, opened drawers and cabinets that were mostly empty. He pulled a small notepad and pen from the pocket of his pristine white shirt and took some notes.

He might be an arrogant, smooth-talking pain in her butt, but he also appeared to be thorough and detail driven, and that was the only thing important to her in this case. Nothing else mattered, as long as he was as good at his job as he looked in his expensive white shirt and the tailored black slacks that fit him to perfection. He wore his gun and holster on a sleek leather belt around his waist, looking both lethal and sexy at the same time.

From the minute she had joined the FBI, nothing had mattered but the job and caretaking for her mother. This particular case hit too close to home, with a fellow FBI agent gone missing.

"Let's take a look at the rest of the house," he finally said when he'd finished checking out the kitchen.

"There isn't much here. Two bedrooms have already been emptied of all the furniture, and there's just a bed and a dresser left in the master suite."

His footsteps thundered down the hallway, and he peeked into each room as they passed, finally stopping just inside the master bedroom.

"Smart man," he said as he gazed at the bed with the navy bedspread. "He's moved most of the furniture out but left a spot for foreplay in the family room and the bed to complete the night." He turned to look at Marjorie and she was horrified to feel a warmth steal into her cheeks. Thank goodness he didn't mention it.

"So, Amberly and Cole came here Friday night to pack things away, and Monday afternoon she didn't show up to pick up her kid from school," he continued. "Do you know if anyone spoke to either of them between those times?" he asked.

"When I left here to pick you up at the airport I had a couple of deputies and another FBI agent canvassing the neighborhood to find out the last time either of them was seen."

She pulled her cell phone out of her pocket and punched in a number. "Adam. Any news?" S[he] tened to the report, acutely aware of Jackson['s] taking her in from head to toe.

The temperature inside the house was a com[fort]able one for the heat of the night, but as her new [part]ner's gaze slid down the length of her, she fel[t the] atmosphere in the room climb at least ten deg[rees] warmer.

"Thanks," she said to FBI agent Adam Forest, a[nd] then hung up. "According to what the officers ha[ve] been able to find out for now, the next-door neig[h]bor, Charles Baker, saw Cole and Amberly arrive he[re] just after five on Friday night. About seven that sam[e] night he saw Cole again when he mowed the lawn. Nobody saw either of them after that…at least that we've talked to so far."

She watched him open the top drawer of the dresser. She hadn't had a chance to check things out this thoroughly before leaving the scene earlier to pick him up at the airport.

"Unless Sheriff Cole Caldwell is an unusual ma[n] for a sheriff, he didn't leave here of his own volition." He pulled a handgun from the drawer, along with [a] gold badge. "No sheriff I know would take off with[out] out his weapon and the very thing that defines him."

Every muscle in Marjorie's body tensed at the sig[ht] of the items. She'd hoped that this was all some kin[d] of a mistake, that little Max and his father had som[e]how misunderstood, and Cole and Amberly had go[ne] off for a mini-honeymoon.

"So, is this like what you were working on in Ba[ch]elor Moon?" she asked Jackson.

"Too early for me to make that jump." He left [the]

lost our first forty-eight-hour window. My gut says they disappeared from here sometime Friday night, and here we are on Tuesday night. Besides, at this point all we have is two people not where they said they would be…nothing to indicate that an actual crime took place at all."

"Trust me, if Amberly told Max she'd pick him up at school yesterday, nothing would have kept her away except something terrible," Marjorie replied. "Max always came first with her."

"Have you checked the local hospitals? Maybe one of them got sick and hasn't had a chance to call." He obviously read on her face that it hadn't been done yet.

"Then that's something you can take care of after you drop me off at whatever place I'm staying while I'm here in town."

"You aren't staying here in Mystic Lake. The director set you up in a motel in Kansas City. Don't worry, there's a restaurant right next door where you can feed your face." She started the engine, fighting a new blast of irritation directed at him.

FBI agents didn't work normal business hours. When in the middle of a case they worked until they physically couldn't work any longer.

To make matters worse, as she began the drive back toward the city, not only did Special Agent Jackson Revannaugh fall asleep, but the car filled with his faint, deep snores.

She was livid that she'd put off beginning the official investigation until this Louisiana man had arrived. She was ticked off that somehow her director thought he could potentially add a valuable perspective on the crime.

As if fate hadn't already delivered enough painful hits in her life, it had now delivered up to her the
partner from hell.

Chapter Two

Jackson shot straight up in bed, his heart beating frantically as early-morning light shone through the half-closed curtains on the nearby window. It took him several minutes to process the nightmares that had haunted his sleep and a little more time to realize exactly where he was.

Kansas City...the Regent Motel. He muttered a curse as he saw the time. Six-thirty, and if he remembered right, Agent Uptight's last words to him after dropping him off the night before were that she'd be here to pick him up at seven.

Coffee. He needed coffee to take away the lingering taste of the nightmares that had chased through his sleep. He spied a small coffeemaker on the vanity and waited for it to brew the single cup. While the coffee was brewing, he unlocked his motel room door just in case Marjorie showed up early.

Once the coffee was ready, he took a big swallow and then carried the cup into the bathroom and set it on the counter while he got into the shower.

He knew Marjorie was angry that he had called a halt to the night before, but he'd also known that he wouldn't be any real asset to her unless he took the night to catch up on some sleep. The case in Bachelor Moon had nearly drained him dry, both physically and mentally, and he'd needed last night to transition, to prepare himself for this new investigation.

At least she'd been right—while the motel wasn't five stars, it was adequate and there was a decent restaurant next door. He'd walked there last night and had enjoyed his first taste of Kansas City barbecue… a pulled-pork sandwich and the best onion rings he'd ever tasted.

Maybe it was the sweet, tangy sauce that had given him the nightmares, he thought as he turned off the water and stepped out of the enclosure.

His dreams had been haunted by Sam Connelly, his wife, Daniella, and their little girl, Macy—the missing family from Bachelor Moon, who had yet to be found. Dashing around the edges of the darkness had been two more figures who he knew in his dream were Cole Caldwell and his wife, Amberly. And then there had been his father.

Jerrod Revannaugh had no place in his dreams, just as he had no place in Jackson's life. The bond between father and son had been fractured long ago and finally completely broken just a little over five years ago.

He shoved away any lingering thoughts of nightmares, especially images of the man who had raised him, and instead wrapped a towel around his waist and got out his shaving kit.

Jackson knew he was a handsome man. It wasn't anything he thought much about, just a fact he saw when he looked in a mirror. He was simply the product of good genes.

He also knew he had a charm about him that drew

women to him, and though he enjoyed an occasional liaison with a sophisticated woman who knew the score, he made certain they also knew he was merely after a brief encounter and not interested in matters of the heart.

He was definitely not his father's son. He might look like Jerrod Revannaugh, and the two men might share the Revannaugh ability to charm, but Jackson would never be the coldhearted bastard that his father had been. He always made sure his partner knew the score, unlike his father who had spent his life taking advantage of naïve women.

While he found his new partner hot to look at, she had a prickly exterior that he had no interest in digging beneath. Besides, it wasn't as if he anticipated Agent Marjorie Clinton jumping his bones. She'd made it fairly clear that she didn't particularly like him and would tolerate him only in order to further the investigation.

He'd managed to razor off the shaving cream on half of his face when he heard a firm knock on his door. A glance at the clock by the nightstand showed him it was ten until seven. He knew she was the type to be early.

"Come on in," he shouted, and heard the door open. He leaned out of the bathroom to see her standing just inside the door. "You're early."

She shot ramrod straight. Her eyes widened and then her gaze instantly dropped to the carpeting, as if unable to look at him. "And it appears that you're going to be late. I'll just wait for you out in the car."

She ran out of the room like a rabbit being chased by a hound dog and slammed the door behind her.

Jackson turned back to the mirror in amusement. He hadn't exactly been naked, but she'd skedaddled out of the room like a virgin.

He quickly finished his shaving, slapped on some cologne, grabbed his white shirt and slacks—neatly pressed the night before and on hangers—and dressed.

He had a feeling the longer she sat in the car waiting for him, the more difficult the mood would be between them. He suspected it was already going to be a long day. Her being cranky with him would only make it longer.

It was exactly three minutes after seven when he slid into the passenger seat of her car and shut the door. "Sorry I'm late. The last thing I would ever want to do is keep a lovely lady waiting," he said with a smile.

"Stuff it, Rhett. I'm uncharmable and you might as well stop trying." She started the car and pulled out of the parking space in front of his unit.

"Why, Scarlett, I haven't even begun to attempt to charm you yet," he replied with his trademark lazy grin.

She frowned. "We have a busy day ahead. We checked all the hospitals last night both here in Kansas City and in Mystic Lake. Cole and Amberly aren't in any of them. I've set up an interview with John Merriweather, Amberly's ex-husband, after nine. He didn't want us at his place until after Max had left for school. I've also directed a couple of agents to check what cases Amberly was working on, and the same with Cole. There are also some other people we need to interview before the day is done. I have a list in my briefcase."

"Wow, you've been a busy little bee while I was getting my beauty sleep."

She ignored his comment and continued, "The crime scene unit worked all night at Cole's house and basically came up with nothing. No fingerprints other than Cole's and Amberly's, and no evidence that anyone else had been in the house."

"That doesn't surprise me. Any chance of breakfast before we get started on this long day you have planned?"

She picked up a white paper bag that was between them on the console and tossed it into his lap. "Two bagels, one blueberry and one cinnamon raisin. I had a feeling you'd ask."

"Gee, I didn't know you cared." He opened up the bag to discover not only the two bagels, but also two small cups of cream cheese and a plastic knife.

"I don't," she replied. "But it appears that your creature comforts are very important to you."

"And your comforts aren't important to you?" he asked as he spread cream cheese over half of the cinnamon raisin bagel.

"Of course they are, but not so much when I'm working on a hot, active case."

"This is already at best a lukewarm case," he replied.

As she had yesterday, she wore a white blouse, a pair of dark slacks and sensible shoes. Her hair was a spill of strawberry silk across her shoulders and she smelled of fresh vanilla and sweet flowers.

She appeared not to be wearing a bit of makeup, but that did nothing to detract from Jackson's physical attraction to her. Chemistry… It was a whimsical animal that usually made a fool out of somebody.

He ate the bagel in four quick bites and wished for another cup of coffee to chase it down. But there was no way he intended to ask her to drive through the nearest coffee shop. He wasn't about to push his luck.

"Last night was more about my survival than creature comforts," he said soberly. "I'd been working non-stop on the case in Louisiana. Yesterday I'd had a plane ride from hell, no food to speak of all day and not enough brain power left to be adequate at my job. This could either be a sprint or a marathon, and I'm betting on a marathon, and so I needed last night to prepare myself for the long haul. Not that I owe you any explanations of my working habits or methods."

He settled back in his seat and stared out the passenger window. "Now, tell me about this John Merriweather," he said, deciding he was far better to focus on solving this crime than imagine what his partner might look like without her clothes.

MARJORIE STOOD JUST INSIDE Amberly's living room, a homey space decorated with pottery and bright colors and woven rugs celebrating her Native American heritage.

The room smelled of sage and sunshine, and it was obvious that a little boy resided here. The bookcases held not only pottery, but also puzzles and children's books about horses and dinosaurs. A large plastic dump truck sat next to the coffee table, the bed filled with tiny army men.

Jackson prowled the room like a well-educated burglar, with booties and gloves to leave no evidence that he'd ever been here. As he moved, she tried not to think about that moment when she'd walked into his motel room and he'd leaned out of the bathroom with just the thin white towel hanging low on his slim hips.

His bare chest, sleekly muscled and bronzed, had been more than magnificent. As she'd gotten that glimpse of it, for a long moment she'd forgotten how to breathe, and she hadn't been able to get the unwanted image out of her head.

He stopped and stared at the large painting above the fireplace. It depicted Amberly as an Indian princess on horseback. Her long dark hair emphasized doe eyes and high cheekbones. She was wild beauty captured on canvas.

Jackson turned to look at Marjorie at the same time she self-consciously shoved a strand of her hair behind an ear. "She's quite beautiful," he said, and then added, with a twinkle in his eyes, "But I much prefer blondes with just a hint of strawberry in their hair."

"Does it just come naturally to you? Kind of like breathing?" she asked sarcastically.

"Yeah, just like breathing," he replied with a genuine grin that warmed her despite her aggravation with him. He turned back to the painting. "Painted by her ex-husband?"

"Yes, John painted it." She'd already told him that John Merriweather was a famous painter who was known for Western settings and beautiful Native American portraits. Most of the Native women he painted looked like his ex-wife. She'd read an article in some magazine where John had talked about how Amberly was his muse.

"How did John take their divorce?" Jackson turned back to look at her.

She shrugged. "According to the local gossip, initially he took it rather hard. But I think they had become more like friends than husband and wife. Amberly once mentioned to me that John's greatest passion was his painting."

Jackson frowned. "I love my work, but I save my passion for living, breathing people."

Women. She knew he meant women. Not that it mattered to her what Jackson Revannaugh's personal passion might be. "Are you married?" The question fell from her lips before it had even formed in her head.

"No, and have no intention of ever getting married. My problem is that I love all women, but I've never found one who I haven't tired of after a week or so."

"So, you are a player," she said, having already suspected as much.

His blue eyes held an open honesty she wasn't sure she could believe. "On the contrary, I only date women who know I'm looking for a passing good time and nothing more serious. I don't toy with hearts or emotions. And now, shall we get back to the case?" He lifted a dark eyebrow wryly.

Heat warmed Marjorie's cheeks in an unmistakable blush. Thankfully he didn't comment on it but rather moved from the living room into the kitchen.

He hadn't even asked her if she was married or if she had a boyfriend. He probably thought she was too much of a witch to hold a man's attention for more than a minute.

She was, and that was the way she wanted it. She had enough on her plate with her job and helping to pay for the fancy apartment where her mother lived and believed she was still a wealthy heiress.

She didn't have time for men. She'd had one brief relationship years ago and he'd turned out to be untrustworthy, as she'd come to believe most men were. She'd been through enough men with her mother, seen what they were capable of, especially the handsome ones full of charm. Nope, she had already decided she'd eventually get a cat, but there would never be a man in the small house where she lived.

Of course, that didn't mean she would never have sex again. Like Jackson, if she did she'd just have to make it clear to her partner that she was a one-night stand—not a forever—kind of woman.

She snapped her attention back to realize Jackson had left the kitchen. It was easy to follow the sound of his heavy footsteps down the hallway to the bedrooms.

Focus on the job, she reprimanded herself, irritated that Jackson had somehow managed to throw her off her normal game, and she'd been working with him less than two hours this morning.

It took them only minutes to check out the bedrooms and return to the living room. "There doesn't appear to be anything here to tie into whatever happened at Cole's house in Mystic Lake," he said. "I think it's time we go talk to John Merriweather."

"He lives less than two blocks away." She checked her watch. It was a quarter after nine. Max would have already left for school and John would be waiting for them.

Within minutes they pulled into the driveway of John Merriweather's neat ranch house. Although John was a respected artist whose work was both expensive and in constant demand, he had remained in the house where he and Amberly had lived as a married couple over five years ago.

"John and Amberly lived here together when they were married," she explained to Jackson. "When they divorced, Amberly bought her house close by so that Max could stay near his father."

"Do they have a court-ordered child custody agreement?" Jackson asked.

"Not that I know of. I think they just winged it and it worked for them."

"We'll see if it was really working out that well, especially when a new man entered the picture," Jackson replied as he got out of the car. "I'll do the interview with him," he said in a clipped tone she hadn't heard before.

She hurried after him, wondering when she'd lost control as lead investigator. She'd allow Jackson to have his moment now, but then she would remind him that this was her case, and he'd simply been invited in to help.

John answered on the first knock. He was a handsome man with dark brown hair and hazel eyes. At the moment he wore a pair of jeans, an old T-shirt and a simmering panic that shone bright from his eyes.

Jackson took care of the introductions, and John sighed in relief. "Have you found them?" he asked as he allowed them entry into the house.

"No, and that's why we're here. We'd like to ask you some questions." Although the Southern accent remained, there was nothing of the lazy charmer in Jackson's demeanor. His eyes were an ice-blue as they gazed at John.

"Ask me questions about what?" John sank down to the sofa as if unable to stay on his feet beneath the intensity of Jackson's gaze.

Jackson remained standing, as did Marjorie, her gaze darting around the room with professional interest. Nice furniture, although the space had a lived-in look with a newspaper spread across the top of the coffee table and several matchbox cars on a highway built of paper on the floor.

The walls were filled with Merriweather's artistic genius, framed canvases of paintings in bright colors, including several of Amberly.

"How did you feel when your ex-wife married Cole Caldwell?" Jackson asked.

"I was happy for her…happy for them. All I ever wanted for Amberly was her happiness. What's this all about? Surely you can't think I had anything to do with whatever has happened to them." John's voice held a hint of outrage.

"Were you worried that your son might start to think of Cole as his daddy, cutting you out of his life?" Jackson's tone held an edge of suspicion that Marjorie instinctively knew he was doing on purpose.

"That's crazy," John scoffed. "My son loves me and I hope he and Cole love each other. A child can't have too many people to love them in their life."

"What did you do over the past weekend?" Jackson asked as he pulled his small notepad and pen from his shirt pocket.

John released an impatient sigh. "I had Max all weekend. Friday night we went to a movie, Saturday we went to the mall and did a little shopping and then ate at the food court, and then Sunday we hung out here all day." His hands clenched tight although he kept his voice calm. "You're wasting precious time here. I would never do anything to hurt Cole and Amberly, especially because they are important to my son. I would never do something like that to him."

He looked beseechingly at Marjorie. "Do you have children?"

She shook her head. "No, I don't." His question created a wistful ache inside her, one she quickly tamped down. In order to have any children she'd have to trust a man, and that wasn't in the cards for her.

"Then you can't understand the love a father has for his son." He half rose from the sofa. "You have to find them. Max needs his mother." Tears filled his eyes and he fell back against the cushions.

"Has Amberly mentioned any problems she's had with anyone lately?" Jackson pressed on.

John frowned. "No, not that I can think of. She went through a terrible trauma last year, but the person who tried to kill her was shot dead. Since then she's just seemed happy with Cole and hasn't mentioned any problems or issues with anyone."

Jackson wrote something down on his pad and then looked back at John. "How was your relationship with Cole?"

"Fine. It was fine." John's control appeared to be slipping. Marjorie saw his hands once again tighten into fists in his lap, and his voice had an edge that had been absent before. "Cole is a good man, and if I'd handpicked the man I wanted in Amberly's life, in my son's life, it would have been a man like him."

He looked at Marjorie again. "Please, find them. Max needs his mother. He doesn't know that they're missing. I just told him his mother was late in coming back from Mystic Lake. For God's sake, don't make me tell him she's missing again." The humble plea in John's voice shot straight to Marjorie's heart.

"Are you seeing anyone now?" Jackson asked, obviously unmoved by John's emotion.

"Seeing anyone? You mean, like, dating?" John shook his head. "Not at the present time."

"Have you dated at all since your divorce from Amberly?"

John's eyes took on a hard edge of their own. "You think I'm so obsessed with my ex-wife and that I killed her and her new husband?" he scoffed. "I've had several brief relationships since Amberly and I divorced."

"Why brief?" Jackson was relentless, and still with the cold demeanor that had Marjorie thanking her stars that he'd never be interrogating her.

"I have my work and I have Max—that doesn't leave me much time for romance." John stood. "Are we finished here? You're wasting valuable time when you could be out hunting who kidnapped Amberly and Cole."

"You think they've been kidnapped?" Jackson jotted something else in his notepad.

John raked a hand through his hair, his features once again twisted in agony. "I don't know. I don't know what in the hell happened to them. I just know that Amberly would never just disappear like this on Max unless something terrible happened. You've got to find them."

"We're going to," Marjorie said, cutting off anything else Jackson might want to say. She stepped toward where John stood and pulled one of her cards out of her pocket. "If you think of anything that might be helpful, if you remember anyone who might be a threat to Amberly or Cole, call me."

John took the card with shaking fingers and nodded. "And you'll let me know what's happening with the investigation?"

"We'll keep you up to date," Marjorie assured him.

"Like hell we will," Jackson said a few moments later when they were back in his car. "Right now John Merriweather is at the very top of my suspect list."

Marjorie shot him a look of surprise.

"Think about it, Maggie. Who has the most to gain from Amberly and Cole disappearing? Max's father, that's who. He has a great motive for wanting them gone."

She didn't want to even think about the fact that he'd just called her Maggie, something nobody else in her entire life had ever done. She didn't intend to reprimand him now, as right now she was considering what he'd said about John Merriweather.

"He might have a good motive to get rid of them in a sick sort of way, but he doesn't have opportunity. He had his son with him all weekend long," she replied.

She pulled out of the Merriweather driveway and headed in the direction of the Kansas City field office where they would next be interviewing Amberly's closest coworkers.

"I saw a picture of Max and his dad on the bookcase. What is he…about six?" Jackson asked.

"Seven," Marjorie replied. "I think he's going to be eight in a couple months."

"I don't know about you but when I was seven my father could have tucked me into bed and then left the house, gone to a movie, slept with a woman and been back home again before I woke up the next morning."

She slid him a curious glance. "And where would your mother have been while your father was out through the night hours?"

"Dead. She died when I was five, of cancer. But that really doesn't matter now—my point is that John could have easily slipped outside the house while Max slept, driven to Mystic Lake and done something to Amberly and Cole and been back before Max awoke the next morning."

"So, supposing he made that midnight run to Mystic Lake, then where are Amberly and Cole? If he killed them, why not just leave the bodies in the house?"

"Nobody said I had all the answers, darlin'. I just have theories."

"I think this one is kind of lame," she replied.

"Maybe," he agreed, the laid-back agent once again present. "John mentioned something about the last time a man tried to kill Amberly. What was that all about?"

"It's actually the case that brought Amberly and Cole together. Somebody was killing young women in Mystic Lake and leaving dream catchers hanging over their bodies. The mayor of Mystic Lake asked for FBI help, and since Director Forbes thought Amberly was the perfect agent to assist, because of the Native American overtones, she was sent to Mystic Lake to work with Cole."

She paused to make the turn into the parking area of the field office, a three-story brick building in the downtown area. "The perp eventually went after Amberly and trapped her in a rented storage unit. It was John's best friend and neighbor who had taken her."

She frowned in thought as she pulled into a parking place. "Ed...Ed Gershner was his name. He had some crazy notion that the only way John would be happy again was if Amberly was dead and John could finally forget her. Thankfully, Cole found Amberly, killed Ed and the rest, as they say, is history."

She turned off the engine and they both got out of the car. "Hopefully these interviews will go fairly quickly. It's got to be getting close to lunchtime by now," he said.

Marjorie hurried after his long strides, successfully stifling the impulse to knock him upside his head.

Chapter Three

Amberly Nightsong Caldwell's coworkers at the FBI field office had little to disclose about anyone who might want to harm her. She wasn't currently assigned to any active case. Her director knew she was in the middle of a transitional time in moving Cole into her home, and so he'd given her desk duty pushing paperwork, and regular hours until she and Cole got things settled.

Jackson had stepped back and allowed Marjorie to interview the players, since they were also her coworkers.

He quickly noticed that while the people they spoke to all appeared to respect Marjorie, none of them seemed to be particularly close to her. She was apparently a loner who didn't require friends.

Jackson had tons of men he counted as close friends in past partners and at the Baton Rouge field office. Jackson wasn't only considered a ladies' man—he was a man's man, as well.

He was the first one to invite a crew over to his place for drinks and chips and dip during a football game, or get together a group to do some horseback riding at nearby stables or head to a firing range for a little impromptu competition.

One thing had become increasingly clear to Jackson as the morning had gone on. Marjorie Clinton was one uptight woman. She smiled rarely and the few she sent his way were filled with either irritation or a strange curiosity, as if he were a species of animal she didn't know and certainly didn't trust.

She intrigued him. He was interested to know her background, what made her who she was today. It was unusual for him to care enough to want to know that much about a woman.

When they'd finally finished up with Amberly's coworkers, he'd insisted they find a place where they could sit and eat lunch before beginning the next phase of interviews in Mystic Lake.

"Don't look so miserable," he told her when they sat down across from each other in a booth in a nearby diner.

"We could have just done drive-through on the way to Mystic Lake and saved some time," she replied.

Jackson opened a menu and shoved it toward her. "Mystic Lake will still be there whether we take ten minutes doing drive-through or half an hour actually sitting and eating."

"Don't you feel any urgency?" she asked, leaning toward him, her green eyes shining brightly. Her lashes were long and dark brown and he noticed, not for the first time that day, that she smelled of the fresh scent of a fabric softener combined with a hint of wildflowers.

"Ladybug, we're past the point of urgency. Urgency should have happened Saturday or Sunday. I wonder how the burgers are here?" He shouldn't be thinking about how good she smelled or the fact that he'd like to see a genuine smile from her directed at him.

"Who cares? I have a case of two missing people, and a partner who only wants to know when his next meal is due."

"Do you have many friends?" he asked.

She blinked twice and sat back. He knew she'd worked up a head of steam about taking the time out for lunch and probably was ticked off by the use of a pet name. His question had caught her off guard.

Her cheeks dusted a beautiful pink. "Actually, no. I don't have a lot of friends. I work all the overtime I can get and I spend my free time either sleeping or visiting with my mother."

"And your father?"

She opened her menu and lowered her gaze. "He died when I was ten."

"I'm sorry. It must have been tough for you and your mother."

"We got by," she replied, and still didn't meet his gaze.

"You're more comfortable if we talk about the case?"

He was rewarded with a flash of her eyes as she gazed up at him intently. "Yes," she said. "Unfortunately I don't think this is tied to anything Amberly was currently working on. Nobody we spoke to indicated she was having problems with anyone."

They were interrupted by the arrival of a blonde waitress with large breasts and a name tag that read June. "Hey, sweet June bug, how about you get us a couple of burgers and fries," he said.

"And what would you like to drink?" She practically tittered the words as she blushed at Jackson.

"I'll take a diet cola," Marjorie said stiffly.

"And I'll take a regular," Jackson replied.

As the waitress left the table with a swing of her hips, Marjorie shot him a wicked stare. "You just can't help yourself, can you?"

"Maybe I don't want to help myself," he replied, and leaned forward. "Do you know how many jackasses June bug probably puts up with on a daily basis? Bad tippers, chronic complainers... What's wrong with giving her a little ray of sunshine. It cost me nothing and made her smile."

She studied him for a long moment. "I'm not sure if I like you or not, Special Agent Revannaugh."

He grinned. "Don't worry. You've really only known me for less than a day. I'll grow on you."

"Right, like moss," she said dryly.

"Okay, just to get on your good side, we'll talk about the case. You're right. I think if we're going to find answers they are going to be in Mystic Lake. There has been no ransom demand, so if they were kidnapped it wasn't for money."

"They were kidnapped," she said with a certainty. "That's the only thing that could keep Amberly away from her son." She frowned thoughtfully. "We don't even know for sure who the intended victim was. One was probably the victim and the other was collateral damage."

"If Amberly was the intended victim, then we already have a suspect with a motive in John," he replied. "We'll see what we turn up in Mystic Lake and see if

Cole might have been working on a case that caused somebody to want revenge of some kind."

"I still can't believe that John would do anything to hurt Cole or Amberly," she replied.

"Yeah, but one of her coworkers mentioned that after Ed the potential killer was killed, John tried one last time to get back with his ex-wife," Jackson reminded her.

"But it obviously went nowhere and Amberly and John remained friends. Cole and Amberly got married and everyone moved on with their lives."

"At least on the surface," he replied.

The waitress returned with their drinks, flashing Jackson a wink as she placed his before him. "Burgers will be right up," she said.

"Thanks, June bug," he replied.

"Do you suffer from multiple personality disorder?" Marjorie asked.

Jackson nearly snorted pop through his nose. "What's that supposed to mean?"

"When you were interviewing John earlier you were sharp, no-nonsense and on top of your professional game, but now you're totally different. You're a laid-back flirting machine."

"Flirting machine. Hmm, I like that," he said in amusement and then sobered. "Maggie, if you play this game too long without being able to compartmentalize, you burn out quickly," he replied. "If I were to make a prediction, I'd guess that you're going to burn out fast if you approach all of your cases with the same intensity you're already using to attack this one."

At that moment June arrived with their burgers, and for a few minutes they both focused on their food.

Marjorie ate quickly, obviously eager to get back on the road and moving.

"So, who are we talking to in Mystic Lake?" he asked as he dragged a French fry through a pool of ketchup.

"Our point person there is Deputy Roger Black. He wasn't at the scene last night but we're to meet him in his office when we hit town. He's acting sheriff until Cole is found," she said.

"Has he managed to get us any suspects? Mentioned anything Cole was working on?"

"I've only had a brief conversation with him and we didn't get into the details. I'm hoping he'll have some information when we meet with him." She looked at her watch and then quickly took another bite of her burger.

"How long have you been on the job?" he asked.

"Two years. I joined the FBI when I turned thirty. I was a cop before that." She used a napkin to dab her mouth. "What about you?"

"Seven years. I was twenty-eight when they tapped me for recruitment. And like you, before that I was working as a homicide cop and working with a behavioral unit to aid in profiling violent offenders. My work there caught the FBI's eyes and here I am."

"But there's no indication that what we're dealing with here is a particularly violent offender." Her eyes shimmered with the need to believe that.

Jackson sighed. He'd made a vow long ago to himself that he would never, ever lie to a woman, no matter how painful the truth might be.

"It's too early to know," he finally replied. "All we

know for sure right now is that it appears that nothing violent occurred at Cole's house."

A look of pain tightened her features. She might appear uptight and in control, but Jackson had a feeling she was soft, too soft for the job she was doing.

"I'm hoping at least Deputy Black can give us somewhere to begin," Marjorie said when they were once again in the car and headed to Mystic Lake.

"Have you considered the possibility that they might be dead?" Jackson asked softly.

He saw the impact of his words in the swift etch of pain that once again crossed her features, in the tightening of her fingers around the steering wheel. "It's too early in the investigation to come to that conclusion. We have a lot of things to accomplish before we even consider that."

"It's been four days since anyone has heard from them." He wanted to prepare her for whatever they might discover. He was also surprised to realize that he somehow wanted to protect her.

He chalked it up to the fact that she was a relatively new agent while he was a seasoned veteran who had seen the horrible things people were capable of doing to each other.

"I know, but we have absolutely no evidence to support that they've been murdered."

"Right now we don't even have the evidence to support that they've been kidnapped," he reminded her.

"All I know for sure is that something bad has happened to them and we need to figure out what it was, who it is who's kept Amberly away from her son."

Jackson didn't want to remind her that the case he'd been working on in Bachelor Moon had involved three people who had gone missing and had yet to be found. No answers, no closure…nothing.

Still, he couldn't imagine how this case in Mystic Lake, Missouri, would be related to the case in Bachelor Moon, Louisiana. The two small towns were about a thousand miles away from each other. It had to be some sort of strange coincidence.

He hoped it was just a coincidence, because if the two cases were tied together he knew with certainty that they were way over their head.

"I'VE GOT A COUPLE OF NAMES of people for you to check out, although I don't have any evidence that either of them were involved." Roger Black looked ill at ease seated in the chair behind the large oak desk that belonged to his boss.

"What I'm hoping is that Cole decided to surprise Amberly with an impromptu late honeymoon and they're off on some exotic island enjoying their time alone," he added.

"Did Cole mention a trip?" Marjorie asked, hoping that there might be a possibility of a happy ending, after all. Maybe John had forgotten plans for a honeymoon that the couple had.

"Nothing specific, but it wasn't too long ago he said he had a mind to surprise Amberly with a trip to the Bahamas," Roger replied.

"Have you checked financials? Talked to airlines?" Jackson asked.

Roger swept a hand through his brown hair. "To be honest with you, we haven't done much of anything since we heard the Feds were being called in. Accord-

·ing to the mayor, you are in charge. I've got my men ready to cooperate and do whatever you tell us to do."

"We've already lost a lot of time," Marjorie said.

Roger shrugged. "We didn't really get worried about them until last night. It's not a crime for two consenting adults to take off somewhere or not be where they are supposed to be."

"The first thing we want you to do is assign somebody to look at both Cole and Amberly's financials, see if anything has moved since last Friday night," Jackson said. "Check back over the last three months or so. If Cole bought tickets to an exotic island, then we'll find proof of that."

Roger nodded. "I'll get Deputy Ray McCloud on it right away. He's our techie freak. If there's a paper trail, so to speak, of anything like that, he'll find it."

"I also want you to assign a couple of officers to walk the streets, ask questions and see if we can find anyone who had any contact with the missing couple after Friday night. And you mentioned a couple of names for us?" Marjorie asked.

She wanted action. She needed to be doing something to move the investigation forward as quickly as possible. Jackson was right—she worked like a dog until conclusions were reached and bad guys were arrested. She was a hare, not a tortoise.

"I know Cole was having some issues with Natalie Redwing," Roger said.

Jackson pulled out his notepad and pen. "What kind of problems?"

"She was kind of, like, stalking him." Roger gave a dry laugh. "Cole thought she was harmless, but irritating." He gave them her address.

"Who else?" Marjorie asked.

"Jeff Maynard. He's a bartender at Bledsoe's on Main Street. He didn't like Cole and he definitely didn't like Amberly. He's a hothead loser, although I doubt he has the brains to kidnap a couple of people and not leave any clues behind. Off the top of my head those are the only two I've ever heard about Cole having any issues with."

Minutes later, armed with address information, Jackson and Marjorie left the small sheriff's office and headed out to interview both new suspects.

"You can do the interviewing with Jeff Maynard and I'll take Natalie Redwing," Jackson said.

"Why doesn't it surprise me that you'd want to talk to the woman and assign me the hothead loser?" Marjorie said dryly.

Jackson gave her that slow, lazy slide of his lips into a smile that heated places inside her that had never been warm before. "I'm hoping you can find a little charm and twist that hothead loser right around your little finger."

"Yeah, right, I've been holding out on you with the charm thing," Marjorie replied sarcastically.

She was aware of Jackson's gaze lingering on her as she focused on Main Street and searched for Bledsoe's tavern. It was late enough in the afternoon that Jeff Maynard should be working.

"I think you might be hiding a little bit of charm under a basket and I've decided it's my goal in life to figure out how to get that basket off your head."

Marjorie couldn't help herself—laughter bubbled to her lips and she shook her head. "You're a funny man, Agent Revannaugh." She pulled into a parking place in front of Bledsoe's, a long, low building at the edge of town.

"You know, that's the first time I've seen a genuine smile on your lips or heard laughter from you. You should do it more often. It definitely becomes you."

"I'm not a laughing kind of woman," she replied as she turned off the car engine. "I haven't had much to laugh about in my life."

"Then my second job is to change that," he replied.

"Duty calls." She got out of the car and slammed the door, more touched by Jackson's words than she wanted to admit. She couldn't let him get to her. She'd seen what men like him had done to her mother's life, to her life, and she was not going to be one of those women who fell for the charm and never saw the callous calculation beneath.

At just after four in the afternoon, Bledsoe's already had a few customers seated on stools at the long bar. It was semidark inside and reeked of booze and a faint underlying hint of urine.

It was the kind of place where the clientele was tough, bar fights occurred on a regular basis and nobody came for a social event. A jukebox played an old country song about a broken heart and a Texas man, but Marjorie was beginning to think it wasn't the tall, handsome cowboys you had to watch out for, it was the smooth-talking Southerners.

As she approached the bar, she pulled out her official identification from her purse, careful to keep the side of her purse that had a built-in gun holster against her body. She went toward the dark-haired bartender, feeling no need to show any more authority than her badge, but she was prepared, should that change.

"Smells like Feds to me," the bartender said as he slowly wiped a glass dry.

"Ah, nice to know you have a good sense of smell," Marjorie said, forcing a pleasant smile to her lips. She almost felt as if she had something to prove to her partner, that she could be as charming as she needed to be while talking to a potential suspect.

"You're cuter than your partner." He set down the glass and jabbed a finger in the direction of Jackson, who stood a couple of inches behind her.

"Thanks. I'm smarter, too. But I let him think he's smarter because he has a huge ego."

Jackson cleared his voice as the bartender barked a dry laugh.

"We're looking for Jeff Maynard," she said.

"You found him, sweetheart, but as far as I know I haven't done anything to get special attention from the FBI." His eyes were dark with more than a hint of wariness.

"What do you know about Cole and Amberly Caldwell's disappearance?" Marjorie asked.

"Only that I'm not gonna cry in my beer tonight over it." He picked up a wet cloth and gave the bar a desultory swipe. "Look, I know you're here because everyone in Mystic Lake knows I don't like Cole. I have a problem with authority figures," he added with a smirk.

Marjorie leaned closer to the bar, closer to the man she knew might possibly have had something to do with Cole and Amberly's disappearance. "All authority?" she asked with a teasing lilt to her voice.

She sensed Jackson leaning closer behind her, but she kept her gaze focused on Jeff, as if he were the most important person on the face of the earth. A small, lewd grin curved his lips. "Well, maybe not all. I wouldn't mind getting over it by maybe handcuffing you to my bed."

Marjorie blinked in shock and leaned backward, bumping into Jackson's firmly muscled chest. "I must protest," Jackson said in his pleasant Southern drawl. "If anyone is going to handcuff this little lady to his bed, it's going to be me."

Marjorie felt as if she were having an out of body experience. "Where were you this past weekend?" she asked Jeff, trying to get her feet beneath her and get the conversation back on track.

The smirk disappeared from Jeff's face. "Friday is my night off. I was out with buddies. Saturday night I worked my usual shift here, from four until close."

"And where did you go with these buddies on Friday night?" Marjorie asked. She didn't bother to pull out her pen and pad. She knew instinctively that Jackson already had his out.

"We were at Jimmy Tanner's place, playing poker. He's newly divorced, thanks to Cole and Amberly and their prying into private lives when they were investigating the murders of those women last year."

"Jimmy Tanner, what's his address?" Marjorie asked, realizing she'd just added another name to a potential suspect with a motive of revenge.

"At the moment he's living at the Mystic Lake Motel on the south side of town," Jeff replied. "His wife really took him to the cleaners in the divorce."

By the time they left Bledsoe's, they had not only added Jimmy Tanner's name to their list, but also Raymond Chandler, who had also been at the supposed poker party on Friday night.

"I'm impressed, Ms. Maggie. I think there's a bit of naughty woman trapped inside you," Jackson said once they were back in the car.

"Don't be ridiculous," she scoffed, cheeks far too warm. "There's no naughty inside of me. I'm by the book, rigid and uptight. Trust me, Jackson, I know who I am."

"I wonder," he mused. She kept her mouth firmly closed, not wanting to know what he wondered. "Let's head on back to Kansas City," he said. "We can drive back out here and start with this Natalie Redwing first thing in the morning."

"Why not do it now?" Marjorie asked.

Jackson looked at his watch. "It's going to be close to six by the time we make it back to Kansas City. I say we order a pizza and sit down and go through what we know, figure out who needs to be interviewed next and get a general idea of where we are."

"Right now it feels like we're nowhere," she replied.

"Exactly. It might surprise you to know that I can be a by-the-book kind of guy despite my huge ego."

She glanced over to catch him smiling that sexy grin of his. "So, what does that mean?"

"It means I'd like to feed my notes into my laptop and see if we really have nothing or if we've already made any connections that might lead somewhere. I also want to utilize some resources I have with the agency to double-check bank records, travel and anything else that might pop up with Amberly or Cole's names."

"But you just assigned that task for Deputy Black to take care of," she replied.

"You know our resources are better than theirs."

"Okay, sounds like a plan," she replied somewhat reluctantly. She had a feeling being in a motel room with Jackson Revannaugh for any reason probably wasn't the best idea.

Chapter Four

He couldn't get the vision of her smile, the sound of her laughter, out of his head. Something about Marjorie Clinton was getting under his skin, Jackson thought as he paid the pizza delivery boy an hour later.

He carried the box to the table and chairs that sat in front of the windows in the motel room. His laptop was open to a file labeled Mystic Lake/Kansas City.

While they had awaited the food delivery, the two of them had sat side by side as he fed into the file the bits and pieces of information they had attained so far in the case.

He'd tried not to notice how shiny her hair was beneath the lamp that hung from the ceiling over the center of the table. He'd tried not to draw in the sweet scent of her that made him think of tangled sheets and slick bodies.

The pizza was a compromise. His half was spicy pepperoni and sausage, and hers was mushroom and green pepper. It was just an indication to him that they were complete opposites and he had no business thinking about what she would look like naked, how her lips would taste or if he could evoke any passion that might be hidden beneath her emotional walls.

Surely these thoughts were only because they were in a relatively intimate setting and there was no question that he was physically attracted to her.

She looked relaxed for the first time since they'd met. Her blouse was unbuttoned at the top, revealing her delicate collarbone, and her body appeared to hold none of the tension of the day.

"So, tomorrow we check out the names we have of people from Mystic Lake," she said as he opened the box and handed her several napkins. She leaned closer to him to look at his computer screen. "Jimmy Tanner, Raymond Chandler and Natalie Redwing—we should be able to have those interviews finished by noon, and maybe one of them will give us more information."

"We also need to check back in with Deputy Black and maybe interview some of the other deputies who worked with Cole." He waited until she took a piece of the pie and then he grabbed a piece for himself. "It's possible that somebody who worked for Cole didn't have his back."

Marjorie frowned thoughtfully. "We might reinterview John Merriweather again to see if he's thought of anything new."

"He's still at the top of my suspect list," Jackson replied and then bit into the slice he had folded in half.

"I'm anxious to talk to Jimmy Tanner and Raymond Chandler to see how well they can corroborate Jeff's poker game alibi for Friday night," she replied.

"He seems so obvious as a suspect," Jackson replied, sorry when she leaned back in her chair and put some distance between them. "He didn't make any bones about the fact that he doesn't like the sheriff."

"Sometimes it's the most obvious suspect that turns

out to be the perp." She wiped her mouth with the napkin and for the next few minutes they fell into silence as they devoured the pizza.

He liked watching her. She had the kind of expressive face that let him know when her thoughts were happy or somber. He found himself wishing he knew what was going through her mind.

He chided himself irritably. Marjorie wasn't a player. She was with him now because she was assigned to work this case with him, and when the case was over she'd probably never think of him again.

And that was the way it was supposed to be, he reminded himself. He glanced up to find her impossibly green eyes locked with his. "You've gotten very quiet," she said. "What are you thinking about?"

"I'm wondering why you don't have some boyfriend ticked off because you're working with an irresistible, handsome devil like me."

She tossed the last of a piece of crust into the box and wiped her mouth once again. "I don't have a boyfriend because I don't want a boyfriend. I'm perfectly comfortable alone." She hesitated a moment and her eyes deepened in hue. "I had enough scheming stepfathers in my life to be done with the idea of relationships or marriage for the rest of my life."

"What do you mean by scheming stepfathers?"

She hesitated, as if weighing how much of herself she was willing to give to him. "When my father died, he left my mother a very wealthy woman, wealthy enough and lonely enough that she was easy pickings for smooth-talking con men to take advantage of."

She worried her napkin in her lap as Jackson's pizza suddenly sat heavily in his stomach. "It took three husbands to swindle her out of her last dime and leave her broke and alone." She shrugged. "I'm not much inclined to share anything with anyone after that experience."

"I'm sorry," Jackson said, knowing it was inadequate and also recognizing that if she ever found out about his own father, she'd hate Jackson and would never believe that he wasn't a chip off the old block.

"It's not your fault, and I have Mom settled in a nice apartment, surrounded by beautiful furnishings so she can feel like she's still living a bit of the good life."

"And what has that done for your lifestyle?" he asked.

Once again she shrugged. "I don't require much. I've managed to get myself a little two-bedroom house that's just right for me."

Although she didn't say it, although she didn't even intimate it, Jackson knew she must be making personal sacrifices to keep her mother happy. An unexpected pain ripped through his heart, along with a lot of guilt he knew he didn't deserve but hadn't been able to shake from his psyche for years.

"You know you shouldn't judge all men by what happened to your mother," he said.

"I don't. I'm a cautious woman, Jackson. I just don't take chances, not in my job as an FBI agent and not in my personal life."

"Being too cautious can close you off from important experiences," he replied.

"I recognize that and I'm okay with it. My life is just the way I like it—predictable and without chaos."

"And love equals chaos to you?" He raised a dark eyebrow.

"Not necessarily." She gave a small, dry laugh.

"What are you doing? Trying to be my life coach? You, who has never met a woman he didn't like, who probably changes girlfriends as often as you change your shirt? You've already told me you aren't the marrying kind, so why is it any different for me not to be the marrying kind?"

He knew it was crazy, but what he wanted to tell her was that she deserved a man who would cherish her, a man who could bring that magical and elusive laughter to her easily and often.

"You're right. I shouldn't give relationship advice to anyone," he finally said.

"So, what are your personal issues when it comes to marriage and long-term commitments?"

Her question surprised him, and he didn't have an answer that he was willing to share with her. "I just don't think I'd do it very well," he replied. He gave her an irreverent smile. "You know, so many women, so little time," he said flippantly.

Her emerald eyes narrowed as her gaze held his. "I wonder what baggage you're carrying around."

He leaned back in his chair with surprise. "What makes you think I have baggage?"

"Maybe it's like sensing like," she replied. "I know what my baggage is and I think I'm not the only one seated at this table who might have some issues."

He could easily fall into the depths of her eyes—*so green*—and he felt as if her gaze was so intense she was looking inside his soul, seeking answers he had sworn he would never give to any woman.

She finally broke the gaze and glanced toward the window, where the sheer curtains couldn't cover the darkness of night that had fallen while they'd talked.

"It's getting late and we need to get an early start in the morning. We have a lot to accomplish tomorrow. It's time for me to head home."

"You're right," he agreed, wondering how the conversation had gotten so personal so quickly. He'd have to be more careful—she was far too easy to talk to, and there were far too many secrets and shames in his life to let down his guard.

They both got up from the table, and the windows in front of them exploded inward. Instinctively Jackson grabbed Marjorie and pulled her to the floor.

He rolled her to the opposite side of the room, where they would be partially shielded by the edge of the bed as the tat-tat-tat of an automatic weapon resounded and bullets shredded the curtains, slammed into the walls, and furniture splintered.

He lay on top of her while the world around them exploded, and knew that there was nothing more he could do but wait and pray that when the shooting stopped they would both still be alive.

PICTURE FRAMES SMASHED and fell from the walls, and Marjorie braced herself for a piercing bullet to find her, even though Jackson's body covered hers.

She could feel his heartbeat, as rapid, as frantic as her own, and the shooting seemed to last forever. A squeal of tires was audible from the broken windows, and after that, utter silence.

For several long moments they remained in place, hearts racing against each other's, the slight scent of pepperoni coming from him. He finally rose slightly and asked, "Are you all right?"

"I…I don't know," she admitted truthfully. "I'm not shot, but I'm a little dazed."

Siren screams filled the night, drawing closer, and the scent of cordite was thick in the air. "I wondered what it might be like for me to be on top of you on a floor or in my bed, but this wasn't exactly what I had in mind," he said.

She shoved him off her and he stood. "Do you always have sex on the brain?" she asked as she got to her feet. "Don't you realize that somebody just tried to kill us?"

Cherry swirls just outside the motel room indicated that the police had arrived. Jackson grinned at her. "Snapped you right out of that daze, didn't I?"

He was right. The fogginess in her brain was gone and she was acutely aware of everything. "It was probably some heartbroken woman who followed you here from Baton Rouge to put a bullet through your black heart."

"Or could be a man you cut off at the knees with your attitude and sharp tongue," he replied.

At that moment several officers raced into the room, guns drawn and terse expressions on their faces. "You both okay?"

"No," Marjorie replied. "He's an egotistical ass."

"And she's an uptight witch," Jackson said. "But other than that, we're both fine. Unfortunately the room appears to be a bit of a mess."

Marjorie looked around and her knees threatened to buckle. "A bit of a mess" was definitely an understatement. The walls were riddled with bullet holes, glass was everywhere and even the bed hadn't escaped the carnage, as tufts of mattress padding peeked out of gaping holes. It was a wonder—no, it was a miracle—that they had survived unscathed.

She sank down on the edge of the bed, unable to take in how near death she had come. She listened as Jackson made introductions to the officer who appeared in charge and then told him what had happened.

"I have no idea what kind of vehicle the perp was in, but it was definitely an Uzi that was used to shoot up the place. I know the sound," Jackson said.

The officer wore a tag that identified him as Lieutenant Larry Segal. "Do you have any idea who might be behind this attack?"

"We're investigating a case of a couple of missing persons in Mystic Lake. Apparently there's somebody who doesn't like the questions we're asking people," Jackson replied.

"Apparently," Segal replied. He yelled to one of his other officers. "Let's get a crime scene unit in here. We need to find as many bullets as possible." He motioned for Jackson and Marjorie to follow him outside the room.

Marjorie grabbed her bag from the floor next to the table and clutched it to her chest, the feel of her gun in the purse holster somewhat comforting. Jackson's laptop computer was toast, exploded into pieces of plastic and metal.

As they stepped out into the darkness of the night, Marjorie's knees still felt wobbly and the sound of the bullets slamming into a variety of items echoed in her head.

"What's going on?" A short rotund man came running toward them. "What in the hell happened here?" He threw out his arms, his round face screwed up in

62 Scene of the Crime: Return to Mystic Lake

anger. "Drug deal gone bad?" He glared at Jackson and then eyed Marjorie. "Are you a prostitute working out of my motel? Did you tick off some john or what?"

Marjorie nearly swallowed her tongue in shock. Never in a million years had anyone ever mistaken her for a hooker. Jackson took a step closer to her, as if to protect her from the angry little man. "This is FBI business," he said.

"I don't give a damn if it's YMCA business, what I want to know is who is going to pay for this damage? I run a respectable motel here."

"Wayne, don't worry, we'll figure it all out," Lieutenant Segal said.

"Somebody better figure it out fast. This is bad for business and I need somebody to get this room back in shape as soon as possible."

Marjorie imagined she could see fumes rising off Wayne's nearly bald head. "I'll call my director and he'll see that the repairs on the room are taken care of after the local officials are finished processing things." She was appalled to hear her voice tremble slightly.

She straightened her back and tried to mentally pull herself together. The last thing she wanted was for Jackson to believe she wasn't up to the job, that she couldn't handle danger when it reared its ugly head.

Wayne's strident voice grew more distant as one of the officers led him back toward the motel office. Jackson and Segal were still talking, and she was just trying to process what had just happened. Two patrol cars were parked in a way to deny entry to any other vehicle into the motel parking lot.

She'd never experienced anything like this before.

As long as she'd been working in the job, she'd never had her life personally threatened.

Death had whispered on the back of her neck, and even now a shiver tried to work up her spine. Surely it was normal to feel this way after such an experience.

"Are you okay?" A deep voice came from beside her, jolting her out of her thoughts.

She turned to see Officer Kevin Winslow standing next to her. He was a young cop and she was surprised to see that his brown eyes held the same kind of horror she felt.

"I'm fine, although it all feels kind of surreal at the moment."

He glanced toward the open motel room door with the shattered windows in the front. "I think I probably would have had a heart attack," he admitted.

They had just been sitting at the table in front of those windows, she thought. If they'd waited another moment to get up, there was no question in her head that both of them would have been killed.

Her gaze shifted to Jackson, who was still speaking with the lieutenant. "I have a good partner. He got me to the floor before either of us was shot."

Kevin nodded. "That's what good partners are for. We're just glad we're investigating a shooting and not a double homicide."

"Trust me, I'm glad about that, too."

Kevin drifted away as Jackson walked toward Marjorie. He held a duffel bag and clothes on hangers. They were surrounded by chaos, swirling lights and the sound of radios, and still he smiled as his gaze locked with hers. "Well, Maggie, darlin', you sure know how to show a man an exciting time," he said when he was close enough for her to hear him above the din.

"That was a bit too exciting for my blood," she replied honestly. "So what happens now?"

"The local authorities are taking it from here, and it looks like I need a place to stay. Didn't you mention you had a nice little two-bedroom house?" Even in the semidarkness that surrounded him, she saw the upward quirk of his eyebrow. The expression only enhanced his attractiveness, by giving him a slightly rakish appearance.

The last thing she wanted was this man under her roof, but it was late and it would take hours to go through proper channels to get him into another motel room.

Besides, it would be churlish of her to turn him away after what they'd just been through. He'd basically saved her life. Surely she could give him a bed for a night. Certainly, he would make other arrangements in the morning.

"I'll warn you, the bedroom is quite small," she finally said.

"Does it have a bed?" he asked. She nodded. "Then it sounds perfect to me."

"Then let's go," she replied.

Amazingly all of the bullets that had flown had been specifically targeted at the motel window. Her car parked in front had no damage, which made her think that the shooter or shooters had been proficient with their automatic weapons.

The minute Jackson slid into the passenger seat, she caught a whiff of his cologne, and her brain exploded with the tactile memory of lying beneath him.

His body had been hard and had seemed to completely surround her in a cocoon of safety, of warmth, that she'd never felt before in her life. Despite the situation, there had been something erotic about his weight on top of her as their hearts beat a frantic rhythm.

"We're going to have to figure out how in the hell this happened," he said once they were in her car and headed to her house. "Who knew where I was staying?"

"Me, of course, and my director and probably a few other people at headquarters." She tried to focus on the conversation and not the thoughts of how she'd felt beneath him. *Be a professional,* she told herself. Obviously Jackson was in agent mode, as she should be, as well.

"The only people we spoke to about this case were agents who had worked with Amberly in the past and they all said she was having no personal issues with anyone. I find it hard to believe that somebody inside headquarters was responsible for what just happened."

"Maybe, maybe not. The only other possibility is that we shook up somebody's cage in Mystic Lake today and we made them damned uncomfortable. If that's the case then we were followed when we left there to head to the motel."

Stricken, Marjorie cast him a quick glance. "I didn't even think about the possibility of anyone following us from there to here. I didn't pay attention to the cars behind us." She squeezed her fingers around the steering wheel, mentally beating herself up for being so careless.

"Don't worry your pretty head," he replied easily. "I didn't think about it, either. But we have now been warned, and we have to proceed from here with caution. We're poking somebody and they don't like it."

Proceed with caution. The words whirled around in her head. Somehow she felt as if she was already abandoning that idea by inviting him into her home.

Chapter Five

She'd told him her home was small, but when she pulled into the driveway of the cracker box–sized place, Jackson was a bit shocked.

He was by no means a snob, but the size of the house reminded him of his earlier thought that she was making sacrifices to keep her mother happy. The entire house would fit into the living room of his apartment.

As they walked through the front door and she flipped on a light in the living room, the aura of sacrifice continued. The room was furnished with a cheap futon, two end tables and a bookcase that looked as if it had been thrown out on somebody's lawn for trash pickup. A small television sat on the top shelf, and he would bet his next month's salary that she didn't even have basic cable.

"It isn't much, but it's home," she said, as if seeing the room through his eyes.

"It's just fine," he assured her. "If you could just show me to my bedroom I'll stow my things away and then we'll talk and see what our next move should be."

"Follow me," she said. She led him down a hall-way that was little more than a few steps and stopped at the first doorway. "This is the guest room, and the bathroom is across the hall."

Jackson stepped into the room, which was just big enough to hold a double bed, a single nightstand and a chest of drawers. The room was painted a light shade of blue and the spread was a geometric design of light and dark blue. Nothing fancy, just functional. He would have expected nothing more from her.

"This is perfect," he said as he tossed his duffel bag on the bed. "Do you have a computer and internet connection here?"

"I do. I have an area in the kitchen where I keep my laptop. You're welcome to use it until you get something to replace your own."

"I'm not doing anything tonight, although I think maybe a cup of coffee might be in order. I don't know about you, but I've got adrenaline firing through me, and there's no way I can go to sleep right now."

"Why don't you get settled in and I'll go make half a pot of coffee," she replied. She got halfway out of the doorway and then turned back to look at him, her eyes simmering with emotion. "Jackson, thank you again for saving my life tonight. When those bullets slammed through the window I couldn't even process what had happened. If you hadn't grabbed me…" Her voice trailed off.

He smiled at her. "Darlin', it was my pleasure."

Her cheeks dusted with color and she quickly disappeared from his sight. He turned to his duffel bag and unzipped it to begin to unpack.

As he stowed underwear, jeans and T-shirts into the drawers, his mind whirled. Somebody had tried to kill them. Faces of the people they'd interacted with since his arrival in town flew through his head. Had they already made contact with the person or persons responsible for Cole and Amberly's disappearance, or had small-town gossip let the perp know they were in town and asking questions?

He'd flung Marjorie down and covered her to save her life, and yet as the bullets had flown all around them he'd been far too conscious of the press of her full breasts against his chest, of the sweet scent of her that made him want to press his lips into the hollow of her throat.

He hung the clothes he'd managed to get from the motel closet in the much smaller closet in the bedroom. He then grabbed the small leather bag that contained his toiletries and carried it into the bathroom.

Staring at his reflection for a moment, he forced himself to change the track of his brain. He couldn't think about Marjorie as a desirable woman now—he had to think like an FBI agent who had just nearly been killed.

The scent of freshly brewed coffee drew him down the short hallway and into a kitchen that had a small table for two, a short counter and a built-in desk that was obviously her workstation. A laptop was on top along with an all-in-one printer/fax machine and phone. She'd probably spent more money on her work equipment than in the entire furnishings of the house.

She turned from the counter as he entered the room. "Coffee is ready," she said.

Her lips pressed tight and her shoulders were tense. Her face was unusually pale. Her blouse had dirt streaks, and a button was missing, and her hair was a riotous mess of shiny red-gold strands.

She looked like a woman who had been to hell and hadn't yet fully realized that she'd really made her way back.

He walked over to where she stood and placed his hands gently on her slender shoulders. "Sit. I'll get the coffee." She opened her mouth to protest, but he quickly slid his finger over her lips. "Trust me, I got this."

She nodded and walked over to the table where she crumpled into the chair as if the weight of the world was on her shoulders.

Jackson turned to face the counter and opened the cabinet door above the coffeemaker, unsurprised to find the three cups nestled side by side. "Cream or sugar?" he asked as he poured the brew.

"Black is fine."

When he turned back with the cups in hand, she was once again sitting upright, the paleness gone and her eyes glittering with a hint of anger. Good, he needed her angry and hopefully not at him. Anger channeled in the right direction would make them both driven to find answers.

He set one cup before her, then took the seat across from her and wrapped his hands around the warmth of his cup. "Tomorrow I want you to get the names of every single person here in Kansas City who knew the motel where I'd been set to stay. First thing in the morning, we're going to check out John Merriweather's alibi for tonight. He's the only person we interviewed here in the city."

She nodded, her eyes gleaming with a steely strength he found ridiculously hot. "And then we head back to Mystic Lake and continue our interviews there, along with checking any alibis of people we interacted with there today."

She took a sip of her coffee and her gaze remained locked with his. "Was this like what was happening in Bachelor Moon and the case you were pulled off?" She set her cup back on the table.

"Nothing like what happened tonight. None of the people working that case came under any kind of a threat. Tonight wasn't just a scare tactic, it was attempted murder."

Her eyes paled a bit. "I know and I darn straight want to find out who was behind that gun."

Jackson grimaced with frustration. "I wish I would have been able to get a glimpse of the car."

She smiled at him and for a moment he wanted to get lost in it, in her. "You couldn't cover the window and me at the same time. I'm grateful you made the decision you did." Her smile faded. "I just wish we knew if we've shaken up somebody here in Kansas City or somebody in Mystic Lake. It would be easier to investigate if we only had one place to look."

"Shame on Amberly and Cole for living in two places and making this more difficult on us," he said wryly. He broke their gaze, glancing around the room in an effort to stay focused on the case and not how much her smile had warmed him or how soft her lips had been beneath his fingers.

He noticed a red light blinking on her telephone answering machine. "It looks like you have some phone messages. Maybe you should check them out, make sure one of the calls isn't from our motel visitors. It would be a boon if our perp was the chatty type."

She took another sip of her coffee and then got

up from the table and approached the answering machine. The first message was an offer for a free estimate from a siding company. She erased it and then a female voice filled the room.

"Marjorie, when are you going to come visit me? It feels like it's been weeks. Oh, and when you come, bring some of those chocolate almonds that you know I like. I don't know why you don't quit that silly job of yours so you'd have more time to take care of things for me. You could easily live on your trust fund—"

Marjorie stopped the machine and took a moment before she turned back to face Jackson. "No bad guys leaving messages," she said with obvious forced lightness as she returned to the table.

"And no trust fund," he replied softly.

This time the smile she offered him had no heart behind it. "Stepfather number two managed to get power of attorney over my trust fund and by the time he left my mother there was nothing left."

"And your mother isn't aware of the fact that you have no money except a paycheck?"

"I've tried to keep her protected as much as possible in financial matters. Besides, it doesn't matter. I'm not exactly the trust-fund-baby type."

"But you could have been," Jackson replied. His stomach twisted with a wave of grief as he saw the residual effects left behind when a con man came to town.

This time her smile was genuine. "No, I could never spend my days buying shoes and fancy dresses and attending charity events. I knew I wanted to be an FBI agent when I was fairly young. I wanted a life of rules and structure. I like having plans and sticking to them, the mundane tasks of filing reports and interviewing suspects."

"But a little spontaneity never hurts. I mean, I'm sure you didn't expect to be thrown on the floor and shot at tonight," he replied.

"I know the unexpected happens on the job, but there's not much room for spontaneity in my personal life, and that's the way I like it. And now, let's firm up our plans for tomorrow."

It was nearly one o'clock in the morning by the time they finished talking and Marjorie carried their cups to the sink. She quickly washed them and placed them on a dish drainer and then turned to look at him. "Since it's so late, why don't we plan on leaving here around nine in the morning?"

"Noon sounds better, but I can do nine," he agreed.

She looked exhausted. Her face had once again taken on a pale cast, and dark shadows rode the delicate skin just beneath her eyes. Her shoulders no longer held rigid tension but rather slumped slightly with the weight of the long day.

As they left the kitchen she turned out the lights and he checked the front door to make sure it was locked up tight. Together they started down the hallway.

"You should find everything you need in the bathroom beneath the sink cabinet," she said as they paused in front of his bedroom. "If you need anything just let me know. Good night, Jackson."

"Good night, Maggie."

She turned to head to her own bedroom, and Jackson realized he couldn't just let her go, not without doing something spontaneous and probably dangerous, as well.

He called her name, and when she turned back to face him, he didn't give himself time to think—he certainly didn't give her a chance to prepare—he simply pulled her into his arms and bent his head to capture her lips with his.

She stiffened and he braced himself for her hands against his chest, pushing him away, or a knee to the groin that would take him down to the carpeting.

But as the kiss continued, she melted into him, became soft and pliant as her arms wound around his neck and tangled in the thick hair at the nape of his neck. The hot, sweet taste of her, the feel of her sexy curves in his arms, was so good it was bad. He knew on every level this was a mistake, but he was unable to deny himself this moment with this particular woman.

She was like nobody else he'd ever kissed before. Her lips were sweeter, her body hotter and he recognized on some elemental level that without trying she was burrowing into his brain, into his heart, where no other woman had ever been before.

This thought halted the kiss. He pulled back and released her and stumbled back a step. She stared at him, a stunned look on her face. She raised a hand and touched her lips with fingers that trembled.

"Why did you do that?" Her voice was husky, and the sound shot a new wave of desire through him.

"Spontaneity," he said. "It's not always a bad thing, even in your personal life."

He didn't wait for her to reply, knew only the need to escape from her before he did something even more stupid. He turned and went into the bedroom and quietly closed the door behind him.

Marjorie tossed and turned for the next couple of hours, cold as she remembered the sounds of the bullets that might have killed them, and heated by Jackson's kiss.

The man definitely knew how to kiss a woman so that her toes curled and desire for more pooled in the pit of her stomach.

The one relationship Marjorie had experienced in her past had lasted only three weeks. He'd been a handsome, slightly quirky computer geek. She'd found his conversation tedious, the sex adequate but nothing mind-blowing, and ultimately had decided what she'd always known: relationships were more trouble than they were worth.

But she had a feeling making love with Jackson might be a mind-blowing experience, not that she intended to allow that to happen. Tomorrow night he would be in another motel room and she wouldn't have to worry...or want any more hallway encounters.

What she needed to focus on was who had tried to kill them and what had happened to Amberly and Cole Caldwell. That was her job, not personal interest in the very hot Southerner who, if she allowed him, just might have the ability to charm her right out of her panties.

She had no idea what time she finally fell asleep, but she awakened to the scent of frying sausage. She frowned. The only food items that had been in her fridge were half a head of lettuce, a couple of eggs and a dozen or so protein bars that helped her get through long days. There had definitely not been any sausage.

She got out of bed, grabbed the clothes she would wear for the day and then skipped from her room into the bathroom for a quick shower before making an official appearance in the kitchen.

It didn't take her long to shower and dress in her usual uniform of a white blouse and black slacks, with her identification clipped to a thin belt around her waist. She liked the fact that each morning she didn't have to think about what to wear, that she wasn't the type of woman to stand in front of a closet and dither about the daily couture.

Before leaving the bathroom she stared at her reflection in the mirror and reached up to touch her lips…the lips that Jackson had taken such possession of the night before.

She wasn't sure what to make of him. She wanted to believe he was a rake, a smooth-talking scoundrel who couldn't be trusted except as an efficient partner. And yet in the brief time she'd known him she'd seen sides to him that had confused her, made her wonder what man she might find beneath the easy charm and sweet talk.

Shaking her head, she left the bathroom, chastising herself for any thoughts of Jackson the man and determined to think of him only as Jackson her partner.

He was just pulling a tray of hot biscuits from the oven when she walked into the kitchen. "Ah, perfect timing," he said with a quick smile. "The sausage is cooked, the biscuits are done and the gravy is bubbly hot."

She noticed he'd already set the table as she walked to the counter with the coffeepot and poured herself a cup. "Where did all of this come from?" she asked.

He plucked the biscuits off the baking tray and placed them on a plate. "Hope you don't mind but I borrowed your car to head to the nearest grocery store. Once I got up and saw the contents of your pantry and fridge, I knew I was in dire circumstances."

She sat at the table and watched as he poured the gravy into a pitcher and then carried the food to the center of the tiny table.

"Did you know you had fourteen protein bars in there, but nothing fit to eat?" He gestured for her to pick up her fork and dig in. "Maybe you can eat those things, but I need real food, so I stocked both the freezer and the refrigerator."

"You shouldn't have done that," she protested. Those weren't the actions of a man who intended to move into another motel room today. They were the actions of a man who had found his roost and had no intention of leaving it.

"Darlin', I had to do it—it's called self-preservation." He grinned and grabbed his fork. "Now, eat. We've got a long day ahead of us, and breakfast is the most important meal to kick-start your body and brain."

Oh, she was kick-started, all right. As she ate, she tried to stay focused off the kiss they'd shared the night before, and tried to figure out a nice way to kick him out of her house.

By the time they were finished eating and had cleaned up the kitchen, she still hadn't figured it out. Hopefully before the day ended she could make him believe that staying in her place wasn't a good plan.

Before they left the house she called her director, who already had the details of what had happened the night before at the motel and was conducting an internal investigation among the handful of people who knew where Jackson would be staying while in town.

With that issue taken care of, Marjorie and Jackson were on their way to Mystic Lake to begin a new round of questioning. Despite the fact that they'd agreed the night before to be on the road around nine, they got an early start. Neither of them had slept in later than usual.

Their first stop would be Natalie Redwing's place. Although they would arrive there fairly early, around eight-thirty, they hoped to catch the woman off guard.

"You can do the interview with Natalie Redwing," Marjorie said, and gave the handsome man next to her a quick glance. "Maybe some of that smooth charm of yours will work its magic and we'll actually get some answers."

"Sounds like a tough assignment to me," he replied lightly.

She laughed. "Yeah, like breathing." She turned onto the highway that would take them to the little town. "We also need to talk to Deputy Black and see if he's heard any gossip about what went down last night and find out if Jeff Maynard has an alibi for the time of the shooting."

"I've got the names of everyone we need to talk to written down," Jackson assured her. "We'll get them all covered today unless something else comes up. What we need to focus on is watching our backs. Last night was a heads-up that somebody is willing to kill to keep us from gaining answers."

A residual chill swept through Marjorie as she thought of those moments the night before when the world exploded around her and terror had shot through her very soul.

"What happened last night doesn't exactly speak well for Amberly and Cole's well-being," she said, the words painful as they fell from her mouth.

"No, it doesn't," he replied after a moment of hesitation. She was grateful he didn't pretend that the couple was probably just fine and being held captive somewhere for some unknown reason.

If they were correct, in that Amberly and Cole had disappeared on Friday night, then tomorrow marked a full week that they'd been missing. A part of her was already mourning the two and that only made her more determined to find out the who and the why of what had happened to them.

It would have been difficult to drive by Natalie Redwing's mobile home in the trailer park located on the west end of the small town of Mystic Lake without taking notice of it. Painted a brilliant orange, with colorful dream catchers and tinkling chimes hanging down from nails at the top of the built-on wooden porch, it was like a brain freeze to the eyes.

No sooner had they pulled into the driveway than a heavyset Native American stepped out onto the front porch, a shotgun lowered to point to the ground, and a wary frown on her plump face. "Friend or foe?" she asked as Jackson opened his car door but didn't step out.

"Depends on what you do with that shotgun," he replied. "We're FBI and we're here to ask you some questions."

She nodded and propped the gun against the doorframe and motioned them out of the car. "A woman alone can't be too careful these days," she said.

Clad in a yellow-and-turquoise muumuu with bright orange flip-flops, she was as colorful as her home. When they reached her porch, she gestured them into two old wicker chairs while she remained standing. "I suppose you're here about the sheriff and his wife. I figured eventually somebody would be by to talk to me."

"And here we are," Jackson said, and flashed her one of his devastating smiles. Instantly the frown across Natalie's face disappeared.

"Why, aren't you a handsome hunk," she said, her voice taking on a softer, almost simpering quality.

"Thanks, you're a fine-looking lady yourself," he replied. "Unfortunately this is a business visit and not a pleasure one. We need to know about your relationship with Sheriff Caldwell and his wife."

"Cole and I were good friends," she said, her gaze never leaving Jackson's face. Marjorie might just as well have been a pet rock on the porch. "I knew Amberly because we occasionally worked together at the Native American Heritage Center in Kansas City, but we weren't real close." She took a step closer to Jackson and leaned toward him. "I thought she was a little bit snooty, if you know what I mean."

Jackson leaned toward her, as if captivated by anything that might fall out of her mouth. "So, were you upset when the two of them got married? I mean, a good-looking woman like you, maybe you had some plans for yourself with Cole."

"I won't lie, I had visions of me and Cole together at one time." The frown creased her forehead again.

"But once I saw the two of them together it was so obvious that they belonged with each other."

As they spoke the chimes tinkled and clanged riotously in a warm breeze, the cacophony of discordant sound making Marjorie's head ache.

"I know this sounds crazy for a lovely woman like you, but we heard a rumor that you were kind of stalking Cole," Jackson said. He shook a quick glance at Marjorie, who had been watching the two of them intently.

"I was never stalking Cole," Natalie scoffed. "But I suppose somebody might have gotten the wrong impression, because it might have looked like I was stalking them both."

Jackson leaned back in his chair. "And why would you be doing that, sweetheart?"

Natalie walked over to the porch railing and leaned against it, her gaze distant for a moment, and then she focused back on Jackson. "Being Native American, I'm tuned into emotions deeper than other people. It's a gift of my heritage. There was something primal between Amberly and Cole, a force, an energy that proclaimed them soul mates. I liked seeing them together."

"When was the last time you saw them?" Marjorie asked, unable to stay quiet another minute.

"I saw Cole on Thursday, but it had been the weekend before they disappeared that I saw Amberly and him together. They were having dinner together in the local diner and I ate at the counter that night."

"Do you know anyone who might want to hurt them?" Jackson asked.

"Jeff Maynard and his group of idiots weren't too

fond of Cole, but I can't imagine any of them doing something like this. You are going to find them, aren't you? What they had between them was something magical, and it would be a shame if they have somehow been destroyed."

Her words were filled with emotion, and tears slipped down her face. "Watching them together made me feel like I bathed in their love. It made me believe that there was somebody out there who I could connect with on that emotional, sexual, loving level."

She gave a harsh laugh. "I know, I'm just a crazy, lonely fat woman living my life vicariously through others. If you came here to find out if I had anything to do with Amberly and Cole's disappearance, then you've come to the wrong place."

Jackson exchanged glances with Marjorie. Marjorie wasn't sure what to believe. Natalie came across as a straight-shooter, but really good liars had the same ability. Still, she knew they wouldn't get any more pertinent information here, and so she stood, indicating to Jackson that as far as she was concerned they were finished here.

Jackson got up and stood next to her. "We may be back with more questions for you," he said.

Natalie's eyes twinkled. "You can come back here whenever you want, you charming devil, but I have a feeling it would still just be business and not pleasure." Her gaze shot from Jackson to Marjorie and then back again. "I sense more than a little primal energy between the two of you." She smiled slyly. "If I were you two, I'd get after it."

"I'm working on it," Jackson said with a laugh as Marjorie fought both the flaming heat in her cheeks and the desire to punch him in the arm…hard.

Chapter Six

"She sensed something primal between us," Jackson said when they were back in the car and headed to find Jeff Maynard's friend Jimmy Tanner.

"The sound of all those wind chimes has obviously scrambled her brains," Marjorie replied.

Jackson grinned, amused by the straight set of her shoulders, the grim set of her lush lips. "Would it be so bad if there was some primal desire between us?"

"Whether there is or isn't doesn't matter," she replied. "You're just a man who is in town until this case is solved and then you'll go back to Baton Rouge and the bimbos you're accustomed to dating."

"Now, what on earth would make you think I'd date bimbos?" he asked.

"All I want to know from you is what you thought of Natalie Redwing. Do you think she's a harmless stalker or somebody more dangerous?"

Although with the memory of kissing Maggie far too fresh in his mind he'd rather talk about primal need, he gave her a pass. "I'm not sure. I think maybe she's no more than a bit of a voyeur, living her life by stalking people who have what she wants. I'd be more inclined to move her up the suspect list if Amberly was dead and Cole was still alive and here."

"Agreed."

"Still, we'll do a full background check on her and see if anything comes to light."

"Maybe Jimmy Tanner will have some answers for us. We already know that we need to check Jeff Maynard's alibi for the night the Caldwells went missing, and we know he might have a motive, in that the last investigation Amberly and Cole worked on together apparently ended Jimmy's marriage."

"And from what Deputy Black told us, Jimmy is now working as a freelance sort of handyman carpenter. We'll see if we can catch him at home at the motel, otherwise we'll have to see if we can find out where he's working for the day."

He could tell she was grateful that the talk had turned to the case, and he knew that was why he was here, that it should be of utmost importance to him. Amberly and Cole were two people who desperately needed help. Jackson wasn't sure at this point if they'd be found alive or dead, but in either case there were also people who needed closure.

Still, he couldn't deny that in the brief time he'd known Maggie, she'd touched him in places no woman ever had before. She made him want to be a better man than he'd ever been in his life, and she'd made him more ashamed than he'd ever been of where he'd come from.

Jimmy Tanner's current residence was at the Mystic Lake Motel. Jackson sighed with relief as he saw the white panel truck parked out front. A ladder was attached to the roof, and it was obviously a work vehicle. It looked as if Jimmy was home.

The motel didn't appear to be a five-star establishment; rather it looked as if it would have to struggle to make two-star status.

Seeing the broken windows of one unit, an old rusty sports car parked nearby, Jackson got out of the car with his hand on the butt of his gun.

The place smelled like danger…like drug deals and hookers and an alcoholic's oasis. It held the scent of crime and lawlessness, and he was glad to see that his partner had the same vibe, for her hand was on the butt of her gun, as well.

They exchanged sober glances as they approached the end unit that belonged to Jimmy. The curtains were drawn over the filthy windows, making it impossible for them to get a glimpse of what they might face when the door opened.

Jackson knocked on the door, tensed as he waited for a response. Marjorie stood on the opposite side of the entrance, her features also taut and sober.

There was no reply. He knocked again, harder this time, certain that Jimmy the handyman was hiding out inside. His suspicion was confirmed when the curtain at the window moved slightly and then fell back into place.

"He's in there," Jackson said softly to Maggie. He banged on the door once again. "Jimmy Tanner, come outside." Before he could identify them as FBI agents, a crash of glass sounded from around the back of the building.

"He's running," Maggie said, and together she and Jackson took off around the side of the building.

The back of the motel was nothing but a field of weeds, and in the distance were two things: the glittering water of the lake for which the town had been named, and a brown-haired man clad in jeans and a white T-shirt running away as fast as his legs could carry him.

"Halt!" Jackson yelled as he raced to catch him. The last thing he wanted was a damned footrace in this heat and humidity.

He was vaguely surprised that Maggie was matching him step for step. Not only sexy, but fast, he thought with admiration.

"Hey, Jimmy," she yelled. "If you don't stop running, then I'm going to shoot you." Maggie stopped in place and pulled her gun from her holster and assumed a shooter stance.

Jimmy glanced backward, his eyes wild with fear, and his feet skidded to a halt. He slowly turned to face them, with his hands above his head. "If she's paid you to shoot me, then just get it over with," he exclaimed. "She's taken everything else from me, she might as well get my life, too."

As Maggie and Jackson drew nearer, Jackson noticed that one of Jimmy's eyes held the faint yellow bruising of a healing black eye, and his lower lip was scabbed over as if he'd taken a beating in the past week or so.

"Who is 'she'?"

"My ex-wife. Aren't you just two more goons she hired to beat the hell out of me?"

"Do I look like a goon who's going to beat the hell out of you?" Maggie asked.

"You never know," Jimmy replied. "My ex is crazy enough to hire some woman just to get me off guard."

"Actually, we're FBI agents, you dumb ass, and we'd like to ask you some questions," Jackson replied. The late July sun was hot, and Jackson was in no mood to conduct an interview in the middle of a field. "We can do this back at your place or we can take you into the sheriff's office. Your choice."

"My place," he replied. "I try not to show my face around the sheriff's station. Just looking at the building makes me want to punch Cole Caldwell upside the head."

They began walking back toward the motel. "Is this about the sheriff's disappearance?" he asked.

"Partly," Jackson replied.

Jimmy eyed him with narrow eyes. "I might have a reason to want to punch Cole in the chin, but really all he did was confirm to my wife what she'd known for years, that I'd been cheating on her all along. For some reason Tara finally went crazy on me. She divorced me, took most everything I owned and has been hiring thugs to beat me up on a regular basis."

By that time they'd reached the front of his motel room. He opened the door and gestured them inside. The space was surprisingly clean, with the bed neatly made and a suitcase half-packed on the floor.

"Packing or unpacking?" Jackson asked as he thumbed a finger at the suitcase.

"Somewhere in between." Jimmy sank down on the edge of the bed while Jackson and Marjorie remained standing just inside the door. "As soon as I get enough money together I'm heading out of this town. I want to get as far away from Tara as I possibly can, but I'm sure you aren't here because of my marital issues."

"We're here to check on an alibi for the time of the disappearance of Sheriff Caldwell and his wife. Jeff Maynard told us that last Friday night, you, Raymond Chandler and he were all here playing poker."

Jimmy rubbed a hand across his sweaty forehead. "You know, a month ago I would have saved his sorry butt by lying for him. But I'm not lying for anyone anymore, and I just want to keep my nose clean and get out of town as soon as possible. Ray and I met here for our usual poker night, but Jeff never showed up. The two of us were here until about one in the morning, playing two-handed card games and drinking beer."

Jimmy's features hardened. "I'm not in the mood to tell you something that isn't true. The three of us have been jokes in this town, losers and cheaters and low-lifes, but I'm turning things around and I don't want to start by lying to Feds."

Jackson exchanged a look with Marjorie. "Then it appears we need to speak to Jeff again."

"I won't lie, I didn't like Cole, but Jeff hated him. I hope he isn't crazy enough to do something stupid, but you never know, where Jeff is concerned, especially if he's been drinking," Jimmy said. "He gets stupid when he gets drunk."

Marjorie pulled one of her cards from her purse and handed it to Jimmy. "Don't leave town without letting us know your plans."

He nodded, and moments later Jackson and Marjorie were back in the car. "I've got to tell you, Maggie girl, you definitely look hot in a shooter stance."

She shot him the look of aggravation he expected, and he laughed.

"I don't know what you find so funny. We're spinning our wheels here and going nowhere fast in this investigation."

"Not true," he protested. "We just found out that Jeff Maynard lied about his alibi. I'd say that's a break for us."

"But everyone we've talked to about him has told us he's not very bright," she replied. "And whoever got Cole and Amberly out of their house in the middle of the night had to be smart."

"Jeff just might be hiding his cunning under a barrel." Jackson thought of the surly bartender. "We'll check him out and then we'll head back to Kansas City. We'll pick up some of those chocolates your mother likes and then take them to her and have a little visit."

She shot him a startled look. "That's not necessary. She can wait until I can get time to visit her alone."

"On the contrary. I'd love an opportunity to chat with dear old Mom," he replied.

He was interested to meet her mother, to find out what kind of a woman would allow herself to be fleeced out of not just her own fortune but her daughter's, as well.

He also found himself wondering what Marjorie's bedroom looked like. If there was a touch of luxury there that wasn't present in the rest of her tiny house. Did she indulge herself in colorful silk sheets or wear an expensive nightgown to bed every night?

He pulled his thoughts back into the case, knowing that it didn't matter if Natalie Redwing had sensed something primal between him and Maggie. It didn't matter that he felt it himself—not just desire, but also need. Not just a sexual pull but an emotional one, as well. None of it mattered, because he knew they would never follow through on it.

The case—he had to remain focused on the case. He needed to find the answers, solve the case and get back home before Maggie got any deeper into his skin.

UNFORTUNATELY THE SHORT DRIVE to Bledsoe's tavern was a waste of time. It was Jeff's night off.

They spent an hour driving around town, trying to chase down his whereabouts, but finally gave up and headed back to Kansas City.

The last thing Marjorie wanted was to take Jackson to her mother's apartment. There was no reason for the two of them to ever meet, no reason for Jackson to invade her personal life to such a degree.

And yet she knew she should probably stop by for a quick visit now. With the information about the lying Jeff Maynard on the table before them she had a feeling the case was about to take on a life of its own and time to visit with her mother might not come again for a while.

It took her only minutes to stop at the specialty store that sold the expensive white-and-dark-chocolate almonds that her mother loved, and then she was back in the car with Jackson and headed to the upscale apartment building where her mother lived.

"You look nervous," Jackson observed.

She frowned and released a sigh. "I guess I just don't want you to judge my mother as some silly ninny who just lets men scam her. My father spoiled her. He took care of the finances and when he died she'd never paid a bill in her life. She was utterly clueless. If she has any faults at all, it's that she trusted too much and trusted the wrong men."

"Maggie, you don't have to defend your mother to me." Jackson's voice was a low, gentle caress. "Trust me, I'm the last person to judge anyone."

She felt herself relax a bit. "No matter what man was in her life at the time, she always made me feel like I was her top priority. Despite everything she was a good and loving mother to me."

"You never wanted kids?" he asked.

A tiny ache shot off in her heart. "In another world, in another life, I might have wanted children. But, considering the fact that I don't want a man in my life, I made the decision that children were out of the question."

She glanced at him, her heart doing a small leap as always at his attractiveness. "You know so much about my early life, but I don't know much about yours."

"There really isn't much to tell. I don't have any memories of my mother, and my dad was kind of a vagabond. We moved around a lot."

His voice held a stress it hadn't before, and it immediately gave her the feeling that there was more to the story than the tiny bit he'd just shared.

"Are you and your father close?" she asked, wanting more details of who he was and where he'd come from.

"No." The single word snapped out of him like a gunshot. He raised a hand and raked it through his thick hair. "We had a falling-out years ago and went our separate ways."

She shot him another glance and he gave her his irreverent, sexy smile. "I'm just a poor, lonely Southern boy with nobody meaningful to fill up the hours of my days and nights."

"I have a feeling that's just the way you like it," she returned. When she cast him another surreptitious glance, he was staring out the passenger window.

She suspected there was a great depth inside him, a place where he allowed nobody to go. A part of her wanted to be invited in, wanted to discover the man beneath the charm, but it was a foolish wish that would lead only to making their parting more difficult when it came time for him to leave and return to his home in Baton Rouge.

As she pulled into a space in the parking lot in front of her mother's apartment building, nervous anxiety tingled through her veins.

She knew it was past time for her to visit with her mother, but it felt strange to have Jackson along with her. They got out of the car and approached the double doors where an intercom was used as security.

She punched the button to contact her mother, who buzzed them in to the small lobby. "Mom's place is on the second floor," she said as she led him toward the nearby elevator. "Her name is Katherine, Katherine Devoe."

They stepped into the elevator and instantly she was aware that he was too male, too close, and the memory of that kiss they'd shared seared through her brain.

"We'll keep this brief," she said as she tightened her fingers on the box of chocolate.

"Whatever," he agreed easily. "We can't do much more about the investigation until morning. Jeff Maynard is my top priority at the moment, and we already know he won't be in at the tavern until late tomorrow afternoon."

The elevator stopped and the doors slid open. If she were smart, she'd make this visit with her mother last until bedtime. It was obvious Jackson intended to bunk with her another night. He'd made no other arrangements to go anywhere else throughout the day.

It was just after six now, and that left far too many evening hours spent in Jackson's company before bedtime. *We'll talk about the case,* she told herself as she rapped on her mother's apartment door.

Katherine Devoe was an older, taller version of Marjorie. She had the same red-blond hair, the same green eyes, and as she opened the door, those eyes lit up with delight.

"Marjorie," she exclaimed, and pulled Marjorie into a quick hug. She released her, her gaze lingering on Jackson, who stood just behind Marjorie. "I see you not only brought me a box of chocolates, but some eye candy, as well."

"Jackson Revannaugh," he said and held out his hand. Katherine slipped her hand into his and released a girlish giggle as Jackson lowered his mouth to kiss the back of her hand. "It's a real pleasure to meet the mother of such an amazing woman," he said as he released Katherine's hand. "I see now where Maggie gets her looks."

"Maggie?" Katherine raised a perfectly waxed eyebrow. "I like it."

He was definitely pouring it on thick, Marjorie thought as she beelined for the white sofa. Jackson followed, sitting far too close to her.

Katherine closed and locked the door and then

turned to face them, delight on her pretty features. "Well, isn't this a special night." She gazed at Jackson. "My daughter has never brought a friend to visit."

"He's not a friend, he's my partner," Marjorie exclaimed.

"Well, then, you've never brought a partner over to visit, either," Katherine said. "May I get either of you something to drink?"

"I'm fine," Marjorie replied.

"I don't suppose you have any bourbon?" Jackson asked.

Katherine flew to the glass-and-gold minibar in the corner of the room. "I do have some bourbon. Straight up or on the rocks?"

"Straight up is fine." He leaned back on the sofa, looking as relaxed as if he'd been here a hundred times before.

"I do believe I hear a little of the good old South in your accent, Mr. Revannaugh," Katherine said as she fixed the drink.

"Born in Baton Rouge and spent most of my time in and around the area," he replied as she handed him the drink.

"What a coincidence—I had a visitor yesterday who was from Baton Rouge. He told me he'd moved up to Mystic Lake to retire."

Every nerve in Marjorie's body jangled with adrenaline. "That is quite a coincidence," Jackson replied. "An old friend of yours?"

"Actually, I'd never met the man before in my life, but he said he was an old friend of Big Bob, my second husband. He was a very nice man, and we had a pleasant visit."

"What was his name?" Marjorie's nerves refused to quiet.

Katherine frowned for a moment. "Edward...Edward Benson— No that isn't right. Bentz. Edward Bentz, that's it."

Marjorie made a mental note of the name as Jackson and her mother visited while he sipped on his drink. It was obvious that Katherine was utterly charmed by Jackson, who was on his best behavior and regaled the older woman with stories of old cases along with his admiration for Marjorie.

Katherine was lapping it up, smiling with motherly approval at Marjorie, as if pleased that her daughter had finally found such a wonderful man.

They wound up staying for an hour, then Marjorie was the one to call a halt to the visit. "Mom, we've still got to grab some dinner and do some work," she said as she stood.

"Your daughter is a tough taskmaster," Jackson said teasingly as he also got up from the sofa.

"She is all about work, but I keep telling her that life shouldn't be just about that." Katherine's eyes twinkled at Jackson, as if she shared a secret with him. "Maybe you can make her slow down a bit and enjoy the fun in life."

"Mom can simper and you can wink all you want, but nobody is going to make me change," Marjorie said once they were alone in the elevator and headed back downstairs.

"It's obvious your mother has your best interests at heart," he replied.

"Whatever," she said as they exited the elevator.

She didn't speak again until they were in the car and headed to her house.

"Something isn't right." Worry simmered in the pit of her stomach.

"Something isn't right about what?" he asked.

"Big Bob was from Texas, not from the South. I'd like to know what a man from Baton Rouge who has just recently moved to the small town of Mystic Lake is doing visiting with my mother."

"Does seem like a bit of a coincidence," Jackson replied, his voice low and heavy with a new somber note.

"I don't know about you, but I'm not much of a believer when it comes to those kinds of coincidences. We need to find Edward Bentz and see what he's up to. I have a bad feeling and I want to make sure that somehow something we're working on now hasn't brought danger to my mother's doorstep."

She swallowed hard, but it was impossible to get the taste of something bad about to happen out of her throat.

Chapter Seven

Jackson paced the floor of Maggie's tiny kitchen, fighting the frustration of three long days without answers, and a simmering desire for the woman that threatened to explode out of control at any given moment.

For the past three days they'd been chasing down people they couldn't find. Jeff Maynard either had skipped town or was holed up with somebody they didn't know about.

According to his boss at Bledsoe's, Jeff had called and asked for a few days off due to a bad case of the flu. Jackson suspected he had a bad case of FBI-itis. Eventually he'd poke his head out or somebody in town would slip up, and they'd find him.

Edward Bentz had also been an elusive character. They'd discovered he was renting a room from an older woman named Betty Fields. They'd checked with her only to discover that Edward had gone back to Baton Rouge to finish up some last-minute business and would be back at her place late that evening.

Jackson had checked with his contacts in Baton Rouge to get a handle on the man, but apparently he had no criminal record and a background search had yielded only the information that he was fifty-five years old, had worked for over twenty years distributing medical supplies in and around the Baton Rouge area and several other states, and had recently retired from that position.

Unbeknownst to Maggie, Jackson had contacted her director and arranged for an agent to sit outside Katherine Devoe's apartment as security until they had an opportunity to check out Edward Bentz.

Meanwhile, nothing had come of the investigation into the shoot-out at the motel except that whoever had fired the shots had indeed used an Uzi…serious firepower that was definitely intended to kill.

He poured himself a cup of coffee and flopped in one of the two chairs at the table. The sun was just beginning to peek up shy, faint beams over the horizon.

Although they had been unable to connect with the two people they most wanted to speak to, the hours of the days hadn't passed with inactivity. Yesterday they'd spent the entire day in the Mystic Lake sheriff's office, interviewing every single person who had worked under Cole's command.

They'd learned that Cole was considered a tough but fair boss. While some of the deputies seemed to have a healthy fear of Cole, it was tempered with an enormous amount of respect. No red flags had presented, leaving Marjorie and Cole to come home each day still confused about who was behind whatever had happened to Amberly and Cole.

It bothered him that they hadn't found their bodies. It was just like the case he'd been working on in Bachelor Moon, where Sam and his wife and their daughter had been missing now for weeks, and their bodies had never been found. The case remained unsolved.

He and Maggie had fallen into a routine, and he knew he probably had about half an hour before she'd make her morning appearance in the kitchen.

Maggie. He took another sip of his coffee and closed his eyes. He had yet to see her bedroom, but last night in the middle of the night they'd accidently bumped into each other in the hallway. The tiny night-light she kept plugged into the socket next to the bathroom had been enough illumination for him to see that she'd been clad in a short deep purple silk nightgown that had fired the red in her hair and showcased every curve she possessed.

Jackson had nearly fallen to his knees with desire. Their eyes had locked in the dim hallway, hers gleaming with a light that made him want to reach out, to pick her up in his arms and carry her into a bedroom and make love to her.

But before he'd been able to move a muscle, she'd scampered like a rabbit back into her bedroom and closed the door behind her.

He'd had a feeling that if they'd remained in that hallway for a second longer, she would have awakened in his arms this morning after a long night of lovemaking.

He blew out a sigh of frustration, both mental and sexual. He felt like a powder keg about to explode. Taking another drink of his coffee, he smelled her before she entered the room, that sweet floral scent that ramped up his testosterone to caveman levels.

"Well, aren't we informal today," she said as she entered the kitchen and her gaze took in his jeans and white polo shirt.

"Yeah, with this heat I didn't feel like doing the

whole agent kind of dress code." He gazed at her navy slacks and white blouse. "You know, you could do casual with me…maybe some shorts and a blouse that actually has some color to it. I have to admit, you look amazing in purple."

He grinned as she ignored him and strode over to the coffeepot. "You can pretend you didn't hear me, but the flames in your cheeks tell me otherwise."

"A gentleman would never mention a lady's nightgown," she replied.

Jackson laughed. "I don't remember ever confessing to be a hundred percent gentleman, and do you realize how often you blush?" He waited until she was seated across from him at the table. "Are you a virgin?"

She slapped a hand across her mouth in an obvious effort to prevent herself from spewing coffee. She swallowed and coughed, all the while glaring at him with those amazing green eyes. "Not that it's any of your business, but no, I'm not a virgin. Why are you even thinking about things like that?"

There was a new wariness in her eyes that told him to back off. He wrapped his hands around his coffee cup and shrugged. "Because I figured it was easier than thinking about this damn case. If it wasn't for that shooting at the motel, I'd be feeling more than a little bit of déjà vu."

"What do you mean?" She was obviously relieved by the change in topic.

"If Cole and Amberly were kidnapped, then so far we haven't figured out a motive. In the case I was working on in Bachelor Moon, we never figured out a motive for what we finally came to believe had to have been a kidnapping. In both cases no ransom notes have been received, everyone couldn't imagine the people having any enemies and no bodies have been found."

"But you said none of the investigators in the case in Bachelor Moon were threatened in any way," she replied, obviously not wanting the cases to be related and still clinging to the hope that they would find the couple alive and well any day now.

"True," he replied. Hell, he didn't want the two cases to be related, but comparing the facts of the crimes gave him pause. The fact that Edward Bentz was from the Baton Rouge area, which was very close to Bachelor Moon, and that he was now in Mystic Lake definitely was too much of a coincidence to ignore.

He got up from the table and headed toward the fridge. "I'll scramble us up some eggs and make toast and then we can get on the road. Hopefully today we'll get some answers that will help make something about this case come into focus."

Breakfast was eaten quickly, with the conversation centered on their visit with Marjorie's mother. "She's a lovely lady," Jackson said.

"She's got a lot of heart."

"It bothers me that you live like a pauper and she's in that luxury two-bedroom apartment," he admitted.

"I don't live like a pauper," she protested.

He raised a dark brow and held her gaze. "Maggie, I know about what you make for a salary and it's obviously you aren't spending any of it on creature comforts for yourself. Hell, since I've been here I've never even seen you in anything but that white blouse and slacks. Do you have any other wardrobe?"

"Of course I do. I'm fine the way things are. I like helping out my mother."

Jackson finished the last of the eggs on his plate and then looked at her again. "But wouldn't it be better if you'd tell your mother the truth of the situation? Have her move to a place that's more within her means and ease some of the pressure off you?"

"I think we need to solve this case, and you should keep your nose out of my personal life." She straightened in her chair and he knew he'd crossed a line with her.

He reached out his hand and covered one of hers. She tried to pull away, but he held tight. "I just want more for you, Maggie. You deserve more from life."

Her gaze searched his, as if seeking a joke, a facade of charm, but he knew she'd find nothing like that there. He'd spoken the simple, stark truth.

She tried to pull her hand from his again, and this time he let go, and she looked down at her plate. "I appreciate your concern for me, Jackson, but I'm doing just fine. I don't require a lot to be happy."

"Are you happy?" he asked.

Her beautiful green eyes met his once again and a frown darted across her forehead. She took a sip of her coffee and then placed the cup back on the table.

"I never really look for happy. I'm satisfied.... Most of the time I'm content with my life, and that's good enough for me," she finally replied.

He nodded, although he wasn't sure why it wasn't good enough for him. He wanted her to have things— scented oils for a bubble bath, a silk purple dress with killer high heels. She deserved dinner in a candlelit restaurant where the prices weren't on the menu. He wanted her to have a luxurious carpet to rub her bare toes in at the end of a long day, a sofa soft enough to cradle her as she watched television to unwind.

He also wanted her to have laughter, and a man who loved her more than anyone else on the face of the earth. There was no question that she'd suffered financial devastation at the hands of scamming stepfathers, but he imagined she wasn't even aware of the emotional trauma that had gone along with it.

She needed a man who could break through her defenses, a man who could find her pain and heal it with a well of endless love. But he knew he wasn't that man, could never be that man no matter how much he might want to be.

She was right. The best thing he could do was help her solve this crime, and keep his nose out of her personal life. Surely when he was back home in his own apartment, living the superficial personal life he'd built for himself, he'd forget all about a green-eyed beauty who had somehow managed to touch the places in his heart he'd thought were untouchable.

"Don't you find it strange that John Merriweather's ex-wife has been missing for a week and a half and we haven't received one single phone call from him?" Jackson asked as they got into her car. "I mean, if my ex-wife were missing, and we were amicable, I'd be camped out on the doorstep of the head investigator and demanding answers every minute of each day."

"Maybe before we head to Mystic Lake we should have another check-in with John," she suggested.

"Sounds like a plan to me," he agreed.

Marjorie backed out of the driveway and hoped that the day forced her to keep her attention on the case and not on Jackson. The touch of his hand on hers, the genuine emotion she'd seen shining from his eyes at the table had both stunned her and sent a yearning through her she'd never felt before.

She didn't care about expensive furniture or luxury items, but as she'd gazed into those blue eyes of his, she'd wanted him.

She headed in the direction of the Merriweather ranch house and tried not to think of that moment in time when the depth of her yearning for Jackson Revannaugh had taken her breath away, made her tingle with crazy need.

She realized that a part of her wouldn't be averse to making love to him…just once, knowing that it would never mean anything, that she wouldn't see him as a threat to the single life she'd chosen for herself.

He had a home to go back to and she had a life to live here. He was probably a great candidate for a single night of hot, mind-blowing sex because she knew they would never mean anything more than that to each other.

As she pulled into John's driveway, she mentally shook herself, needing to get sex and Jackson off her brain and work the case that had gone nowhere so far.

It was strange that John hadn't contacted anyone since Amberly's disappearance. Surely, even though he was her ex-husband, it would be normal, since he and Amberly shared a child, for him to be rattling cages to find her. So why wasn't he?

She didn't realize how early it was until the door opened and a young boy with jet-black hair and big brown eyes answered. John was behind him in a second. "Any news?" he asked as he ushered the two of them inside.

"We have a few leads we're following," Jackson replied.

Marjorie sat on the sofa, and Max sidled up next to her. "Are you looking for my mom and Daddy Cole?" He leaned into her, bringing with him the scent of soap and innocence that shot a stab of pain straight through Marjorie. This was the victim of whatever had happened, a little boy who desperately needed his mommy back where she belonged.

"We're trying our very best to find them," she replied, fighting her impulse to wrap him in her arms.

"You haven't heard anything?" Jackson asked, his features set in stern lines, reminding Marjorie that he still believed John was their number one suspect.

"Nothing," John replied, his voice holding misery. "I've reached out to all her friends, people she'd mentioned working with, anyone I can think of, but nobody knows anything about what's happened."

He sank down in a chair and motioned Max to his side. "I've been making her welcome-home cards," Max said. "But I need her to come home so I can give them to her."

"We're doing our best to make that happen," Marjorie said. Max nodded, his expression far too somber and grown-up for such a little boy.

"We were just wondering why we hadn't heard from you," Jackson said, his gaze still focused on John.

John shrugged. "I haven't contacted you because I don't have any information to help you. I'd much rather you spend your time working on finding them than talking to me." He raised his chin slightly, as if he felt Jackson's suspicion. "If it would make you feel better about me, I'll start calling you six or seven times a day for a progress report."

Jackson's jaw clenched. "I don't think that's necessary. We'll keep you informed of any new developments, and you let us know if you learn anything that might be helpful." His glance at Marjorie indicated he was ready to leave.

As Marjorie stood up, Max returned to her side. "When you find my mom, would you please bring her home as soon as possible?" His dark eyes filled with tears. "I miss her really, really bad."

Again her heart squeezed painfully tight as she placed a hand gently on his shoulder. "We're doing the best we can, Max."

He nodded and stepped back to his father's side. "We'll be in touch," Jackson said.

Once they were back in the car Marjorie slammed the steering wheel with the palm of her hand. "Who would be so evil to take away that little boy's mother?"

"Let's hope we get some answers in Mystic Lake today," Jackson said, a hint of emotion thickening his voice.

They didn't speak again until they reached the small town. The first place they stopped was at the sheriff's office, where they found Roger Black seated in Cole's office.

"Any news on the missing Jeff Maynard?" Jackson asked the middle-aged head deputy.

"Actually, I have a tip from the rumor mill that he's holed up with Tara Tanner."

Marjorie looked at him in surprise. "Jimmy's ex-wife?"

Roger nodded. "That's the word out on the streets.

Apparently they were seen together last night at the liquor store."

Marjorie's head spun as she remembered their talk with Jimmy. Had Jimmy lied about Jeff not being at the poker party because he was ticked that Jeff was with his ex-wife?

Roger shoved a piece of paper toward them. "This is Tara's address. Be careful—she's a bit of a firecracker."

"So we've heard," Jackson replied.

Roger looked tired, with dark circles beneath his eyes and his brown hair standing on end as if it had felt the rake of frustrated hands through it too many times.

"I wish somebody would find Cole. This job was his, not mine. He's a good sheriff and everyone wants him back behind this desk, where he belongs."

"Right now we have three people in our sights as potential suspects," Marjorie said. "Hopefully in the next hour or so we can either remove Jeff from that short list or confirm that he had something to do with Cole and his wife's disappearance."

"I wish all of us could be more help," Roger said as he stood. "I've got all my men out on the streets, pounding the pavement in an effort to find some kind of answers, but so far we've come up empty-handed on our end."

"We're going to check in with good old Jeff now, and then we have another person of interest we intend to check out this afternoon," Jackson said. "And in be-tween those interviews we'll be walking the streets, as well, seeing what scuttlebutt we might be able to pick up."

"As you both know, we're at your disposal at any time. Whatever you need from us, you've got," Roger replied.

With that Marjorie and Jackson left with directions

to Tara Tanner's house. "Jimmy was mad at Cole for outing his cheating. I wonder what Tara's feelings are about Cole?"

"She should probably consider he did her a big favor," Jackson replied. "I've never understood women who put up with men who cheat on them."

"Maybe it's a matter of a bad man is better than no man at all," she replied.

"I'll bet you wouldn't put up with a cheater," he said.

"You've got that right. If by some miracle, at any point in my life I would decide I wanted a meaningful relationship with a man, I'd expect monogamy. I'd far rather be alone than just have a male body in my life who wasn't committed to me body, heart and soul."

"Apparently Tara Tanner has an addiction to bad boys, if she's moved on from Jimmy to Jeff," Jackson replied.

"We're about to find out," Marjorie replied as she pulled into the driveway of a neat ranch house.

Together they got out of the car and approached the front door. Remembering Roger's warning about Tara being a firecracker, and the fact that it was possible Tara had hired men to beat up Jimmy, Marjorie made sure her gun was easily accessible, if needed.

Jackson knocked on the door and they waited. When there was no reply, he knocked again, harder this time. "Hold your damn horses," a husky female voice called from inside the house.

The door flew open to reveal a bleached blonde wrapped in a red silk robe that had several cigarette burns down the front. The air that wafted out of the door smelled of stale smoke and booze and dirty clothes.

"Yeah? What do you want?" Tara pulled a cigarette

and lighter from the pocket of her robe, lit up and blew smoke at both of them.

"We're here to talk to Jeff," Jackson said.

Tara frowned in fake confusion. "Jeff who?"

"Are we really going to play that game?" Marjorie asked dryly.

A tall shadow appeared behind Tara, and as he came into view he gave them a guilty smile. "Hey," Jeff said.

"We need to talk to you," Marjorie said.

"I figured as much."

Tara stepped back with a shrug of her shoulders, and Jeff gestured them into the semidark living room. Marjorie and Jackson stood just inside the door, looking at the bartender who was dressed only in a pair of plaid boxers and a stained white T-shirt. He wore bed-head badly, and it was obvious they had awakened them.

"Tara, put some coffee on," he said, and she scurried out of the living room.

"None for us," Marjorie replied. She wasn't about to put her mouth on anything that came from this house.

"It's for me," Jeff replied. "We went on a little bender last night and I have a headache from hell. So, guess you're here about the poker party on the night that Cole and his wife disappeared."

"Your alibi sucks, buddy," Jackson said. "Your friends say you never showed up that night. You didn't even call them to say you weren't coming."

Jeff raked a hand through his hair, making his bed-head even worse. "Yeah, well, I hooked up with Tara that night and I couldn't exactly call Jimmy and tell him I was boffing his ex-wife. That was the first night Tara and I hooked up, and I've been here ever since."

Tara came back into the room. "He's telling the truth."

"And we should believe a woman who has been hiring thugs to beat up her ex-husband?" Marjorie said.

Tara's cheeks grew dusky with color. "I don't know what you're talking about." She averted her gaze to the wall.

"I think you do, and we could take you in right now and have you arrested for conspiracy to commit bodily harm or even attempted murder." Marjorie glared at the woman.

Tara's gaze shot back to Marjorie. She folded her arms across her chest, a mutinous expression on her face. "Okay, so maybe I wanted Jimmy to get banged up a little for all the hurt he caused me over the years, but I didn't want him hurt too bad."

Jeff looked at her with stunned surprise. "You actually hired people to beat up Jimmy?"

"It doesn't matter what I did, I'm telling the truth when I say that Jeff was with me on the night that the sheriff and his wife disappeared," Tara said.

She took a deep drag of her cigarette, ignoring the ashes that fell on her ample breasts. "Besides, no offense, but Jeff is too much of a dumb ass to pull off the kidnapping of two people. He couldn't even figure out that it was smart to tell the truth about where he was that night."

"Hey," Jeff said in protest. "I'm not a dumb ass."

Yeah, he was, Marjorie thought and there was no way in hell she'd believe that he had anything to do with whatever had happened at Cole's house almost two weeks ago.

She looked at Jackson. "I think we're done here."

He nodded and inched toward the door as if he couldn't wait to escape the confines of the house. "If we have more questions we'll be in touch. Make sure you both are available," he said.

"Whew, I couldn't wait to get out of there," Jackson said once they were back in the car.

"Did you see the look on Jeff's face when he found out that Tara had hired people to beat up Jimmy?" She laughed. "I don't see a happy ending for Jeff with Tara." Her laughter lasted only a moment and then she sobered. "I also don't think Jeff had anything to do with Cole and Amberly's disappearance. I think we need to take him off our short list of suspects."

A wave of discouragement swept through her. Their list of suspects was dismally small for the length of time they'd been working the case.

For the first time since she'd been handed the case she began to wonder if they'd find the answer they sought, or if this would wind up being like what Jackson had been working on in Bachelor Moon…an unsolved case with collateral damage in the teary eyes of a young child.

Chapter Eight

After leaving Tara's house, Maggie parked her car on the street in front of a business that sold knickknacks and trinkets, and they took off walking.

The heat was unrelenting, the humidity like a sauna, and Jackson wasn't sure what he hoped would happen as they interacted with some of the people of the small town, but he knew with certainty that the investigation was in trouble.

Cell phones had yielded no clues; the bank accounts and credit card activity had remained untouched. It was as if Cole Caldwell and his wife had been levitated into an awaiting spaceship. Just like Sam and Daniella and Macy from Bachelor Moon. He shook his head to dispel the thought.

It was important they continue to work this case by itself until the time came that they either found some answers or had to reach the horrible conclusion that somehow, someway, the Bachelor Moon crime and this one were related.

He shouldn't be confused by attempting to combine the two cases together even though so far they had only one person who had motive for getting rid of Amberly—and that was her ex-husband.

At the moment he was attempting to focus on the chicken fried steak dinner in front of him. He and Maggie had ducked into the diner twenty minutes ago for a late lunch.

Maggie picked at her salad as if without appetite, and he knew the lack of forward motion in the case was affecting her, as well.

"Don't look so depressed," he told her.

She looked up and offered him a small smile. "I just can't get Max's little face out of my head."

As he had that morning, he reached across the table and covered her smaller hand with his. He liked touching her. He wanted to give her comfort, but he knew as far as the case went, he had no words of support to offer her.

She surprised him by twining her fingers with his. "We're doing the best we can, right?" she said.

"Maggie, honey, we're doing everything humanly possible."

She squeezed his fingers a little tighter. "I just don't understand why we haven't found their bodies yet. Deep in my heart I can't imagine a kidnapper keeping them alive for this length of time. That takes planning and work, and even though John might have the best motive for something happening to Amberly, I also believe it would be in his best interest just to kill them and let them be found." She finally pulled her hand away from his.

"He has a lot of resources," Jackson said. "Despite his modest home, he's a very wealthy man. He may have properties we don't even know about, people working for him who aren't even here in town. I've got people from your field office trying to dig deeper into John's life and finances."

She looked at him in surprise. "Working behind your partner's back?"

He shook his head. "Just using whatever resources are available. I know your gut instinct is that John had nothing to do with whatever happened, and to tell you the truth, my gut instinct has completely stopped talking to me. I'm starting to believe in aliens abducting people for scientific studies."

He was rewarded with one of her infrequent but charming laughs. "If that's the case then maybe both of us need to make some aluminum foil antennae to make contact with the alien species."

He grinned. "I think you'd look beautiful in a pair of aluminum earpieces."

"Stop that," she chided him.

"Stop what?"

"Don't flirt with me. I want to know the real Jackson Revannaugh, not the superficial one who spews compliments like the peeing boy statue sprays water."

"I can't believe you just compared me to a little boy statue in Brussels," he said with a laugh. "And just for your information, that wasn't a superficial compliment. That one came straight from my heart."

Her gaze held his and then she looked down and stabbed a piece of carrot with more force than necessary. "You make me a little bit crazy," she said.

"I think you're making me a little crazy, too," he admitted.

They finished their meal in silence and then once again hit the sidewalks for more interaction with the locals. Edward Bentz's landlady, Betty, had told them that she expected Edward back around dinnertime.

Jackson was eager to talk to the man who had ties to both Baton Rouge and Mystic Lake, a man who had visited Maggie's mother before he'd left town.

Certainly, there were elements of this case Jackson found quite troubling, elements that weren't like what he'd investigated with the Bachelor Moon disappearance.

Everything that could be done was being done, both at the federal and at the local levels. There was nothing more they could do but what they were doing.

They spent the next couple of hours going in and out of stores, chatting up people about the sheriff and his wife. Everywhere they went, everyone they spoke to had only good things to say about Cole and Amberly.

Spinning wheels, he thought in disgust. They were hamsters running as fast as they could and getting nowhere. Somebody had been threatened by them, but who? Who had been holding on to the Uzi that shot up their motel room?

He believed the threat had come from this small, pleasant town with its sparkling lake and friendly people. He believed that whoever had shot the gun had followed them from here with the intent to kill them both.

At five o'clock they headed back to Marjorie's car. "I'm hot and my feet are killing me," Marjorie said as she leaned against the driver door. "I'm not used to doing this kind of pounding-the-sidewalk investigation."

"I told you it might be a good day to go casual," Jackson replied, although his feet were aching, too, and his polo shirt was damp with perspiration.

The sun was relentless and the humidity was like a living entity trying to suffocate him to death. "Is it always this humid here?" he asked as he slid into the passenger seat and she got behind the steering wheel.

"This feels worse than usual. I heard somebody say we're supposed to get storms tonight. The atmosphere is definitely soupy enough for them." She started the car and turned the air conditioner on high blast.

It blew hot air for several seconds and then began to cool. Jackson moved his vents to shoot on his face and neck and looked out the window where the sky remained cloudless. "I don't see any signs of rainstorms anywhere," he said.

"Give it another hour or two," she replied. She backed out of the parking space. "Look to the southwest, that's usually where they come from. I just hope we've given Edward Bentz enough time to get from wherever he's been to Betty Fields's place. I'm eager to see why he was visiting my mother."

"I'm eager to ask him a lot of questions," Jackson replied. He hoped there was a reasonable explanation for Edward Bentz's sudden move to Mystic Lake. He hoped they'd discover that the man had family here, that he'd grown up here and decided it was the place he wanted to retire.

Otherwise Jackson would have to consider if he was a potential link between the crime that had occurred in Bachelor Moon and what had happened here in Mystic Lake.

By the time Maggie pulled up in Betty Fields's driveway behind a white panel van, Jackson's head was spinning. A high dose of adrenaline pulsed through him at the sight of the van, which hadn't been in the driveway when they'd been here before.

If somebody was going to kidnap two people, they would need transportation, and a panel van was the perfect vehicle for such an undertaking.

Betty answered Jackson's knock. She was a petite older woman with a head of snowy-white hair and the smile of a gentle soul. "Come in and get out of the heat," she exclaimed. She ushered them into a small, cool formal living room with a sofa, two chairs and a polished coffee table.

The scent of pot roast rode the air, and Jackson's stomach rumbled despite the fact that they'd had a late lunch.

"I know you're here to speak to Edward. He's just gone to his room until dinnertime. I'll call him and you all can talk in here." She gestured them to the sofa and then disappeared down a hallway.

The sound of a knock on the door, a murmur of voices, and then she returned with a tall, broad-shouldered man following at her heels. "I'll just be in the kitchen if you need anything," she said, and quickly scurried from the room.

Edward Bentz was a handsome man with sandy hair and hazel eyes. He gave them both a pleasant yet curious smile. "You wanted to speak to me?" he asked.

Jackson did the introductions, noting the slight dilation of Edward's pupils as he realized they were FBI agents. "What have I done to warrant the interest of the FBI?" He sank down in the chair opposite the sofa.

"The first thing is that you visited my mother before you left town," Maggie said.

"Your mother?" His brow wrinkled and then

smoothed out. "Of course, you're Katherine's daughter. I should have recognized the resemblance."

"What was your business with her?" Maggie asked, her tone more aggressive than usual.

"Business? No business. I knew Bob Stevenson. I used to deliver medical supplies all over the southern portion of the States. I met Bob and we became friendly and then a year went by when I didn't see him. I saw him again about three months ago and he mentioned that he'd married and divorced a woman from Mystic Lake. I got the impression he'd done her wrong, and so when I came to town I decided to look her up. She's a lovely lady, by the way."

Jackson could tell Maggie wasn't sure if she believed him or not. "I understand you're from my neck of the woods," Jackson said. "Baton Rouge?"

Edward grinned. "I'd know that accent anywhere. I called Baton Rouge home for a long time, although my roots are here in the Midwest."

"Ever hear of a place called Bachelor Moon?" Jackson asked.

Edward frowned again. "No, I don't believe I know the place. Is it near Baton Rouge?"

"Not far from there," Jackson replied. "So, why does a man move from Baton Rouge to Mystic Lake?"

"I came into a little money, an inheritance, and decided my traveling-salesman days were over. I was sick of the big city and remembered passing through here once when I came to a conference in Kansas City. I wanted a small town, and this seemed to be the perfect place."

Although he spoke earnestly and his facial features showed no signs of lying, as he'd talked his body had shifted slightly away from Jackson, and his feet pointed toward the door.

When Jackson began to question him about his whereabouts on specific dates, Edward got downright shady, not remembering where he'd been or who he'd spoken to, professing that since he'd been making trips back and forth to Baton Rouge he wasn't sure what days he was where.

He couldn't provide receipts for gas or travel, didn't have records of what motels he'd stopped at on his trips. "I didn't know any of this would be important," he exclaimed. "I'm just a retired salesman looking for a quiet life. Why would I want to hurt a sheriff and his wife?"

Why indeed?

By the time they left Edward, Jackson was more confused than ever. There was something about the man he didn't trust, but he couldn't make the pieces fit. According to Bentz, he'd never even met Cole Caldwell.

Dammit, they needed a break, he thought as he slammed out of the house when they were finished with the interview. He got into the car and noted the dark clouds gathering in the sky.

Maggie had been right. It looked as though a storm was brewing, and he felt it simmering inside him. The frustration that roared through him was the same that he'd felt when he'd been working the case in Bachelor Moon, only bigger and stronger.

He couldn't imagine working back-to-back cases that yielded no answers, no closure. He was used to solving crimes, not allowing crimes to beat him, and at the moment he felt totally beaten.

Maggie slid into the car and turned to look at him. "Food," she said. "I sense a raging beast not only in the sky but also in the seat next to me. I can't do anything about the coming storm, but we need to feed the beast before he fully emerges. We'll stop at the diner before we leave town."

He looked at her in surprise, wondering when in the time they'd spent together she'd come to know him so well.

"I just feel like we can't get a damned break," Jackson said when they were seated in the Mystic Lake diner, where they had eaten lunch earlier in the day.

They'd already ordered burgers and fries, but even the promise of imminent food didn't relax the tense lines on Jackson's face.

"You'll feel better after you've eaten," she said. She took a sip of her water as outside the window where they sat, the sound of thunder rumbled, and lightning flashed in the distance. Hopefully they could eat quickly enough to get back to her place in Kansas City before the rain came.

"What did you think about Bentz's story?" he asked.

She released a tired sigh. "To be honest, I don't know what to think. I definitely believe we need to dig a little deeper into his background, confirm his previous employment and whatever we can find out through legal channels. We don't have enough on him to get any kind of a warrant to dig too deep."

"I did a cursory background search on him already. He has no criminal record. The man has never even gotten a speeding ticket," Jackson said with obvious disgust.

"Maybe it is just a coincidence that he showed up in town around the same time Cole and Amberly went missing. Maybe he really is exactly what he says he is, a traveling salesman from the South who decided to retire to a small Midwestern town." She sighed once again. "And maybe the moon is really made of green cheese."

"So, you didn't believe him," Jackson replied. He paused as the waitress arrived with their orders.

"I don't know what to believe anymore," she admitted. "I feel like my brain has been taken out, scrambled and shaken and then set back in place. Maybe I'm just exhausted. I haven't been sleeping very well."

"That makes two of us," Jackson replied.

She had a feeling he wasn't sleeping well for the same reason she wasn't. Each night that he'd been beneath her roof, she'd tossed and turned, trying not to think about him in the next room, trying not to play and replay the kiss they'd shared. The energy between them snapped and crackled, and fighting it had become exhausting.

He picked up a fry from his plate without enthusiasm and glanced out the window where the storm clouds had created a false sense of twilight.

It was the first time since she'd met him that he appeared discouraged, without a smart quip or that twinkle in his eyes. His unusual demeanor made her even more afraid for Cole and Amberly.

"You aren't giving up, are you, Jackson?" She voiced her concern.

He smiled and shook his head. "No way. I'm a persistent man when I'm going after something I want, and I want answers. No, I'm not giving up, but I am discouraged by our lack of progress."

He picked up another French fry, but it was obvious that food wasn't going to solve the problem of his frustration. He took a bite of his burger and then shoved his plate away with a deep sigh.

"Actually, I thought I was hungry, but I guess I'm not," he admitted.

She raised a brow. "Take note of this moment… Jackson Revannaugh isn't hungry." She looked down at her plate and then back at him. "To tell the truth, I'm not really hungry, either."

He gazed toward the window where it appeared darker than it had moments before. "Maybe we should just get out of here and try to beat the storm to Kansas City."

"Sounds like a plan to me," she agreed. "We can always eat later at home, since you stocked my pantry and fridge with enough food to feed a small army for a month."

Thunder crashed overhead as they left the diner, followed by a sizzle of lightning that slashed through the dark sky. Thankfully the rain hadn't begun, although it threatened to fall at any minute.

Marjorie had just pulled out of the diner and started down Main Street when she noticed in her rearview mirror that a motorcycle was following too close for her comfort.

"Crazy drivers," she muttered under her breath. At that moment her rearview mirror on the outside of her door exploded. She screamed at the same time Jackson flew into action. He unbuckled his seat belt, pulled his gun and turned to look out the back window.

"He's got a gun. Don't let him pull up next to us. Keep him behind us." Jackson rolled down his window and leaned out as Marjorie fought down panic.

The back window exploded inward and Marjorie stifled another scream while Jackson cursed and fired back. "Get us off this main road," he said. "Make a turn and try to lose him."

Marjorie didn't know the town of Mystic Lake well, but she stepped on the gas and then took the next right turn at a speed that had them nearly riding on two wheels. She quickly made another turn to the left, but could hear the whine of the motorcycle still behind them.

Jackson popped off a couple more shots, but in her rearview mirror Marjorie saw the motorcyclist zig and zag in erratic movements to dodge Jackson's assault.

As he made a move to pull up next to the side of the car, she turned the wheel and rode along the curb to thwart his actions, grateful that they were on a residential street with no oncoming traffic. Numb with fear, she turned left, then right and then left once again, lost in the maze of quiet neighborhood streets while the cyclist remained behind them.

She realized that as long as she was driving fast and taking corners at breakneck speed, he had no opportunity to shoot but instead had to focus on his own driving.

The fear dissipated when she focused on the simple act of survival. Training kicked in and a cold wash of determination swept over her. As Jackson fired again, the motorcycle fell back.

Marjorie didn't slow her speed or her evasive driving. She continued to race down streets. Disoriented as to place, she was stunned to find herself back on the road that led to Kansas City. A glance in her mirror showed her nothing, and an edge of relief coursed through her. It lasted only seconds, since the motorcycle roared into view once again.

"Just don't let him get next to us," Jackson said, his voice half lost from the wind blowing in the open back window. He was leaning so far out the passenger window she feared if she veered too sharply he'd fall out.

Once again the motorcycle roared forward, heading for the other lane of traffic. Marjorie jerked her wheel to keep him from coming up alongside the car.

She knew that if he got next to them he'd have a perfect shot to kill either her or Jackson, and she wasn't about to let that happen. If he was going to kill them, she was going to make him work for it.

As she saw the approaching lights from a car, she swerved back into her lane, and the motorcycle fell back. She was aware of her own breaths coming in small gasps, but she focused on keeping the car on the road.

If they could just make Kansas City there would be enough traffic that it would be much easier to lose their pursuer. She knew the city well, knew the best streets to take to throw him off.

Just get to Kansas City. It became a mantra in her head as her gaze shot from the mirror to the road. Raindrops began to splash on her window, and she had to turn on her wiper blades in order to see the road ahead.

She had no idea what Jackson was doing, only that he'd lowered himself back in the passenger seat but was still turned to face the back, where he could shoot out the busted window.

Her fingers were so tight around the steering wheel they cramped in pain, but she didn't dare relax her hold. She didn't even have time to wonder who was chasing them. All she could think of was getting to familiar territory where it would be more difficult for the man chasing them.

The rain came down harder, making visibility more difficult as the skies grew darker. She didn't want to turn on her lights, didn't want to make them a well-lit moving target.

Ten more miles and they'd reach the city limits. Ten more miles and she was certain they would find safety. If nothing else, she could drive right into the parking lot at the FBI field office, where she was certain a murderous motorcyclist wouldn't follow.

Seven miles, she thought. Six miles. She was eating up the highway at a reckless speed, despite the rain and the darkness.

Almost there. Surely she could get them to safety. The front windshield exploded outward and instantly another bullet found one of the tires. With a scream she twisted the wheel, bumping them over the edge of the highway and down an embankment, where the car rolled to its side.

Stunned, she remained buckled in place as she heard the whine of the motorcycle coming closer... closer.

"You okay?" Jackson's voice came from someplace next to her.

"I...I think so."

"We've got to get out of here."

The car lay on the driver's side, and she unbuckled her seat belt as Jackson climbed out the window. She fumbled around and found her purse, grabbed it and then allowed him to pull her up and through the window, as well.

The motorcycle appeared on the lip of the highway and went silent. "Run," Jackson whispered, and pointed in the distance to a stand of trees.

He grabbed her hand and together they ran like the wind, rain pelting them as danger got off the motorcycle. Apparently the lack of good visibility worked in their favor. They made it to the trees at the same time a tall, well-built figure started down the embankment toward their wrecked car.

Jackson squeezed her hand. "We can't stay in the area. Which way is the city?"

Marjorie paused a moment to get her bearings and then pointed. They took off running, aware that within minutes the motorcycle man would realize they weren't in the car and would come after them.

Chapter Nine

Jackson had no idea how long they ran. It felt like forever. At any moment he half anticipated a bullet to the back, but as they got farther and farther away from the car, some of the fear that had lodged in the back of his throat began to wane, the rich, comfortable and familiar emotion of anger taking its place.

He'd heard no sound of the motorcycle that might indicate they'd been followed. They finally landed in an alleyway between a pizza joint and a tattoo parlor, where they leaned against the brick wall of the restaurant and drew in deep, gulping breaths.

The rain had stopped for the moment, although both of them were soaking wet. Wet was better than dead, he told himself as he waited for the stitch in his side to go away.

"I can't believe I wrecked the car," she finally gasped.

"You didn't wreck the car—a man with a gun wrecked the car. You drove like a professional racecar driver until he blew out that tire."

She gave him a grateful smile. Her blouse was wet and torn at one shoulder; the bottom of her slacks were covered with muck. Her hair hung in a bedraggled fashion, slicked to her scalp, and yet she looked beautiful.

He'd admired her as a gorgeous woman, but a new admiration for her as an FBI agent filled him. "We need to get someplace dry and safe," he said.

"I'll call for a car to pick us up." She started to open her purse.

"No, don't do that," he said quickly. She paused, and in the darkness of the alley, her eyes glittered like those of a jungle animal. "Right now I'm not in the mood to trust anyone but ourselves."

"You think that guy might be able to track us?"

"I don't know, but I'm not taking any chances. First the motel room and now this—things have definitely taken an unexpected turn. Do you have any idea where we are?"

"I know we're someplace downtown, but I'm not sure exactly where."

"You wait here. I'm going to go into the pizza place and get an address and use their phone to call for a cab." Her eyes lit with a touch of fear. "Don't worry," he assured her. "I'll only be gone a minute or two." She drew her gun and nodded. "Just don't shoot me when I come back," he said dryly.

The pizza joint was empty except for a young man with bad acne behind the counter. "Help you?" he asked in a tone of voice that indicated he'd prefer not to have to help anyone.

"I need this address and a phone to call a cab."

The kid rattled off the address and then picked up the receiver of a cordless phone on the counter and handed it to Jackson. "Cab numbers are taped to the wall by the front door. Our usual clientele like their beer more than their pizza."

Jackson walked over to the door and dialed the first number that connected him with a cab company. Assured that a cab would be there within the next fifteen minutes, Jackson hung up. He handed the kid behind the counter the phone and a ten-dollar bill.

"Hey, thanks."

Jackson didn't reply. He left and returned to the alley, where Maggie was huddled against the back. "Cab will be here in fifteen minutes or so."

"I can't wait to get home and get out of these wet clothes," she said as she put her gun back into its holster.

"We aren't going home."

She moved closer to where he stood at the mouth of the alley. "Then where are we going?"

"A hotel, and I don't want anyone on earth to know where we are for the night—not your boss, not mine and none of the law enforcement in Mystic Lake or here. Just you and me, darlin', for tonight we disappear off the face of the earth until we can fully process what just happened."

"I'm not sure I'll ever be able to process what just happened."

He heard the faint tremble in her voice. The adrenaline that had kept her functioning was apparently beginning to wear off. He wrapped an arm around her shoulders and pulled her close against him, their clothes slapping together wetly.

"I guess we should be grateful it was just rain and not hail or a tornado," she said, leaning into him.

"We should also be grateful that the shooter managed not to wound either of us."

He hugged her closer while they silently awaited the arrival of the cab. Although the night air was warm, she shivered against him and he mentally cursed the fact that they'd once again been caught off guard.

Whoever had been on that motorcycle had to have been watching them, waiting to follow them onto the highway, where he could hopefully kill them by either shooting them or causing a wreck that would render them helpless.

This was the second murder attempt they'd survived. He had to admit that he was a bit superstitious. How many lives did they have? Would the third time be a charm for the assailant?

There was no question in his mind now that the threat came from somebody in Mystic Lake. But who? They had spoken to dozens of people that day as they'd meandered the streets and stopped into stores.

It had begun to rain again, a soft patter that, at this point, couldn't make them any wetter. Nor did the rain distract from Jackson's thoughts.

Two things he knew for sure—the person who had chased them had been on a street-legal motorcycle, and he was left-handed. Jackson pulled out his cell phone and called the sheriff's office in Mystic Lake.

"Deputy Black," he said to whoever answered the phone. "Tell him it's Agent Revannaugh."

A moment later Roger Black's deep voice filled the line. "What's up?" he asked.

"First thing in the morning I want you to have ready for me a list of everyone in Mystic Lake who owns a motorcycle," Jackson said.

"Okay, want to tell me what this is all about?" Roger asked.

"We'll talk in the morning when we come in to get that list." Jackson disconnected and slipped his cell phone back into his pocket.

At that moment a cab pulled to the curb, and he and Maggie slid into the backseat. The driver was a bear of a man, with a full head of fuzzy red hair and a nose that looked as if it had been broken more than once. "Where to?"

"What's the best hotel in the city?" Jackson asked, and felt Maggie's surprised gaze on him.

"Best as in most expensive?" the cabbie asked. "Definitely the Woodbridge Hotel on the Plaza."

"Then that's where we want to go," Jackson said, and then leaned back in the seat.

Maggie leaned toward him, her eyes worried. "Jackson, that place is really expensive, and I'm not sure the agency will cover that kind of accommodations."

"Don't you worry," he assured her. "I've got this."

"Are you sure?"

"Positive. Just sit back and enjoy the ride. It won't take long and we'll be someplace safe and dry."

She leaned back against the seat and closed her eyes, and Jackson studied her in the light of street lamps they passed.

Once again her face was unnaturally pale, and even though her hands were clasped in her lap, he couldn't help but notice their slight tremble.

Adrenaline still pumped through him, wild and intense. He knew it would go away eventually, but not until he and Maggie were safely ensconced in a place where nobody would find them for the night.

He checked his watch, surprised that it was only just after eight. The chase had seemed to last forever, their run for safety even longer, but the entire thing from start to finish had lasted only about forty minutes.

He plucked at his wet shirt, looking forward to a shower and then a big towel to dry himself off. His mind clicked and whirred with his plans for the night.

By the time the cabbie pulled around the circular drive in front of the high-rise, high-dollar hotel, he'd made his plans and felt good about their safety for the night.

They got out of the cab, and Jackson paid the driver, who then zoomed off to head toward a staging place to await the next call.

The hotel lobby was tastefully opulent, gold and black being the main color scheme. Jackson led Maggie to an area near the concierge's desk. "Wait here," he instructed. "It should just take me a short time to arrange things for the night."

He strode toward the front desk, aware that both of them looked like something the cat had dragged in.

"Good evening, sir." The man behind the reservation counter didn't blink an eye. "How can I be of service to you tonight?"

Jackson told him exactly what he wanted, and within minutes the room had been paid for and he held two keys in his hands. "There are also several other things we'll need." As Jackson explained, the man behind the counter pulled out a pad and took notes.

"We'll be glad to accommodate you with everything you need," he said.

Jackson thanked the man and then went back to Maggie. "We're all set."

"I still can't believe you came here," she said as they walked toward the elevator bank. "A no-tell motel would have been just as safe as long as nobody knew where we were."

"My taste for motels has changed since somebody tried to kill us in one," he replied.

They stepped into the awaiting elevator, where Jackson used a key in a slot. "Trust me, nobody will think to look for us where we're going."

The doors whooshed closed and he watched Maggie's eyes as the elevator reached the top level of buttons and continued upward.

When the door finally opened it was on the quiet top floor. There were only three rooms here, and he led her to the door on the far left and used a card to open it.

"Welcome to your home for the night."

She stepped into the lush two-bedroom suite with a living room that boasted a white stone fireplace, a red plush sofa, two chairs and, to the side, a dining room table that would seat twelve.

She turned back to face him, her eyes gleaming and a smile of disbelief curving her lips. "Are you serious?"

He laughed. "As serious as a heartbeat. Tonight we live in luxury. I'd say we've earned it after barely escaping with our lives."

Her smile fell and her body began to tremble. He wasn't sure if it was because she was wet and the air-conditioning was cool or if it was the aftermath of trauma. He suspected the latter.

He pulled her into his arms and she pressed against him, as if seeking any heat that might remain in his body. He held her for several long moments and then released her.

"Go on, go check out your suite. There should be a jetted tub in there, complete with complimentary bubble bath. While you're indulging in that, I'm going to shower and order up some food. I'm suddenly starving."

She laughed, the first carefree burst of laughter he'd ever heard from her. "Why am I not surprised? I'll meet you back here after I'm clean and dry."

She practically skipped to her suite and he heard her excited gasps. She returned to the doorway, her eyes opened wide. "There's even a television in the bathroom," she exclaimed.

"Turn it on and watch something," he replied, delighted by her excitement.

"I'm going to get spoiled and then I'm probably going to have to order cable television when I get home." She flashed him a quick smile and then disappeared back into the suite once again.

Jackson turned and headed for his own room, a sinking feeling in his heart. Not only did he have to figure out who had tried to kill them not once, but twice, he also had to admit to himself that he was more than a little bit in love with Maggie Clinton.

MARJORIE LOWERED HERSELF deeper into the hot pear-scented bubble bath and released a deep, cleansing sigh. Awaiting her was not just a big fluffy towel, but also a pristine white robe that would serve as her clothing until bedtime.

She'd hung her blouse and slacks over the top of

the shower stall, hoping they would be dry enough by morning to put on again.

She frowned and sank lower in the oversize tub. The last thing she'd want to do in the morning was pull on the torn blouse and nasty, dirty slacks, but at least for tonight she'd be clean and comfortable in the provisions offered by the hotel.

The television was turned on to an all-news channel, the volume just loud enough to be heard above the bubbling jets that gently pummeled her body in pleasurable waves.

Never had she been in a place like this, and she wondered how on earth Jackson had managed to afford it. She used her toe to turn the knobs that would add more water, and then grabbed one of the complimentary bottles of shampoo and lathered up her hair.

She turned so that she could use the faucet water to rinse the shampoo and then reluctantly turned off the water, shut off the jets and pulled the plug. If she stayed in any longer she feared she might grow a tail.

The big towel was heavenly, soft and fluffy and enfolding her entire body. She moved from the tub to the enormous marble vanity complete with two sinks and a mirror that showed her tangle of hair and the paleness that still clung to her skin, making the handful of freckles on her face stand out more than usual.

As she finger combed her hair, she tried to keep her thoughts off the events of the night. At the moment she was warm and comfortable, but she knew if she allowed her mind to drift back in time, a new chill would not only sweep through her, but take complete possession of her.

One minute at a time, she told her reflection in the

mirror. Soon enough she knew that she and Jackson would be discussing what had happened. But for right now, she just wanted to indulge herself.

She found a small bottle of complimentary lotion that smelled of the fresh, slightly spicy pear bubble bath, and she rubbed it liberally over her shoulders and down her arms and legs.

She thought about using the hair dryer, but heard a knock on the front door and froze. Her purse with her gun was on the king-size bed in the bedroom.

She relaxed as she heard Jackson answer, the murmur of voices and the sound of a tray being delivered. She'd been so long in the bath apparently Jackson had already showered and ordered them a meal, which had just arrived.

It took her only minutes to discard the towel and reach for the robe that easily wrapped around her. She belted it and then eyed her reflection in the mirror one last time.

Twice they'd eluded death, but at least for tonight they would be safe. She left her suite and returned to the living room, where the table had been set for two. The plates were covered with metal containers hiding the visual sight of the food but unable to hold in the amazing scent that emanated from the plates.

Jackson wore a robe like hers and he looked hot as hell with his dark hair still damp and slightly messy and the material stretching across his broad shoulders.

"Just in time," he said as he caught sight of her. He smiled and pulled out one of the chairs at the table for her.

"Something smells delicious." She slid into the chair

and he removed the metal cover to reveal a beautiful steak, mashed potatoes and perfectly grilled asparagus.

"I wasn't sure what you'd want," he said as he took the seat next to her. "I figured this meal hits most of the food groups—meat for protein, potato for starch and veggies just because I figured you'd want some."

A basket of hot rolls and slabs of butter were also on the table, along with tall glasses of water. He'd poured her a glass of red wine, assumingly from the bar, and he had a glass of what she knew was bourbon in front of him.

He raised the bourbon glass and motioned for her to pick up her wineglass. "To us, for surviving." They clinked glasses, and then she took a sip of the wine. It warmed her from her mouth to her stomach.

"I say we eat and don't talk about anything too grim until we're finished with our meal," he suggested.

"Sounds perfect to me," she replied. She cut into her steak and took a bite. "I feel like I've died and gone to heaven."

"Not heaven." He grinned. "Just the Woodbridge Hotel."

They ate in silence for a few minutes, and then Marjorie looked at him in speculation. "Are you wealthy?"

"I suppose in some social circles I'd be concerned wealthy," he replied.

"Family money?"

"God, no." He laughed, as if finding the very thought amusing. "More like lucky money."

"What does that mean?" She cut a piece of asparagus and tried to tell herself she really wasn't that interested in his life, she was only making dinner conversation.

"I left home when I was sixteen. I continued to go to school, and after school I worked whatever jobs I could find. I slept in bus stations, showered in truck stops and did everything I needed to survive." He set his fork down and stared just over her shoulder, as if lost in the maze of his past.

"I managed to get through college on scholarships and still working whatever jobs I could find. When I graduated I had a little nest egg put away and I invested it in a company one of my roommates was starting up, a computer security company.

"By the time I joined the police force the company was widely successful and my buyout gave me more cash than I knew what to do with. Since that time I've invested smart and been lucky with those investments."

"So, if you're so rich, what are you doing working for the FBI? Why work at all?"

"The job is in my blood." His eyes flickered the dark blue that made her want to plumb their depths. "I can't imagine doing anything else."

She nodded, understanding exactly what he meant. She couldn't imagine anything else she'd rather be doing than working this job. She liked taking bad guys off the streets and making sure they were locked up where they belonged.

"I especially like the profiling aspect of the job, although I seem to be failing miserably at the moment," he added.

"The very best profiler wouldn't have enough information to work well in these circumstances," she replied. "And we said no talking about work while we ate."

"Right," he said easily, and took another sip of his bourbon. "I will say this, though—this is the first time I've felt completely relaxed, completely safe, since the night of the motel shooting."

She raised a brow. "You didn't feel safe at my house?"

"To be perfectly honest, I wondered when the bad guy or guys would figure out where you lived and attack us there."

She sucked in her breath at the very thought of the sanctity of her little home being compromised.

As they finished the meal, rain pattered against the windows and an occasional rumble of thunder was heard, but it was obvious the storm was passing and would soon be gone.

Once they had eaten they moved to the sofa. He sat first and patted the space right next to him. As she sat next to him he wrapped an arm around her shoulder.

"It's been one hell of a night," he said softly. "Was the car your personal vehicle?"

She nodded, trying to ignore the fresh scent of soap and male that emanated from him. "But I'm not worried about it. I have good insurance."

As she thought of the car...the bullets and how lucky they had been...a new chill took form in the depths of her, a chill that forced a shivering she couldn't control.

"Hey." He pulled her closer against his side. "It's over for now and we're still here."

Unexpected tears burned at her eyes and as they fell down her cheeks she swiped at them with an embarrassed laugh. "I don't know what's wrong with me. I suddenly feel like an emotional mess."

He tightened his arms around her. "You're crashing, darlin', and it's okay to do it right here in my arms." His voice was a soft caress that only made her tears flow faster.

Instead of attempting to suck them up, mentally realizing she couldn't do anything to stanch them, she turned so that her face was in the front of his robe and she sobbed into the fresh scent as he held her tight and caressed her back.

He didn't say a word and she was grateful for his silence. All she needed were his strong arms around her and the safety of his nearness.

When the tears had finally stopped, she sat up and swiped her face. "Sorry, I didn't mean for that to happen." Her gaze searched his. "I was just so scared," she admitted painfully.

He smiled and gently reached out to tuck a strand of her hair behind her ear. "I'll tell you a little secret—I was positively terrified."

Her eyes widened in astonishment. "But you seemed so cool."

"Inside I was quaking like a young man meeting his girlfriend's parents for the first time." Once again he reached out, this time to place the palm of his hand on her cheek. "Fear is good, Maggie. Fear is what keeps us alive. If you had no fear, then I wouldn't want you as my partner. You'd be dangerous not only to yourself but to me, as well."

She curled against him once again and released a deep sigh.

They were safe for tonight, but what happened tomorrow? Were they at risk staying in her home? They certainly couldn't stay here indefinitely.

Tomorrow new arrangements would have to be made, but she wasn't sure where they could go to escape the danger that felt as if it moved closer and closer.

Chapter Ten

Jackson didn't want to move. With Marjorie snuggled against him on the sofa, finally relaxed enough that she was no longer crying or shaking, he was reluctant to break the embrace.

But he knew they had to talk about the case, to discuss what had happened tonight and what it might mean. Hopefully tomorrow Roger Black would have a list of everyone in and around the Mystic Lake area who owned a motorcycle, and with that list he and Maggie could potentially figure out who had chased them through the rain with the intent to murder them.

She must have sensed that his thoughts were going in darker directions, for she sat up and wrapped her arms around herself, as if preparing for the discussion they had to have.

"It's obvious that the guilty party lives in or around Mystic Lake," he said.

She nodded. "I agree. Unfortunately we talked to dozens of people today, so it's impossible to single out any one person we might have spooked."

He frowned. "You know what bothers me about all of this? We aren't the only FBI agents asking questions. We aren't the only law enforcement people investigating. So why target us specifically?"

Her frown mirrored his. "What are you thinking? That these attacks are somehow personal and not about the case at all?" She shook her head. "You aren't even from around here, and I can say with confidence that there's nobody who cares enough about me to kill me."

Nobody cares enough about me…. The simple, stark words once again touched Jackson's heart despite his desire to the contrary. He raked a hand through his hair and tried to remain focused on the real topic of conversation.

"I don't know, maybe it's just a crazy thought. But Black has deputies walking the streets, and nobody has tried to kill them. Don't you have an agent working with you…Agent Forest?"

She nodded. "Adam Forest. But he hasn't been in touch with me about any threats or near-death experiences. Should I call him and double-check?"

"Not tonight and not from here. I don't want either of us using the phones here, or our cell phones for the night. Call me paranoid, but I don't know the enemy well enough to know what his resources might be."

"That's a scary thought," she replied.

"Better safe than sorry. We get to just talk to each other until it's time to go to bed." He looked at his watch. It was already after ten, but he didn't feel the least bit sleepy.

What he felt like was taking Maggie into his suite, stripping the oversize fluffy bathrobe off her body and making love to her, but he knew it was not only a natural reaction to stress, but also a bad idea all around.

Still, the spicy pear scent of her, the softness of her

hair and the memories of her sweet curves pressed tightly against his own, stirred that primal desire that Natalie Redwing had spoken of so eloquently.

"I just think you're wrong in believing this is anything personal," she said. "We have been the face of the investigation since it began. If our perp is from Mystic Lake, then the law enforcement there might be his friends or relatives, while we are strangers and easily disposed of."

He grinned. "Not so easy, after all. We're cats with nine lives."

"I'm not willing to trust our luck a third time. We need to figure this out, Jackson." Her eyes were so emerald and so earnest.

"We aren't going to figure it out tonight," he replied. "I arranged for a late checkout tomorrow so we have until noon to get out of here. I suggest we both sleep as late as possible and prepare for whatever surprises come next," he suggested.

"And there will be surprises, won't there?"

"Probably," he replied honestly.

"Should we plan on going back to my house or figure something else out instead?" she asked with obvious worry.

Once again Jackson released a deep sigh. "To be honest, I don't know the answer to that. It worries me that somebody found us in my motel room and then again on the road in your car."

"But nobody would be able to get my address from anyone at headquarters, and I'm not listed in the phone book. My neighbors don't know me well and certainly don't know what I do for a living." A wrinkle creased her brow. "I still think we'd be safe at my place as long as we don't unintentionally lead anyone there."

"I'm not willing to take that chance," he replied. "An internet search would cough up your address in an instant to somebody who was digging around for it. I think we need to go off the grid altogether," he said. "I'm thinking a motel somewhere and we don't tell anyone where we are."

"What about a car?" she asked.

"Do you trust Agent Forest?"

"With my life," she replied without hesitation.

"Then when we're ready to leave here tomorrow, call him and tell him to get us a rental under one of his friends' names, nothing that can be tied back to you or me. I'll make sure the fees are paid for in cash and we'll do as much work as we can out of your house. Let Roger Black and his men handle things in Mystic Lake under our advisement, but we stay away from that place until we have some better leads on who is willing to kill us."

He got up from the sofa and went to the well-stocked bar, where he poured himself another shot of bourbon. "Let's face it, darlin', at the moment we're just too hot, too visible to be seen in Mystic Lake. It's time to lie low and see what shakes out."

She unfolded her legs from beneath her. "I know you're right, but it makes me mad. I want to be out there. I want to have the pleasure of handcuffing the person who shot up my car."

"How about you go to bed and dream about it," he said. "You look tired, and it's been a very long day."

"What are you going to do?" she asked as she stood

and tugged her robe belt more firmly around her slender waist.

He picked up his glass of bourbon. "I'm going to finish this and then I'm going to hit the hay."

She smiled at him. "Those beds don't look like hay. They look big and luxurious and have pillow tops and cloudlike comforters."

She sighed and he took great delight in her obvious pleasure. "Then I'll just say good-night, Jackson."

"Good night, Maggie. Sleep well and we'll figure things out in the morning."

She disappeared into her suite and closed the door behind her. Jackson walked back to the sofa with his glass of booze and sank back down amid the accommodating cushions.

The bourbon was good, smooth and spreading warmth through him, but his thoughts remained dark. He couldn't shake the feeling that there was something more going on here than the investigation of the case of Cole and Amberly. But damned if he could figure it out.

Maybe it was actually a better idea to go back to Maggie's house rather than hide out somewhere. If the perp was as good as Jackson suspected he was, then eventually he'd figure out where Maggie lived, and some sort of attack would happen there.

They could be bait. They could be prepared and instead of chasing after their tails just wait for the bad guy to come to them. It was risky and he had to make sure Maggie was on board, but it made more sense than any other plan that had entered his mind since they'd arrived at the hotel.

First thing in the morning he'd contact somebody

to set up a security system at her place. *Fool me once, shame on you. Fool me twice, shame on me.* Twice they'd had close calls, and if they intended to stay at her place, then he wasn't going to make any careless mistakes.

They would be ready for the attack when it happened, and once they knew who was behind it they'd maybe get the answers they sought as to what had happened to the missing couple.

He finished his bourbon and carried the glass to the sink, then headed for his bedroom. He'd declined turndown service. He didn't want a maid coming in and disturbing their conversation by leaving a chocolate on the pillow and turning down the sheets.

His gun and holster were already on his nightstand and he took off his robe and slid naked into the bed. The mattress was heavenly, with just enough support to be comfortable.

He turned off the bedside lamp, and the only illumination was the faint moonlight that spilled in through the window, an indication that the storm had moved out of the area.

Closing his eyes, he tried to empty his mind, but flashes of the evening shot off like a kaleidoscope of pictures and scents and feelings.

He loved that Maggie had been so excited about the room, but he also knew she was a woman who didn't need this kind of opulence. She liked simple things, but he had a driving need to give her more.

It was crazy—she obviously didn't need anyone to take care of her, and yet he wanted to. He wanted to make sure her fridge held more than protein bars. He wanted her to have scented bubble bath and cable television.

He'd never felt like this before and he wasn't at all sure if he liked it. What he needed to do was solve this case as quickly as possible and hightail it back to his real life.

He smelled her before he saw her, that sweet pear scent that instantly aroused him. She stood in the doorway of his room. "Maggie?" he said softly.

"I'm looking for a nice Southern gentleman named Jackson," she said, her voice slightly husky.

"That would be me," he replied, his chest suddenly tight with anticipation.

"I thought you might be interested in a night of uncomplicated sex with a woman who isn't looking for anything more than this night and this night only."

"Maggie…" He said her name in hesitation. God, he wanted her. He thought he might even need her. But he knew things she didn't know, things that would forever stand between them and make any future impossible.

He didn't want her to pretend that she could be a one-night kind of woman if at heart she wasn't.

"It would only be a one-night deal," he finally managed to say.

"I wouldn't have it any other way," she replied. Before he could respond she shrugged out of the robe, leaving her gloriously naked in the moonlight.

Chapter Eleven

There was not a fiber in Marjorie's being that felt any hesitation as she approached the side of Jackson's bed. She knew that probably part of what had driven her to his room was the fact that they'd both nearly died, that she was probably suffering some innate need to connect and affirm life.

But there was also a huge dose of desire that had been burning inside her soul for him that she'd finally decided to give in to. The primal energy that Natalie Redwing had spoken of had exploded, and she wanted to burn in those flames.

When she reached the side of the bed, he threw back his covers to invite her in. She didn't hesitate. Even though she knew he wasn't a man for her lifetime, he was the man she wanted for this night.

She slid between the sheets and instantly he drew her against him. His naked body was hot and hard against hers as their lips met.

The kiss was wild, desire untamed and unleashed. Their tongues lashed against each other. He tasted of command and possession and bourbon, and she couldn't get enough of his mouth.

At the same time their hands moved frantically,

caressing naked flesh in exploratory strokes. She loved the way his broad back felt beneath her fingers, the muscles that moved and bunched beneath the palms of her hands.

His hands played down her back, as well, forcing a shiver of pleasure to sweep through her as he used first light and feathery touches and then harder, more determined ones, sliding down to the base of her spine.

Their kisses continued until finally he slid his mouth down her jawline and she gasped for air, feeling as if he had stolen all that there was in the room with his intimate nearness.

His body was hard and she liked the way her soft curves fit against him. She'd expected complete mastery, a sense of utter possession. What she hadn't expected was the tenderness.

His lips moved down her throat, lingering as if he loved the taste of her skin. "My sweet Maggie," he murmured. "I've wanted you since the moment you picked me up at the airport."

"And I think I've wanted you even before I met you," she replied, knowing it didn't make sense. But she'd been hungry for a man like him, a man who would challenge her, a man who, with his sexy smile and twinkling eyes, could weaken her knees and make her want him to take her to bed.

She gasped again as his mouth possessed one of her nipples, his tongue swirling around the hardened tip and creating a river of sensation that shot straight to her center.

Tangling her hands in his hair, she was aware of his complete arousal, that he was physically ready to take her at any moment. But he seemed to be in no hurry, his mouth attending to one breast and then the other. This raised her desire for him inside her to an unrelenting ache of want.

She moved her hands to his smooth chest, loving the heat and hardness of his taut muscles. He lay half on top of her, giving himself room to maneuver his hands and lips to explore her body.

His mouth left her breasts and trailed a blaze of fire down the flat of her stomach. She attempted to lie still but couldn't, and instead shivered from the sheer pleasure he evoked.

Reaching a hand down between them she grasped his hardness and he raised his head to gaze at her, his eyes glittering with raw emotion in the nearly dark room.

With their gazes still locked, he caressed a hand down to touch her between her legs. A moan escaped her as she raised her hips to meet him.

She was a firecracker ready to fire, and he was the detonator that would make her explode. He moved his fingers a little faster against her sensitive skin.

She moaned again, this time louder. Heat flooded through her, and every nerve ending in her body tingled with imminent release. And then she was there, exploding into a million pieces and shooting out to space.

Before she returned to earth, Jackson positioned himself between her thighs and entered her. This time he moaned as he buried himself deep within her.

He hovered just above her, holding the bulk of his weight on arms that trembled. Taut neck muscles let her know he fought for control as he moved his hips to thrust him slowly in and out of her moist heat.

He paused a moment, looking down at her, and he smiled that sexy grin that shot straight to her heart. "I feel like I'm finally home, Maggie."

She raised her legs to wrap around his back, drawing him in deeper and also trapping him against her. "For tonight you are home," she replied softly.

Her words seemed to galvanize him back into action. He stroked in and out of her with a quickened pace, and a new release built up inside her. He was all that mattered at the moment, the taste of his mouth, the feel of his hands on her skin, her hands on his. She was ravenous and he fed her hunger.

Tears sprang to her eyes as waves of pleasure threatened to drown her, and at the same time he stiffened against her, climaxing with a groan of her name.

She'd expected him to roll over and out of the bed. He'd gotten what he'd wanted, was finished with her. But instead he rolled to the side of her, leaned up on one elbow and gently stroked a strand of her hair away from her cheek.

Maybe he was just waiting for her to get up and leave his bed, his room, she thought. She started to sit up, but he pushed her back down.

"Don't be in such a hurry," he said with that lazy grin stretching his lips. "After-sex conversation is almost as important as presex talk. You were amazing."

"I never knew it could be like this," she said as she relaxed back into the sheets. "I mean, I never before... uh... It's never been so intense for me before."

He looked at her in surprise. "You mean you've never had an orgasm before?"

Her cheeks warmed and she was grateful for the

darkness that hid the blush. "My previous partner was more interested in his own pleasure than mine."

"Then he definitely wasn't a gentleman," Jackson replied. "In fact, I believe that makes him an ass."

She laughed. "He was kind of an ass. In fact, he was worse than that—he was a boring ass."

He reached out and stroked his hand against her cheek. "You're too much woman for that kind of a man."

"You mean I need somebody who aggravates me, who has a ridiculous Southern charm and is totally hot to look at?" she teased.

"And that would be me," he agreed.

"You do realize you're quite arrogant."

"Not arrogant," he protested. "I'm just good and I know it. I'm confident."

"And I'm sleepy now. I think it's time for me to use the bathroom and say good-night." She slid out of the bed, not self-conscious in her nakedness after what they'd just shared.

"Use my bathroom and then come back to my bed." He sat up, the sheet falling down to expose his beautiful chest. "I'd like to wake up in the morning with you in my arms."

She hesitated. There was nothing more she wanted at the moment than to crawl back into his bed and wake up with him next to her in the bed. But her desire for it scared her. He wasn't supposed to mean that much to her. This was just supposed to be a sex thing, not a warm and fuzzy continuance until morning.

Desire won over good sense. She went into his bathroom and when she returned to the bedroom he lifted the sheets to once again welcome her into his bed.

The minute she was beneath the sheets, he pulled her into his arms, spooning her as if they'd been lovers for years. She hated to admit to herself how much she liked the feel of his body against hers, his arm possessively around her waist and the soft warmth of his breath against the back of her neck.

She didn't want to admit that he had managed to crack the shell that had encased her heart since the time of her father's death, that he'd made her not just like him, but love him more than a little bit.

It was a feeling she didn't want to have, a feeling she knew would only lead to heartbreak. She knew her partner and she knew his life was far away from her life in Kansas City, not just in miles but in emotional distance.

She knew their case was in bad shape. They'd been nearly killed twice and yet she felt as if the clearest, most present danger she faced at the moment was the luxury of loving Jackson.

It was just after seven when Jackson awakened, Maggie a warm pillow he'd wrapped in his arms as he slept. Although he knew they had a hundred things to accomplish today, he was reluctant to leave the bed.

He'd suspected there was a wealth of passion hidden deep inside her and last night she'd released it all, giving to him the gift of her vulnerability and her fiery need.

It was funny that she'd been the one to remind him that it was a one-time deal. That was all he'd ever wanted from the women in his life, but he found himself dissatisfied and wanting more from Maggie.

But, of course, he knew that more wasn't possible. If he ever bared his soul to her, she'd run for the hills.

The sins of the father would come back to haunt him, and he'd rather walk away from here without her ever knowing where he came from and the choices he'd ultimately made that should have been made long before.

With these thoughts in mind, he silently slid from the bed and padded into the living room where several boxes had been delivered at some point during the morning.

He opened one of them to find underwear, a pair of jeans and a polo shirt all in his size. He carried the items into Maggie's suite, where he showered and dressed without awakening her.

Once showered and dressed, he called room service for coffee, deciding to wait for Maggie to wake up to order breakfast. He hoped she slept late. He had no idea what time they'd eventually gone to sleep, but he knew it had been the wee hours of the morning.

He stood in front of the expanse of windows in the living room and stared outside, trying to keep his mind off Maggie and instead focused on the work that had to be accomplished that day.

If they went through with his plan to return to Maggie's house, then the first thing he had to do was arrange for a state-of-the art security system. He wanted outside monitors so they could see who might approach the house from any direction. He wanted to arrange for extra firepower besides their two handguns.

Last night's attack had led him to believe that somehow things were coming to a head. The assailant had taken a million chances in chasing and shooting at them on the open highway. Witnesses might have seen him, somebody might have recognized his motorcycle. Somebody was getting desperate to quiet him and Maggie.

But surely whoever was behind the murder attempts could reason that even if he killed the two of them, more FBI agents would take their place.

That meant either their perp wasn't that bright or something deeper was at work. Either scenario worried him, and this morning he was filled once again with the frustration of the entire case.

Two people missing now over two weeks, no clues, no bodies. What were they missing? The frustration was a familiar one, the same that he had felt while working the case in Bachelor Moon.

A soft knock on the door announced the arrival of coffee. He opened the door, handed the man dressed like a butler a twenty-dollar bill and took the tray from him.

He carried it to the table, noting in satisfaction that there were two cups and the silver coffee carafe was huge. He poured himself a cup and then returned to the windows where he stared unseeing outside.

Maybe he should stash Maggie someplace safe and use himself as bait. The instant the idea entered his head he knew he was thinking like a protective lover and not as a professional agent. Besides, there was no way she'd agree to such a plan. She would want to be involved as a trained FBI agent on the case, not tucked away like a delicate piece of china.

While he didn't regret a minute of the night before, it concerned him that making love to Maggie had only made him want more from her. He knew they were ill-fated lovers at best.

As if drawn from her sleep by his thoughts, she

appeared in the living room, clad in the hotel robe. "Ah, coffee," she said, beelining toward the table where the carafe and a cup awaited her.

"And a good morning to you, too," he replied with an amused smile.

She poured the coffee, took a sip and then flashed him a bright smile. "Now it's a great morning."

He gestured for her to sit at the table, and he joined her there. She took another sip of her coffee and quirked one of her eyebrows upward. "Where did you get the clothes?"

"It's amazing how accommodating the concierge at a hotel can be when persuaded with cash." He pointed toward the sofa. "That box has fresh clothes for you."

She sighed in obvious relief. "Thank goodness. I was really dreading having to pull on the stiff, torn, dirty clothes from last night." Her eyes gleamed as she held his gaze. "You better not have ordered up some red silk cocktail dress for me to wear out of here today."

He grinned. "It crossed my mind, but I figured why start the day on a bad note after such a great night."

She eyed him over the rim of her cup. "It was a great night if you forget the motorcycle maniac and the trek through the rain. So, what are the plans?"

"First up is breakfast." He moved a room service menu in front of her. "Personally, I'm going for the Woodbridge special—bacon, eggs and toast with pancakes on the side."

"I'll take the same without the pancakes," she replied. "I seem to have worked up an appetite overnight." Her eyes twinkled teasingly.

Jackson placed the order and then returned to the

table. "After we eat, and we're ready to check out, you can call Agent Forest and see if he can get us a car. I noticed out the window that there's an outdoor restaurant named Willie's, with a dedicated parking lot about a block away. Tell Agent Forest to leave the car there with the keys under the mat."

"Okay, and then what?"

"First thing we do is drive to Mystic Lake and get the list of motorcycle owners from Roger, and then how do you feel about heading back to your place and setting us up as bait?"

Her eyes narrowed. "I like it. You're banking on whoever is after us being able to find us at my house. And we'll be waiting for them."

"Exactly. I'll use some of my own resources and see to it that by the time we get back to your place, we'll have a security system in place." He stopped talking as a knock fell on the door. "That should be breakfast."

The food was delicious, the conversation not so much fun as they discussed the pitfalls and perils of their plan. "I'll make sure we have monitors to give us vision of all areas of your yard. If anyone approaches we'll see them before they get too close."

"The monitors will have to be watched 24/7," she replied. "We'll have to take shifts."

"We'll do whatever we need to do." He poured a liberal dose of syrup over his stack of pancakes and then cut into them. "We'll put everything in place, but what I'm really hoping is that once we see that list of motorcycle owners Roger has prepared, we'll have the name of our suspect, or at least more people to seriously look at."

"I'm glad we've decided to do this. I'd much rather

take chances and work the case than hide out somewhere and let others do our job for us," she said. "I
want this solved, Jackson, and I want to be a part of
the solution."

She got up from the table. "I'm going to shower and
get dressed and then we'll get out of here and back to
work. I might just like being a worm dangling on a
hook waiting for a shark to bite."

He watched her as she grabbed the box from the
sofa and then disappeared into her suite. He took a bite
of his pancakes, but his appetite was gone.

Was this a mistake? Intentionally placing themselves
in a spot where a killer might come to call? He didn't
mind taking the risk himself, but the idea of anything
bad happening to Maggie set his heart plummeting to
the ground.

He just hoped that when or if the time he might need
to save her came, he would be the agent he thought he
was, the man he believed himself to be.

Chapter Twelve

Purple. He'd bought her a jewel-tone purple blouse and black jeans that hugged her legs as though they'd been tailor-made for her. In the box there had also been a lilac bra and silk panties.

He was incorrigible, she thought as she pulled on the clothes after having taken a long, hot shower. She'd thought she wouldn't like him. She'd believed that within two days his charming talk and easy ways would force her to strangle him. But instead, he'd captivated her.

Despite all her intentions to the contrary, she knew without doubt that Jackson Revannaugh was going to be her very first heartbreak, and she might as well prepare herself for it now.

Once she was dressed and they were ready to walk out the door, she made the call to Adam Forest to arrange for the car, and at the same time, Jackson spoke to somebody about the security system he wanted installed at her house. "We'll meet you at Maggie's in half an hour or so to let you inside," he said.

With plans made to begin their day, they left the luxury suite of rooms and headed out the hotel. "By the way, you look gorgeous," he said as they walked side by side to the restaurant where they'd pick up the new car.

"Thanks. I've never had silk underwear before."

He shot her a glance that threatened to melt her into a puddle of goo. "Don't even talk about it—the image I get in my brain will force me to throw you down right here on the sidewalk and have my way with you," he teased.

"One-night wonder, that's what we were," she replied lightly, needing to remind not just him but herself that what they had shared the night before wouldn't happen again.

Once again the late-July sun beat down with unrelenting heat, although the air wasn't as humid as it had been the day before.

They walked briskly. With their plans made for the day, Marjorie just wanted to stay focused on the work and not on how hot Jackson looked in his tight black jeans and white polo shirt. He wore the shirt untucked, with his belt and gun making a slight bulge on his side.

She'd always felt safe in her home, but Jackson was right—if somebody wanted to find out where she lived all it took was an internet search. She'd worked enough cases that she was surprised she'd never considered how easily somebody could find her for some sort of retribution before.

She should have had a security system in her house a long time ago, but money was so tight and she'd never felt the need for one until now. And when this case was over, she'd figure out a way to keep the security system in place.

She'd made arrangements with Adam to leave a black rental car at the farthest end of the parking lot from the restaurant. She was surprised, when they spied the car, to see Adam sitting behind the wheel.

He got out of the car when he saw them approach. Adam was a handsome man, with slightly long blond hair and pale blue eyes that looked cold and distant.

Marjorie knew he was anything but that. He was definitely one of the good guys, a talented profiler who loved research and was brilliant with a computer.

"I thought you were just leaving the keys under the mat," she said as they reached the car.

He nodded a greeting to Jackson, and then looked at Marjorie. "I just wanted to make sure the two of you were okay. You both had your phones off last night."

"We had a little encounter with a Mad Max character who tried to kill us," Jackson explained. "We decided to take the night and lie low. Was there a reason you tried to call?"

"No, just a check-in." He held out the keys to the car. "It's rented in the name of Charles Bachman and paid up the next two weeks."

Jackson took the keys. "Thanks."

Adam looked at Marjorie once again. "Let me know how I can help."

"Actually there is something you can do. Check and see if John Merriweather knows anyone who might own a motorcycle. If you find out anything give me a call." Aware that Jackson apparently intended to drive, Marjorie slid into the passenger seat and waved at Adam, who stepped back from the car.

"He's crazy about you," Jackson said once they were in the car and headed to Mystic Lake.

Marjorie looked at him in surprise. "Don't be silly. We've worked together on several cases. He trusts me."

Jackson had almost sounded jealous, but surely she'd misinterpreted his tone.

"Adam is a talented agent who overcame a horrible childhood. He doesn't trust easily and he's, for the most part, a lone wolf. But enough about Adam."

"So, you've come around to my thinking that John Merriweather remains a solid suspect," he said as he pulled onto the road that would take them to Maggie's house.

"I'm keeping an open mind," she replied. "It occurred to me this morning that all John would have to do was sell a couple of his paintings under the table for cash and he'd have enough money to hire himself a hit man. There would be no way to follow the money and he could keep himself distant from the violence."

"Smart thinking, but if that's the case he hired a local yahoo instead of a professional hit man. If this was a professional, we'd probably both already be dead."

She couldn't help the small shiver that swept through her at his words. He glanced at her and caught her midshiver. "Are you sure you're up to this? I'd love to drop you off at some out-of-the-way motel and let me be the worm on the hook."

"We're partners, remember? There's no way I'm going to let you go all macho on me. Is this about what happened between us last night?"

He shot a quick glance at her. "Maybe a little," he admitted. "I have to confess that a little protective streak I didn't know I had has reared its head where you're concerned."

"I'm an agent first, Jackson, and then a woman."

He grinned. "Darlin', you were all woman last night."

Her cheeks warmed in a familiar blush. "But that was then and this is now. Whether you like it or not, I'm dangling on that hook right next to you."

"I figured that would be your answer." He pulled into Maggie's driveway, where a panel truck was already parked. "Sit tight," he said as he opened his driver door. "This should just take a minute."

She watched as he met with the tall bald man who got out of the truck. Interesting that there was no writing or graphics on the side of the truck to indicate that it was part of a home security business. Jackson handed the man a key she assumed was the copy of the one she'd given Jackson to her house.

"Everything should be done by the time we get home from Mystic Lake," he said when he was back behind the wheel. "I told him to go subtle but effective. I don't want the bad guys to know we have anything in place."

"Sounds like a plan."

They fell silent as he headed toward Mystic Lake. For no particular reason she felt as if they were approaching the end, that the list of motorcycle owners they got from Roger might hold their answer.

Their list of suspects was still rather pathetic, with Jeff Maynard, Jimmy Tanner, Edward Bentz and John Merriweather, but if one of those names appeared on Roger's list, then they could potentially have enough evidence to get all kinds of warrants to execute to gather even more personal information.

Even the FBI had red tape and rules that had to be followed, but Roger might hold the clue that would get them past the red tape.

Once the case was solved she saw no happiness for

anyone. Cole and Amberly were probably dead, which would scar little Max for years to come and leave behind many people to mourn.

Jackson would return home, taking with him a source of energy, of life that had filled the little house with his presence.

She had a better understanding of her mother now. It wasn't stupidity that had driven her mother into the arms of con men, it had been loneliness and the need to believe she was all the wonderful things they told her she was even as they fleeced her out of what money they could get.

As Marjorie thought of being held in Jackson's arms the night before, of the magic of their lovemaking, she realized that despite her fight against it, she had fallen for his smooth charm, his sexy smile and the bits and pieces of the man she'd seen beneath his facade.

The case would eventually be solved, and Jackson would go home, but she knew it would take her a very long time to get him out of her system, to not think about him and ache for what might have been.

DEPUTY ROGER BLACK was in his usual spot behind Sheriff Caldwell's desk. Next to the desk were wooden file cabinets, the tops stacked with files. A photo of Amberly and Cole sat on the desk, and Jackson knew that picture would be a constant reminder of his missing boss.

He stood as they entered his office. "I was just about to get some coffee. Would either of you like a cup?"

"No, thanks, we're good," Maggie replied.

Roger sat back down. "It took me half the night, but I got the information you requested." He shoved several documents aside and grabbed a sheet of paper and handed it to Jackson. "I included not just the street-licensed bikes, but also the names of folks I know who have dirt bikes."

"Thanks, I appreciate it." He took the list and folded it up in his pocket, making the decision that he and Maggie would pore over it when they got back to her place.

As the three of them caught up with the case as it stood, Jackson tried to ignore Maggie's presence. He should have never bought her those tight jeans and that purple blouse. The purple was a perfect color for her red-blond hair and intense green eyes.

Most of the time when he woke up after having sex with a woman, he was ready to bolt as quickly as possible. But Maggie was different. She was special, and each time he looked at her, a new desire returned to torment him.

They had to get a quick solve and he had to get away from her. She threatened the very lifestyle he'd chosen for himself. When he'd seen her with little Max, he'd immediately seen her with another dark-haired little boy—his child.

He'd never thought about having a family, having children, before in his life, but Maggie made him think about those things. And he couldn't go there, especially not with her.

He focused back on Roger's musings about the case. "I just don't understand any of it," he said. "Usually when something bad happens here in town, eventually we hear rumors that yield clues. But this time we've heard absolutely nothing. Even the drunks down at

Bledsoe's haven't given up any information that might be useful."

He reared back in the chair and shook his head. "Cole wasn't just my boss, he was my friend. He was a good man who most folks in town liked and respected. He had no dark secrets that might have come back to bite him. I knew him."

"You're speaking about him in the past tense," Maggie said.

Roger shrugged. "After all this time, it's my belief that they're dead. Nobody would keep them alive so long without a ransom note filled with some sorts of demands."

"And yet we don't have their bodies," Jackson said.

Roger frowned. "I figure at some point in the future some farmer will stumble on the bodies in the middle of a field or hidden in some woods."

"And you don't have any theories as to why the bodies wouldn't be just left out in the open for somebody to find?" Jackson asked.

Roger shook his head. "I'll be honest with you, we've been out of theories and ideas about this case since the very beginning. We were hoping the officials in Kansas City might come up with something."

"So far, we have nothing," Jackson said. "Except for somebody who has Maggie and me in their sites."

"And you don't know for sure where that threat is coming from?" Roger asked.

"I'm guessing somebody from here, but the first attack happened in Kansas City, and last night's attack came from somebody who was here in town and followed us. We're working the case from both ends," Jackson replied.

"And I'll keep working from this end. Hopefully that list I gave you will help." Roger stood, as if aware that their conversation had come to a natural end.

Minutes later they were back in the car and headed home. Jackson was grateful for Maggie's silence, as his head spun with suppositions and possibilities.

They had a meager list of potential suspects, and it was quite possible that the person responsible for Amberly and Cole's disappearance wasn't even on that short list.

It was possible that they hadn't even made personal contact with the perp, that he was flying far enough below their radar to be completely off the screen.

Every person on the list in his pocket would have to be fully investigated. Even though he had no real evidence, he still believed the person responsible for the crime, the person who had attempted to kill him and Maggie twice, was from Mystic Lake.

"Home, sweet home," he said as he pulled into Maggie's driveway. There was no sign of the panel van that had been there before.

Jackson cut the engine on the car and pulled his cell phone from his pocket. It took him only minutes to connect with the tech who had done the work on the house and learn the details of what had been done.

"Okay," he said as he dropped his cell phone back in his shirt pocket. "We're all set."

Together they got out of the car and as they approached the house he saw Maggie looking at the structure carefully, as if expecting to see trip lines and big cameras.

He laughed and she looked at him. "What? Were you expecting rolls of barbed wire and steel bars?"

She grinned sheepishly. "I was expecting something."

"The eyes that protect us are no bigger than a fly. We aren't hooked up to any monitoring system. I told him to put the camera monitors in your bedroom, and if anyone tries to breach the house through a door or a window, a siren will sound that should not just awaken us but the entire neighborhood."

"The wonders of modern technology," she replied as she unlocked the door. They stepped inside and he immediately moved to a keypad on the wall and punched in a series of numbers.

"The code is random. I'll write it down for you and you need to memorize it. Too many people make the mistake of making their codes their birthdates or part of their social security or some other sequence of numbers that a determined bad guy could ferret out."

Maggie nodded and headed down the hallway to her bedroom. Jackson tried to ignore the sway of her hips in the tight jeans as he followed behind her.

He hated to admit that he thought maybe he'd told the tech to set up the system in her bedroom just so that he could actually see the room where she slept. He had a feeling that this visit would be his first and his last to the room that belonged to her alone.

The bedroom was a shock. He'd expected monotones of black or gray and instead he walked into a flower garden. A floral spread covered the bed, with pink throw pillows in the center. A pink shaded lamp stood proudly on the nightstand, next to a creased paperback written by a famous profiler.

The dresser top held an array of lotions and perfumes and a picture of her and her mother. Above the dresser, the wall now held several medium-sized television screens that gave views of the front of the house, the back and both sides.

"We should be snug as two bugs in a rug in here," he said.

She turned and her lips turned up in knowing amusement. "You did this on purpose. You had him mount the monitors in here so that we'd have to spend time together in my bed if we wanted to see what was happening outside the house."

"You wound me to the core," he protested. "I just figured if you wanted to keep this system after I'm gone it would be easier for you if the monitors were in here."

She eyed him dubiously, and love for her buoyed up inside him, unwelcome and unwanted but there nevertheless. "Let's head to the table and take a look at this list that Roger gave us," he said gruffly.

He needed to be out of this room, where glimpses of her femininity showed, where her scent filled the air and made his desire to possess her again surge.

Once they were in the kitchen and seated across the small table from each other, he pulled out the list that Roger had prepared and scanned the names. Disappointment flared through him and he shoved the list in front of Maggie.

Her brow wrinkled as she read, and the wrinkle turned into a sigh of frustration. "None of our potential suspects are on it. That means we're going to have to investigate all these people, because it's possible the perp is one of these names.

"I'll fax the list to Adam and he can get on the investigation from the office," she said, her disappointment evident in her voice. "I'd so hoped that we'd have an answer by now, or at least a path to follow."

"Maybe Adam will be able to sort out who could be a potential threat on the list and who definitely isn't," Jackson said thoughtfully. "It would have been nice if Roger had given us not just names but ages, as well."

"It would have been nice if that motorcycle would have hydroplaned in the rain last night and crashed," she said dryly. "But nothing about this case has been nice so far."

"Last night was nice." He couldn't help himself. The words were out of his mouth before his brain was engaged.

She looked up at him, and her eyes held a soft vulnerability he'd never seen before. "You're right. It was nice, and the truth of the matter is I've allowed you to get deep into my heart, Jackson."

She raised a hand to halt his response, though he wasn't even sure what he intended to say. "It's my problem, not yours. You have no ownership in it other than you are who you are. Women find you irresistible, and I guess this just confirms that I'm a normal woman at my core."

"Maggie…I…"

Once again she stopped him from speaking, this time shoving back from the table and talking over him. "I didn't realize how empty my life was until you came along. When you leave here I will be making some changes."

She gave him a small smile, defusing some of the tension in the air. "First thing I intend to do is order cable television. The second thing is that I'm going to have a long, difficult talk with my mother and get her settled into someplace more affordable."

"I'm glad to hear that," he said, surprised to discover a lump in the back of his throat.

"I'm also going to stop eating so many protein bars and learn how to cook. I'll miss you desperately when you're gone, but eventually I'll get over you because I'll have to. You'll break my heart when you leave here, Jackson, but we both know we weren't meant to be anything but partners. And now I'm going to go check out the monitors."

She didn't wait for him to say anything, but scurried out of the kitchen and disappeared down the short hall. Jackson remained at the table, his heart twisting like a flag in a windstorm.

She loved him. That was basically what she'd just confessed. She loved him and he loved her. But he would leave her brokenhearted. What she didn't know was that she wasn't the only one who would have a broken heart when Jackson returned home to Baton Rouge.

Chapter Thirteen

Four days. It had been four long days since the security had been installed and she and Jackson had been cooped up together waiting for something to happen.

Four days since she'd foolishly confessed her feelings for Jackson, and since that time they had been stiffly polite to one another, unnaturally impersonal.

She hadn't intended to tell him how she felt about him, it had just happened, and now she wished she could take it back, return their relationship to the easy, slightly flirty and effective partnership they'd shared before.

Equally as difficult was the fact that nothing new about the case of Amberly and Cole's disappearance or the attacks on her and Jackson had come to light. They were dangling themselves out there like worms on a hook, but the shark hadn't even circled them yet.

They'd stopped throwing out theories and ideas to each other, having exhausted the topic to death. Jackson paced the small confines of the house like a caged animal, his frustration and pent-up energy nearly driving her mad.

They both needed something to happen. A blip on the monitors, the ring of an alarm would almost be a relief. At least it would break the tense monotony of waiting for something to occur.

She'd been in touch with her director several times during the past few days. She'd learned that the case in Bachelor Moon was still an open one, that the three people who had gone missing from the Bachelor Moon Bed and Breakfast had yet to be found.

Both the FBI in Kansas City and Baton Rouge were still reluctant to draw the conclusion that the two crimes were related, especially given the attacks that had happened on Marjorie and Jackson...a distinct difference from anything that had happened in Bachelor Moon.

It was early afternoon and Marjorie was seated at the table, staring unseeing out the window. She sat up as Jackson came into the room. "I feel like a shriveled-up worm left dangling on a hook that nobody wants to bite," she said.

"Trust me, I feel the same way." He threw himself into the chair opposite her and raked a hand through his hair. "I don't know, maybe this hole-up-and-wait idea was a bad one."

She shrugged. "It made sense to me at the time."

"Yeah, it made sense to me, too, but I didn't expect it to take so long for somebody to come after us."

"Maybe he's intentionally torturing us," Marjorie said. "Maybe he knows we're holed up here just waiting for an attack to happen and so he's decided to wait us out."

"Maybe," Jackson said absently. He stared out the window, obviously lost in thought.

Why did he have to be so handsome? Why couldn't they have sent her an overweight, belly-scratching, beer-burping agent to work as her partner? Why did it have to be Jackson?

He looked at her, his eyes a fathomless midnight blue that let her know his thoughts were deep and dark. "I can't help but believe that the case in Bachelor Moon and this case are related."

"But nobody else seems to want to make that connection, and then there's the difference of the attacks on us," she replied.

"The cases themselves are virtually identical. Missing people obviously taken unaware, no clues left behind, no ransom communication from the kidnapper... nothing varies from case to case except the two attacks on us." His frown deepened.

"So, you're back to believing that maybe the attacks weren't about the case, after all, but somebody who wants one or both of us dead for another reason." She leaned toward him, trying not to notice the familiar scent of him. "But neither of us can think of anyone who would want to hurt us."

"I know, I know," he exclaimed irritably and got up from the table to pace the small confines of the room. "I feel like I've lost all my instincts as an agent, like I'm floundering in a vast sea and not seeing the rock right in front of my boat."

Even though she knew it was the worst thing she could do, she got up from the table and walked over to where he'd finally stopped pacing and stood by the refrigerator.

His arms were folded across his chest, his eyes hollow as he stared at her. She placed a hand on one of his arms, wishing she could take away his frustration, wishing she had the answers that would take that hollowness out of his eyes.

What she really wanted to do was take him by the hand and lead him into her bedroom, fall into bed with him, where they could both escape the frustration and sense of time being stopped by losing themselves in each other.

But she knew that wouldn't help anything; it would only make matters worse. Instead she laid her hand on his arm and gazed deep within his eyes. "Jackson, we're doing what we think is right. Whether somebody is trying to kill us for personal reasons or because of the case, we're here, and eventually they'll get tired of waiting and will make a move. We just have to be patient."

He uncrossed his arms and she dropped her hand to her side. "Patience isn't something I consider a virtue," he said dryly. "In fact, I find it a real pain."

She smiled at him, grateful to hear a bit of humor in his voice. "Maybe we need to decide what we're going to cook for dinner," she suggested, hoping to lighten his mood even more.

"I'm not in the mood for food at the moment," he replied. He walked back over to the window. "Besides, we're out of milk." He turned suddenly. "Isn't there a convenience store at the corner?"

"Actually, it's two blocks away."

"I think I'll drive up and get a gallon of milk." His eyes were no longer hollow but instead held a glint she hadn't seen before.

"What are you up to?" she asked warily.

"Nothing. Just a fast trip to the store, that's all." He grabbed the car keys from the counter. "I'll be gone five minutes. You know the drill, keep the doors locked, the security system engaged and I'll be back before you know it." He set the keys back on the table. "On second thought I think a quick walk will do me good."

He didn't wait for her reply, but headed for the door, his footsteps heavy and determined. She followed behind him and locked the door, then engaged the security after he left.

Instantly she felt two things…an immediate loss of energy and life in his absence, and a bit of relief that his frantic energy was momentarily gone.

She walked back into her bedroom and watched on the monitor, spying him as he walked down the driveway and then disappeared from her sight.

Just watching him walk away from the house shot a tiny stab of pain through her heart…a precursor of what was to come when the case was solved and he went back to his home in Baton Rouge.

She left her bedroom and went back into the kitchen. Maybe she'd surprise him and she'd do the cooking for dinner tonight. She opened the freezer door and stared at the packaged meats, trying to make up her mind between pork chops and chicken breasts. She finally settled on the pork chops. She pulled them out of their packaging and placed them in a baking dish, and at that moment the doorbell rang.

She nearly jumped out of her cotton underwear at the sound. It was too soon for Jackson to be back already. She raced to her bedroom and looked at the monitor that viewed the front porch.

A man stood there, a man who looked like an older

version of Jackson. As he knocked, she raced from the living room to the front door.

"Who is it?" she called.

"My name is Jerrod Revannaugh. I'm looking for my son, Jackson, and was told that he was here." The voice was deep, smooth and Southern.

She hesitated a moment, fingers paused over the security keypad. There was no question in her mind that the man on her front stoop was Jackson's father. He not only sounded like his son, but looked like an older model of Jackson.

All she knew was that father and son had suffered some sort of falling-out years before, but surely Jerrod Revannaugh wouldn't be here if he didn't want to make some sort of connection with Jackson.

Decision made, she punched in the numbers that would disarm the security and then unlocked the door and opened it. In person, the resemblance between Jackson and his father was nearly breathtaking.

Surely she had nothing to worry about in letting him in to wait for Jackson. She had no idea what had caused the break between father and son, but it had to be a good thing that Jerrod was here.

"Mr. Revannaugh, I'm Marjorie Clinton," she said as she stepped aside to allow him into the small living room. "Jackson just went down the street for a minute and should be back anytime."

"Well, then, I'll just have to hurry a bit, won't I?" He gave her a charming smile and then stuck her in the side of the neck with a needle.

She yelped at the sting, and immediately the effects of whatever he'd given her took hold. Her legs turned to rubber and she reached out to grab him around the neck to keep herself from falling to the floor.

Without effort, he scooped her up in his arms. "It's okay, darlin', I'll take good care of you."

Her last conscious thought was that she hated Jackson's father...because he'd called her darlin', and the only man in the world she wanted calling her that was Jackson himself.

JACKSON WALKED BRISKLY, breathing in the air that smelled of fresh-cut grass and sunshine instead of the sweet floral scent of Maggie.

They were out of milk, but his walk had two goals. Retrieve the gallon of milk and make a phone call where he knew Maggie wouldn't be able to hear him.

Maybe he was being paranoid, but he couldn't shake the fact that the attacks they had survived had been somehow personal in nature. There was only one person in Jackson's life who might have a motive to kill him, and that was his father.

Last Jackson had heard, his father was behind bars at the state prison just outside Baton Rouge. Jackson knew he was there because he'd been one of the people who had been responsible for putting him away.

Jerrod Revannaugh had been a con man for all of Jackson's life. He could have easily been one of Maggie's stepfathers, a man who scammed women out of their life savings through fraud and deception and danced away unscathed...until the last time.

At sixteen years old, Jackson knew what his father was, and he'd walked away from him without a backward glance. Jackson had gotten on with his life and rarely thought about the man who'd raised him, a man who had attempted to instill the same lack of morals in his son.

They'd met again six years ago, when Jackson was contacted by law enforcement officers who were investigating the death of an elderly woman. Although it appeared to be a tragic slip and fall in a bathtub, the fact that her much younger husband had been married five times before to older women who'd found themselves nearly destitute after encountering the same man made them suspicious. The dead woman's husband was Jackson's father.

Jackson clenched his fists at his side as he reached the convenience store. Instead of going inside, he walked around to the side of the building, pulled out his cell phone and punched in a number he'd called several times over the past couple of years.

The murder charges hadn't stuck in the case against Jerrod Revannaugh, but a dozen counts of fraud by deception had, and he'd been sentenced to six years in prison.

When his call was answered, he asked to speak to the warden and then identified himself. "I'm calling to check on prisoner 22356," he said. The pause on the other end of the line tensed every muscle in Jackson's body. "What's up, Warden?" he asked when the pause went on too long for comfort.

"Somebody should have contacted you. Prisoner 22356 was released at six o'clock this morning."

Jackson nearly dropped his phone. Jerrod was out of prison, and he definitely had a reason to hold a grudge against Jackson, who was a prosecution character witness in the trial.

He hung up and slipped his phone back into his

pocket and then went into the store and bought the milk. As he walked back to Maggie's his head whirled.

Jerrod was Jackson's dirty secret, a secret he hadn't shared with Maggie because of her past with her mother and men like Jerrod. He was afraid of being judged, afraid that she would somehow believe the apple hadn't fallen far from the tree.

Jerrod was a threat to him, but if Jerrod had been released from prison in Baton Rouge early that morning, there was no way he could be behind the shooting at the motel or the chase by the shooting motorcyclist.

Unless he had an accomplice. Unless he had somebody on the outside who would be willing to do his bidding for part of the fortune Jackson guessed his father had hidden in some offshore account.

As he thought of all the people they had spoken to, all the people who had been potential suspects, the name Edward Bentz exploded in his forehead. He was a man who had traveled back and forth from Kansas City to Baton Rouge over the past couple of weeks… in the time that Jackson had been here working on the case.

Was it possible Edward had been behind the attacks? He'd certainly been vague about where he'd been during to two incidents. They should have dug deeper, they should have looked harder at him.

Suddenly he couldn't get home fast enough. Knowing that his father was out of jail put a whole new spin on things, and he needed to come clean to Maggie.

If there was anything that would put a halt to any feelings she might have for him, surely it would be the fact that he came from the same kind of men who had scammed her mother out of her fortune.

Still, it was information she needed to know, because Jackson had a feeling he'd realized the answer behind the attacks on them…his father wanted him dead, and Maggie would have just been collateral damage.

He started to unlock the front door, but realized it was already unlocked. Had Maggie forgotten to lock it when he'd left? Damn, he needed to remind her that locks and security systems didn't work if they weren't used.

"Maggie?" he called as he walked toward the kitchen. She wasn't in the living room or in the kitchen. He put the milk in the refrigerator, noted the pork chops in the baking dish and then went in search of her, assuming she was probably back in her bedroom.

"Maggie," he called again. This time when there was no response, his heart began an irregular rhythm of anxiety. Her house wasn't big enough for her not to hear him.

He paused at the bathroom long enough to check that she wasn't in there and then headed on to her room. Empty. His heartbeat accelerated.

He knew there was a door in the kitchen that she'd told him led down to a basement she used for storage. He raced back to the kitchen, flung open the door and thundered down the stairs into a small basement that held nothing but a couple of boxes labeled Winter Clothes.

Gone.

She was gone.

There was no way she would have left the house alone. She knew the dangers of being outside without having him along as backup.

He raced back up the stairs and went to the video equipment in her bedroom. He knew the security tapes were looped and he could replay them to see if anyone had come to the door.

His hands trembled as he punched the buttons to rewind the tape and he gasped in shock as he saw his father on the front porch. "Don't open the door. Please, Maggie, don't open the door." He whispered the words desperately even as he saw the front door open.

He froze, watching the monitor and moments later his father walked out of the house, carrying an obviously unconscious Maggie in his arms.

Instinctively he grabbed his gun, wishing he could shoot his father's image and make him drop Maggie. He wanted her safe, away from the man Jackson knew was a sociopath.

The monitor didn't show Jerrod getting into a car—he simply walked out of sight with Maggie in his arms. Jackson remained immobile, unsure what his next move should be, as terror threatened to burst his heart right out of his chest.

He knew he should be doing something, searching for her, but he didn't even know where to begin. Edward Bentz…Mystic Lake.

Edward Bentz had to have the answers. There was no doubt in Jackson's mind that the mild-mannered traveling salesman had been his father's minion. Jackson had to get to Mystic Lake. Hopefully, Jerrod would keep Maggie alive as a bargaining chip, for Jackson knew what his father wanted most was to kill Jackson.

Within minutes he was in the car and driving faster than he'd ever driven in his life toward the small town. If Bentz wasn't in his rented room, then Jackson would head straight to Roger Black and see to it that every law enforcement official in Mystic Lake was looking for Bentz and the newly released prisoner who had Maggie with him.

Dammit, he should have realized what was going on the minute it entered his mind that the attacks on them might be personal. But he'd been certain his father was still locked up and he hadn't thought of Jerrod being devious enough to hunt Jackson clear across the country to a case he was working.

He hadn't tried anything like this in all the years he'd been behind bars. Why now? *Why not now?* he countered. Who knew what drove Jerrod Revannaugh besides naive, lonely, wealthy women?

Maggie. His heart cried her name and the love he'd never felt for any woman before filled his soul. Maggie. She had to be all right. He had to find her and make sure she survived this horror he'd brought to her doorstep.

Chapter Fourteen

Maggie came to and with a dazed semiawareness realized she was bound at her ankles and wrists, and tape covered her mouth, making it impossible for her to scream for help.

Dark… She was in the dark in a small space that smelled of oil and gasoline, and through her groggy hangover she realized she was in the trunk of a moving vehicle.

As the full implication of her predicament exploded in her brain, panic fluttered her heart and surged bitterness up the back of her throat.

She swallowed against it, knowing that panic would accomplish nothing. She remained still, lying on her side, and took several deep breaths in and out through her nose.

Think, Maggie, don't panic, she told herself. Thankfully her hands were bound in front of her with what felt like duct tape. She knew the futility of trying to slip or rip the tape away. She assumed her ankles were bound in the same way. She tested the strength of the tape, attempting to pull her ankles apart, but there was no give at all.

He must have been watching the house, she thought.

When he saw Jackson leave, he took the opportunity to engage her. She'd been a naive fool, thinking that maybe he was there for some sort of happy reunion with his son.

She should never have opened the door to him. But she had, and now she was in the back of the trunk of a car carrying her to an unknown destination for some unknown purpose.

Her heart raced faster. One thing was clear. Jerrod Revannaugh didn't intend for her to walk away alive from whatever he'd planned. Not only had he kidnapped an FBI agent, but he'd introduced himself to her, allowed her to see his face.

She was already a dead woman.

The minute she'd opened her front door, she'd signed her own death certificate. The only thing she didn't know, that she couldn't understand, was why this had happened.

Why her? She'd never met Jackson's father before, knew virtually nothing about him. So why had he taken her instead of just waiting and dealing with Jackson?

Somehow she knew she was a pawn between father and son. Jerrod probably believed that Jackson loved her, that she would be a useful tool to get his son to do something. What he didn't know was that Jackson didn't love her. And now she understood why he was probably incapable of loving somebody too deeply. Who knew what kind of childhood he'd had with a man who could drug and kidnap a woman?

She shoved away thoughts of Jackson, thoughts that caused pain as her love for him remained undiminished by the current events.

She had to figure out a way to get out. She'd read somewhere of a case of a woman who'd been imprisoned in the trunk of a car and she'd managed to punch out a back taillight and get another driver's attention.

Disoriented in the darkness, the first thing she did was scoot around the small space, trying to get her bearings. She was sideways in the trunk and she tried to position herself so that her fingers could search for a trunk release inside.

She didn't even think about what she might do if she did manage to pop the trunk. At the very least she could potentially sit up and maybe get somebody's attention. Worst-case scenario was that they were traveling in an area where there were no other people around, and her actions would only enrage Jerrod Revannaugh.

Deciding anything was better than just lying there waiting for whatever he had planned, she wiggled and squirmed until her fingers had traced every place she thought a release would be and found nothing.

Unwilling to be defeated, she located one of the back taillights and began to use her bound feet to bang against it. Again and again she slammed her feet into the back of the taillight, until she had to stop to catch her breath, a difficult thing to do with her mouth taped closed.

Sweat ran down the sides of her face, and the T-shirt she'd put on that morning stuck to her. The temperature in the trunk had to be nearly a hundred degrees. If Jerrod kept her in here too long she'd die of the heat and dehydration.

She made several more kicks at the taillight and

then gave up, unwilling to expend the energy for what appeared to be a futile attempt.

Where was he taking her? She had no idea how long she'd been unconscious and so had no idea how long she'd been in the trunk.

Was he behind Amberly and Cole's disappearance? She frowned. No, that didn't make sense. He couldn't have done something to them to bring Jackson to Mystic Lake. There was no way he could have guaranteed that Jackson would be sent here from Baton Rouge. Unless he was a company man...unless he'd had a hand in appointing Jackson to his current assignment.

Her heart began to hammer once again as the car turned onto a gravel road, the rocks pinging beneath her. The car went over a short distance and then stopped. The engine went silent and Maggie could hear the sound of her own heartbeat filling the trunk. It was the sound of terror.

Every muscle in her body tensed as the trunk opened. She blinked against the sunshine that momentarily blinded her. Jerrod was nothing more than a tall, well-built silhouette as he leaned forward.

"We can make this easy, or you can make it hard," he said. "I'll pick you up and carry you, but if you fight me, I'll fight back, and with you trussed up like you are, it wouldn't really be a fair fight."

She nodded to let him know she understood. She would be a fool to fight right now. She'd have to wait and see if an opportunity presented itself later...if she had a later.

He leaned down and picked her up as if she weighed no more than a child. As she got her first vision of where they were, her heart sank.

In the middle of nowhere, that was where they were. She didn't even see any landmarks that she recognized. Ahead of them was a large shed with a tractor stored inside and a smaller shed to the side that was probably used for a variety of equipment.

He carried her to the smaller shed and as they drew closer she saw that it was solid and well built on a slab of concrete. He laid her on the ground and then unlocked the padlock on the door.

Once again sheer, unadulterated terror filled her. She tried to roll away, even knowing in her head that it was nothing but the pathetic move of a desperate woman.

He turned back to her and laughed. "Where you going, darlin'?"

She wanted to scream at him to stop calling her that. There was only one man in the world who had the right to call her darlin', and at the moment she feared for his life as well as her own.

Once again Jerrod picked her up and carried her into the dark confines of the shed. It was completely empty and the concrete floor was hard against her body.

He left her there but returned only moments later, this time with a flashlight and a couple bottles of water. He set them on the floor just inside the door.

"You can scream your head off out here and nobody will ever hear you," he said, and to her surprise he pulled out a knife and sawed through the tape on her feet.

He motioned toward her hands and she quickly held them out. She watched him cautiously as he removed the tape from her wrists and then ripped off the piece that had been across her mouth.

She thought about rushing him, but she was too weak and he had not only the knife in his hand, but she suspected he also had a gun somewhere on his person.

"Why?" The word croaked out of her dry throat as she managed to raise herself to sit on her butt. "Why are you doing this?"

"Why?" He laughed, although there was no warmth in his cold blue eyes or in the tone of his mirth. "I raised that boy and taught him everything I knew and he turned his back on me, became a damned FBI agent. Six years ago I got myself into a little legal problem and my son, my own flesh and blood, testified against me. I wound up being sentenced to six years in jail. He betrayed me, and the price for that is his death."

"What did you do with Amberly and Cole?" she asked, her mind reeling with all the information she'd just learned.

"Who?" His handsome face twisted into a confused frown as he stared at her.

"The sheriff of Mystic Lake and his wife."

"I don't know anything about them. All of my energy, all of my resources have been used to keep tabs on my dear son. You two have had the luck of the Irish so far. The men I've hired have been unusually inept in completing a simple death or two. But I'm here now, and to be honest, this is the way it should be. I should be here when it's time for Jackson to pay. I've had six years to stew and plot, to enjoy the vision of his death."

For the first time as he spoke of killing his own son, his eyes lit with life, and Marjorie recognized that she was looking into the eyes of pure evil.

"I'm leaving you with a flashlight and some water. I'm not inclined right now to kill you, but I do take great joy in the fact that for the next couple of hours my son will have no idea where you've gone or if you're dead or alive."

"Jackson won't care. He's nothing more than my partner," she protested.

"Oh, he cares, and once I contact him he'll come for you. Your white knight riding to your rescue, but unfortunately, the white knight won't survive to see another morning."

"Wait!" she cried as he stepped out of the shed.

As a reply he slammed the door closed and she heard the sound of the padlock being clicked into place and once again she was plunged into utter darkness and despair.

JACKSON REACHED BETTY FIELDS'S house in record time, a new fear crashing through him as he saw that Bentz's panel van wasn't in the driveway.

Of course it wasn't, he thought. Because Jackson was relatively certain that the panel van had carried Maggie away. He had no idea where his father might be holed up with Maggie, but he knew in order to get some answers he had to find Edward Bentz.

A knock on the door was answered by Betty. "Agent Revannaugh, how nice to see you again." She smiled sweetly.

"Where's Edward?" he asked, politeness gone beneath urgency.

"Well, I'm sure I don't know. He left earlier but didn't mention where he was going." Betty's forehead wrinkled. "Is there a problem?"

"Call the sheriff's office if he shows up here," Jackson said, his feet already moving him back to his car.

Panic simmered in his veins, a panic he refused to allow to blossom into its full potential. Panic didn't allow rational thought, and he had to think.

With Edward gone, his next stop was at the sheriff's office. He was led into the office where Roger Black sat behind the large desk. Roger must have sensed something, for he stood, his brow wrinkled. "What's happened?"

"Maggie is gone."

Roger's frown deepened. "Gone? What do you mean she's gone?"

"She's been kidnapped by my father. I saw it on the security video at her house."

"Why would your father want to kidnap your partner?" Roger asked as he sank back down in the leather chair behind the desk.

"Look, I don't have time to give you all the reasons why. We don't have the luxury of chatting about my father or my past with him. All you need to know is that he took Maggie and I believe Edward Bentz is involved."

"Bentz?"

Jackson wanted to reach across the desk and slap Roger upside the head. "I need you to get off your ass and get your men out looking for Bentz's van. I want him found sooner rather than later."

"No need to get all riled up." Roger stood once again and walked around the desk to stand before Jackson. "Just take a breath, man, and tell me what else you need from us."

Jackson sucked in air, trying to calm the nerves

that had his body on fire. "My father's name is Jerrod Revannaugh. He was released this morning from a prison in Baton Rouge. I believe he's now either in Kansas City or here in Mystic Lake."

His chest tightened and he clenched and unclenched his hands into fists at his sides. "I'm guessing he's here because I believe he hired Edward Bentz to keep track of me."

"What does he want from you?" Roger asked.

"He wants to kill me, but at the moment I'm more afraid for Maggie's life than mine."

"Have you got a picture of your father?" Roger asked.

"No." Jackson sighed impatiently. There was too much talk and not enough action going on. "You can get a photo of him off the internet, but right now you need your men to be looking for Bentz's van. My gut says if we find Bentz, we'll find my father and Maggie."

"Excuse me a minute and I'll get the process started." He walked around Jackson and disappeared from the room. Jackson assumed he was going to talk to his dispatcher and get the word out to all units working the streets.

Something had to happen fast. He knew his father, he knew the black soul Jerrod possessed. With every minute that passed, Maggie's life was in danger.

As he waited impatiently for Roger's return, his gaze darted around the office, thinking idly that all the clues to everything that had happened in the town might be here.

Hopefully one of Roger's men would see Edward's

van seconds after the call went out. If Jackson didn't get to Maggie, if he couldn't save her, then he'd be worth nothing.

Shame and humiliation had already made him keep the secret of who his father was, what kinds of crimes he'd committed. Now his shame and humiliation might be the very cause of Maggie's death.

"No," he whispered, his knees nearly buckling at the thought of losing her. Rage and fear forced his eyes closed for a moment as visions of Maggie filled his head.

Her childlike excitement in the hotel suite, the laughter that was a rare and beautiful gift and the unbridled passion of her lovemaking all combined to create his love for her, a love that was too deep to explain.

He opened his eyes and his gaze instantly fell on the top of the wooden file cabinets. He frowned as he saw something there he hadn't noticed before.

A pair of black gloves.

A pair of black motorcycle gloves.

He took a step around the desk and saw a gray helmet half-hidden next to the wastebasket. His blood ran cold. Roger hadn't been on the list he'd given them of motorcycle owners. Why would he leave himself off?

He moved back to where he'd been standing when Roger left the room. As the deputy returned, Jackson stopped him before he could get all the way into the room.

"You own a motorcycle, Deputy Black?"

Roger's face paled. "Yeah." He gave a forced laugh. "Guess I didn't put myself on that list I gave to you.

I didn't even think about it. I keep it in storage most of the time."

"What's that?" Deputy Morsi joined the conversation.

"I just learned that Roger here owns a motorcycle," Jackson said, his voice deceptively pleasant.

"Yeah, he rides it most days, but hasn't ridden it for the last week or so," Morsi replied.

Something snapped inside Jackson. The motorcycle chase...the near-death drama. Roger's guilt-ridden expression. With a roar of rage unleashed, Jackson attacked Black, tackling him to the floor as his hands wrapped around the big man's neck.

"Hey...hey," Deputy Morsi exclaimed in panic as he drew his gun, obviously unsure who he should point it at, his fellow deputy or an FBI agent.

"You're part of it," Jackson growled out as his hands pressed tighter against Roger's neck. "You were the one who tried to kill us."

"I don't know what you're talking about." Roger had to work to get the words out as his face reddened from a lack of oxygen.

"I'll kill you right now if you don't start talking," Jackson said.

Roger's face grew even more red as his fingers scrabbled to loosen Jackson's hold on his throat. Realizing he couldn't break the contact, he hissed out an okay.

Jackson released his hold and as he got up he pulled Roger's gun from his holster and held it pointed to the lawman's chest. "You'd better start talking or I'm going to start shooting."

Jackson ignored Fred Morsi and several other deputies who had gathered behind him in the hallway. "Where's Maggie?"

"I don't know." Roger remained on his butt on the floor, rubbing his raw throat.

Jackson took a step toward him and placed the barrel of the gun against his forehead. "Jeez, I swear I don't know. I was hired by your father to get rid of you. I never wanted to be sheriff. All I wanted to do was retire, and he offered me enough money to make it worth my while. You're right, I was the one who chased you on the motorcycle, and I was in contact with Bentz, who was hired to keep track of your movements, but I swear I don't know where Jerrod has Agent Clinton. I swear to God I don't know."

Jackson took a step backward and handed Roger's gun to Deputy Morsi. "Arrest this man for attempted murder. We'll figure out more charges as we wind up this case."

He left the office as Morsi was locking handcuffs on his coworker. He stomped back to his car, got inside and realized he had no idea where to go.

His head dropped to the steering wheel, and hot tears burned at his eyes. Maggie. His darlin', Maggie. Where was she? Was she already dead? He hated his father, but he hated himself even more for not being man enough to tell Maggie the truth about the man who had raised him, a man capable of killing not just his own son, but the woman his son loved.

Chapter Fifteen

The dim shine of the flashlight did nothing to penetrate the dark corners of the shed. Maggie sat in the very center, having exhausted every means of escape she could think of.

She'd tried to break down the door, had checked every area of the walls and the flooring to see if there was a weakness she could exploit, but there was nothing.

Tonight she would die.

She'd come to a final resignation about it, although a million regrets came with her acceptance of her fate. She wished she would have laughed more and worried less. She wished she would have taken more chances, reached out for more happiness.

She should have told her mother that all their money was gone and it was time for Katherine to live within her means. Marjorie wished she'd enjoyed her time on earth a little bit more. Dammit, if nothing else she should have allowed herself to get cable television.

A giggle bubbled to her lips. She knew it was a hysterical reaction to her circumstances. She was laughing to keep from weeping. She wanted to weep for Jackson. Even though she knew they hadn't been meant to be together, she could cry for what he'd given her. He'd opened her up to trusting. He'd made her realize she could love a man deeply.

She wished she'd had a chance to tell him she loved him one more time, but if even given the chance she wouldn't do it. She belonged in Kansas City, and he would go back to his home in Baton Rouge. She'd known there wasn't a future with him, but surely as she waited to die she could pretend.

Having already drunk one bottle of water, she was reluctant to open the second bottle that Jerrod had left for her. She had no idea how long she'd been inside the shed or how much longer she might be captive here.

She knew instinctively that this shed would not be her coffin and the only tiny modicum of hope she had left was that somehow when Jerrod came to get her out of here, she could escape.

What hurt the most was the certainty that she would be used to give Jackson as much pain as possible. Jerrod would twist Jackson's feelings for her, no matter what they were, into something ugly, something that would haunt Jackson if he lived or would be the last thing he'd know before his death.

She jumped to her feet as she heard the jingle of the padlock on the door. Maybe if she rushed him, she could bowl him over and run. She lowered her shoulder and prepared to attack.

The door opened, displaying two things—night had fallen outside, and Jerrod stood before her in the beam of her flashlight with a gun pointed at her chest.

"Don't get any smart ideas, girly," he said. "It doesn't matter to me if I deliver you to Jackson dead or alive."

For a moment she wanted to rush him anyway, let him shoot her now so that Jackson wouldn't have to watch her die. But that tiny survival instinct kicked in, that single ray of hope that somehow, someway, she and Jackson could get out of this together and alive.

"Turn around," he commanded. She hesitated only a moment and then did as he asked. He quickly tied her wrists together and then grabbed hold of her shoulder and spun her around. "Come on, we've got a date. I'll let you sit in the passenger seat as long as you behave, but if you give me any trouble I'll backhand you into unconsciousness. Got it?"

She nodded as he shoved her toward an awaiting SUV. He opened the passenger door and she slid in, wincing at the uncomfortable position of her arms behind her.

He circled the vehicle and slid in behind the steering wheel and started the engine. "This would have all been so much easier if you could hire good help these days. Black had two chances to kill you and he bungled both of them."

"Black? You mean Roger Black?" she asked in stunned surprise.

Jerrod chuckled. "You'd be amazed how easy it is to buy a greedy man."

They hadn't even considered the top-dog deputy as a potential suspect, but then why should they? She knew by Jerrod's answer to her question about Amberly and Cole that he didn't have anything to do with whatever had happened to them.

Jackson's gut instinct that the attacks on them had been personal had been right, and the attacks had nothing to do with the case they'd been investigating.

That meant they had no clues at all about Amberly and Cole's disappearance and moved her closer to believing that somehow the case was related to what Jackson had been working on in Bachelor Moon.

They drove only a short distance and then he stopped the SUV and put it in Park. Every nerve in Marjorie's body went on high alert.

She looked around the area, but still couldn't discern where they were in the darkness of the night. There were no lights to indicate any kind of civilization nearby.

Jerrod pulled a cell phone out of his pocket and flashed Marjorie a smile that was visible in the dashboard illumination. "Time for the games to begin," he said and then punched in a number.

JACKSON HAD DRIVEN up and down each and every street of Mystic Lake, seeking Edward Bentz's van. Not only could he not find it, none of the deputies on duty had managed to locate it, either.

Darkness had fallen and along with it his hope. Maybe this had been his father's intention all along. To take Maggie away from him and place her somewhere that Jackson would never, ever find her again, either dead or alive.

Maybe the true torture was the not knowing what had happened to her…if she was alive, or if she was dead. And if Jerrod had killed her, had she suffered?

He'd been in touch with Deputy Fred Morsi, who was now acting as head deputy, several times through the course of the past couple of hours. Roger was locked up, and although Fred had continued to elicit answers from him, he still swore he had no idea where Jerrod, Edward or Maggie might be.

Jackson was now parked once again in front of the sheriff's station. Night had fallen, and his despair had grown to mammoth proportions as if fed by the darkness itself.

He didn't know where to go. He didn't know what to do. He tasted grief, but refused to acknowledge it. He refused to grieve for Maggie without positive confirmation that she was dead.

He jumped as his cell phone rang. He fumbled it out of his pocket. "Revannaugh," he answered.

"Isn't that a coincidence, it's Revannaugh on this end, too."

The familiar sound of his father's voice churned up a combination of rage and hatred in Jackson that he knew he had to control. "Where is she?"

"The lovely Agent Clinton is right here by my side."

Jackson pressed the phone more tightly against his ear. "If you've hurt her I'll kill you."

Jerrod laughed. "Big talk from a man who doesn't hold the cards."

"What do you want, Jerrod?" Jackson asked the question although he already knew the answer.

"Do you have any idea the indignities I've suffered over the past six years? A man of my stature, in a prison cell with monsters? You put me there, son."

"You put yourself there," Jackson replied.

"You put the final nail in my coffin, my own flesh and blood testifying against me. You want your girlfriend back? Meet me in thirty minutes on the north bank of Mystic Lake, and as they say in the movies, come alone."

"Thirty minutes. I'll be there." Jackson dropped his phone in his pocket, started his car and headed directly toward the lake that was the namesake of the town.

He had no idea what his father intended, had no idea what would go down on the banks of the lake this night. There was a near-full moon that would make it difficult to depend on the darkness of the night for cover.

He had no idea if his father would be alone with Maggie or if Edward Bentz would be with him to provide backup. He didn't even know if Maggie was still alive or if Jerrod intended to deliver her body to his son.

Jackson was certain of just one thing…only one Revannaugh would be leaving the banks of Mystic Lake tonight. Jerrod had pushed him into a corner where he had no options. He would kill his father to save Maggie, and he knew his father would kill him without blinking an eye.

On the north shore of the glittering lake was a thick grove of trees. Jackson pulled into the area and got out of his car, his gun in his hand.

The night was hot, muggy and completely silent, as if Mother Nature knew something bad was coming and had hidden all the insects and night creatures from harm.

Nerves jangled inside him. He waited, unsure from which direction his father would come, uncertain if he might already be here.

He'd been foolish to come without his own backup. He didn't exactly trust the Mystic Lake sheriff's department, given the fact that their top deputy had turned out to be an ineffectual hit man.

He pulled out his phone and dialed the number for Agent Adam Forest. Maggie had given him the number to use in an emergency, and he figured this definitely qualified as an emergency.

It took him only moments to explain the situation with Adam and then hang up. It would be at least twenty to thirty minutes before Adam would arrive, and Jackson was expecting his father within the next ten minutes or so.

Those minutes clicked by in agonizing slowness. During that time, Jackson removed all emotion from his head. He couldn't think of Jerrod as his father and he couldn't think of Maggie as his partner or the woman he loved. The two of them were simply hostage taker and hostage. As long as he thought that way and kept his emotions in check, he would function better in doing whatever needed to be done for a successful outcome.

Despite the heat of the night, Jackson was cool as an unnatural calm descended upon him. He gripped his gun tighter as an SUV approached. The vehicle pulled to a halt, the high-beam lights pointed directly at Jackson, half blinding him.

He squinted and saw a tall man get out of the driver's seat. Jerrod. He held his gun on the man who was his father, but there was no way he would shoot, not without knowing where Maggie was.

He got the answer to that question as Jerrod walked to the passenger side and pulled Maggie out of the car, using her as a shield in front of him as he approached Jackson. He held Maggie with one arm around her neck, and in his other hand was a gun pointed at Jackson.

"Let her go," Jackson said. He kept his gaze on

Jerrod, knowing that one look at Maggie would undo him to the point that he wouldn't be able to function.

"Drop your gun," Jerrod replied.

"You drop yours and let her go. It doesn't have to be this way," Jackson said.

He knew he would shoot Jerrod if he had to, but in a flash, old memories shot through his brain. Jerrod teaching him to ride a bicycle, buying him ice cream and taking him to a movie.

There had been flashes of a father in the monster, but Jackson had never been fooled. He knew exactly what his father was capable of, the kind of man he was at his very core.

"Just let Maggie go and we all walk away from this," he said, although he knew at the very least he'd make sure his father was in custody.

Jerrod laughed, a dry, humorless sound. "Now, we both know you aren't going to just let me walk away from this, and I'm definitely not in the mood to let you walk away. I've had years to think about your betrayal, to wallow in my need to see my own brand of justice served."

He moved the barrel of his gun and pressed it against Maggie's temple. "Maybe if I kill her you'll understand the depth of my unhappiness with you."

For the first time Jackson allowed himself to look at Maggie. He was surprised to see that she appeared calm, as if resigned to whatever happened.

"If you kill her she'll be dead, but then you'll be dead, too," Jackson said, pleased that his voice remained cool and calm.

Jerrod appeared to study him, and once again he moved his gun to point at Jackson. "Then I guess you leave me no choice. I'll just have to kill you first, and then after you are dead I'll take care of your partner."

A shot rang out and Jerrod roared in pain as he dropped his gun, released Maggie and fell to one side on the ground. "You shot me," he screamed at Jackson.

"No, I didn't," Jackson said in bewilderment as Maggie ran to his side.

At that moment, Agent Adam Forest stepped out from behind the SUV. As he walked past the writhing Jerrod, he kicked Jerrod's gun out of reach and smiled.

"I saw an opportunity and so I took it." He looked at Jackson. "No man should have to carry the burden of killing his own father through the rest of his life."

"I'm bleeding to death," Jerrod screamed. "For God's sake, I need help."

Adam returned to the man on the ground and checked out his wound. "Don't be such a baby. It's a clean shot through and through and didn't do any permanent damage." He rose to his feet. "I'll call it in."

Jackson nodded, numbed by the unexpected help. It was only when he grabbed Maggie into his arms that his numbness went away, along with the iciness that had been inside his heart for what felt like days.

He cupped her face, her beautiful face in his hands. "Are you all right? Did he hurt you at all?"

"I'm fine," she assured him. "But I'd love it if you'd unfasten my wrists so I can wrap my arms around you."

He whirled her around and with a pocketknife he sawed through the tape that bound her. She turned around and threw herself at him, her arms wrapping around his neck while her body pressed tightly against his.

"I was so afraid for you," she murmured against his chest.

"I was terrified for you," he replied as he stroked her hair, then caressed her back and breathed in the scent of her.

"I was a little worried myself," Adam said, his voice breaking them apart. "I broke every speed limit to get here and then I was afraid he was going to shoot Jackson before I got a clean shot at his leg."

Jackson looked over to where his father was still on the ground, only now he wore a bracelet of handcuffs. He looked back at Forest. "I don't know how to thank you."

"All in a day's work," Forest replied.

At that moment the sound of sirens rose in the air. "I've got both FBI and local authorities on their way. From what I've heard, Mystic Lake law enforcement is going to need some help getting their stuff together."

As Jackson thought of Roger Black, he nodded his head. "They definitely have some problems." He frowned thoughtfully. "But nothing that went down here tonight had anything to do with the case of Amberly and Cole Caldwell's disappearance."

Maggie moved closer to his side. "At the moment I just want to celebrate the fact that we're both still alive and your father is probably going back to prison for a very long time."

"He'll be facing attempted murder charges, kidnapping and conspiracy—yeah, he won't see the light of day for years to come," Jackson replied.

At that moment a flurry of cars pulled up. Jackson and Maggie were separated as the area swarmed with law enforcement officials. Maggie found herself in the backseat of her director's car.

Daniel Forbes questioned her about not just the events of the night but also what she had known about Jackson's father. She confessed that she'd known nothing about Jerrod Revannnaugh until the moment he'd shown up on her doorstep.

Jerrod had been taken away under armed guard to a hospital to have his wound tended to, then he would be taken to a federal holding cell in Kansas City.

Director Forbes questioned her for a long time, their talk interrupted several times by phone calls he had to take. By the time they were finished, he offered to take her home. Seeing Jackson nowhere in the sea of men and women in the area, she agreed.

When she arrived home, Jackson wasn't there. She went inside, set the security and locked the door and then stumbled to the sofa and collapsed, trying to process everything that had happened, everything that she had learned over the course of the long, tension-filled evening.

It was no wonder Jackson hadn't wanted to talk about his father with her, and it was no wonder that at sixteen Jackson had left his father behind and began to build a different life, a righteous life, for himself.

Thank God Adam had arrived in time to save Jackson the trauma of having to kill…or be killed…by his father. She stood as she heard the sound of a key in the lock, and then Jackson came in. He punched in the code on the keypad, then locked the door behind him and opened his arms to her.

She ran to him, needing to be held, needing to be close to him as the aftermath of the night washed over her. He wrapped her tight in his arms and there were no words necessary as they simply held each other.

She didn't know how long they stood in the embrace, but finally he broke it and led her back to the sofa where they sat side by side.

"I should have told you," he said, his gaze focused on the coffee table. "I should have warned you, but I had no idea that he was plotting against me or that he'd been released from prison."

He finally looked at her, his eyes dark pools of misery. "He was a con man, the kind of man who might have scammed your mother out of any money she possessed. He had married at least six times, and each time he divorced he was wealthier and the woman was destitute. Knowing your history, I never wanted you to know that I got my charm from him. I wasn't sure you'd really believe that that's all I got from him."

"Jackson." She took one of his big hands in hers. "You can't possibly be like your father. If you're a con man you're a very bad one. I don't have any money." She smiled at him teasingly. "That means you've wasted all your charm working it on me."

He gave her a faint smile and pulled his hand from hers. "I've been called back to Baton Rouge."

She looked at him in surprise. "When?"

"I'm on a ten o'clock flight tomorrow."

"But we haven't solved the crime. We still have people missing," she protested.

"I think the powers that be have decided that the two cases might possibly be linked. The Kansas City FBI will continue to follow up here, but I'm heading home tomorrow."

And now the heartache begins, she thought as pain

pierced through her. Tomorrow she would no longer have him in her life. Tomorrow he would be back in Baton Rouge, charming the ladies, and in no time at all he'd forget all about her.

"I hate to see you go," she said softly.

"Then come with me." He grabbed her hands and pulled her closer to him. "I'm sure you're due some time off. If I was to guess, you haven't taken a real vacation since you started the job. Come with me, Maggie. Let me show you my city, let me show you how much I love you."

She stared at his face, expecting to see a teasing twinkle in his eyes, an indication that he was joking, but there was only love and want in the depths of his eyes.

"I love you, Maggie. I love you like I've never loved anyone else in my life. I want to give to you, to make you happy. Come visit and let's see where this all goes. You can get a transfer and we can buy a big place with a carriage-house apartment for your mother."

Marjorie pulled her hands from his. Wasn't this what she'd wanted? For him to love her as much as she loved him? And yet it all seemed too fast. Her head was spinning. Things were going far too fast.

"Jackson, I...I don't know what to say."

He stared at her for a long moment. "I'd say that says it all," he replied as shutters fell over his eyes. He stood. "I'd better get packed up. I'll need to be at the airport by eight-thirty or so. You want to drive me or should I arrange for a cab?"

"Of course I'll drive you," she said.

"Then I'll see you in the morning." He turned and went into his bedroom and closed the door behind him.

She remained seated on the sofa, a million words unsaid, a thousand regrets already forming. But it was crazy to believe that they could build a life together. They weren't meant to be, they'd never been meant to be anything more than partners.

She wasn't his Maggie, she was Marjorie Clinton, a Kansas City FBI agent who was good at her job and didn't take chances in her personal life.

THE RIDE TO THE AIRPORT the next morning was silent and awkward. Jackson knew Maggie loved him. She'd told him how she felt about him, that he'd managed to get deep into her heart, and yet not so deep that she wanted to take it any further.

It was a bitch, that the first woman Jackson had fallen in love with apparently wasn't as deeply in love with him. First love, first heartbreak. He hadn't expected either of them. But then, he hadn't expected Maggie.

When they reached Terminal A, she circled around to the drop-off area and halted the car. She got out of the driver's seat as he got out and retrieved his duffel bag from the backseat.

She joined him on the curb. She was dressed in a yellow blouse, which enhanced the beauty of her red-gold hair, and the pair of black jeans he'd bought when they'd been at the hotel. She was an ache inside him.

"Then I guess this is goodbye," she said. "You have your ticket and your boarding pass?"

"I have everything I need," he replied. *Except you.* "Goodbye, Maggie." Before he could stop his impulse, he dropped the duffel to the ground, pulled her into his arms and kissed her with all the love, all the emotion that was in his heart, in his soul.

When he released her, he didn't look at her again. He grabbed his duffel and went through the doors that would take him into the terminal.

He found his gate and passed through security easily, then sank down on one of the padded chairs to wait the hour and a half for his flight.

Maybe he'd pushed too hard. There was no question in his mind that Maggie loved him. And now there were no more secrets between them. She knew about his father and had judged him as his own man, not for his father's sins.

Maybe he should have told his director he needed a little downtime, hung around here and allowed their love to grow a bit more before encouraging her to leave everything behind and come with him to Baton Rouge.

He knew Maggie. He knew the kind of woman she was, and he'd been wrong to press her so aggressively. Maybe the best thing to do was to cancel his ticket home and pursue the woman who was the love of his life.

He stood from his seat at the same time Maggie came running toward him. He stared at her in surprise. "I have a ticket," she said. "I'm going with you." She laughed in carefree abandon. "I don't have any clothes, I don't even have a toothbrush, but I'm not letting you leave without me."

Still stunned, he fell back into his chair. "I was just about to go cancel my ticket," he said. "I didn't want to leave you. What changed your mind?"

She sank down into the chair next to his. "The whole time I was locked up in that shed waiting to find out if your father was going to kill me, I had a thousand regrets, and one of those regrets was that I hadn't taken more chances in my personal life."

She reached for his hand. "I'm taking a chance now, Jackson. I'm taking a chance on you…on us. I love you and I want to see if we can make this work. I need a man who brings me laughter, whose kisses make me weak in the knees. I need a charmer who flirts with his eyes and has a smile that melts my heart."

"And that would be me," he said.

He stood and pulled her up and into his arms. As he kissed her once again, she knew in the very core of her being that they were meant to be together, that some-how, someway, this magic between them was going to last a lifetime. Primal energy, that was what Natalie Redwing had called it, but in truth it was simply love.

Epilogue

Amberly Caldwell woke to small fingers stroking the long length of her dark hair.

"Macy, stop bothering Amberly." Daniella's voice came from nearby.

"I just wish sometimes that I had long pretty black hair," Macy's childish voice said.

Amberly turned over on the small bunk where she'd slept and faced the little blond-haired girl, who was on a bunk next to her. Iron bars separated the two beds. She smiled at Macy. "There were lots of times when I was little that I wished I had pretty blond curls just like yours."

She reached through the bars and gave Macy's slender shoulder a gentle squeeze and tried not to think of her son, Max.

Cole was already awake and out of his top bunk. He and Sam Connelly stood at the back end of the prison-like cells they were each held in, talking through the bars in low whispers.

Each cell was identical, with bunk beds built into the steel, a stall shower and prisonlike stool and a curtain that could be pulled around the bathroom area for a bit of privacy.

She and Cole occupied one cell, and Daniella, Sam and little Macy occupied the one next to them. None of them knew where they were or why they had been taken from their homes and brought here.

Sam and Daniella had lost track of the time they'd been held captive, and although Amberly knew it had been a couple of weeks since she and Cole had been brought here from his home, she didn't know specifically how many days it had been.

All she knew for certain was they were in trouble. Twice a day a man clad in black and wearing a ski mask brought them trays of food, but he'd never spoken to any of them.

The men had finally stopped asking questions. "A waste of breath," Sam had said. "He'll tell us what's going on when he's ready, but he obviously isn't going to be goaded into speaking before then."

The men had already searched the cells for any weakness, they'd tried to figure out escape plans, but none appeared to be viable. The only way in and out of the cells was through the locked doors, and since their arrival the doors had never been unlocked.

The food trays were slid through a slot without the need for their captor to open the doors. The only thing she knew about the man who held them was that his eyes were the coldest ice-blue that she'd ever seen.

They had speculated on why they had been kidnapped, why they were being held, but nobody had come up with any viable answers.

The only small sense of relief she had was the fact that none of them had seen his face, none of them had heard his voice. There was no way any of them could identify him, and as long as that remained true, they had a chance for surviving whatever plot was in progress.

But Amberly knew that the minute he came without his ski mask on and they saw his face, none of them would leave this place, wherever it was, alive.

* * * * *

"You have a lot of nerve coming back after twelve years and trying to pick up like nothing ever happened after you left."

Alicia closed her eyes, inhaled deeply. "I get it. You're a naval officer who probably has a gal in every port. Well, Lieutenant Sloan, my little part of the world doesn't have a dock. It's centered around a four-year-old child. I'm her whole world. And I don't take risks with it."

"I get it."

"No, I don't think you do. I have responsibilities to Lauren and have no intention of jeopardizing that by dating. Let alone having sex in a dried-up field with a man I haven't seen or heard from in over a decade."

"Don't worry about Lauren. We'll get her back."

"I don't want you to hate me."

"Never." He'd never hate her. He'd also never stop wanting her with every part of his being. *Never.*

NAVY SEAL SURRENDER

BY
ANGI MORGAN

Published in Great Britain 2014
by Mills & Boon, an imprint of Harlequin (UK) Limited,
Eton House, 18-24 Paradise Road, Richmond, Surrey, TW9 1SR

© 2014 Angela Platt

ISBN: 978 0 263 91358 3

46-0514

Harlequin (UK) Limited's policy is to use papers that are natural, renewable and recyclable products and made from wood grown in sustainable forests. The logging and manufacturing processes conform to the legal environmental regulations of the country of origin.

Printed and bound in Spain
by Blackprint CPI, Barcelona

Angi Morgan writes Mills & Boon® Intrigue novels "where honor and danger collide with love." She combines actual Texas settings with characters who are in realistic and dangerous situations. Angi has been a finalist for the Booksellers' Best Award, *RT Book Reviews* Best First Series, Gayle Wilson Award of Excellence and the Daphne du Maurier Award.

Angi and her husband live in North Texas, with only the four-legged "kids" left in the house to interrupt her writing. They recently began volunteering for a local Labrador foster program. Visit her website, www. angimorgan.com, or hang out with her on Facebook.

Many moons ago, I graduated high school with a small group of kids. Brian & Johnny are fictional characters but named after two men who won't be returning at our next reunion. Several of the names in the Sloane brothers' stories are familiar to my friends, but do not reflect any of their true personalities. All the characters are fictional, but not my friendship with my classmates.

Chapter One

Join the navy. See the world.

"I don't think they meant the sandboxes I've been playing in." John Sloane had met and helped a lot of great people around the world. He'd been to several cool cities, nice ports and seen a lot of water. But he never wanted to see most of the places his unit had been deployed again—even in the news.

Back in Texas. Right back where he'd started wasn't exactly what he'd had in mind when he was eighteen. But right now he didn't care about choices or destinations. He just wanted information on his dad.

He'd returned from a training exercise and was told that his father had suffered a major stroke. When he couldn't reach the house or his dad, he'd called the police station with no luck. They'd refused to help.

From the message, he knew that his father was alive and at the ranch. He'd arranged extended leave and a ticket back to his hometown. Taking as much time off as he wanted wasn't a problem. He had a lot stored up. He wanted to be here as long as needed to get his father back on his feet. The only objective so far was to get home.

Two hours in triple-digit heat with the rental's AC whacked-out had added to his building frustration. He was sailing blind with no information, since his brother hadn't returned his calls and the home phone seemed to be out of order.

If John was being honest—no sense lying to himself—he hadn't been the most dependable brother. Or the most communicative. Since they'd learned to open their mouths, Brian had been the twin to tell the world what they needed. Brian had been the responsible one keeping him out of trouble, right up to his last words to him, "Leave and never look back."

That was exactly what he'd done.

John had followed through on his promise, joined the navy, left the ranch and had never come back.

In the navy, he wasn't Brian's twin or Johnny Junior or the baby. He'd quickly risen to chief petty officer and was the man you went to with a problem. He was the guy who got things done. Action, not words.

Then things changed. Promotions after online classes and a college degree. Instead of solving the problems, he followed orders. Now a lieutenant, he was the man responsible if someone got shot. A man who'd been doing too much thinking recently.

Texas? California? Navy? Private sector? Which road should just simple *John* choose? Too much thinking.... Right now he would help his dad, work the horses and maybe—just maybe—reconnect with his brother. That was the mission.

Deciding his future could wait.

His hometown was just ahead, and suddenly he didn't feel so confident. Since that short good riddance right after graduation, he hadn't seen or spoken to Brian. John hadn't seen his father in almost three years. How would the town see him now? Who would he be after twelve years? The man he'd become, or the kid the town remembered?

Aubrey looked like a busy small town instead of the bus-stop intersection with one red light he'd left. Lots of changes, and yet the most familiar thing in the world to him. He knew what stool old man Searcy would be sitting on for his lunch at the café, and he knew who would be serving him his blue-plate special. His stomach growled, emphasizing his lack of lunch. Another ten minutes and he'd be home.

Home.

The word felt good. He'd stay, help his dad around the ranch, work with his back instead of a weapon. He'd welcome every minute of mind-numbing grunt labor. And somehow he'd figure out what to do with the rest of his life.

He raised a finger off the steering wheel, acknowledging those driving past. A friendly custom in north Texas, like tipping your hat. Or at least it used to be. People stared at him and quickly looked away when he caught their eye. He drove through his little town, now full of fast-food restaurants and an outdoor mini shopping mall. He turned off the main road, took the familiar turns and passed the mailbox—faded with one of the letters missing from his father's name.

Parked on the side of the driveway was a cherry-red Camaro. A car he knew inside and out. The car had always hummed perfection. Mark Miller had won many drag races with that engine. When Mark had left for the army, John had tried to buy it from Mr. Miller many times. He slowed as the driver—obviously waiting on him—opened the door of the car he'd wanted throughout his teenage years. His tires crunched on the gravel as he pulled to a stop.

"Wow." The word slipped from his brain to his mouth.

"You still haven't gotten over this car?" the woman said, caressing the hood with long strokes.

Thankfully, she thought he was gawking at the muscle car. The vehicle was a nice backdrop to the curvy medium-height babe with long wavy dark brown hair and eyes hidden behind aviator shades. Dressed in old worn jeans that hugged her hips and a tank top that hugged everything else, he couldn't focus on the car if he wanted to.

And he really didn't want to. If he had air-conditioning, he would have cranked it to high. Instead, the sweat beaded on his forehead. He grabbed the button-up shirt he'd tossed on the seat next to him to wipe his face.

"Driving with the windows down? Braving the Texas heat, Johnny? You forget how hot it gets here in July?" the babe asked, crossing the road in worn boots. She slid her glasses to the top of her head, tucking her hair back in the process. Bright smiling eyes laughed at him.

"Alicia?" He recognized her voice, but none of the curves she currently sported.

"Welcome home." She leaned on the open window, giving him a great view straight between her breasts. A much better view than he'd ever seen in high school.

"How did you know I'd be here?"

"I was already at the house. Wanda thought she saw Brian in a new car and sent a text asking if he'd come into some cash." She shrugged her bare, tanned shoulders. "I knew Brian was in the barn. So I assumed and waited." She stepped back, pulling the door open. "Get out here so I can give you a proper welcome home. It's been a while."

Alicia Miller, now Adams. Or had she gone back to Miller after her husband had died? Either way, he barely recognized his high school sweetheart. She'd definitely filled out in all the right places. He popped the seat-belt release and stood, towering over her in a white undershirt that probably smelled as bad as the horse stalls. She wrapped her arms around his middle and squeezed. He hugged her back.

Home.

They separated, and the pearly-white smile he expected was gone. He missed her hand swinging upward, until it connected with his cheek. Connected hard. He rubbed it, not ashamed to let her know the slap had stung. Caught off guard by a girl. Or maybe he deserved it. Time enough to contemplate later.

A fitting welcome home.

"Before you ask, that was for your dad. J.W. will never say or do anything to make you feel ashamed, but you deserve that and more for just leaving. It broke his heart."

The little fireball choked on the last word. But she was right. And he was grown enough now to admit he'd made a mistake by not calling more often. "You've seen him? Is he okay?"

"He gets stronger every day. I'm his nurse and help him with physical therapy. That's what I do, at-home nursing."

"Just for the record, that's the one and only time you'll slap me and get away with it." He leaned against the rear door, crossing his arms to keep them in check. He didn't know if he wanted to drive away or reach out and pull her back to fill the emptiness he suddenly experienced.

"Are you okay? I didn't mean to hurt you. I'm not even sure why I did that. I never do that. And now I'm just babbling."

"Really?" Had it been too long to tease her? She'd been a junior in college the last time he'd heard anything. Their lives had changed when he hadn't chosen that route. Really changed when Brian had taken the blame for the accident. They hadn't spoken since his twin had accused him of being irresponsible and leaving a campfire burning.

After boot camp, his dad said Brian had decided not to attend college. Brian's taking public blame for the fire meant John could achieve his dream of entering the navy. It wouldn't have happened otherwise, and he owed his brother his entire career.

Join the navy. See the world.

It had been his dream, and his brother had pushed him toward it, sacrificing everything to let him keep it. *That* was the problem. The closest people to him had believed the accusation.

"I should be…" She gestured toward her car. "Your father's waiting."

"You said Brian was in the barn?"

"He was earlier." Alicia stuck her hands into her front pockets, creating a shrug whether she wanted one or not. "Sorry I slapped you, Johnny."

"I'm sorry you needed to." He rubbed his cheek again, scraping the three days of growth.

Alicia took a step toward him, awkwardly pulled him down for what he thought was another hug. He didn't reach for her. Instead, supersoft fingers caressed him from the bottom of his ears down both lines of his jaws. The sting disappeared faster than a radar blip.

Before he could react, she'd kissed his lips, lingering just a second too long for it to be just a friendly welcome home. Then she waved and returned to her car.

"See you around."

The dust from the road stuck to his arms and face as he stood there like an idiot while she drove away.

"Wow."

The Double Bar had been around for over a hundred years, supplying its fair share of cutting horses and rodeo stock. Oak trees had towered over the winding gravel driveway, since just after the Civil War. They'd formed a canopy and should have been a sight for his weary eyes. It was normally one of the coolest places on the ranch. The trees stretching above his head looked gnarly. Had anyone trimmed them since he'd left? He had to slow to avoid the potholes. The pasture looked more like West Texas desert than grazing potential for a herd.

"What the hell's happened?"

Granddad's old Dodge truck was loaded with feed and supplies. No doubt his work would start this afternoon, no waiting around. The ranch never let you take a vacation. John parked the rental, dropped the tailgate of the truck and slapped a bag.

Wham. Slammed to the ground, he spit dirt from his mouth. A punch to his kidney caused him to tighten his gut and pull his arms tight against his sides. The attacker shuffled off and away. John scrambled to his knees and popped up to both feet.

"You've got a lot of nerve showing up now!"

"Brian? What the…" He wiped the dirt from his face just in time to block a punch. His hands automatically formed fists. He resisted throwing his right at the last minute, but his shoulder momentum took him a step closer to his brother. "Cut it out or find yourself on the ground."

"Yeah, who's going to put me there? Oh, right, the son who's been gone twelve years. Think you can take me with all your fancy military training?"

John couldn't start his return home by teaching Brian a lesson. He relaxed his body enough to appear nonthreatening, but didn't lose eye contact. Brian would always give his punches away by dropping his gaze to the ground before he swung. Better to avoid being hit than make things worse by hitting back.

"Come on, man, I just got here," he said. Home for fifteen minutes and already he'd been slapped and eaten a face full of dirt. His lower back didn't feel all that great, either.

"That's the point. Dad's stroke was over a week ago."

"No excuses. I was on a mission and got here as soon as I could. How is he?"

"Busy saving strangers and can't be bothered at home." Brian grabbed a fifty-pound bag of feed, throwing it to his shoulder like a bulky pillow, then stomped toward the shed. "Go see for yourself. Alicia usually leaves him in front of the television."

Guess it wasn't the right time to remind his brother he'd called a couple of dozen times in the past two days. John rubbed his side, then his jaw, and dusted some of the dirt from his body. *What a welcome.*

"Dad?" He pushed the screen door open with the hesitation of entering the unknown. He didn't know what to expect. Light on his feet, soundlessly moving through the kitchen and sitting room, he was afraid of what he'd find in front of the loud television.

A severe stroke ten days ago when he'd been working horses. That's all John knew. He'd left messages on his dad's cell, but no one had called back. His dad kept him up-to-date. Sad, but he didn't know his brother's number.

Bad communication skills were nothing new before he'd left for the navy. More bad habits had formed when he'd been in training and not allowed to call. Then long missions with no communication. Different time zones. Easy after that to avoid calling home by just being too busy— or pretending to be. His father had accepted the excuses. His brother had told him never to look back and meant it.

He was a different man. They both were. They had time to fix what was wrong. Later.

Right now it was about his dad—who was asleep in a wheelchair in a room that no longer resembled his mother's favorite in the house. Full of a hospital bed, pulleys, a portable toilet and other medical stuff, everything familiar had been removed. There was a flat-screen TV hanging on the wall.

He heard the water running in the kitchen behind him and jerked around, surprised Brian had entered without making a sound.

"Dad, wake up." Brian shoved a shoulder into John as he passed. His angry twin turned a gentle hand to touch their dad's shoulder and not startle him awake. "John's home."

He understood the pain. His brother had a right to be

upset, from the serious look of things. He'd been here taking care of the ranch and their dad. Alone.

The last time they'd been face-to-face, they were skinny kids eating their dad out of a ton of groceries. Identical twins who could have passed for each other—and had fooled more than a teacher or two. Not to mention the girls. There were differences now. The most obvious was their hair. His was the navy regulation, high and tight over his ears. Brian's was longish, touching his collar.

John knew the tense jaw-clenching muscle all too well. Strange seeing what it looked like to others. Their bodies were toned from different types of exercises—his PT and Brian's ranch work. Weird that they still looked so much alike.

"I got here as soon as I could. I had no idea," John apologized. He would not complain about the lack of information provided by his brother. It would just upset his dad.

"That's an understatement," Brian mumbled.

His dad shook his head. Upset. Brian patted his shoulder. "I know, Dad. I told you I'd explain things when he got here."

He kept his mouth shut, stunned at the fright he saw in his father's eyes. The stroke had left him paralyzed. He couldn't talk. Brian lifted a straw to the left side of his dad's mouth and patiently waited, that angry gleam still in his eyes when he connected with John.

"Dad had a stroke and was lucky to survive. Recovery's going to take a while, but he's doing great." He put the mug on the table. "Looks like Alicia wore you out as usual, old man. Time for a nap, right?"

Brian moved swiftly. John moved in to help but was waved off. In two shakes, J. W. Sloane was back in bed. Brian maneuvered him quickly and with the same calm ease he handled troubled animals.

"I got this. Go get cleaned up and I'll get him settled. I'm sure you have things to explain."

Things hadn't changed; his brother issued orders for him to follow. And just like every day of his life, he followed orders well. Stowing his gear back in a room that hadn't changed except for the layers of dust, he wondered if the day would ever come where he'd be deciding his *own* fate.

Chapter Two

"Hey, beautiful."

"Mommy! Mommy! Look, I'm a princess."

Alicia Ann Adams watched her four-year-old daughter run across the playroom, dodging toys and playmates. Her yellow sunflower dress had a purple stain on the front—most likely grape jam from a snack. She lifted her over the gate guard in her day-care room to squeeze her close. "What did you do today?"

"We painted and dressed up. I was a princess and gots to wear the crown all the time."

"Well, that was appropriate for my very own Princess Lauren. Did you put your toys away?"

"The other girls are still playing with everything, Alicia. Don't worry about it this time."

She put Lauren down, dreading the next part of the conversation. "Go pick up a bit, sweetie. I need to talk with Miss Mary."

"Is something wrong?" asked the woman responsible for her daughter's daily care.

Mary Fitz had owned and run the day care forever. Alicia had stayed here before starting kindergarten, and had worked here in high school. There was nowhere else she wanted her daughter to stay. Which made not being able to pay Mary all the more difficult.

"I'm afraid tomorrow's our last day. It isn't fair to ask you to let Lauren stay when I can't pay you, Mary." What was she going to do? She couldn't take Lauren with her to her clients' homes, and she had to work.

"Nonsense. I've told you before just pay me when you can. I trust you. I know what you're going through. Working on your own to spend more time with your daughter is admirable, dear. Starting this place wasn't easy, either. Everyone thought I was a crazy widow. So don't fret. She's safe here." Mary turned back to the children. "Lauren, time to go, sweetheart."

Alicia was going to cry. She hadn't been able to think of Dwayne without all the problems he'd left when he'd died four years ago. Leaving her with a newborn and without a will had created chaos in a once-happy life. Those thoughts seemed utterly ridiculous compared to his death. Nevertheless, they were true.

The tears were building, so she pressed the palms of her hands to her closed eyes, attempting to stop the waterworks. Mary had saved her life. Again.

"It won't be too long. I have to drive a bit farther, but there are two more patients in Sanger."

"It's really not a problem, Alicia. I'm glad to help." She lifted Lauren over the doorway gate. "She had so much fun playing princess today. Such an imagination. Keep the crown, sweetie."

"Say bye-bye to Miss Mary." They both waved to one of the nicest people left in their lives. "See you tomorrow."

Unfortunately, she wasn't branching out on her own willingly like Mary thought. She'd been forced to resign from the Denton hospital.

After years with a spotless record, her patients' exit questionnaires were suddenly full of mysterious complaints. Complaints that had all begun at the same time

Dwayne's trust fund was frozen and her mother-in-law sought control.

Coincidence?

And then an anonymous caller said they'd witnessed her selling drugs. *Anonymous? Not hardly. It has to be Shauna.*

She'd never believed anyone could be that cruel. Especially family. She didn't *want* to believe Shauna, her mother-in-law, was responsible for the loss of her job at Denton Regional. But if she hadn't been, she wouldn't have known about Alicia's dismissal and wouldn't have filed for custody of Lauren the same day.

Ugh. I certainly wish I wasn't forced to refer to her as my mother-in-law.

Dwayne had never called Shauna Weber his stepmother. She was the same age and had even gone on a couple of dates with him their junior year. She'd married a man two years younger only four months after Dwayne's father had died.

Think about the extra time you have with Lauren today.

With only a couple of home clients on her Monday schedule, she should be rejoicing about the light load and playing with her daughter. But a light load meant light money. Next on her list was to speak with her landlord. He'd be upset splitting the rent again, but her paychecks just weren't large enough for her to get a couple of weeks ahead.

A real shame they couldn't head straight to the park, but it was 107 degrees outside. Almost as hot in the car, even with the AC on high. Store first, then dinner, then a cooler playtime on the swings before her bath.

It was hard to enjoy anything. She was still shaking. Money—or the lack of it—always got her this way. Then throw in what happened with Johnny and she was a nervous wreck.

How in the world had she ever thought she could welcome him home? She could still feel the sting of that slap on her hands. Feel the strength in his arms around her waist. Feel the tingle down her spine from kissing him.

She glanced in the rearview mirror to watch Lauren playing in her car seat.

It had been a major mistake kissing him. Really kissing him. Add a shot of guilt and disloyalty to her deceased husband, and her hands wouldn't stop shaking. If Johnny didn't know how she felt about his return before—he did now. Well, there was always the possibility he might be as thickheaded as when he'd left. Was he the only thing she could think about?

"Great. Just great. I was not supposed to kiss him. Ugh."

"Like a princess kisses a frog, Mommy?"

"Just like that, sweetie. Mommy did kiss a frog today, but he didn't turn into a prince. What do you want for dinner?" *Think about the park. And ice cream. Real ice cream from the Creamery. That would be nice. Getting cool. Don't think about the money or Johnny Sloane.*

"Chicken nuggets."

"You want those every night." She laughed at the nightly conversation.

It was definitely hard not to think about how great her high school boyfriend had looked. And felt. He'd been a solid rock under her hands. Why it seemed he was taller than Brian, she didn't understand, but it did. Not once, for as long as she'd known the Sloane brothers, had she been attracted to Brian. They'd never been able to fool her like they had so many of their teachers and friends.

Nope, she could always tell them apart.

She liked how John's hair was short over his ears, but not cropped completely down to the skin like it had been the last time she'd seen him. He looked fantastic. Strong. Sturdy. Like a man. She'd been thinking about him all day and had to stop.

It was Lauren time.

"I like nuggets. McDonald's nuggets." Her daughter giggled again.

Probably the dinner menu on those rare visits alone with a babysitter—without her mother-in-law's supervision. She turned into the store parking lot.

"How 'bout chicken nuggets from scratch? We have lots of time today, but first a stop at the store."

It didn't take long to get down the street to the grocery. She parked by the far basket return, always protecting her father's Camaro from dings and scratches. "Looks like you'll get to ride in your favorite play shopping cart. There aren't too many people here."

"Can we get real chocolate milk?"

"We have the stuff at home to mix it up."

"But Grandpa Weber's gots real chocolate milk straight from the cows," her daughter whined, sounding just like Shauna. How was that possible at the age of four? And she wasn't even blood related.

"Honey, it doesn't come that way." She was forever correcting the things Shauna's husband, Patrick, assured Lauren were true.

Alicia went to the passenger side to get Lauren. Cool-looking cars were absolutely not family cars. She pulled down the front seat and removed the shoulder restraints from Lauren, who waved to someone passing by.

"Hi," Lauren said.

Shoved just as she'd lifted Lauren, they both fell into the car. Her feet were kicked from under her. She couldn't stand.

"Somebody help!"

Thick material was yanked over her head, smelling like a burlap feed sack. She couldn't see. The pressure in her back grew sharp, like a knee. It moved to her neck. Someone forced her face into the hot leather. Lauren screamed behind her, kicking her side as she was dragged from the car.

They were taking her baby!

"Stop hurting my mommy," Lauren screamed.

"What do you want?"

Pushing. Shaking. Choking her from behind. She couldn't move. *Dear Lord in heaven, please send someone to help me.*

"Mommy!"

"Shh," a deep voice said.

Lauren continued a muffled scream.

"Please don't…don't hurt her. It'll be okay, baby."

"Shut up," a second gravelly voice whispered close to her ear. Her hands were quickly taped behind her.

"Don't do this. Please," she pleaded.

Shoved into the back floorboard, her boots removed, her ankles taped. She heard the lock being pushed down. The door slammed. The windows had been up. The keys were in her pocket. It was a scorching triple-digit day outside, but she was not going to die!

They'd kidnapped her little girl.

She felt the adrenaline rush through her body, but still couldn't tear the tape from her hands. She closed her eyes from the grain dust and shifted closer to the window. Then kicked and kicked some more. But the bastards had pulled off her boots and left her with only socks. Her heels couldn't touch the glass, just her toes. It was doubtful she could break the glass, but someone would hear the pounding.

Someone would see her. They'd call the police. They could break the window and get her out. Something. Something fast so they'd find Lauren.

Who could do this? She'd never give up until she found her daughter.

Sweat beaded over her face, making it itch. It was hard

to breathe without inhaling the feed dust left in the sack. She choked, coughed, gagged. All the while twisting and using the carpet to slowly work the suffocating material from the bottom part of her face.

Kick. Keep kicking.

Don't stop.

"Don't. Give. Up. On me. Baby!"

Kick.

"Help! Can anybody hear me?"

Try to sit up. Impossible. She couldn't twist enough and was hooked to something. "The seat belt." They'd taped her hands to the front seat-belt strap.

Kick.

"Help." The dry, hoarse whisper was all she had left.

The tears wanted to come. They started. But it was so hot in the car she could barely catch her breath. *No tears.*

Kick.

Kick again.

A customer will bring their cart to the return. Someone would hear her. She just had to keep kicking. Someone would wonder why her dad's car was here. Wouldn't they?

Kick. *God, let me kick.*

Lauren....

Chapter Three

"No witnesses. No physical evidence. No ransom demand. The Amber Alert is still active. But it's been thirty-two hours since the kidnapping, and we've got nothing, Alicia."

County Sheriff Coleman had escorted her home from the hospital after recovering from heat stroke. Thank heavens someone had seen her through the window after she'd passed out. The excessive heat inside the car could have killed her. She'd hated to call the county sheriff to bring her home, but the press had made it impossible for her to leave unescorted, and the Aubrey police had refused to help.

Now he stood in her humble living/dining room like he had a dozen times in the past four years. Same humble sheriff, just a different house than when he'd notified her Dwayne had died at the scene of his car accident.

"I don't understand. We both know the only person who could be behind this is Shauna. She's publicly threatened to take Lauren from me." Her husband's stepmother had put on a good distraught act for the television cameras, but Alicia knew the truth.

Knew the Webers wanted her little girl's trust fund. Knew in her heart they were involved with the abduction. The gleam of dollar signs in their eyes proved it to her over and over again.

"Why can't anyone see past the fake tears she has only

when the press is around?" There was something else just behind Shauna's heavy-lidded eyes. Gloating. The same look she'd had when they'd successfully frozen all of Dwayne's assets.

"Lauren isn't at the ranch or the Frisco house, where Shauna lives now. We've checked. We've followed Weber. We've searched every property remotely associated with either of them." The sheriff shook his head as he had each time he'd told her the same results while she'd been in the hospital.

"What about the FBI? Did you contact the Texas Rangers like you said? Or are you telling me to give up?" She wouldn't.

"I'm telling you I won't stop looking, but there's little I can do. The rangers are on watch and are conducting the investigation. They feel like this is a domestic dispute and haven't called in the FBI yet."

"Did Shauna stop them? Does everyone believe her and the lies she's telling the press? I did *not* kidnap my daughter for her trust fund." Vultures.

He hung his head, letting her assume it was true.

"It might be time for a private investigator," he said.

"I checked into them yesterday from the hospital. They all want a lot more money than I have access to. And they want it up front before they'll even begin." She went to the window to see if any cameras were still parked out front. None. "Shauna says she's hiring her own and swears if they find her, she'll take her away. Isn't that grounds for a search warrant or something? You've searched here based on the accusations of the press."

"Now, Alicia, that's not why the task force looked around and you know it. Shauna invited us to search all the property without a warrant."

"You know that in the media, I've already been found guilty of kidnapping my own daughter, but I'm not sure how I did it. I think of all the times I judged those mothers being crucified by the news stations. You never hear about them being found innocent. But I'll take the blame, Sheriff. I'll let them call me whatever they want to get Lauren home safely."

If she wasn't so tired, she'd pace the carpet. Sitting and waiting was driving her crazy. Too exhausted to stand any longer, she fell into the chair and couldn't stop the tears.

Lauren was gone and there was no one to find her. The light pat on her back reminded her that the sheriff was politely waiting.

"Alicia, you know that wasn't me. I don't think you're using Lauren for publicity."

"I don't know what to do, Ralph." She needed to pull herself together one more time so he could leave. "Sorry I had to call you again, but I couldn't get out of the hospital door with those vultures wanting a statement."

The press had hounded her, comparing her to a desperate, unstable woman. Implying she'd kidnapped her own little girl for the ransom. The local newspaper had made the first insinuations in their weekly editorial. Reporting that she was broke, unable to pay her bills because she was in the process of suing her sweet mother-in-law for Lauren's trust fund.

"It's all so stupid crazy, Ralph. If anyone is hungry for cash, it's Shauna. Everyone knows she married Dwayne's dad for the money. Goodness, she was the same age as her stepson. She hated me in high school and especially hated me after I married Dwayne. Even more after Roy left everything in a trust to Lauren."

Another slow, awkward pat.

Pull it together.

"You should go. I'm fine. Really," she finally managed.

"Lock the doors, Alicia. I don't think it's safe."

She nodded, but if the kidnappers had wanted to kill

her, it would have been much easier when they'd taken her baby. As it was, they were successfully framing her for their actions.

"I mean it, girl. They may be back to finish what they started. You could have died from being locked in that car."

"I'm fine." She feared her own neighbors more. That people she'd known all her life might take a mob mentality and throw bricks through her windows. Hadn't that happened to a mother of another kidnapped little girl?

"As long as you stay inside, you'll be fine." He patted her shoulder again, following with a little squeeze before heading to the door. "Lauren will be fine, too. We'll find her. I promise you that."

"Without any idea where she's been taken? Who's really looking?"

He dipped his head again, raised his hat to his head and stood on the outside of the screen, tapping the doorknob.

Alone. No one to hold on to.

Alicia dropped her face into her hands. "What am I going to do?"

"Find someone without connections to the Webers," he said through the glass, still waiting and pointing until she locked the door.

The silence was deafening after his car pulled away. How many nights over the past three and a half years had she begged for a moment alone? With no responsibility? Each moment spent away from Lauren, she'd been working doubles at the hospital. And now? Just one sweet giggle asking for another drink of water. That was all she wanted to hear.

She wiped more tears and stood straight. What she needed was money. Shauna had Lauren hidden somewhere. She watched the sheriff drive away and turned the dead bolt. Money would help her find her daughter.

She had to break her promise and sell her dad's Camaro. There was one person who might want it just as badly as she did.

Johnny.

"You can't avoid this forever. I've already given him his meds. Next round is written on the schedule. He needs his exercises after lunch." Brian grabbed his gym bag off the back porch and tossed it over his shoulder. "I've got to go."

"Where are you headed?" John asked, letting the screen slam behind him. He wanted Brian to answer the question instead of ignoring him like he had since he'd returned. Other than instructions about their dad, Brian hadn't said anything except "pass the butter," at breakfast. John's brother worked from sunup till past midnight every day, breaking only for meals and to take care of their dad.

And now he was taking off to go to "work" for four days?

"All you need to know is written down. Since Alicia can't be here, call Mabel if you need something."

"Shouldn't we hire another nurse or a proper physical therapist?" His brother's announcement last night that it was John's turn to take care of their dad had thrown him for a loop. He had no training for this sort of duty.

Helping his father—other than in and out of the wheelchair—wasn't like facing down the enemy. But for some reason making a mistake scared him to death.

"I won't do that to Alicia. And neither will you." Brian shook his head, adding to the disgust already plain on his face. "Truth is, we can't afford it. Dad doesn't have insurance. Alicia's been coming by without payment until I get some cash. She insisted. I'll pay her eventually, but I have to sell one of the mares. I've been having problems, since she's in Dad's name."

"I can pay. How much do you need?"

"Keep your money."

"It's for Dad," John said, stopping before he spouted what he really thought about his brother's pride.

Things were a lot worse than John had imagined, but even then, his brother's loyalty to Alicia wasn't a battle he was willing to wage. *Stick to Brian's plan and negotiate peace when the time is right.*

"Four days. Then we'll suffer through a discussion," Brian grudgingly mumbled.

The ranch and his dad were a different story. Brian couldn't keep him from looking at the financials while he was gone to "work."

"I'm not sure of what to do with Dad."

"There's a list of exercises on the stand next to his bed. It will give you a chance to talk to him without me around. You can complain all you want." Brian shoved his hair off his face and pulled an old beat-up straw hat onto his head. "Mabel said she's glad to help with Dad and is five minutes across the road."

"I remember where Mrs. Standridge lives. Why are you wearing Dad's hat?" His brother shot him a look and stuffed the hat harder on his head. "You could drive the rental to wherever you're headed. I don't have to return it for another couple of days."

"Now, why would I want to do that?" He tossed his gym bag into the front of the truck and climbed in. "Don't call her unless you really need to impose."

"Don't impose. Right," John mumbled to a trail of dust mixed with gas fumes. "Four days without a freaking clue. Is that a reason to impose?"

Talking to his brother was more difficult than facing a terrorist. Brian was right about one thing—speaking to his dad had always been easy. But that was a long time ago, before two-minute conversations or voice-mail tag had become their routine. Long before his dad had such a hard, frustrating time just communicating that he wanted a sip of water. Maybe he could talk about some of his war stories? His dad might enjoy those.

But storytelling would have to wait until he'd checked forty sets of hooves. Made certain the rest of the herd was moved to the front pasture—what was left of it—and had plenty of water. Checked the fence line, which meant saddling an unfamiliar horse and riding for the first time in twelve years. In between the three-page to-do list, he was supposed to check on his father every half hour.

How had Brian kept up with the work four hired men had accomplished while they'd been growing up? And why had he left with only a small bag for four days?

Well, if Brian could do it, he could do it. He *wanted* to do it. If he could handle hotheaded naval aviators, he could handle some chores he'd done most of his childhood.

Piece of cake.

Chapter Four

He couldn't do it.

Saddle sore, John wanted to drop in a chair, turn on a mind-numbing rerun of an old television show and drink a beer. If he'd been in San Diego, that was exactly what he would be doing. Or hitting the beach.

Of course, if he'd been at home in front of his TV, he wouldn't be frustrated at not completing any task on Brian's list. He'd consistently been aware of each minute slithering by. The stops and starts of checking on his dad had disrupted each job he'd begun. As a result, he hadn't finished anything.

After a couple of hours he'd admitted he was out of his element. He'd run and trained almost every day since leaving home, but every part of him was sore in a different way. By lunch he'd called Mrs. Standridge. He wasn't ashamed to ask for help. He was used to teamwork, admitting his shortcomings and working to improve.

As soon as she'd arrived, he'd seen the look in his dad's eyes change. Brian could have been a little more specific that their father was embarrassed for anyone to see him. Mable had let him know a couple of hours ago she'd fed his dad breakfast for a late lunch, something J.W. could eat almost on his own. J.W. clearly didn't want her in the house, but there wasn't a choice. They needed help.

The excruciating one-hundred-plus temperature had climbed along with the sun. By the heat of the afternoon, it had hit 109. Might just make it down to ninety-eight later that night. Finally some relief. Ha! He hadn't experienced a Texas summer since his teens. He'd like to see Brian survive after being dropped in the middle of a desert, dressed in full gear. He missed the ocean breeze and his run along the beach in California.

Different life. Time to concentrate on this one and see if Brian would allow him to return home more often. Yeah, he was seeking permission from his brother.

Which meant getting inside and tackling more things on the list. But first, he needed to get some of the sweat off him. One bathroom meant no shower until Mabel left. He crossed to the watering trough he'd just filled, pulled his shirt off and stuck his head under. The water cooled him like the shock of jumping in the Pacific.

He shook his head and swiped his hand over his face to sluice the water off before he headed to the house. The distinct hum of his favorite Camaro pulled behind him and stopped.

The last person he'd expected to see was Alicia. When he turned, there she was, one hand gripping the steering wheel, one hand gripping her cell. She didn't make a move to get out of the car. According to the news he'd just heard, her kid was still missing. Why was she here?

Lost. He'd seen that look before.

The petrified stare of someone who had no options.

"Alicia?" He opened the car door, reached across and turned the engine off then leaned on the roof. "Hey, you okay?"

"No."

A whisper of desperation. Tears trickling from swollen eyes. She barely resembled the confident woman who'd met him in the driveway.

"They can't find her and…"

"I want to help, but I'm not certain what I can do."

He could see her trying to keep control by blowing air through her puffed cheeks. It wasn't working. Again, out of his element. Should he get her out of the car and take her inside or bring Mabel out here?

"They— I thought— I have to sell the car, but he just called.…" She shook her head. Tears streamed from her red-rimmed eyes. "They've arrested him."

"Who? Did they find your daughter?"

"No. It was— Brian just called."

"Is Brian buying the car? He's not here." He should get Mabel. Maybe she could understand and tell him what this was all about.

Alicia turned to him, took a deep breath before she made eye contact. "They arrested Brian for Lauren's kidnapping."

ALICIA LOOKED AROUND the faded yellow kitchen in the Sloane house. She'd spent lots of summer days with the twins' mother here. Waiting on fresh lemonade or homemade peanut-butter cookies. More recently, she'd spent time cooking simple meals for J.W. and Lauren while Brian handled ranch stuff.

Or at least she'd thought he'd been handling ranch stuff.

Of course he was. Don't start doubting him. He's not the kidnapper or a drug dealer like half the town thinks. Shauna's behind the kidnapping. You just have to prove she's guilty.

"Here you go, dear. I have dinner for you both whenever you're ready."

"Thanks, Mabel. I'm not really hungry." Alicia took a cool wet cloth and placed it over her eyes. She was so tired of thinking. So tired of trying to decide how or where to start.

"Did you find out anything?" John asked.

"Well, that silly receptionist or whoever they have answering the phones said they won't let anyone talk to Brian until after he's been formally charged." Mabel continued to move around the kitchen as she spoke. "I wanted to send Dave Krueger over for representation, but they told her Brian didn't want a lawyer and then mentioned your brother was being cheap and stubborn."

"I can't believe Brian refused a lawyer or that the situation has spun out of control so rapidly." *Cheap and stubborn.* She totally understood those two words. She heard Johnny grunt from the doorway. "Did they arrest him based on an anonymous tip?"

"That's why they initially pulled him over. Then they found Lauren's toys behind the seat," Mabel said, patting her shoulder once and moving away.

Alicia used her palms to keep the cloth in place. Her eyes were swollen and burning from the constant crying. "We told her not to play in the truck. This is all my fault he's in jail."

"No, dear, it's not," Mabel said. "And tomorrow morning he'll be charged or free. I'll make certain he has a good lawyer whether he wants one or not."

"I'm so glad you're here for J.W.," she told Mabel, removing the cool cloth and feeling calmer just sitting at the old dining table. Her insides still shook, but she could talk rationally again. The anxiety wouldn't leave until Lauren was back safe and sound.

"I am, too." John's deep voice rumbled softly through the room. "Thanks for calling the police station. I moved Dad back to bed. I'd like to see Brian ASAP. Can you stay? I hate to ask, but I'll probably need to be gone tomorrow as well if he's not released."

"Not a problem." Mabel folded the kitchen towel and laid it on the dish drain. "Let me run home and feed the dog. I believe the jail opens at eight in the morning. I'm an early riser but I don't think you'd want me at five, so I'll come at seven-thirty. Be right back."

Alicia replaced the washcloth against her face while Mabel gently shut the door and left. Hot air from outside drifted across the room. She didn't know how to look at this man. Or how to talk to him. Or how to apologize or explain her behavior. So much had happened since he'd left home, and he seemed to be clueless.

Where did she begin?

By looking at him.

She wiped her face one last time and set the cloth aside. He'd put a shirt on. His hair was still wet, but she'd heard the shower while Mabel had washed dishes.

"You doing okay?" John asked.

She watched by peeking through her fingers as he turned one of the old metal dining chairs away from the table, sat and leaned across the back.

"Brian sits exactly like that. But I'd never think you were him."

John's bland expression subtly switched to annoyance as he tapped the table. Easily spotted on a man who didn't really show much emotion.

"You and Brian a thing now?"

"No. It's not anything like that."

"Why don't you explain just how it is? If you're up to it." John didn't move. He was tall enough that when he sat in a chair he still seemed to tower over her. "You should probably start with why the police booked him for your daughter's kidnapping and why the first person he told was you."

"Shauna's responsible for the anonymous tip. I'm certain she's trying to frame Brian and me. Sheriff Coleman thinks so, too, even though he can't say that to anyone else."

"*Did* he say it to you?" John remained steady, his arms

crossed over the top of the chair. His eyes constantly moved between her and his dad.

"No. But he didn't disagree when I said it. You need to take care of Brian. I just came to see if you wanted to buy the car."

"Shauna who? And why do you need money?"

"Shauna Weber was Dwayne's stepmother and the reason my accounts are frozen."

"Why would his stepmother freeze your assets?"

"Because she's a money-hungry bi— Sorry, I can't talk rationally about her. Look, Johnny, can you buy the car? I need money for a private investigator. It's the only way I'll ever find Lauren before Shauna pretends to find her and takes her away from me."

"That's quite an assumption, Alicia."

"I'm not assuming anything." Shoving the chair backward, it hit the kitchen wall. She was losing it. She forced herself to sit and take cleansing breaths before she babbled again. She couldn't look at him to see what he thought of her outburst and couldn't imagine why he wasn't lecturing her, like anyone else she'd tried to confide in. "It's the only explanation. Shauna has frozen Dwayne's assets, including Lauren's trust fund, and I...I just need the cash for the car. If you still want it, that is. Then I can get out of your hair."

"You mean the court froze everything," he corrected.

"Shauna took me to court. As if she has a right to any of that money. It belongs to my daughter. I hate having to use it, but it was our only support while the will was being contested. Now there's nothing except a few home-care clients who stuck with me."

Would he remember the same friendship they'd had as kids? Be sympathetic enough to give her more than the car's estimated value? She gathered her courage to make eye contact with him. But his gaze was toward the living area and his father.

"The house wasn't built for wheelchair access." She attempted to draw his attention again. "Brian set J.W.'s bed there so he could work here at the table and still see him."

"Back to Brian's arrest," he said, lowering his voice. "Why my brother? If you're just friends, what does he have to do with your daughter?"

"Shauna and Patrick Weber have made several accusations that we're having an affair. That we kidnapped Lauren for ransom."

"We. Meaning you and Brian. But there hasn't been a ransom note."

"One showed up last night at the Weber show barns. They tried to blame me, but didn't know I had a solid alibi. The sheriff was at my house. So they immediately accused Brian of working with me."

"That's ridiculous. He was out with the horses until after dark."

"The note was left at their stables that back up to your property line."

"You mean Pat Weber owns old man Adams's stables? He used to work there."

"Shauna married him four months after Dwayne's father died. If that doesn't prove she just wanted the money, I don't know what does. Marrying Roy Adams was another way she could get close to Dwayne after high school. With both of them gone, she's selling off everything."

"Wait. Are you talking about Shauna Tipton, the cheerleader a couple of years older than us? Didn't she date Dwayne? This sounds like a damn soap opera."

"Tell me about it. I've been living this nightmare for years. Brian's a good man. Shauna will use anything that can be taken out of context."

"Right. I still don't see why the police would arrest my

brother. If there's nothing between you guys, how did they connect Brian to the kidnapping?"

"I've always been his friend and I stayed here with J.W. while Brian worked his four-day shift in Fort Worth last week."

"Shift?"

"He's a paramedic. Wasn't that where he was headed this morning when they arrested him?"

"He didn't mention where he was headed. Just that he'd be gone four days."

Spoken just like his brother. Same attitude, tone, inflection. If they tried to fool people, not many would be able to tell them apart. But she could. She also recognized the stubbornness that kept them from speaking to each other after Johnny left for the navy.

"I'm not reprising the role of mediator between you two. You can talk to him at the police station."

He nodded once. Curt, not rude. Just like he accepted her words and there was no need for any more. "That still doesn't explain why they'd think Brian kidnapped your daughter."

"Lauren. Her name is Lauren, and I want her home. She needs to be home with me." Fear blocked the last words, cutting them short.

"Do you know why they're assuming he took Lauren, tried to kill you and then just hung around the ranch until he was arrested?" He'd raised his voice just a tad and looked toward J.W., who still appeared to be sleeping far enough away not to hear the conversation. "It isn't a logical plan of attack and would mean that you involved a third person to hide Lauren somewhere. It doesn't make sense."

"They don't need a reason. There are townspeople who have been trying to send him to jail for twelve years."

John's brows drew together. He shook his head, compressed his lips and appeared genuinely confused.

"You don't know? You're Brian's twin and you're telling me you don't know what happened after you left?"

"Would I be asking if I did?" He sounded very annoyed.

Technically, he hadn't asked, but she saw the visible tick in his jaw muscle. He was obviously upset. She could barely believe her two best friends had grown so far apart. Identical twins who had shared secrets and pranks all through school.

"Brian admitted to starting the fire that killed Mrs. Cook."

"I know. He thought I caused the accident and took the blame."

There was some emotion Johnny couldn't hide. He stiffened and blinked his eyes a smidgen too long. They'd both changed over twelve years, but some things never would. The man sitting with her was just as hurt as the eighteen-year-old boy had been when his brother had believed the lies spread about the fire.

"They've never forgiven him."

"Who?" He looked genuine asking his question, like he really didn't have a clue.

"Everybody. Other than the sheriff, Mabel and me, no one talks to him. Ever. No one ever told you why he didn't go to A&M?"

"I assumed he changed his mind. Neither of us were good in school."

"But you knew he lost his scholarship, right?"

John's poker face melted.

"Your dad never said anything?"

"He didn't talk too much about Brian." John dropped his gaze to the tabletop.

"In other words, you didn't ask because you didn't want to hear."

"I'm listening now."

"The town was upset about Mrs. Cook's death. It didn't

matter that it was an accident. They wanted Brian punished. So there were outcries and editorials demanding consequences. Teachers withdrew their letters of recommendations."

"They could do that?" he asked in a hurt whisper.

"The university suddenly didn't have a full scholarship. They reduced it to about a thousand dollars. He couldn't finance the rest."

Disbelief, astonishment, anger—a ton of emotion took charge and marched across his face. "You can count on my help. Whatever it takes. We'll find your daughter and clear Brian."

"I don't know what you can do, John. The police and rangers have an Amber Alert. No one saw anything, no clues, no prints, no way to find her. It's like she just disappeared."

Alicia saw his fists tighten, ready to do battle to defend his family. It had been a while since she'd felt someone was completely on her side.

"I can help. Trust me."

The harsh tightness across his face softened. His hand took hers and she saw a glimpse of a friend. It had been a while since she'd depended on anyone. She nodded, realizing that trusting him was second nature. She'd run to the Double Bar because he was home.

Chapter Five

"Tell me what happened after I left and what we're up
against." John paced the kitchen, keeping his dad's napping
form in his peripheral vision. He didn't want him upset.

After the first couple of stories, John barely listened to
Alicia's recounting of how the town had treated Brian. He
was still stuck on his brother's arrest. Instead of calling a
lawyer, Brian had phoned Alicia.

What was up with that? Was it his way of keeping his
family informed without talking to John? Warning Alicia? She thought they were being framed. "Do the police
know who Brian called?"

"I'm not sure." She looked as confused as he felt.

Cute and confused, with that worry line emphasized
between her brows. Now wasn't the time for an attraction, and neither was the future. Alicia claimed there was
nothing between her and Brian, and she thought they were
only friends. They were clearly closer than either wanted
to admit. They always had been.

"What did Brian say, exactly?"

She put her fingertips to her temples, concentrating.
"They pulled him over, found Lauren's bear and crown behind his seat—the one I said she had with her when they…
when they took her. The Aubrey police would be coming
to the house to talk to me."

"You sort of buried the lead, Alicia. I think Brian called to warn you not to go home."

"Do you think they left something at my house?" She shook her head and her long hair fell forward, covering her face. "The media has already taken Shauna's side and is insinuating that I arranged for Lauren's kidnapping to get the ransom money. Do you believe they're going to arrest me? I haven't done anything."

He didn't have time to be sensitive, so blunt would have to work. "If Shauna's gone to the trouble to frame you for faking a kidnapping, don't you think they'd plant evidence to implicate you?" He let that info take root. "You've got two choices. Turn yourself in and hope it can all be sorted out legally."

She looked up, eyes wide with fright. "If I'm in jail, no one will be looking for Lauren."

John didn't correct her. Everyone had looked for her daughter. To clear Brian, he would do more than just look. He'd find her. "Then hide."

"How can I hide? I don't have any money and I can't go anywhere. Dad's car is fairly easy to spot."

"I can help with that." He stood, glancing to the living room to verify his dad was still asleep. When he turned back, she stood touching distance in front of him. But she didn't reach out, and neither did he.

"Johnny, I can't ask you to help more than just buying the car. Your dad needs you."

"Don't bother, Alicia. You need my help. More important, the only way to clear Brian is to find your daughter. And I need *you* to make that happen."

"Thanks isn't enough." She launched herself and hugged him. "What should I do?"

John awkwardly set her away, not trusting himself to hold her close. The next few days were going to be hard enough. "We'll put your car in the shed, and if they look, I'll tell them you sold it to me."

"What's next?" She removed the key ring from her pocket, clutching it like a lifeline.

"Do you have a smartphone?"

"Yes."

"Book yourself on the next flight to San Antonio. Don't browse anything out of state. If the FBI's not involved yet, we want to keep the search for you in Texas. When you're done, take the battery out and leave it in Dad's things. Someplace you'd normally have access when you check on him."

"You want them to think I'm running. They won't believe it. They know I wouldn't go anywhere without Lauren."

"Did you think you'd be set up for her kidnapping?" He could see she was terrified. Her daughter had been abducted. Even if she was certain of who took her, there was still a deep fear of making a mistake. Doubt that she could be wrong.

It happened to him on every mission. Especially the ones that cost a man's life. Questioning your decisions would drive you insane. So you couldn't question. Someone like Alicia needed someone to help make those decisions. As long as he was around to take the blame, she wouldn't have to question if *she* did the right thing.

"And what if they release Brian or if asking me questions would help them find where Lauren is?"

"I don't know if they have enough evidence to hold Brian. They might release him, watch who he contacts, hoping they're right and that he'll lead them to the person holding your daughter. But more important, I need you with me to find Lauren."

"You really think this is the best way? Running?"

"Hiding. Staying under wraps until we gather all the

facts and know who's involved. There are a lot of places to disappear on the ranch tonight. I'll get you somewhere safer tomorrow."

"Where?" The word was muffled in defeat as she covered her mouth with slim fingers.

"Adams's property tonight. Brian and I played there all the time. They won't think you're arrogant enough to hide right under their noses."

"Johnny." She gently took his arm before he could walk past her. "What happens if they find me?"

He sank into the bluest eyes he could remember. A face that he'd tried his best to let go. She'd never lied to him, always had faith in him. He was the one who'd turned his back on her, not trusting.

"Believe me, they won't. I know what I'm doing. I've hidden in a lot places worse than Aubrey, Texas. No one finds me when I dig in."

He reached for his cell, dialing the number Mabel had written on the notepad stuck to the fridge. "It's John. Change of plans—can you pack a bag and come stay with Dad overnight? Thanks."

"Brian called to warn me. Did he keep you out of the loop on purpose? No one knows you're here, do they?" Alicia asked once he'd hung up.

"That's our ace in the hole. They'll all be watching Brian and they think you're alone. I won't lie to you, Alicia. It's going to get rough, and plenty of people are going to say worse things than the accusations on television."

He glanced over his shoulder into the living room. His dad looked straight at him, smiling, and gave him a thumbs-up. If there had been doubts about leaving his dad to help Alicia before, there weren't any longer.

"I want my daughter back and I'm willing to do anything to make that happen. I trust you, Johnny."

"Good."

The real question was if he could trust himself.

Chapter Six

"Where's my mommy?" the kid asked for the hundredth time since she'd been hauled here kicking and screaming.

Tory had been sure they'd be caught before leaving Aubrey. But the dark windows and loud speakers of her ex's car had covered their escape and the kid's screaming. Then country back roads had hidden them again.

Lauren had cried until they'd convinced her of the lie. Part of the cover-up. Part of Patrick's brilliant plan. Part of their attempt to never be caught. Tell the kid her mother was testing her and would "rescue" her after they finished the game. It was no big deal. She could pretend she was on an adventure.

"Can't you make that kid shut up?" Her ex-boyfriend charged toward the little girl, but Tory stepped between them to calm him down. He turned and threw himself on the tattered cushions of the broken-down couch.

"What do you want me to do? You know if we hurt her we don't get paid." She should never have told Patrick that she'd help. And should have never have gone back to her ex to assist her pulling off this stupid plan. The bum always thought he was the boss, and he had the muscles to convince you. "Go back in the bedroom, honey, and play with your new toys."

"But can't I have a drink?" the kid asked. "When's this game going to be over?"

"Later, sweetheart." Tory scooted her inside the room and flipped the newly installed bolt to keep her there.

She passed too close and her ex's thick hand wrapped around her wrist. The same one he'd fractured last spring. It still hurt if she twisted it the wrong way and especially hurt when she tried to pull free. The bastard knew that. She'd yelped loud enough the first couple of times he'd grabbed her like this.

"The news thinks that kid's mother snatched her for the money."

"It's working just like I said it would," she agreed, hoping he'd let go before she cried from his tight grip.

"So I've been rethinkin' our arrangement. We can get more money. That idiot Weber is loaded."

"I'm not so sure. Seems kinda dicey." How would she explain this to Patrick?

"What can he do to us if we demand more? It's not like he can waltz to the police or his wife and tell them everything. This is a sure bet. We're in charge and he has to do what we say."

"I don't know if we should. My way seems like it's safer. We take the money and the mom takes the blame." She had to convince him to stay with the original agreement. She wasn't risking everything for half the pittance he thought they'd agreed to last week. She'd follow the plan, take all the money, leave this blustering jackass hanging and run off with Patrick.

"My way, we get lots more dough. I've seen them do this on TV lots of times."

He wanted to be in charge. How could she make it *his* plan? Her wrist was aching but she didn't pull away. She cozied up to the slime bucket, giving him full view of the extra cleavage in the tight shirt Patrick couldn't resist. "Don't they always get caught on TV?"

"Only if they leave DNA or somethin', and we're in the clear. That stupid Weber left his prints and gave us the bear to plant. We used gloves."

"But, honey." She tried to sound sweet in spite of the shooting pain in her arm. "You know I already took the ransom note you worked so hard on."

"We can make another."

Patrick had instructed them to let Lauren cut and glue the letters together. It had taken a long time, but only the kid's prints were on the paper. That one little thing had taken a four-year-old two solid mornings and afternoons to put together. Small pieces of paper needed to be thrown away and it had been her idea to leave them at Alicia's house. The scissors, magazines and scraps had been left on the kid's play table in Lauren's very own bedroom.

"Getting the kid to do it again will take a couple of more days," she said sweetly.

The lummox heaved her to his sweaty chest. Tory couldn't deny he had a great body. And wasn't bad to look at. That was why she'd been with him so long. If he could just control his mean streak and stop stinkin' like horses, she wouldn't mind getting together with him while she waited for all this to be over. He grabbed a handful of her hair and yanked backward. His hot breath landed between her breasts as she landed on his lap.

She knew what would come. She'd told Patrick, practically begged him to let her ask someone else. This was their best option, he'd explained. No one would look too closely if her ex moved back in, but they'd ask lots of questions if it was a stranger. Especially a stranger who moved in at the same time the kid disappeared.

So this way was smarter, and Patrick couldn't get mad if the inevitable happened. She'd let her ex have his way.

Keep him happy and hopefully get him to forget about changing the plan. With any luck, he wouldn't knock her around too much in the process.

Tory bit her lip and held her breath, preparing herself. Three more days and she'd be flying first-class to Paris with Patrick. Her imagination drifted, picturing another lover, more skilled, gentler. She fell backward, dropping to the floor when suddenly released.

"What did I do?"

"You don't ever do nothin'." He shoved off the couch, kicking out with his boot.

Tory saw the red-faced rage burst from her partner and covered her face, prepared for the mean left punch she'd received many, many times. It didn't come. She timidly stood, uncertain what would happen. She'd never seen him like this. A backhand to the side of her cheek spun her across the arm of the couch.

"Get out of here before I really show you what I think," he bellowed.

Tory ran to the kid's door, twisted the bolt and darted inside. She'd been frightened of the jerk before, but never like this. That anger she'd seen ripped into his heart—if he still had one.

The bastard who exploded wasn't her ex-boyfriend. He was worse. She didn't know what he'd become or what drugs he was doing now, but he'd turned into an angry striking machine.

She shrank to the floor, leaning against the thin wall, her mind whirling with ways to get out of this mess. She couldn't go back out there and pretend to like that monster.

Three more days. Could she do this for even one?

For Paris? For Patrick? She could do it for him. She would do it for a million dollars. But now she had to come up with a story about her face. She was certain it would be black-and-blue when she went to work the next day. She needed to pretend everything was normal and not give the police any reason to question her.

A cool little hand soothed her hot cheek. "Are you okay, Tory? Your face is sunburned."

"Yeah. Just a little scared. I'm going to sleep in here tonight."

"Are you scared of the big man, too? He yells loud like Grandma Weber." Her small four-year-old hand covered her mouth. "Oops. She yells more when I call her Grandma."

Lauren's embarrassed giggle was sweet, but not enough to make Tory forget who'd just hit her into the next county.

Nothing in the room would slide in front of the door. Nothing to use for protection. Just a mattress on the floor and plastic blocks in the corner. Tory heard determined footsteps heading their direction. She braced herself against the thin door.

Silence.

Click.

The bastard had locked her in with their prisoner, and her cell was in her purse in the kitchen.

"I'll take care of the money arrangements, Tory. You manage the runt," he shouted through the wood. "And you ain't going to work no more. I ain't no babysitter."

She allowed Lauren to crawl in her lap, hugging the little girl close. This wasn't the plan.

Lauren tugged on Tory's shirtfront to get her attention. "How long is Mommy going to be gone? I don't like it here."

"Me neither, sweetie. Me neither."

Chapter Seven

The dilapidated barn stall still held the smell of manure after years of nonuse. Alicia was hot, sticky and had no intention of lying under the cover of the sleeping bag, until Johnny reminded her rat snakes loved barns. The horrible creatures could actually climb into the rafters and wait. So, of course, she couldn't close her eyes and was stuck searching the decaying wooden beams.

"You just had to mention snakes," she complained, hearing him actually laugh.

"You ever going to sleep?"

She noticed the flick of an LED watch from his direction.

"What time is it?"

"Twenty-three minutes after the last time you asked," he mumbled.

He sounded muffled, maybe facedown with his mouth pushed into his muscles. Johnny wasn't worried about the nasty snakes that bit when they were provoked. He'd never been afraid and had constantly irritated the cold-blooded things when they were younger.

"Are you sure we can't sleep outside? It's sweltering in here." She tossed the bag off her, keeping the zippered end only over her bare feet. "There's absolutely no breeze."

"I was only teasing about the snakes, you know." His

clear, rich voice came from slightly higher, like he was raised on his elbows.

He was bare chested, just like he'd been when she'd arrived at the Double Bar earlier that afternoon. The memory of his sculpted muscles sent her thoughts in a wild direction. She chased her thoughts back to slithering, long things hanging above her.

Snakes were a safer subject to concentrate on. The cold eating machines weren't nearly as likeable as a man who had promised to find Lauren.

"The thought of snakes isn't really what's bothering me. I'm letting my mind fixate on it so I don't think about other things." *Lots of other things.*

"Like?" he asked, sounding resigned they were talking in the dark instead of sleeping.

"Lauren's been gone less than a week and I feel so alone. Every part of me aches."

"I'd be worried if it didn't. You've taken an emotional beating. Hurting's a lot better than feeling nothing at all," he said softly.

"Is that what you feel? Nothing?"

"Me? Negative. I'm confused more than anything."

She heard the slick of the nylon rustling, gave up and looked at him. The crescent moon still spilled enough light to see a few old wounds on his shoulder. He sat, one arm wrapped around a knee that he'd brought close to his chest.

"Confused? I don't understand. You were very decisive ordering me what to pack and what to do. I witnessed exactly what your dad is always telling me. How you're such an in-charge leader and all."

"My dad?" He drew his brows together, a permanent crease between them now that hadn't been there in his teens.

"Yeah. I mean, he'd tell me before the stroke."

He stretched his back by raising his arms above his head.

Goodness, he had muscles on top of muscle. There couldn't be an inch of fat on him anywhere. She couldn't watch and looked out the door to the star-studded sky.

"Did you spend a lot of time with Dad?" he asked, settling back against the stall post.

She sat, leaning on the wall opposite him. "Sure. J.W. and Brian checked on me after Dwayne's dad died and I was alone with Lauren."

"I didn't know."

"There are a lot of things you don't know."

"I get the picture. I missed quite a bit around here. Hey, we should get some shut-eye. It might be the last sound sleep we get for a while."

"I don't think I can sleep. There's just too much going on in here." She pointed a finger to her head. "The thoughts are so random. Mixed with a desire to be held. When we hugged out on the drive, I realized just how long it had been since I've been in a man's arms."

"Alicia."

"But the guilt mixed throughout all those thoughts makes me want to cry. Lauren's gone and...and...there's nobody. I can't do this alone." She covered her face with her hands, drawing her knees to her body, suddenly chilled at the prospect of never seeing her daughter again.

"Alicia. Come here."

John gently tugged her hands into his. He'd moved next to her and wrapped her in his arms, kissing the top of her head as it dropped to his chest. His gentleness warmed her heart. He smoothed her hair and she felt his breath close to her ear.

"Go ahead and cry, just let it go. I've got your six."

THE WOMAN IN his arms had cried herself to sleep. She'd forgotten about snakes, only to replace one worry with several more—fright, attraction, the unknown. Fatigue had finally claimed her around two in the morning. Earlier, he could have been out like a flipped switch. His life in the navy had taught him the importance of sleeping upon command.

So why couldn't he sleep?

He was wound tighter than a coil of wire, that's why. Alicia was more than just a beautiful girl who needed help changing a tire. He was her *only* chance at finding her daughter. Not to mention freeing his brother.

If his guess was correct, he was the only chance she had at staying alive. It was logical that her enemies wouldn't want her around to continue fighting them. If caught, she'd conveniently meet with a fatal accident or suicide, leaving behind a note clearing the Webers. Telling her about the danger wasn't a current option, but he'd need to sooner or later.

A plan of action was what they needed. Maybe that was what his brain had been searching for before it could rest. What did he have to work with?

Weapons. Just the revolver his dad owned.

Stealth. One thing on their side was that no one knew he was in town. He hadn't shared with the police department he'd been headed home. Alicia had commented that her friends thought they'd seen Brian drive through town. They could assume Alicia had an accomplice, but they wouldn't know who. And Mabel had sworn herself to secrecy without being asked.

Communication. He could call his team for information. No one would be monitoring his cell. No. He couldn't involve the team. He was the lieutenant who'd come up through the ranks. Not only an officer, but a friend. They'd feel obligated to help. This op had to stay off book and had dire consequences if he was caught. It was the end of his career.

Alicia shifted and he let her slide down his ribs, cradling

her head in the crook of his arm until she rested on his lap. It was still warm in the barn, but he draped his sleeping bag over her legs anyway. She turned her head and shifted to her side, drawing her hands under her chin.

He could remember another night they'd spent under the stars. Having fallen asleep at the lake, they woke up with the sun and tried to sneak back to their respective homes. Man, oh, man. They'd received a tongue-lashing up one side and down the other from his mom. It was all about how they needed to be responsible. And what if anyone else had seen them?

His mother's voice was in his head as clear as if she were standing in front of him. *You've got to take care of the ones you love, Joy-o.* How many times had she said that? Boy-o and Joy-o, her nicknames for them. *B* for Brian and *J* for John.

How quickly he'd forgotten. Put out of his thoughts to avoid the hurt as soon as she'd been gone.

Was that what Alicia wanted to do? No. She cared too much. But why was she facing this on her own? Where were her brother and dad? What had happened to their property?

More questions that somehow he knew would cause her pain if asked. He couldn't do that yet.

Alicia was family, according to his mom. She had been since the first time she'd come over for cookies. He hooked her long waves around her ear and stared at her nose, at the freckles that had been there as long as he'd known her. *Is she worth losing your career?*

"Absolutely."

His whisper caused Alicia to stir again. He gently placed her head on the sleeping bag and eased away. If he was going to be awake, he might as well make good use of the time. Pulling his phone from his pack, he walked into the field.

He'd debated since leaving the ranch whether to call for assistance. He knew his limitations. There was no doubt he could protect Alicia. And he would find her daughter. But finding the proof to clear his brother of the accusations meant finding the proof that would convict the actual kidnappers.

He owed Brian after everything he'd sacrificed. He'd been mad all this time, and for what? He dialed a number on his way from the barn, walking toward a familiar tree where he, his brother and Dwayne had attempted to build a tree house.

Devlin McClain picked up on the fourth ring. "This had better be good, Sloane. Do you know what time it is?"

"I've got a problem, Dev."

"What's her name?" His bunkmate laughed.

"Cut the crap. Do you know any former SEALs or specialists in Texas?"

"Texas?" His response sounded much more alert. "Just what kind of trouble are you in?"

"Maybe somebody gone private security? I need some quiet research and fieldwork."

"I think I can find someone. Seriously, you going to tell me what's up? Don't pull that 'it's better if you don't know' stuff."

"A friend's little girl has been kidnapped."

"Runaway dad? You want me to do a search—"

"No. It's about the money. I think the kid's close by. Alicia's being set up to take the fall."

John heard a string of words on the other end and couldn't agree more. "I hate it when they use kids."

"I can't take any risks with this one, Dev. Nothing with the team, but I need someone to check out the possible suspects. Someone willing to bend the law a bit."

"And if you don't get anywhere? You know who to

call?" Dev declared, he didn't ask or suggest. "With you gone, the team's been given leave."

"I can't ask that, man."

"How many times you save my hide, John? Anything you need, you've got it."

"Thanks."

"I'll have someone contact you ASAP. This number secure?"

"Should be. I'll call if I switch."

"You should hear from me in a couple of hours. You got someone watching your back?"

"This can go south all sorts of ways. Stay clear. You hearing me?" He hoped his friend took his words seriously. A team of SEALs loose in the area wouldn't be easy to hide.

"How's your dad and, um…you see your brother yet?"

Dev was the only person he'd shared a split second of concern with regarding coming home. "Dad's going to make it. The stroke left him slightly paralyzed and unable to talk."

"That's tough, man."

"Yeah. It's also something I can't talk about. I need my battery."

"Right. Two hours and you'll hear from me with a time and place to meet locally."

"There's a lake nearby. Just tell me when. And thanks, Dev."

He powered down the cell and stuck it in his back pocket. There was no way he'd be attempting to sleep now. He looked up in the tree, saw an old board still secure at one end and rusty nails on the other. He pulled himself up and yanked, jerking it free.

He could see the entire field from the lower branches. It looked the same as it had the summers he'd played there, with a major exception. No horses. This place used to be full of them.

"John?" Alicia called from the barn door.

"Right here." He swung down and jogged the fifty yards or so back.

"What were you doing up in the tree?"

"Grabbing this." He tucked the board in a safe place inside the half-rotten door. "Where are the horses? Have things gotten so hard around here they were shutting down the horse farm and selling the stock?"

"Shauna sold it off."

"Dwayne's grandfather must be turning in his grave." He wanted to tilt her head back to look at him, but he was afraid to touch her. She was vulnerable and attractive, and he knew exactly what he wanted to do. It was not what she *needed* him to do. "Why are you awake?"

"Same to you. Why are you awake?"

"SEALs rarely get eight hours of shut-eye."

"Neither do mothers."

The teasing in her eyes was gone. A look of hopelessness filled her eyes with tears again. She was thinking about Lauren.

"These probably seem like empty words to you, Alicia. But you've got to be strong. All the time. Never let your guard down and let the emotion get the better of you. If you do…they win."

"Right." She pressed her lips together and joined him leaning on the decaying wood. "What do we do now?"

"That is a very good question."

Chapter Eight

"Are you sure this is the best of plans? I'd rather be looking for Lauren." Alicia had mentioned that fact in every other sentence, and John had seemed to ignore her. "Maybe we could be doing anything other than illegally entering a house I lived in for a short time."

She'd gladly stay in the sun waiting. It was much better than heading inside.

"Each visit to this house reminds me of how Shauna manipulated Roy into getting married. Visiting after that was horrible. The first Christmas Dwayne and I were here was excruciating. We were forced to listen to Roy compare Dwayne's mother to every decision Shauna made. I actually felt sorry for her at one point. But I'm still uncertain this is the best way to use our time."

"I've got a former U.S. Marines specialist looking into the Webers. We're meeting him at fifteen hundred. He'll locate every property. Pull their phone and bank records, their emails. We're going to find Lauren. Trust me."

"Then what are we doing here?"

"It's reconnaissance. I need to familiarize myself with the lay of the land again. Maybe find a safe place for you to lay low." He put a pair of binoculars back to his eyes.

"I told you that the Adams farm is for sale. Shauna lives in Frisco now. The horses are ready to be auctioned tomorrow. She emptied the house of anything worth money and promptly called a local Realtor. It's still listed, but can't be sold, much to that witch's frustration. The house may belong to Shauna, but the land around it belongs to Lauren."

"Then why are there three cars here?"

"It's probably the cleaning staff." Alicia knew one was her father-in-law's. He'd left the classic to her, but it was caught in probate court. It deserved better care, but she couldn't afford to professionally store it in the garage. Shauna's lawsuit prevented her from touching it at all.

She was with John at the edge of the yard, having hiked from the old barn where they'd stayed the night. With no stables to run and no one living in the house, it may have been the safest place for them to hide after all.

They had enough food for a couple of days, and they weren't in the wilderness by any means. John had grabbed a fishing pole. Hiding wasn't the problem. He'd convinced her to come with him because they'd be searching for Lauren. But they weren't.

"What do you expect to find?"

"Man, Alicia. Just trust me. This is what I do."

"I have to take your word that you're good at what you do, John Sloane. But you don't have carte blanche over my life. I appreciate everything. Just remember that it's my little girl who's missing. I'm a little bit anxious, especially since the police think *I'm* responsible somehow."

She hadn't intended to huff when she crossed her arms. But she had. She wanted to sound slightly indignant and was afraid she'd sounded spoiled instead.

"I apologize. I'm not used to people questioning my orders."

"This is a joint effort," she reminded him.

"Right." He placed the binoculars to his eyes, letting the one word sound like three or four syllables as it slipped through his lips.

It was far from being a joint effort. She didn't miss the sarcasm.

"There's only one person moving around. A young woman. Got any idea who she is?"

She adjusted the binoculars and saw a short blonde wearing jeans and a T-shirt. "That's probably Andra's Angels. I recognize the swirly *A*s on her shirt. It's a cleaning service."

"It looks like she's packing up. We'll wait down by the gulch."

With each ray of sun poking through the cooler shade, she could feel her skin baking and her temper boiling. She wanted to *do* something. Be proactive. Not sit around and wait at a dried-up creek bed.

"While we're waiting, you can explain more about your plan and why it's so dang important to hide."

"All right. Here are the facts. You're being framed— along with Brian—for the kidnapping of your daughter. Once they take you to jail, they'll probably insist you go to Denton County, where you'll be involved in a fatal fight or feel such remorse you'll commit suicide."

Totally deflated, she plopped on the hard ground next to him. He sounded so matter-of-fact recounting his supposition. He'd clearly thought through the options and jumped to a dismal end. "And with me gone, they get control over Lauren's trust. To get Lauren back, I'd sign over the trust fund this minute and walk away forever. Don't they know that?"

"They don't. Whoever they are, they don't think that way. They believe everyone desires money as much as they do. Just remember, we're assuming it's Shauna and Patrick, but right now, everyone's a suspect."

"How do you plan on finding my daughter?"

"There are a lot of variables they need to control. Since the police have been watching them, other people must be involved and doing the dirty work. There must be details somewhere. We'll find their trail, but we have to keep you alive along the way." He set the binoculars to his side and patted her knee. "Don't worry, I'm actually good at this."

He looked concerned, but didn't smile to reassure her. Not a grin noting confidence that he knew all the answers, not even a slow tilt of his lips showing comfort. Come to think about it, he hadn't grinned since they'd been in the driveway together that first day and he'd seen her. Had she? She couldn't smile with Lauren gone.

"What happened to you, Johnny?"

"It's been twelve years, Alicia."

"You've changed. You're so serious and realistic. You're certainly not pulling any punches."

"Do you want me to sugarcoat the reality of the situation?"

"No. I... I've been sugarcoating much too much of my life as it is. I want Lauren back and I'm willing to do anything and every—"

"Shh." His finger went unerringly to her lips as his eyes searched behind her. "Someone's coming."

"What do we do?" she asked in a panicked whisper.

His strong arm dropped around her shoulders and in an instant her back was on the ground. Her head was in the bend of John's arm, bringing his body on top of her. For a split second she thought he was just protecting her, but then he grinned. A teasing gleam from their teenage years reached his eyes as his lips captured hers.

"Stop being shocked and pretend to kiss me," he whispered against her lips. He slid a knee between her legs, supporting himself so she could breathe, but leaving no breath of space separating them.

It wasn't shock at kissing him that she was experiencing. It was a shock at realizing twelve years could pass and desire for this man could rush back so fully.

Even after loving Dwayne. This was different. She wanted to feel, to be held, to be desired. It was like capturing a stolen moment from her youth.

She parted her lips, hungry for the contact. His tongue danced with hers. She slid her hands around his back, wanting to lift his shirt and feel the contours of the muscles she'd seen last night. The familiar feel of a strong body protecting her from the world was a heady sensation.

Footsteps crunched sticks and dried leaves that fell from the elm trees earlier that spring. John's body tightened becoming more rigid, more alert.

"Oh, I beg your pardon," a somewhat familiar older voice said.

"Mr. Searcy?" John asked, breaking their contact and lifting his chest from hers.

"Brian, boy. I didn't recognize you with that head of hair gone. Looks good. Is that you, Miss Alicia?"

Joe Searcy had worked for the Adams family all of their lives. She'd witnessed him breaking up many fights between the boys and escorting them to their parents more than once by holding their ears.

Alicia shoved at John's pectorals and scrambled to a sitting position, straightening her tank top. All the while both men chuckled.

"It's about time you two got together," Joe said with his cigarette-battered vocal cords. "I remember catching you around the property a time or two."

"That was John, Mr. Searcy." John laced his fingers through hers and smiled goofily while pretending to be his twin. Pretending unsuccessfully. Brian was never goofy.

"You're really reminding him of that?" she whispered, knowing Joe was hard of hearing.

How anyone ever got them confused was beyond her. That goofy mischievousness was 100 percent John.

"What's that?" the older man complained. "And, Brian,

why so formal? You've been calling me Joe since you've been stopping by to help around the place for Miss Alicia."

"Yes, sir," John said.

"Sorry I mumbled, Joe. It's good to see you outside, but where's your walking stick?" She disengaged from John, stood and brushed the dirt from her jeans. "John, would you—" She stopped herself, remembering at the last minute he was pretending to be his brother. "John would get so embarrassed when you caught us. Remember?"

She went to Joe and gave him a hug. John stood and hunted for a stick, quick to understand what she'd been about to ask him.

"Miss Alicia, I don't need a walking stick."

"Now, Joe, we agreed after the fall you took last March that you'd get a walking stick for uneven ground. It's either that or a cane. You promised."

"Always looking out for everybody. How long you two been seeing each other?"

She shook her head at John, warning him not to answer. He handed Joe a sturdy-looking stick, smooth enough for his callused but weaker hand to grip.

"Thank you, Boy-o. I forgot the one you brought by the house. No need to make another. And I'll remember to use it. Now, you two should think about finding a cooler place to cuddle. Why, out here, you could have a sunstroke getting all hot and bothered." Joe waggled his bushy eyebrows at them.

Heaven help me.

Certain she'd changed several shades of embarrassing pink in a few seconds, she watched John smile and nod in agreement. She attempted to dart her eyes and jerk her head away from Joe to indicate she was ready to escape. John didn't seem interested or just flat-out ignored her. He seemed to be having a good laugh at her expense.

"How's your father, Brian?"

"Better, sir. Thanks for asking. Alicia's taking great care of him. In fact, he's the one who suggested we take a break today."

"Good. Good. He up for visitors yet?" Joe finally took a step away.

"Probably do him good to see you, sir." John helped the old man up the slight incline.

"I'll plan on it. Bye now, I'm off to lunch."

"Oh, Joe. Would you mind keeping this a secret?" She pointed to John and herself. "We'd like to keep it quiet awhile."

"Mum's the word, Miss Alicia. You should try that old storage barn on the Kruegerville acreage for some privacy. You might have to saddle a ride, but no one goes there since Mr. Adams…passed." He leaned on the stick and took several steps. "Mum's the word."

John stood next to her as an icon from their youth meandered back the way he'd come.

"That brought back some memories," John said, scratching his head. "I don't get it. He didn't ask about Lauren, but he knew about Dad."

"I told him about J.W. He refuses to have cataract surgery, and his vision is blurry. So he doesn't read the paper or watch television anymore."

"Was he talking about the barn we had that haunted house in one year? That thing still standing?"

"I guess so. I had no idea Roy went there. He never mentioned it to me."

"That should go on our list of things to check out."

John turned away from her and jogged back to get the binoculars he'd set on the ground. She had no clue if he meant to check out the barn for potential information or to use it as Joe had suggested.

But she knew that her first thought leaned heavily toward the latter. And that both frightened and excited her at the possibility John's thoughts had gone there, too.

Chapter Nine

The short visit with Mr. Searcy hadn't brought up too many memories of getting caught in their youth. John was still thinking about the kiss in the gully today. It took top-notch self-discipline and concentration to stay sane enough to continue looking for the approaching threat. How had she gotten to be a better kisser? And man, if they hadn't cooled their heels over the past fifteen minutes in the presence of the old man, he might have thrown her onto her back— kissing her into oblivion again.

"Joe will probably mention seeing me at the lunch counter today. He's there every Monday and Friday and bound to hear about Lauren. We can only pray that he doesn't mention seeing you."

"Yeah, pray." He didn't really expect fate or luck to be working on their side. "I'll lose my anonymity as soon as Joe has lunch if Mabel doesn't get Brian out of jail."

"Are we heading to the house?" Alicia asked.

"Affirmative."

They walked into the bright noon July heat, across a field as dry as fire tinder. *What had happened to everything?*

"Say *affirmative* around other people and they'll know you're not Brian for sure. Of course, I still don't know how anyone could get the two of you confused."

"The hard thing to believe is that you don't. How?"

"How what?"

"How do you tell us apart? Besides the obvious haircut."

She shrugged. He stopped them at the backyard to verify the maid had left. One car now. The other must have been Joe's. He hopped the wooden fence and waited for Alicia to climb.

"Show-off. What are we looking for once we're inside?"

"I don't know. Let's find an entrance and then think about it." He tried a couple of windows. All locked. He was about to put his elbow through the glass on the back door when Alicia pulled it to a stop.

"Why don't we just use this?" She dangled a lone key at the end of her tanned arm.

"You could have said something."

"And where's the fun in that?" She slipped the key in the dead bolt and a second time in the knob. "I warned you that the place has changed a lot."

"Yeah, it's empty. What happened to everything?" He shut the door and had to flip on the light to see.

More than just furniture was missing. There weren't any mementos, knickknacks, family pictures...nothing. Objects that had been there the entire time they'd grown up. Dwayne had lost his mother at a very young age. His grandparents had moved back in and had no reason to change things around. His dad had told them more than once that he liked keeping his wife's belongings close to their everyday life.

Alicia gave him a look and he knew the answer. Roy had married Shauna and she'd changed the open kitchen area into a dark cave. Heavy drapery blocked the sunlight.

"She didn't like seeing the barn and constantly complained about how her eyes hurt in the sun."

"Was she hungover or high?"

"That would have been understandable. I don't think

so. Honestly, I have no idea." Alicia's voice sounded older, sadder.

More than the room was dark. Gone was the tenderness this woman had shown for Joe Searcy. She walked through the house with her arms crossed and hands tucked into fists.

"A lot of things were packed away as soon as she moved in. She told the movers to donate it someplace. Roy had it stored somewhere for Dwayne to look through one day. Less than a year later he was gone. Roy followed not too long after."

She squeezed her eyes shut and he patted her shoulder, afraid of the thoughts passing through his head. Inappropriate thoughts of desire shot through his body and made him drop his hand.

"The court said she could sell anything that they'd bought as a couple."

"There's not much left." He gestured to the near-empty everything. "I know it's difficult, but I've got to ask. Why did Roy marry someone young enough to be his daughter? Was he that lonely?"

"She went through a divorce just after Dwayne and I married. I talked to her one day at the grocery store. Then she asked to come over. And kept asking. We didn't want to be rude and I actually thought she was lonely. She must have come over when Roy was alone one night. I think she tricked him into thinking she may be pregnant. He never said anything to anyone. Especially not Dwayne."

"Is there a wall safe?"

"No, I don't think so. And even if there was, he never kept anything here. All his papers were in his office at the show stables. I told you earlier you wouldn't find anything." Her voice choked up a little and he could see tears flooding her eyes.

"Sorry for putting you through this. I didn't mean to

upset you more." *Don't touch her, man.* He didn't listen to himself. Pulling her into his arms and letting her cry was probably the worst idea he'd ever had. Right up there with that failed maneuver in Afghanistan.

A bad idea, because he couldn't trust himself. He wanted a second kiss and more. They were both adults. They could handle a real relationship now. He rested his chin on her head and encouraged her cheek to lie against his chest. Wisps of her curls caressed his hot skin. Hard to believe less than a week ago he'd been halfway around the world in mock maneuvers.

What the hell was he doing?

Waiting here was putting her in danger. Bringing her inside with him put her in danger. They should have been in and out. Fast. And he was delaying so he could hold an old girlfriend.

Emotion had no place in reconnaissance and was not allowed in rescues. Period. There was no room in his lifestyle and career for emotional attachments. He'd seen too many of his buddies lose their families. Partial custody or not seeing their kids for months at a time tore them up and made them lose their edge.

Man, she has a little girl. Dwayne's kid. He couldn't do this.

"If you're okay, let's get out of here." He held her shoulders and kept looking over the top of her head, to keep from seeing the sadness in her eyes. Sadness for another man she loved—even if he was gone.

"I'm fine."

Words with no substance, if wiping away tears was an indicator. And yet she stood straight and didn't complain.

Was it strength? Completely different from what he experienced with his team. A kind that he hadn't seen in a long time. Not since his mom died and the community had rallied around his family.

Alicia should come with warning signs. Emotional ties were dangerous ground for a SEAL who traversed the globe and never knew if he'd return. He needed to build a wall too high for her to climb. He never surrendered. Never would.

A car door shut and he jerked to a stop. Alicia froze. He didn't have to tell her to be quiet or to remain calm. She was. He saw it in her questioning expression. He pointed upstairs. She turned, pulled her shoes off like they had each time they'd snuck up those same stairs as teenagers and soundlessly left him.

About to follow, he turned off the lights and from the corner of his eye spotted the key Alicia had left on the counter. *Damn.* He had training on his side and nothing else. Moving quickly, he swept the key into his pocket and turned the bolt. Good thing the drapes were heavy and no one outside could see shadows.

He peered through the minuscule view available at the window and saw two policemen—one older and one younger. They were both looking in the flowerpots.

"I'll find the key," the experienced officer said. "Go keep a watch out front to see if anyone leaves."

"It's hot out here. She's long gone, sir. Everyone knows she took off to San Antonio and left Sloane to take the rap. Let the Texas Rangers locate her. Coming here doesn't make sense."

"Randall, I swear, if you backtalk me one more time today, you'll be looking for a new job. She left her keys in the car, son. The keys to the houses were missing. Use your noggin."

The older officer was smarter than John had given him credit for. And Alicia hadn't followed his instructions. The patrolman, a kid he didn't recognize, reluctantly shuffled his feet around front. They couldn't get out of the house without being seen.

Fighting the kid out front wasn't an option. If he didn't know him, the kid knew what Brian looked like and that he was in jail. Assuming it was John he'd fought wouldn't be a giant leap for anyone. He hated hiding, but he couldn't risk the police announcing that he was back in town.

He got upstairs, heard the door in the kitchen creak open. Where was she? Dwayne's room was empty. He felt the wave of heat. Window? It was open a crack. They couldn't get to the ground without being seen, but they could hide in the tree next to the house. Alicia could think on her feet. Good to know.

The climb up the giant oak took little effort on his part. He'd shut the window behind him and caught sight of Alicia as high up as the tree would support her weight. She sat in the V of a branch, lacing her shoes.

He got far away from the window and the woman he was trying to protect. If they looked out and spotted him, they might miss Alicia. All they needed was a little luck and for him to screw his head on straight. *Start thinking, man.*

Searching the house didn't take long for the chief. They hadn't disturbed anything—there was nothing to mess with. No one could tell they'd been there. The two men grumbled as they got in the squad car and drove off.

He waited a full five minutes, checking his watch every thirty seconds, before he climbed down to the ground. Alicia followed.

Silently, they proceeded across the open field, choosing the shortest distance they'd be exposed. They hit the far tree line with a barbed-wire fence and followed it just as quickly down to the gully.

When they stopped, Alicia was bent at the waist and gulping air. He was used to running in the heat and could make it to the old barn where their gear was stashed.

"Wait here and catch your breath. I'll get the binoculars.

Then we need to clear out of the barn before they check all the property again."

"Sure." She sat.

It wasn't long before he saw her lie on the ground.

"Why do you think they were looking at the house?" she asked when he returned. "Do you think Joe told the guys at lunch?"

"The key."

"Shoot. I'm so sorry—I didn't think they'd notice. I'll listen to you from now on. Promise."

"Time to get moving." He'd given her time to catch her breath, and neither of the police officers had doubled back. He'd been careless enough with her safety today.

From this point forward, he'd treat her as he would any other civilian he was ordered to escort to safety. No more distractions. No more emotion. No more holding. And definitely no more kissing.

Chapter Ten

SEAL versus SEAL. There had been nothing but an over-abundance of testosterone since John had met his contact. The man obviously wasn't the stranger who John had earlier explained they'd be meeting at the lake. They clearly knew each other, and John was furious.

"Nice to see you, too," the young man said as John grabbed the younger man's shirtfront.

John released him, but neither man backed away. "What are you doing here? I told you not to come."

If either of the men puffed out their chests again, she would push them both in the water to cool off. She watched, sitting at the end of the walk where she'd been tempted to pull her shoes off and dip her feet in the lake. Right until John reminded her they might have to climb another tree—referring to their narrow escape from the police chief.

"You need my help," the stranger shouted, staying nose to nose.

Good thing they'd rendezvoused on a deserted boat dock on Lake Ray Roberts. If she hadn't been worried about being discovered, their classic posturing might even be comical.

"I asked for a favor, Dev. You weren't supposed to hitch

a ride with a pilot and bring the gear personally," John answered tersely. "You said you understood that."

So his name was Dev, and her assumption about him being part of John's unit was correct. They were similar in height and haircut, but nothing else except perhaps some navy SEAL arm muscles.

The water looked very inviting. Jeans weren't the best thing to be wearing in this heat, and being this near the water made her sticky from the humidity. But it was nothing compared to the images that kept playing through her head of where her daughter might be. She wanted her back.

These two needed to do more and argue less. Or not at all.

"The equipment stays with me. It's my personal gear. I'm here and that's the end of it."

"Excuse me." She hesitantly approached them, attempting to interrupt. Both men ignored her. "John? Dev?"

Two sets of SEAL jaws were visibly clenched in determination. Neither one seemed about to flinch. John's hands were fisted. Dev's legs were braced to take a shove or a punch. She had to stop this before it came to blows and someone reported them to the police.

"I thought you guys were friends," she said, laying a hand on John's arm.

He turned toward her so fast that she jerked backward. Her feet tangled under her and sent her flying. She watched John's eyes grow large and his mouth open. He said something as she fell. She was grimacing at the punishment her bottom would endure when she hit that solid wood, so she couldn't comprehend his words.

She kept falling. No wooden dock. She was headed for the water. She inhaled deeply, but too late. The splash caught her at the same time her mouth was open and she sucked lake water. She kicked hard, ready for air, and popped her head above water.

Coughing, sputtering, floundering.

"You okay, Alicia?" John asked.

Hands grabbed her shirt and hauled her to sit on the edge. Strong hands patted her back. Her hair was plastered to her face, so she couldn't see. Her wet shoes tugged at her legs with their weight.

"You okay, sweetheart?" Comforting hands were at her elbow, trying to help her stand.

She twisted some of the water from her hair and began to smile at the endearment. Wait. *That* voice, sounding so Texas, was the *other* SEAL.

"Back off, Dev." John sounded just as angry as before.

"I was just asking." Dev's hands held firm.

"Shut up. The both of—" cough "—you just shut up." She cleared her throat. "Or I'll send you into the water—" cough "—to cool down." She managed to raise her croaky voice a little and slapped the boards on either side of her for emphasis. Then she coughed a couple of times and cleared more water from her lungs, losing all the emphasis she'd gained.

It took a minute, and they patiently tapped her back until she thought she'd be black-and-blue. "This is ridiculous. Back off and don't touch me."

Both men stood, took a couple of steps in opposite directions and were silent. Blessedly silent.

She took her time arranging her hair where it belonged behind her head. She wiped the lake droplets off her face and arms. She toed off her shoes and ignored the warning look from John. It would take forever for her shoes to completely dry, especially if her feet were in them. It was enough that she'd be miserable in the wet denim and underwear.

On the bright side, she was much cooler and no longer sticky.

"Now, boys," she said sweetly as if she were talking to

six-year-olds. She braided her hair before it dried in a wild frizzy mess. They both turned, standing similarly. "How sweet. You're both at attention."

John immediately relaxed. Dev stood more like he was at morning roll call or something. She crossed to John's friend, who had come to rescue her daughter, and extended her hand.

"I'm Alicia Adams, and I can't tell you how much it means to us that you've come to help. Thanks just doesn't seem enough."

"My pleasure, ma'am. Lieutenant Devlin McClain. Sloane and I are on the same team."

"And obviously friends. Thank you."

Then she turned to John, shooting him a forceful look with every indication he should also thank this man who had come to help, putting everything on the line for them.

"Thanks," he said, looking to the water at the last minute.

At least he'd gotten the message. She clapped her hands together. "Okay, then. Here's how it's going to be."

"Actually, I think I should take it from here," John said.

"I rented a cabin and I have the gear. Maybe I should tell you what I've discovered." Dev didn't flinch or break eye contact with his teammate.

"No more arguing," she warned, pointing fingers at them both. "Lauren's been missing five days. Time's running out. She's scared, and who knows what else has happened."

All the sturdy walls she'd built to hold the trouble at bay started dissolving. The tears threatened. Then filled her eyes. Her throat tightened, this time from emotion. She pressed her palms against her eyes to prevent the meltdown.

It didn't work. John's arms engulfed her. She recognized his comforting stroke on her hair and hated that a simple hug from him could make her feel better. She had no right to feel better while Lauren was gone.

"We'll find your daughter, ma'am."

"Dev, what we're doing is illegal." John spoke over the top of her head. "If you get caught, it's a court martial—dishonorable discharge if we're lucky. Maybe military prison."

"Then let's not get caught," Dev replied matter-of-factly.

John sort of growled. She felt it under her hands. He cared so strongly for those around him. How could he have turned from his brother twelve years ago and never thought twice about any of them again?

She sniffed and backed away. John's T-shirt was wet with an imprint of her body. "We need his help. I certainly can't break down a door or overpower those men who tied me up. Please, Johnny. I have to find her."

She pleaded with him. She'd beg again if that was what it took. She desperately needed to hold her baby. They'd lost so much and were so alone. She was all Lauren could remember. Her little girl had to be scared to death.

"WE SHOULDN'T HAVE left her all alone," Tory complained, hoping her ex would turn the horrible truck he'd stolen around and forget this wild demand for more money.

"The brat was happy with the new toy. If you're all worried, then remember to be quick about this and not screw around."

"I hope nothing happens to her. She could choke on that dry sandwich we gave her or something else. Then what would we do?"

"Same thing we're doing now, collect a million dollars and give them the kid."

She saw something in his eyes that hadn't been there before. He wasn't just angry, he might actually kill Lauren. God, she didn't want to go to jail for murdering a kid or anybody. "You're sure it's a good idea to ask for more money?"

"They're going to pay." He hit the steering wheel with his thick fists. "Every rich son of a bitch that's screwed me is going to pay through this guy."

She wondered which rich men he was talking about. He'd never had anything worth taking from him, but she didn't want to rile him more. They were minutes away from delivering the second ransom note, which Patrick knew nothing about.

All hell was about to break loose.

It had been his idea to become real kidnappers instead of remaining the hired help. All her plans for Paris seemed further away than ever before. She recognized the Frisco side street. "You want me to walk three blocks to get to the Weber house?"

"Get goin'. You look stupid with that wig. No one will recognize you, so stop being scared."

His crazy idea for walking down the street with a stroller might just work. She already had a long dark wig, big sunglasses that covered half her face and boots. She'd sweated through the tight-fitting shirt, but she wasn't trying to impress anyone.

"Don't forget this." He threw a huge straw hat they'd gotten at the Dollar Mart across the cab.

She shut the door, grabbed the stroller they'd found in a truck bed and put a sack of trash under a blanket. She fluffed it around until it looked close enough to a fake baby.

It crossed her mind to run as she took off quickly down the sidewalk to round the block. She could knock on someone's door and ask for help. Tory Preston could be the hero, tell the police where Lauren Adams was being held and watch her brutal ex be placed safely behind bars. Then he'd tell the cops all about how it was her plan to start with. She couldn't go to jail. She wouldn't waste this shot by being stupid.

Shauna Weber thought she was so smart with her fancy education and all her husbands. She'd show her who was the real boss and the smartest woman. *But most important, I'll show her who Patrick really loves.*

The house was on the right, and empty. It had been her idea to pick a time when Shauna was giving another plea to the press. The TV had been talking about it all morning. But they'd held the talk at the Aubrey police station. No one was here in Frisco. No gawkers. No press. And it was hot enough that no one was outside.

At least Patrick could see through the money-hungry bitch he'd married. She'd been so lucky to have met a man like him. And even more lucky that he'd fallen in love with her. If only that stupid wife of his would give him a divorce when he asked.

Her ex's instructions were to put the ransom note in the mailbox when no one was around. It didn't make sense to think no one was watching the house. But she wasn't stupid. She had an idea of her own.

Tory rolled the stroller the opposite way from the Weber house and then down to the driveway to cross the street. She boldly went up to a door and slipped the message behind the screen. Acting like no one was home, she casually walked away without anyone being the wiser.

If Lauren hadn't been alone, she'd be in no hurry to return to the car. But the kid was only four and could get into a lot of trouble by herself. Even locked inside a small bedroom with nothing but a plastic cup and some blocks. Or Tory would have to clean up the accidents. She hated that.

Why did her ex have to get greedy?

It had all been so simple before and would have been over tonight. This was her one time to make it big. So she had no choice. Follow his stupid new plan and somehow

keep the ending the same. She'd have her happily ever
after with Patrick.

But even then, she might never feel safe if her ex was
left alive.

Chapter Eleven

"Please don't hurt our baby. Lauren's just an innocent child in all this."

The TV station cut back to the reporter, talking live in front of an empty police station. "That was Shauna Adams Weber, pleading with the kidnappers to return her step-granddaughter alive. Kidnapped four days ago from the grocery parking lot, here in Aubrey, Texas. If you've seen this little girl, please call the number on your—"

John clicked the mute button so they wouldn't hear any more of the blather regarding the kidnapping. Silent tears rolled down Alicia's cheeks. She sat close enough to the screen to touch the picture of Lauren, almost caressing the beautiful little girl who looked just like her. Long curly dark hair. Freckles across her nose. Same frame. No doubt who that kid's mother was.

"How dare that woman call my child her baby?" Alicia whispered hoarsely.

"So that's the target? The dude standing behind her doesn't look like much. Why don't I just ask him real polite like?" Dev asked under his breath, and plugged another auxiliary cable into something electronic.

"Negative. Too many unknowns."

"Gotcha. Hey. Isn't that you?" His friend began laughing. "You never said your brother was a twin."

"Turn it up, John."

He did. Knowing they all had to hear the details, but not liking a minute of it.

"With no evidence of a kidnapping and the fleeing of Alicia Ann Adams, police were forced to release Brian W. Sloane earlier this morning. When asked about the kidnapping, Sloane's attorney shrugged and said his client refused to comment."

He hit the mute button. "Give me your cell."

"You could ask," Dev said while reaching into his pants cargo pocket.

"You can leave."

Dev tossed it to his hands. "So demanding," he said to Alicia.

John left the cabin. "Hi, Mabel."

"It's about time we were hearing from you, Johnny. Is this number— Oh, what do they call it on those shows? Secure. Can we talk?"

"Yes, ma'am." He smiled, all the while dreading the conversation with his brother. They hadn't managed more than arguing since he'd returned. "This number's good to reach me. How's Dad doing?"

"He's just fine, Johnny. How's our girl, she safe?"

"Missing Lauren and threatening to beat me to a pulp at every turn."

"Oh, I just bet she is. There's someone here who wants to talk with you." The noise on the phone sounded like it was being passed around. There was a long delay.

"Where are you?" his brother asked.

"You don't need to know."

He'd been expecting his brother, but for some reason hearing himself on the phone had always thrown him for a loop. People thought that being a twin was like seeing yourself in the mirror. It wasn't. In person, the sides of your face are on the wrong side. Hearing himself on the phone was unnerving.

"I see you got out of taking care of dad."

"I'll try to make up for it."

It was hard to explain. Creepy to some. Cool to others. For him, he'd instantly missed the connection with his brother. Maybe he'd been missing it a long time. Though the moment was awkward, it was good. A calm start that neither of them could control. Neither could order the other around.

"They treat you okay in jail?"

"A couple of bruised ribs. Nothing I couldn't handle. Nothing I haven't handled before. One thing they didn't do was talk around me about the investigation. I'm assuming you're the one who figured out they were waiting at Alicia's house to arrest her."

"Yes. Quick thinking to call her instead of your lawyer." *Handled before?* Had the chief or other officers beat his brother?

"I didn't have much time. The deputy had his boot in my back by then. What do you need from me?" Brian asked.

Son of a— What had his brother endured while he'd been gone and why hadn't anyone said anything? *Because I never asked.* "A haircut."

"Already done. Mabel fainted when she walked through the door and I'd used the horse trimmer. Hasn't been this short since we were kids."

In the background there was a distant, "I did not faint, you flirt."

"Stay visible around town, Brian. Let people see you."

"I get it. If they see me, they'll think Alicia really left. Leaving your presence here as a surprise. How do you plan on getting Lauren back?"

"To be honest, I'm not completely sure. But I will." Any

luck and Dev would find some property or a money trail. Something. Soon.

"You can't do this alone," Brian said in a low growl.

John recognized the mix of pain, frustration and clenched jaw in the delivery. He spoke that way when he wanted to argue with commands given to him on a mission.

"I've got an expert here. I promise, Alicia's secure and we *will* find Lauren."

"Don't mess this up." Same growl. "A piece of pie from the café might be exactly what we need for dessert after all that chicken, Mabel," he said louder and in a fake worry-free tone. "John." He lowered his voice again. "Weber's as guilty as sin."

"How do you know?"

"I saw him with a chick in Fort Worth one weekend. It wasn't his sister, if you know what I mean. Find her and I bet you'll find Lauren."

"I've got somebody digging into their financials. Did you tell the cops you'd seen him?"

"I didn't bother. They wouldn't believe me, man. Take care of my girls."

"I'll send a message if we find anything."

Brian disconnected. John stuck the phone in his pocket and cracked his neck from side to side. *My girls. Handled before*. Things had changed a lot.

"Did they say anything about Lauren to Brian?" Alicia asked.

He spun around. He'd been so deep in his thoughts he hadn't heard her come outside. That had to stop. "He gave me a lead about Weber."

"Isn't there anything I could be doing? Making phone calls, pretend to check on references or something?"

"Have you thought about how you're going to prove you had nothing to do with this mess?"

"Why? I'm innocent. Why would I have to prove anything? You know I didn't arrange this. You believe me, right?" She plopped onto the porch swing, looking totally defeated.

"What I know doesn't amount to much in court, Alicia." He joined her. "Will you let Dev look into your accounts?"

"What do you expect to find?"

"If Shauna is framing you and Brian for the kidnapping, she might have arranged for more damning evidence."

"I, um… I hadn't thought of that." She began to stand but he caught her arm.

"There's something else."

She waited. Mentally preparing herself for bad news. The expression on her face went from terrible to worse. Tight. Strained. He wanted to be cool with it and not show any emotion one way or the other. At least he thought he did. Jumping out a chopper with a full pack into the Indian Ocean was easier than this conversation.

"I think my brother's in love with you."

"ARE YOU OUT of your ever-loving mind? Brian and I are just friends. We see each other almost every day when leaving instructions or getting leftovers from the fridge. End of discussion." She shook free from his hand.

If she hadn't been so furious, she'd laugh so hard she might fall down. But she was furious. After all these years, John's interpretation was still the same.

"He just told me to take care of his girls."

"When are you going to grow up, Johnny Sloane? It's just an expression."

She jumped to her feet. If she wasn't so exhausted and anxious, she might just give him a dose of reality. Shoot, she was tired enough to go ahead and give him a full heaping helping. "You know this is the same reason neither one of us went to the senior prom. And the same argument we had when we broke up."

"That's not how I remember it."

"You and Brian were arguing. As usual, neither of you said what you really wanted to say. You both interpreted the other and as much as I wanted to stay out of all those stupid arguments, you sucked me in and I didn't ever wear that prom dress."

"You don't know what was going on then. What he thought about me."

"I really thought you'd changed, Johnny. Don't you get it? We were friends. You and Brian both talked to me back then. Both of you. I know both sides of the story. So I think I got the full picture."

"Why aren't you mad at him?" He tensed his body.

"Only one of you left without a word."

"We'd broken up. I didn't think you said you never wanted to talk to me again."

She crossed her arms and tried to stay. Tried to listen. But she needed to get away from him and all the emotion that his return made bubble to the surface. Good or bad emotion, it was just too much.

The words faded the faster she ran, even if she couldn't get far. The cabins sat on the edge of the lake, and she was soon out of path. When she slowed down, she heard the brush crunching. John was directly behind her.

"Don't go off on your own, Alicia. It's not secure."

"It's at least 110 on a weekday. There aren't that many people out here tanning. Actually no one's here to notice me. Is that all you can think about?"

He coolly walked closer. She, as casually as the tension strumming through her would allow, took steps away.

"You have to be careful. Your face is being flashed on

every television network and someone's bound to recognize you." He kept his voice low, sounding sexy and dangerous.

"Yours, too."

"It's Brian's, but point taken." He stopped advancing and stretched his arms above his head, yawning. "I don't know if you heard me back there, but I don't know what you mean. You knew I was leaving for the navy. We said goodbye."

What was she supposed to say? "We broke up the night of the fire. I never really thought you'd leave without making things right or that you'd leave without ever coming home." Should she just answer the question that he'd been incapable of verbalizing? "You never asked me wait."

More crashing through the dry leaves had John expertly shoving her behind his body to protect her.

"Dude, you guys can't take off like that. They found another ransom note."

"What?" She'd heard the concern in Dev's voice and asked, "Why would they up the ransom demand on themselves?"

"They wouldn't." John spoke low, sounding more than a little worried. "If they abducted Lauren, they'd want to be the heroes in all this."

"I don't think *they* did. I couldn't record it and don't know them as well as you, Alicia, but they looked genuinely surprised. They kept looking at each other like 'What the frankincense is going on?'"

They all ran back to the cabin. The ransom note was breaking news and being repeated by every local station. So they were able to watch the video replay over and over again. And with each play she fell further into an abyss of despair and hopelessness.

"You're right. They look surprised." Her eyes burned.

She wanted to curl into a ball, give up and cry, but that wouldn't accomplish anything. It wouldn't get Lauren back.

"Watch when she turns to him. He shrugs." Dev pointed to Patrick the third time the station played the video behind whatever the broadcasters were saying.

"Or he's shifting his jacket in the heat." John continued his walk around the cabin.

She couldn't call it pacing, per se. He was thinking and moving. He seemed to always move, always be aware. This afternoon, it was walking around the room, tapping the remote with the palm of his hand or rubbing it on the bottom of his chin.

"Dude, unmute it."

"...stunning development. Witnesses say they saw this woman—" the screen flashed an unflattering driver's license picture of her face "—Alicia Ann Adams, mother of the missing little girl, who was thought to be in San Antonio after reservations were discovered in her name. Witnesses report her pushing a stroller with a child through the neighborhood around two this afternoon. The Amber Alert for Lauren Adams continues—"

The TV went silent again.

"Well, we know that's a lie," Dev said. "You've been here. So who's been there?"

"That's the million-dollar question. Any luck running down Weber's phone records and bank accounts?" John asked.

"I can see why the police didn't suspect them. They both look clean." Dev waved them over to look at his laptop screen.

"But..." John added.

"There's a *but*? You really found something?" A spark of hope? It was amazing how fast her mind could latch on to the smallest glimmer that this ordeal might end well.

"Alicia, your accounts aren't so squeaky."

"Mine? I don't understand. I barely had twenty dollars to buy chicken the other night."

"In checking, yes, but your savings account's a different matter." Dev pointed to an insane amount of money.

She looked at both men. "I don't have any savings. I emptied it."

"Actually, you're a cosigner. This account is Lauren's."

That shiny glimmer of hope that had been just out of reach quickly became a far-off pinprick of light in the sky. Again, the images of all those women found guilty in the press... Were any of them ever innocent like her? She couldn't remember hearing of anyone cleared. If she was watching the evidence on television or found this bank account, she'd probably think the mother was horrible and didn't deserve to be reunited with her child.

"Whatever you're thinking, stop." John's hand was on her shoulder. A strong plea was in his eyes to not give up.

"Don't worry, sister, I'm good at what I do." Dev typed on his laptop.

"Is that a navy SEAL motto?" she asked, trying to put on a brave front. A look shot between the men. Perhaps it was their motto, or they were just surprised they'd both said it.

More screens and code flicked across the monitor. She had no idea what he was doing, but had to trust that he was very good at what he did. John trusted him. And she trusted John to get her daughter back.

"Meanwhile in Dev's world, I've found a couple of rental properties that the Webers' parents own for you two to check out."

She sort of moved through a haze watching John add the addresses to a map application on Dev's phone. The men whispered indiscernibly and she stared at a television now showing the evening programming. She had no point of reference to draw from to try to understand the mind of someone so horrible. No amount of money in the world would make her put an innocent child through this ordeal.

Chapter Twelve

"I thought we were going to check on those two properties Dev told you about. Ponder is the other direction." Alicia pointed west.

"Plenty of time for that." John turned east on Highway 380 and realized they hadn't spoken since pulling away from the cabin. "Finding those properties seemed a little too easy and something the police would have known about. Besides, it's almost dark."

She huffed, crossing her arms and dropping them to her chest.

Did she know she pushed her breasts higher in the air when she did that? If he told her, she'd get embarrassed and stop. He liked it, along with the little puff of air that escaped.

"Please explain your plan."

"Sure. We've all agreed that the Webers seemed surprised at the second ransom demand. Well, what if they're spooked? What if they want to know what's going on and plan on visiting the kidnappers? What if the fake drop is tonight?"

"Do you really think they'll react that way? I mean, surely the police are watching their house, have their phones monitored, et cetera."

"There's always a way. Especially when someone thinks they're smarter than the police."

"I just don't see how—"

"First off—" he hated to bring his world to Alicia's, but he had experience dealing with people she'd never understand "—you should trust me. I've dealt with more than my share of scum who think their plan is foolproof. There's always a way to bring these people down."

"And the second thing?" she asked.

"Don't try to understand them, Alicia. You won't. The price for trying to think like sleazebags is too high. It does something to a person, and you don't deserve that."

He drove Dev's rental for several minutes, watching her peripherally, unable to stop expecting a reaction to his words. An argument? An agreement? More questions? Nothing. Not a hitch in her breathing.

"Is that what happened to you, Johnny?"

"Huh?"

"Do you understand them? The sleaze and scum?" she asked.

"Yeah, I do. Unfortunately."

"I'm sorry."

She pitied him. After everything she'd been through, she pitied *him*. What did anyone say after that conversation? Him? He had nothing, so he kept his trap shut before he said something to confuse their relationship further. He didn't want her to care. He wasn't her problem. When Lauren was back, when his brother was cleared of the charges and when his dad was back on his feet...

There was no reason to care. Hell, Lieutenant Sloane would be out of here and back in a third-world country for another six months. He couldn't afford to care when he'd be right back with the sleaze and scum and away from Alicia's goodness.

Join the navy and rescue strangers all around the world.

Yeah. It didn't surprise him he had no desire to further his military career. The more time he spent here, the less he appreciated his lifestyle of the past twelve years.

Hard to believe it was less than a week ago that he'd received word his dad had suffered a stroke. The first wave that struck him had been relief hearing his dad was still alive. The second, anticipation. His dad's illness justified a confrontation with his brother. He'd no longer needed an excuse to come home.

That hadn't gone as planned.

"How are we supposed to watch a house that's being watched by the police?"

"They won't be expecting us to be watching. That's one thing on our side. The cops are watching Brian hang out in the café. They aren't looking for me here."

"And the cops believe Lauren is safe with me, not kidnapped at all. Do they think I'm sitting around San Antonio, sipping margaritas, waiting for the ransom money to be delivered?"

"I don't think they took it that far, Alicia." He put the car in Park at a stop sign. "That car, second from the end of the block. That's the surveillance team. I can only see one guy in the car, though."

He turned the corner and parked their car a couple of blocks away.

"So what do we do now?" she asked.

"Take a walk."

"You've got to be kidding, John. They've had my face all over the news. What if someone sees me?"

"I need to see the back of the house." *Get closer. Evaluate Weber's expressions, his gestures, his level of anxiety.* But he couldn't get into all the details.

"It's a six-foot fence."

"There's a utility alley between the houses. A six-foot fence means no one will be watching the back for them to leave. No one should notice us and there will be plenty of room for a walk."

"So do you want me to stay here?"

"You're coming with me. A couple is definitely less noticeable." He shoved the pistol Dev had brought him into the back of his pants and opened his door.

"It's okay, no one will see us."

"Leave the gun in the trunk, please."

"Alicia, I know you aren't afraid of pistols."

"We're just a couple out walking. You don't need a gun. If we're noticed, we're running. Right? You wouldn't shoot at the cops."

It wasn't the cops he'd been thinking about. He nodded, wishing he had a piece of gum. Something to chew and work out the nervous tension in his gut. He didn't like venturing into unknown situations. Exposed. Defenseless. He wanted well-thought-out plans to execute, and hated flying by the seat of his pants. That was exactly when things went wrong and someone got killed.

He put the pistol in the trunk and sent a text to Dev, also at Alicia's insistence. His reply couldn't be repeated in polite company.

Feeling naked without a weapon, he laced his fingers through Alicia's. She took a step, but he spun her to face him, drawing her in close so he could lower his voice.

"I say run and you run. No discussion. We'll meet back here at the car. Here's the key." He watched her stuff it into the back pocket of her jeans. "Run means run."

"No debate," she agreed, without convincing him she would follow any directions from him.

"Get the smile out of your eyes, woman. Think about Lauren. The objective is to find her. If we're caught, it'll be a whole lot harder to achieve that goal."

"You're worried?" She gripped his biceps, silently demanding an answer.

"Five days is a long time for kidnappers. They're either feeling confident and getting cocky or they're starting to lose their nerve. My gut tells me they'll make a move soon. Probably tonight."

"I guess I should have asked before now what it is that you do in the navy."

The laugh escaped before he could hold it back. "Let's just say I have experience and you can trust me."

She cupped his cheek with her palm. "Thank you."

He caught himself leaning into her caress and wanting to capture her lips. "Come on."

No one was in sight. No cars parked on this street. People were in their air-conditioned homes with their vehicles locked in their garages. Patrick Weber shouldn't be any different. All the news reports they'd seen had been with the couple standing in their empty driveway. The steps leading up their walk had made it inconvenient to tape them in front of the door.

John had memorized the local landscape this afternoon. Technology and the internet made espionage too easy. The Webers lived on the north side of the street, four houses from the end. At the entrance to the utility ally, John pulled Alicia into his arms again.

"Drop your head against my chest, hon. I need to see over you."

She did as instructed and he verified they were still alone on the street. He grabbed her hand again and darted into the dying weeds. They ran, staying close to the fence. First yard. Second had a dog that barked once or twice. Third yard was behind them. Target yard. No gate. No lights. No noise.

He motioned for Alicia to stay down and close. His eyes were almost level with the top of the fence. He lifted himself to get a full view of the yard.

Professional landscaping and no pool. That would work

in his favor. It was only nine o'clock, and yet no lights were on, with the exception of the television glow from the front room. He lowered himself back to Alicia.

"I need you to go back to the car quickly." He placed the phone in her palm. "Pull around to the other end of the alley in six minutes. If I'm not there, go back to the cabin and tell Dev what happened. On the way, call Brian and tell him to get the hell out of Aubrey. When he's sure no one's following him, pick him up somewhere he can leave his truck."

He saw the frightening questions in her expressive eyes and caught the slight shaking of her head. He took her shoulders and whispered, "Nothing's going wrong. You just need to know what to do if it does. I've got this covered."

He kissed her forehead and pointed for her to go.

"Be careful," she said for his ears only.

"Always."

She left the same way they'd come in, remembering the dog and switching to the other side of the alley. He marked his watch with a five-minute countdown. In the corner of the yard, he hopped the fence and got to the back of the house without an alarm sounding.

He slid to the side of the kitchen window and had a perfect view of Shauna stacking bundles of cash into a gym bag. And next to the bag, a set of two keys that would fit a much older truck, reminding him of the one his brother still drove. From Shauna's rich tastes, it didn't seem likely that either of the Webers would be caught dead driving something that old.

He flattened himself to the brick and listened. Shauna left the room. She'd been barefoot, so they weren't leaving immediately. He glanced at his watch. Three minutes. One last glance and he was out of the yard the way he'd come. He hid in the shadows behind a telephone pole until

Alicia slowly approached. She didn't come to a full stop as he opened the door and jumped inside.

"My gut was right."

Chapter Thirteen

I'm tracking my daughter's kidnapper. How did this happen?

The surrealism of the situation didn't escape Alicia. She wasn't qualified. Could only do as she was told. And each time she deviated from John's instructions, something bad happened. Her shoes were still wet from the dunking she'd received trying to stop an argument between two men who were on her side.

She couldn't claim to have been doing a wonderful job on her own prior to the kidnapping, but she'd survived. She'd battled all the obstacles of the past four years, and she'd figured it out. Enough that Lauren and she were happy.

I still don't know what to do now.

A couple of minutes driving around in the subdivision and they found the truck on an empty lot at the end of a cul-de-sac. They parked in view of the subdivision entrance to watch for the truck to leave.

John convinced her to drive, since he had other things to prep. He retrieved his gun, stuffed it into his waistband and texted Dev. He sat next to her, leaning back in the seat, keeping watch and thumbing through screens on the smartphone. She was so anxious to get Lauren back she could hardly think about any of the details he'd been going over.

"Are you playing solitaire? How can you be completely confident this is going to work?" she asked after forty-five minutes.

"I'm never *completely* confident. Solitaire keeps me from thinking about things that can go—"

"Wrong." There was a long list of things that could go "south," as he constantly put it.

John put a hand on her shoulder, deeply massaging the tight muscles. "You're tense. Relax. The steering wheel can't possibly escape that death grip of yours."

Two cars passed and had her leaning forward, jumping to start the car. John's hand stayed her from turning the key. Her heart beat so quickly she checked the mirror to see if the vein in her throat was bulging. She rubbed her shaking hands up and down her thighs, feeling the adrenaline tremble through her body.

Doubt crammed into her mind and blocked her ability to think straight. She had to know if she was as clueless as she felt.

"Did I miss something? Could I have prevented the kidnapping or bank transfers or any of this from happening?"

"No," John answered quickly, but stiffened.

"How can you be so certain?" Questioning her movements and decisions was a big part of the apprehension building inside her chest. If he knew something... If he had an answer... Maybe that would ease the tension and allow her to function better.

He shifted uncomfortably. His gaze seemed to drift. Then he looked sad, like a memory he didn't want to face wouldn't leave him alone. She'd seen that faraway look a couple of times now. He was physically fit and looked like Brian, so she'd sort of *seen* him for twelve years. But something big in him had changed. She'd known Johnny. This man was Lieutenant Sloane. She didn't know him at all.

"Whoever kidnapped Lauren, they've thought this

through and planned her abduction for a long time. Framing you and Brian took months. I think they planned for you to die in the car. Then the Webers would rescue your daughter and have custodial control over the trust fund without any questions."

As hot as the evening still was, her skin was covered in goose bumps. He'd spoken with chilling reality, logic and confidence.

I think they planned for you to die, his voice echoed in her head.

The sheriff had said something like that, too. And still, she'd shrugged it off, been optimistic, unable to think the worst, and she definitely didn't want to believe Shauna could really hate her that much.

"Your theory makes perfect sense. I just can't begin to think like you and I'm so grateful you came home. Without you, I'd be in jail and lost to Lauren forever."

"Don't think about that possibility. Besides, why should a nurse who spends her time caring for others think like me? I'm glad you can't wrap your mind around this situation. Really glad. I like who you grew up to be."

"Are they going to hurt her? Be straight with me, Johnny."

"I don't know. If you concentrate on the unknowns, it sort of makes you crazy. Just remember that we *will* get her away from them."

No tears. Not even a threat of them. She was all cried out. Too worried about making another mistake. John twisted to face her, taking her chin in his fingers, nudging her to stare from the street toward him.

"Wherever they lead us—if they go at all—you know there's no guarantee Lauren will be there." The crease between his brows grew prominent with his concern. "If she is, it might get messy. Maybe I should drop you off and—"

"No. I'll do anything necessary to keep my daughter

safe. Don't worry about me. I've been on my own for a while now." And she had. Her father, Dwayne's accident and then her father-in-law. "Talk about something else while we wait."

"Dev said the money in Lauren's savings was a series of small cash deposits over the last four months. Different branches. Nothing electronic."

"Alicia, you okay?" he asked after a minute of silence. "I'm fine."

"I wanted to ask before, but where's your dad and brother through all this? I expected them to show up sooner."

"Alzheimer's. Dad had a slow progression in the beginning. I took care of him as long as I could. But he doesn't recognize me anymore. He mistook me for Mom for a while. But he hasn't had many lucid moments in a very long time. He was in a nice place in Denton, but when Shauna got me fired, I had to move him to a state facility about four hours from here."

"I'm sorry, I didn't know." His large hand covered hers, squeezing. "My dad never mentioned it. I shouldn't have brought it up."

"It's okay. You didn't know. J.W. was pretty upset. He lost his two best friends in a short amount of time. My brother's never been close and is stationed in Germany. He volunteered to go shortly after Dad needed round-the-clock care, and I haven't called him about Lauren. It doesn't make sense. What could he do?"

"Alicia, I can't begin to understand what you've been through. What about Roy? Dad said he died from a broken heart. I asked what that meant, but he never said."

"He shot himself three months after Dwayne's accident."

"Son of a— That can't be true. They're certain? Who found him?"

"Shauna." She hated saying the woman's name. It was bad enough thinking about her. "This isn't exactly the subject to help relax me." She forced a short nervous laugh and relaxed her fingers again.

"You're right. That was stupid of me."

"What are we going to do when we follow them to where they have Lauren?"

"There's no *we*. I'll go inside and do what's necessary. You'll stay in the car and call Dev if something goes wrong."

"I can help. Believe me."

"I'm sure you can, but we're going to have to grab Lauren and hightail it into hiding."

"I don't understand. Why can't we just go home? Or at least to the county sheriff. He'll believe us. We have to tell someone what we know and let the police arrest them."

"We haven't proved that you didn't orchestrate this from the start. It's their word against yours."

"But Lauren can tell everyone the truth."

"No, that won't work. At this point, you won't win."

She was stunned into silence. Where could she take Lauren that was safe? How would they survive without any money? It didn't matter. She meant what she'd said. She was willing to do anything to get Lauren back. That included becoming a fugitive and hiding until she could prove her innocence.

"You need to prepare yourself for another scenario."

His tragic tone shouted and screamed *what if*.

"No, don't say it. Don't think it. I won't accept that they could hurt her."

"Alicia. We have to be reasonable."

"Wait. Isn't that the truck?"

She started the car, putting it in Drive after the truck passed and they knew which direction he was heading. The older truck could have been mistaken for the one Brian drove. Very distinguishable among the newer models on the road. It made it easy to keep two or three cars between them and not lose sight of its direction.

"Looks like Patrick's alone. Why would he pay them without Shauna?" Alicia asked.

"Probably the same reason I should be alone right now. It's dangerous."

They followed on the main road, being led farther away from the larger cities and even small towns. Onto rural roads, where it was harder to keep the truck in sight without giving their presence away. Sometimes they depended solely on the vehicle lights ahead of them in the distance. Then brakes.

"Alicia, can you see the road in the dark?"

"I think so." The sandy gravel reflected enough moonlight that she could see and not drive into the ditch.

"He's slowing down," John confirmed. "Stop here. It must be the driveway of a house." He tapped the phone and put it to his ear. "Dev, I need info on a property. Just texted coordinates....Extraction. Solo....Negative....No, I can't wait. No second pair of eyes. She'll be secure in the car."

She was amazed at how matter-of-fact every aspect of Lauren's rescue was to John. Was this what he did as a SEAL? *Where will you be safe, Johnny?*

"Hide the car," he mumbled as he pointed. "See that spot behind us where the side of the road is flatter? We need to get behind those trees."

"But there's a fence. Won't the car still be in the road?"

"Not for long. And you're staying in it. You promised to follow orders." John reached into his pocket, then jumped from the car.

By the time she'd reversed onto level ground, he'd cut the barbed wire and she could park it in the field hidden from other drivers. He pulled the wire mostly back together and motioned for her to join him. The truck hadn't moved from next to the mailbox.

"Stay close to the car and keep this." He handed her the phone. "There's a map of the area and you'll be able to let Dev know where to pick you up. You can trust him."

"I'm going with you."

He just shook his head and smiled. "Not this time, sweetheart. I'm in. I get Lauren. I'm out."

"What are you—"

John cut off her words with a quick kiss. Not supersexy, but the surprise was effective and shut her up.

"I can't wait to explain. I want in before Patrick. I'll be back soon with your daughter."

John ran. His dark T-shirt and jeans were stark against the light brown of drying hay. The large round hay bales set randomly throughout the field gave him the cover he needed to avoid being seen. Hopefully.

She had to do something. She couldn't just sit and wait. But what, she had no idea. No frame of reference. No experience. Only one thing—Lauren was her daughter.

Thank God this man had come back home. If it weren't for him, she'd have no way to prove Shauna's involvement. And no one to save Lauren.

Too antsy to stay in one place, she wanted to view the map sent earlier. She darted across the road out of view, ducking behind the bushes until no lights from the house could be seen.

Oh, no. There were more headlights slowly turning from the main road. Like a car wanting to remain unseen or a person who might be lost. She ran hard, making her lungs hurt. Across the rows of dirt and grass until she could hide in the trees.

The car turned the curve and went dark. It took several seconds to pass the bend in the road and roll to a stop close to the drive. Alicia could make out only the silhouette of a head. It didn't take someone with John's experience to understand whoever was inside that second car didn't want to be seen.

The person in the car was waiting. The sound of the engine filled the silence. Had Patrick been followed? Had she and John been followed? Or was the stranger Shauna and this part of their plan all along?

The car loomed like a demon waiting to pounce.

What are you up to? It didn't matter.

John was nowhere in sight. She had no way to contact him and he wouldn't know about this additional danger. Patrick finally drove his truck toward the house. She had to help John, so she ducked farther into the brush and covered the brightness of the phone. The map appeared on the screen.

The objective was to stop these people from hurting Lauren. No matter what happens.

Chapter Fourteen

John crossed the hay field without any problem. He approached straight down the fencerow next to the drive, using the trees as cover.

There were actually two old houses, both probably built before indoor plumbing. The southern one closest to him, just a box with steps, had no lights and no activity. Storm cellar to its east. Barn to the north, then a shed, tractor and some baled hay.

Between him and the main house was a circular drive with a large oak in dead center. All laid out just like the gridded map in his head.

The larger house had started small with rooms haphazardly stuck to it. One of those additions was definitely the bathroom. He could see pipes and a hole in the ground from plumbing work. Two he could assume were bedrooms. They each had a small window air-conditioning unit identical to the one in the front room.

Weber had taken his sweet time pulling up the driveway. He parked near the smaller house and was still in the dang truck. No one reacted to his arrival. No doubt due to the window unit and blaring television.

A blind rescue. He hated being without intel on how many assailants were inside or where the hostage was located. What he wouldn't give for some heat imaging to locate hostiles.

When Weber finally got out of the old truck, he was covered from head to toe, including gloves. Not good. It had to be almost a hundred degrees still. Obviously, he didn't want to leave evidence behind. The situation had all the markers of going south fast.

Pictures. Video. Why hadn't he brought Dev's cell to record the exchange? He'd thought only of rescuing Lauren, and that Alicia needed the phone for her safety. Nothing else. It was too far to run back and retrieve the thing. He'd taken images of Weber in the truck, but a recorded conversation would be damning and convict the Webers, clearing Alicia. It couldn't be explained away as easily as a ride in an old truck.

After the rescue, mother and daughter would be together. At least that met his priority objective.

Weber appeared nervous and hesitant walking up the steps to the wide well-lit porch. He shifted the gym bag from shoulder to shoulder. If he and Shauna had nothing to do with the kidnapping, delivering the ransom without police involvement wasn't a good idea. They had to be guilty.

Then where's the money? Dev was the best, and he was having problems finding it.

The outside light flicked on. Weber was greeted by a surprised young woman. A man yelled. As soon as he walked inside, an argument began. Indistinguishable words, but John could guess what it concerned.

John darted behind the darkened house, pausing at the raised earth of the cellar. No outside guard. No one standing watch. No cattle or horses in the field. No dogs and not even a sign of a cat. He zigzagged the open twenty yards to the corner of the bathroom.

Words like *in charge* and *highfalutin* popped through the thin walls, along with a host of four-letter words. Unless Patrick Weber's voice had shifted from a tenor to a deep bass, the man he'd joined wasn't a happy camper. Weber showing up—especially without the extra cash—wasn't to their liking. But neither was the surprise demand for more. The way the men discussed the details was additional proof that Lauren's step-grandparents were in charge of the entire kidnapping. But there still wasn't evidence that would clear Alicia or Brian.

John kept his back to the paint-peeling wood, glancing into the windows of each room. At the rear of the house, one of the window units had plywood over the glass. *Bingo.* Lauren had to be in that room. The wood was new and the nailing sloppy, but he couldn't pry it loose with just his hands or the multitool that lived in his back pocket. There wasn't anything lying around to help. He couldn't risk losing time searching the barn.

Just past the window was another porch. Kitchen. Back door. He tried the knob. Unlocked. He cracked it open. No squeak.

Weapon ready, John crept inside, leaving the door open behind him, and silently got his back to the cabinets near the main room. Only one way into the rest of the house. In fact, there weren't any hallways. All the rooms opened onto the front room, where everyone was located.

"You ain't gettin' the kid till I get the rest of the dough," the second man screamed.

The yelling grew louder. More erratic. Covering several subjects. About staying in an old rattrap of a house. About Tory, the woman who had answered the door. About how tired he was of babysitting a kid. The woman screamed back, seeming to hold her own until the big guy backhanded her. And Weber remained silent, looking edgy.

The anxiety landing in the pit of John's gut wasn't good. This second man seemed to be strung out—no telling what drug he was high on or what he was capable of doing. Tory kept trying to appease him, calm him.

It didn't work. And after a second brutal slap, she pressed against the wall and out of his reach. Getting Lauren out of the house fast was imperative.

"Take the money," Weber encouraged. "There's twenty-five grand here."

"We decided we need more, and you gotta pay to keep us shut up."

"Then leave it." Weber shrugged.

John surveyed the living room via a wall mirror he could see from where he stood. The girl was blond, petite and had a deeply black eye. There were bruises up and down her arms.

"Come on, babe. This is what we've waited for." The girl tugged on the man's arm. "Twenty-five thousand gets us on a beach in the Bahamas."

"Stop hanging on me, you whore." He propelled her away and she collided with the TV stand. The old set crashed to the floor and Weber didn't cringe or react. "I told you, you ain't getting the kid for less than half a mil."

"You're certain about that?" Weber dropped the bag from his shoulder.

John heard the zipper. Did Weber really think he could convince this guy to take the money by showing it to him? Aw, hell. There must be a gun in the top of the bag.

Should he wait for Weber to draw and hope the big guy could defend himself? Then he'd proceed to where he thought Lauren could possibly be located. Or should he stop Weber before he killed the only two people who could prove Alicia's innocence?

"Hold it." John spun around the corner and aimed his 9 mm at Weber.

"Who the hell are you?" The big man took a step closer to him.

"Far enough." John shifted his aim between the two men. The second was easily five inches taller than John and outweighed him by a good eighty pounds. The man was a damn giant.

"What are you doing here, Sloane?" Weber asked.

"You know this bastard?" the other man said to Weber, but advanced toward John.

"Stay back and, Weber, show me your hands." He gestured with the gun for them to move to the outside wall. "Slowly stand up and back away from the bag."

"I'm going to tear you both to shreds."

"Back to your corner, Gargantuan." He kept both men in his view, but lost sight of Tory. Served him right if something hit him over the head for being so careless, but it wouldn't help Lauren.

"You should leave. I'm here to get the kid back and you're mucking everything up." Weber stood, but suspiciously slipped his hand into his pocket.

"I know why you're here, and it won't work."

"I disagree." Weber dived for the bag, rolled and fired.

John couldn't discharge his weapon for the same reason he'd tried to prevent Weber from shooting. He couldn't risk injuring Lauren or the kidnappers. But that wouldn't stop the others from taking the risk.

When Weber dived toward the front door, Gargantuan dived straight into John. The woman who cowered in the corner scurried in the opposite direction. John lost sight of Weber when a thick shoulder hit his kidney, stunning him with the force. He kept his grip on his gun, hitting the giant of a man in the side of the head.

Gargantuan didn't flinch, just locked his arms around John's midsection and started squeezing. He wasn't just huge, he absorbed all the hard-hitting blows John could deliver. The deadlock around his ribs had him struggling for air. He couldn't get any traction with his feet dangling. Then the giant shoved him into the wall.

The gun flew while old picture frames banged to the floor. John watched his defense land close to the front door. Hand to hand it would have to be.

John used his legs to do his own shoving. They both shot across the room. Gargantuan lost his balance but not his grip as they crashed between the chair and couch. John could only see the nicotine-yellowed ceiling, but the voice of a child was very distinct behind one of the doors.

"Help."

ALICIA RAN TO the farm, imitating John's movements, and following as much of the path as she'd watched earlier. The car she came to warn John about was still parked— waiting for something. Just like when they'd run from the house that morning, she got close to the fence and tried to blend in with the trees. Once she reached the open yard, she skirted around the edge of the houses before getting close to the back porch.

The door was open. She heard thrashing inside and then distinct sounds of a car door out front. Could John already have Lauren?

JOHN THRUST HIS elbow under Gargantuan's ribs. Again. Then again.

Blessed relief around his chest was followed with direct hits simultaneously to his ears. He saw two women—or maybe it was one and he was seeing double—twist a dead bolt on one of the doors.

They were moving Lauren. He had to get free.

A quick shake of his head, attempting to clear it, just made the double vision worse. His ears burned as much as his anger at being taken by surprise by Weber's bully. And Weber.

He flipped around and landed a couple of punches to a massive chest. He saw the woman running, dragging Lauren behind her. Escaping.

Time to end this.

AFRAID SOMEONE WAS leaving with Lauren, Alicia ran around the house to stop them. The porch light was enough to see Patrick running to the driveway, waving an arm above his head. He carried a bag, but didn't have Lauren. She stayed in the dark at the edge of the porch. Should she go in the house? Where was John?

More crashing. Shadows of bodies hit the curtains. Two men were fighting. It must be John. She searched the darkness, trying to get her eyes to adjust to find Patrick, but he'd disappeared. A car—most likely the one from the road—was headed toward the house.

A tiny, frightened whimper. Alicia's attention snapped to the porch.

"Patrick, wait," a woman shouted, shoving the screen door against the wall as she ran through.

"Lauren." Though a little dirty, her daughter seemed uninjured.

"Mommy! Mommy!" Lauren struggled to free her wrist from a familiar young woman. The struggling forced the woman to pause and get control. When Lauren couldn't get free, her daughter threw herself to the porch, taking her captor to her knees and turning her face toward Alicia.

"Tory?"

GARGANTUAN WOULDN'T STAY DOWN. John threw his head backward, connecting with the man's nose. He heard the familiar crunch of cartilage breaking and took advantage of his opponent's momentary stunned state to scramble to his feet.

Twelve years in the navy had taught him a couple of

things about hand-to-hand combat. It was time to let some of it kick into high gear. There was no guilt at a few dirty tricks to get this kidnapper on the floor.

Another punch caught him in the chin, but he returned with three quick jabs of his own. He hit a bloody nose twice, obtaining a groan of pain from his opponent. He spun, kicked, connected. Boot sliced flesh.

Gargantuan finally looked dazed. Another kick to the head. He fell through the kitchen doorway and didn't get up.

Where the hell is my gun?

ALICIA WATCHED AS Tory waved the handgun like an inexperienced teenager afraid of what she held. She yanked Lauren onto her side, the gun so close she could accidentally hit her little girl.

Lauren squirmed on Tory's hip.

"Be still!" the frightened young woman shouted. "Stay away. Just stay back."

"It's okay, princess." Alicia tried to sound calm while coaxing her baby to keep out of the line of fire. "Stay there and be still, sweetheart. Do what Tory says."

"I don't want to stay with her no more, Mommy."

"Shut up," Tory hysterically screamed, pounding the gun against her skull. "I can't think what I need to do."

"Princess, please be still and let me see if Miss Tory will let you come home."

"That ain't never goin' to happen. Not until— Patrick?" Tory searched the dark, the gun pointed casually toward Lauren again. "God, Patrick, don't leave me."

Nervous, anxious, uncertain… Alicia shoved a stopper into those emotions before they clouded her judgment. But whatever she felt, Tory was horrifically worse. She'd clearly been beaten and was terrified. She searched the yard, pointing the gun practically everywhere, including at Lauren.

Alicia couldn't wrap her mind around who held the hand of her daughter. Shauna had to be responsible for the kidnapping. Tory worked for minimum wage at Mary's day care. She didn't have enough money or influence to create a money trail that would frame her.

It was Shauna. It had to be.

"We're going to get in that car and drive away from here." Tory wrapped Lauren tightly across the front of her body, using her daughter as a human shield. "Do you hear me, Alicia? Nobody comes near me or I'll shoot. I don't want to, but I will."

Lauren cried, chanting, "Mommy, Mommy, Mommy."

It broke her heart not to sprint to Tory and lock her daughter into a tight embrace of love.

"You don't have to do this, Tory. We can work things out. No one will ever know."

Flashing police lights spun into the night near where they'd left the rental. Lights from the car that had been lurking for so long popped to life at the end of the driveway, heading toward the house.

"It's too late. I'm not going to jail. I'm sorry, but Lauren's my only chance."

"Don't be crazy, Tory. Patrick and Shauna have to be behind this. All you have to do is tell the police what happened. You can make a deal."

Tory took the steps to the yard fast and ran to the parked car. "I'm not going to jail. Stay there. I swear I'll shoot." Her voice was full of panic as she jerked the gun around, her finger on the trigger, Lauren still in her arms. "We're going."

"Mommy, please," Lauren sobbed. Frightened tears streamed down her little cheeks as her hands stretched past her captor toward Alicia.

Alicia watched in horror as Tory tripped and fell behind the car. She heard a petrified scream from her little girl. Gun or no gun, she ran to rescue her daughter.

On the far side of the car, two bodies struggled, outlines until the beams from the car drew closer. Tory sat on John's chest, a crazed look on her face, her hands swiping at him like bobcat claws.

"Go. Find your daughter. I've got this," John said as he locked his long fingers around one of the wrists still slapping at him.

Lauren was nowhere in sight. She couldn't help him; she had to find her daughter.

"Lauren! Where are you, princess?" she called with no success. "Are you hurt? Lauren, baby, where are you?"

Movement at the edge of the darkness, near the trees. Lauren. Headlights momentarily blinded her before the car cut her off from her baby.

"Mommy, help me."

"Get her, dammit," Shauna shrieked from the driver's seat.

Alicia ran, following her daughter's wails. Near the car that had just stopped, she saw Patrick grab Lauren from her hiding place under his parked truck and lift her into his arms, slapping a hand over her mouth to keep her quiet. She started to run toward them and the car door opened, broadsiding Alicia to the ground, knocking her breath from her lungs.

"No! I don't want to go with you. I want my mommy."

A shot echoed between the house and trees.

Oh, my God. The last she'd seen, Tory had the gun and had been struggling with John. But she had to get Lauren before Patrick left with her.

"Baby." Alicia rolled away from the car door to her knees. Just as her feet were under her, she was pulled back to the ground. *John*. Relief blasted through her as sharply as that shot had pierced the night.

"Let me go."

On the ground with her, he clapped a hand across her mouth to keep her quiet, but kept them moving to the edge of the house. "Don't fight me. We can't get her. Believe me."

The police sirens blasted into the yard. The cars stopped, blocking the drive at the top of the circle. John half dragged, half rolled Alicia into the complete blackness cast by the house's shadow. He covered her with his body and waited. What was he doing? She had to get Lauren.

"Thank God you're here. It was them." Shauna yelled at both officers who approached her. "They're here. She was just here with her junkie boyfriend. Find and arrest them before they get away!"

There was no way to escape, lying under him. He remained motionless and didn't bother to relieve some of the heaviness of his muscled body, which cut off her oxygen.

She could still see the charade being played out in front of her eyes. An intense drama with no comic relief or happy ending in sight.

Chapter Fifteen

"Is she dead?" Shauna asked the first officer who pulled up, now kneeling by Tory.

From next to the house, John had a decent view of the action playing out in the driveway. Just like the situation he'd been in a couple of years back when a buddy got wounded with hostile fire on both sides. He clamped his hand tightly over Alicia's mouth and froze.

No movement. No sound. It was crucial not to draw attention to themselves right now. If they did, they might as well surrender. He didn't surrender.

"Hang tight or they'll see us," he whispered directly into her ear.

"See when backup's going to get here," the older officer commanded his much younger counterpart. "Then check the house without destroying all the evidence."

Patrick Weber stared at the woman lying there, motionless. He didn't utter a sound or show any remorse.

"Shouldn't we look for those other two who got away?" The younger officer drew his weapon and walked directly to where John was trying to control a squirming Alicia.

"Do what I said," the older officer yelled, reversing the younger guy in his tracks. "We've rescued the girl and can't leave the scene."

Shauna ran to Weber and jerked Alicia's daughter from her husband's arms. "Oh, Lauren, thank God we found you."

Weber walked a little less hesitantly to the rear of his truck and dropped the tailgate. John could no longer see his face, but he saw a puff of smoke. The distinct smell of cigarettes drifted to their hiding place.

Lauren looked surprisingly like a miniature Alicia. Her face was grimy and tear streaked, clothes filthy, curly hair a tangled mess. The kid definitely had the will to fight like her mother. She squirmed, tugged on hair and slapped. When Shauna swatted her behind, Lauren silently cried, drawing in huge gulps of air around her two middle fingers she'd stuck in her mouth.

He hoped Alicia couldn't see what was happening. If he could, he'd cover her ears to keep her from hearing, too. What if Lauren cried for her again?

"Let me up," Alicia mumbled, twisting violently under him and moving until she could whisper clearly. "It's over. Lauren's safe. We caught them with those kidnappers. They can be arrested. All we have to do is give ourselves up."

"Nothing's over," John whispered. "Surrendering is not an option."

"I don't understand. You can't let them— I've got to get to Lauren." She spoke strongly into his ear.

"We still don't have any proof you're innocent."

"Nonsense. You can't keep me here, John Sloane. She needs me."

"Your daughter needs you for longer than it takes to put you in handcuffs." He replaced his hand over her mouth. "I'm not letting you go. Period. The younger one is so skittish, he may shoot us on sight."

Her body went limp in defeat, not moving, with the exception of the silent crying. Good. He needed to find a safe way back to the car. They were too close to Tory's body to make a run for the fence line. They'd be heard or seen before they could get out of sight. If either officer walked the perimeter of the circular driveway, they'd be discovered before they got to their knees.

The extraction route would be the back of the main house, then the barn and out through the far pasture. It would take longer, but it was the only way.

Shauna pivoted from the dead woman, meeting the younger officer at his car. "I agree with you. Alicia and Brian need to be found and caught. Are you really not going after them? They can't be far. They were just here when you pulled up. If you don't hurry, they'll get away."

Her daughter fought Shauna just as hard as Alicia fought for her own freedom while pinned beneath him. As difficult as it must be for her to draw a breath with his two hundred pounds on her back, she gathered strength and tried to throw him off several times. He jerked a little when she tried nipping at his fingers. He ignored it and kept her snug to the ground, not trusting her to break free and take off after Lauren.

"Orders, ma'am." The young officer holstered his weapon and leaned into the car, grabbing the radio.

"I want my mommy!"

Alicia's body jerked under him. She bucked violently trying to get free.

"But they're getting away," Shauna whined, and returned her attention to the older officer still at the side of Tory's body. "You *have* to go after them. This little girl isn't safe. None of us are safe."

"Stand back, Mrs. Weber. I've told you we have to wait here." The older officer spoke loudly over Lauren's cries.

"You're just going to let them escape?" Shauna harped.

"Don't worry about that. We'll set up road blocks and get them before they leave the county," the officer in charge said. "So you got a good look at them?"

"It was them, Brian and Alicia. Oh, my God, he just shot that woman. I can't believe it. She…she… I think she worked at Lauren's day care, and must have helped them, but she didn't deserve to die. Brian just turned the gun and shot her point blank when she tried to get away."

"We'll find them, Mrs. Weber." The older officer spoke loudly over the cries of the four-year-old. "Weren't you instructed when you phoned earlier to wait for our arrival before approaching the kidnappers?"

Shauna should have gone to Hollywood after graduation. She never skipped a beat. "If you hadn't taken so long we wouldn't be in danger now."

Lauren pulled Shauna's hair.

"Ow! You stup— Don't be a bratty child." She said the words, but looked at the officer as she held Lauren as far from her body as possible.

The officer in charge stood and placed a hand on Lauren's back, patting her, then held out his arms. Lauren went to him without any coaxing. He walked in circles, trying to calm her sobbing.

"When they turn their backs to us, we're going," John whispered. With all the distractions in front of the house, they could crawl safely to the back side of the barn.

"No." He felt her mouth form the word beneath his palm and felt the defeat rip through Alicia's torso. She struggled to push him from her.

John couldn't lessen his grip around her waist. There was no way he'd let her go. Gargantuan hadn't left by the front door and was probably in the woods by now. Weber hadn't told the cops he'd seen the big guy in the house, so the police wouldn't be looking for him. But the giant would definitely be looking for them.

With the death of the young woman who had taken Lauren, it was evident the Webers had no intention of leaving anyone alive who stood between them and the money. Until the money was legally in their control, Lauren was safe.

No one faced their direction.

John stood, tugging Alicia farther into the darkness, and she lashed out at him the entire way. He had to throw her over his shoulder before running behind a hay bale near the barn. He let her slide down his chest, back to the ground.

She took a step toward the circular drive. John clamped his arm around her thin waist and tugged her face into his shoulder. He'd watched the artificial way Lauren was being held. It broke his heart, but not half as much as Alicia's if he let her see it. There was nothing he could do.

"Now's not the time. It's suicide if we go back there."

It would be easier if she was unconscious. He'd had to do that once before on a rescue. It had been absolutely necessary and had saved six lives. But John had never forgiven himself for hitting the hysterical hostage to knock him out. No way could he hit Alicia.

Shauna's show of hysterics continued as she ranted to the younger officer, telling him not to listen to his superior. The officer issuing orders still held a crying Lauren. It was enough of a distraction without any help. Then she ran to Weber demanding he do something or chase them himself. When he stood, both officers raced to the tailgate.

They'd be in the clear for a solid couple of minutes, with the argument commencing. So long as they could make it behind the barn and possibly across the field. He caught Alicia's attention and pointed to the next hay bale, then gave a hand signal that they'd run in three, two—

"I can't leave her," she pleaded. "John, please. You have to get Lauren. Do something."

"Don't argue with me."

He ordered his heart to ignore her pleas. He didn't know how much time they had before the police backup arrived. He'd get Lauren. He just couldn't at this particular moment.

There were too many unknown variables. Only one gun, one clip, one chance at their vehicle. And if a cop discovered the rental on their way to the scene, they'd be stuck in the backwoods. Even if they managed to make the main road and call for an extraction, the rental would be discovered and they'd know John was in Texas via his best friend's name on the agreement.

Bottom line—he needed that anonymity edge to ensure Alicia was safe whether she liked it or not. He dragged her along with him until they were far enough away for her to concede. She ran next to him—silent, quick, physically okay. He knew she'd have a hard time forgiving his failure.

"We've got to get out of here before additional cops show up." He said it sternly. Whether for her benefit or to ease his conscience about leaving Lauren behind, he didn't know. He would assure her somehow that he'd rescue her daughter soon.

The car was where they'd left it, key in the ignition, phone on the seat. He went to remove the cut fence and she latched on to his arm.

"You're really not going back for her?"

He shook his head, unable to utter the word *no,* which had stuck in his throat. The defeat washed over her like a spray from a water hose, drenching her belief in him faster than that dousing in the lake.

"I thought you were a hotshot navy SEAL. You can help strangers all over the world but not my daughter." She shoved him away, covering her face to hide the silent tears.

The dig caught him unaware and right in his vulnerable spot. Around the world, but never at home. Same opinion Brian had of him.

She ran to the wire and yanked it back while he moved branches out of the way. He started the ignition and crept the car from the field. Once around the corner, he bolted down the dirt road, constantly watching for an approaching vehicle.

Their luck held and they were on the main road in less than three minutes.

"She begged me to help. How could you just leave her? What am I going to do now?" Alicia pressed her palms to her eyes, turned to the window. "How will she ever forgive me?"

John asked himself the same question about Alicia.

It took all his restraint not to turn the car around, rush onto the scene and remove Lauren by force. He wanted to swear he would—right then—or swear that he'd bring Lauren back no matter what. But he'd taken that oath before and been unable to keep it. She'd find out sooner or later that he wasn't the hero she needed.

John drove around the corner and continued another mile before turning on the headlights and calling Brian.

His brother answered Mabel's cell on the first ring. "Did you find Lauren?"

"Mabel's with you?"

"Why?"

"You need an alibi," John stated, thinking the same four-letter words his brother muttered into the phone.

"Did something happen to Lauren or Alicia?"

"No. We prevented whatever they had planned. We were also close to getting caught. There was a confrontation and I underestimated the opposition."

"Explain."

He recounted everything he'd seen, even that he had no idea why Alicia had followed him to the house. A vague idea that she'd never keep her promise to follow orders. Not that it mattered to the way he'd messed things up. But she might not be shutting down if she hadn't seen just how close he'd been to Lauren without rescuing her.

"Shauna identified us. Naming you and Alicia as the

kidnappers. I need to find a place that's safe while I clear Alicia's name. You need to delete Mabel's call history. The police can access it eventually, but it'll take a warrant instead of just a glance. It'll slow them down awhile. Give us some time to finish this thing."

"Got it. I'm assuming this is the last call for a while. I activated Dad's cell this afternoon. Use that number to call or text. You know, if Tory worked at the day care, I should be able to check her out. Maybe I can find out who this giant is. You said he stunk like horses? Only twenty or more horse ranches in the area."

"Alicia seemed to know her, but stay clear of it, Brian. I've got someone who can handle searching for info." He glanced at his silent passenger. Still crying. She hadn't uttered a word.

"That huge monster beat the girl up. Regularly. Fresh bruises on her face."

"Does Alicia recognize him?"

"I don't think she got a look at him."

"Did anyone actually see you?" Brian asked.

"If anyone did, it was Weber, but you shouldn't—"

"I was at the diner until it closed. Plenty of witnesses to back that up. No way I could get to the McKinney area to fight Weber's man. Mabel's here to verify what time I got home."

"I was so close, Brian."

"Do you need help? I've got a place where I stay in Fort Worth they don't know about."

"They'll be all over you even with the alibi." He watched Alicia out of the corner of his eye, wishing he knew what to do. "We should be fine. I need to make a call and will get back to you with details or if something else happens."

"Gotta go. Looks like the police chief is pulling up."

Alicia hadn't moved. He reached across her and snapped her seat belt. He needed to call Dev soon. That had been the plan. But he was disappointed in his personal failure. He'd let this woman down, badly.

"What's going to happen now?" she asked and sniffed, wiping her face.

"I'm not sure. We need to see what the locals do and regroup."

"You should have let me go to her."

"The police wouldn't have treated you well, Alicia. There was nothing either of us could do. You understand that, right?"

"I don't want to talk about it," she said with another sniff.

"But we have to."

"Did you shoot Tory?"

"Do you think I'd shoot her?"

"I… I'm— I didn't think you'd walk away and leave Lauren there, either." She shook her head, dropping her face in her hands again. "I don't know what to think. You're not the same man I knew twelve years ago."

"I hope I'm not. I was just a kid without a good head on my shoulders, who took advantage of his brother." *Not for the reasons everyone believes, but I still took advantage of his admission.* "Dammit, I didn't *want* to leave your daughter with those people."

He had no more explanations. *Excuses, you mean.* Better word choice, more accurate. Poor planning. Caught with his pants down. Disbelief when the woman sitting on him fell to her side, shot in the head. The strong emotions associated with this op overpowered his ability to think straight.

"For the record, I didn't shoot anyone. My weapon hasn't been fired. Check it." He leaned forward, pulled it from his back waistband and held it out to her. She'd been cleaning handguns since she could pull a trigger and knew what to do without any instruction, but she didn't take it from him. "It's a safe bet that Weber used one of Brian's or even Dwayne's."

"Patrick shot her? But when I heard the shot, he was holding Lauren. You mean she heard, maybe even saw him?" She tugged on his arm. "Turn around. Now. I'm begging you not to leave her with them. Oh, dear God. What are they going to do to her?"

"She's safe." *For now, at least.*

They couldn't go back. She acknowledged that in a matter of seconds with a deep, hurtful roar of hopelessness. It didn't matter that he was the person who'd made the decision to leave her little girl behind. It didn't matter that they needed to leave the area as fast as possible.

From here, he could keep them off the main roads and away from the search that would ensue. None of it mattered as much as the pain he heard next to him. He swung the car onto a dirt road, yanked the keys and jumped outside.

Right this minute, Alicia needed him as a friend, someone to hold her as she grieved. He'd never comforted a civilian before. It would be a new experience for him, but it was necessary. They weren't exactly touchy-feely in the navy. He'd compensate his lack of know-how with sheer willpower to take whatever she dished out without a negative response. Surely she'd get it together before he needed to say anything. Right?

Hoping any effort from him would help her, he opened the door, knelt awkwardly with a knee on the floorboard and pulled her into his arms. She resisted at first, grabbing the steering wheel with one hand and the seat belt with the other. When his strength won out, she collapsed against his chest.

"I don't want you to touch me," she said as her arms contradicted her, landing on either side of his neck. "Oh, God, Johnny. How could you let this happen?"

The words she muttered changed to giant sobs. He

just held her. None of her dislike of how he'd handled the extraction mattered. The physical stress mixed with the emotional upheaval of the past few days. She just needed someone to hang on to. And he was her only choice.

As her crying shuddered through her body, the strain tightened his muscles. He held her closer, skintight to keep her from breaking free. His jaw cracked with his own apprehension. If he had done something differently, would Alicia be holding Lauren instead of him?

Did she believe the failed rescue was his fault? She didn't really want an answer about how it had happened. Right? He could provide it. He'd written a hundred reports answering the hard question of how the best-planned op had detoured into a nightmare.

He didn't know what to say—if he should say anything at all. He'd never dealt with failure in a good way. It didn't sit well in his gut. But other botched operations didn't hold a candle to this one. Her crying shuddered to a stop as she pounded on his shoulder. She continued to chant, "Why, why, why," again and again. He could always push the doubt aside and eventually lock the memories in a place they didn't surface.

Very few ever involved children.

Not this. Not Alicia.

Someone as caring and giving as she was deserved to be protected, pampered. Deserved something to go right in her life. There was a long list of how he'd underestimated his opponent tonight. Another list of what he'd done wrong afterward. But there was only one promise he could make.

"No matter what it takes." No matter what it cost him—family or career. He'd give anything and everything. "I'll reunite you with your daughter."

She drew a deep, shuddering breath and tilted her questioning eyes in wonder at him. Instead of wanting to gently set her away and get back on the road, he wanted to keep her tucked close or kiss her into oblivion.

Damn it to hell, he was falling in love with her all over again.

Chapter Sixteen

Straighten up and fly right. Her dad's phrase from one of his favorite songs.

Why the words were in Alicia's mind at this particular moment, she had no idea. Was she ready to sit straight and stop lamenting over what had happened?

But John had left her child in the hands of murderers. Could she forgive him long enough to accept his help? She had to. She had no choice. She would rescue her daughter no matter what it took. *No matter what it took.* That was her answer.

It was time to leave the protection of his strong arms wrapped securely around her and determine what they needed to do next.

"You okay now?" he asked. The phone vibrated on the console.

"No. But I'll function." She tapped his shoulders, hoping he'd release her before she lost it again. "It's probably Devlin with news. You need to answer it."

"We have a lot of work ahead of us, you know." He stood, sweeping the phone into his hand at the same time. "Yeah?"

John walked to the front of the car and finished his conversation. The serious look on his face didn't really indicate whether the news was good or bad. The look was almost always there. She couldn't remember anything he'd asked Devlin or Brian to do before they'd gotten to the kidnappers' house. She'd been focused on following Patrick, on getting Lauren away from the monsters who had stolen her. She hadn't been listening to John's plans or if she'd been included.

Since this debacle had begun, he'd been multitasking, thinking ahead, planning the next move. Totally unlike the young recruit who had graduated from high school and left for boot camp without any plans to return. She'd admitted he'd changed.

So had she.

She'd become an adult, so it was logical that John had done the same. Gone were the boyish grin and the never-grow-up attitude. Replaced by a complete and focused concentration, along with a speak-when-spoken-to response.

She could handle that. Maybe. She wasn't as completely immune to the attraction between them as he seemed to be. Lying under him, even in a dangerous situation like minutes before, she'd found it hard not to remember the lean, sinewy muscles his body had developed. If he had any response to her, he hid it well.

Even when being in his arms gave her comfort, he seemed to pull back the passion. With one exception—their kiss in front of Joe. Both times she'd kissed him had jump-started her heart in a way she hadn't thought would ever be possible again after Dwayne died.

But she wasn't ready. There was too much chaos in her life, too many problems with no foreseeable solutions.

No matter what happened with her, John would leave anyway. He was here to help save his brother and Lauren. And when J.W. was better, he'd return to his mysterious assignments protecting the world. He'd never be satisfied pinned down with a family in their little country corner.

No, she was far from ready to fall for anyone. Especially him.

Don't read anything into those hugs other than their intent to keep you from falling completely apart. She was a soldier to him. Someone who needed to accomplish his goal. Nothing more. Nothing less.

John got back in the car in silence, turned it around and headed northeast—the opposite direction from the lake where Devlin was staying. She didn't mind a change in plans, but being included in the discussion every once in a while would be nice.

Who was she kidding? She had no experience and would follow his instructions and advice. She understood her limited role. And at the back of her mind there was the question of whether he'd dump her someplace safe to get her out of his hair. She needed to be mature, gain control of her emotions and be helpful. A faithful sidekick, not a hindering fool who screwed things up.

"Where are we going?"

"Dev checked the scanners. We're avoiding the police. Looks like the cops received a call from the Webers earlier, saying they'd been contacted by the kidnappers and had chosen to deliver the ransom themselves. By the time the police got to the ransom-exchange address, Patrick supposedly would have Lauren back."

"So they staged the entire event to make themselves look like heroes. But we interrupted and reinforced their claim that I was behind the abduction. I'm sorry I messed everything up."

"How do you figure that?" he asked, his voice deep and quiet.

"I couldn't sit in the car and wait. I thought you should know there was a second car. I thought Patrick had an accomplice who would get the jump on you or something. So I tried to warn you."

"I get that."

"Did Patrick plan to kill Tory before we showed up? Or was she killed because of me?" she asked, full of guilt that her presence may have caused the young woman's death.

John rubbed his free hand across his mouth and jaw stubble. Contemplating something. "Tell me about Patrick and Shauna."

"Like what?" He'd avoided her question, but she wouldn't forget to ask it again. She wanted to know the truth and take responsibility. Had Patrick hired Tory and her boyfriend to handle the kidnapping? If he had, then why had he brought a gun to pick up her daughter? It didn't make sense.

"For starters, did you think Weber was capable of shooting anyone?" John draped his wrist over the top of the wheel. Casual. Relaxed. Yet there was a tension in the way he sat and the way he constantly searched the mirrors.

"No. I'm still having a hard time absorbing it. You don't think it was an accident or that he was aiming at you? I mean, he knew Tory from Lauren's day care."

They were in the middle of nowhere. Illuminated only by the dashboard lights, John's face was all sharp angles and serious glare. Either deep in thought or terribly irritated. She couldn't tell. Either way she had a strange feeling she wouldn't like what he was about to say.

"Alicia." He pulled to a stop sign and faced her. "Weber didn't hesitate to shoot that woman, and he did it with Lauren on his hip."

"What does that mean?"

"I think he's done it before and had gone there with the intention of killing the two witnesses to the actual kidnapping. Then there'd only be Lauren, who would sound confused since she knew Tory from her school."

"Oh, my gosh. Who do you think he's killed before today?" Fear clogged her throat, but she swallowed the lump and pushed it away. She could be scared later, when she was alone. Not now. Now she had to help get her little girl back. Who could it have been? A slow realization filled her. "You think he killed Roy Adams."

"It's a logical assumption. Dwayne was...gone. If Roy was dead, Shauna would inherit. Did she know about Lauren's trust fund receiving the bulk of the money?"

"No. I mean, I don't think so. I didn't know about it either, honestly. Roy probably changed his will after Dwayne died."

"Where was his body found, again?" His free hand rubbed his chin in thought. It softened his chiseled features.

"At the old barn Joe told us about."

"Why was he out there when the stables are nowhere nearby?"

She shook her head. "I'm sorry, John, but I really don't know. I was sort of in a daze after Dwayne's accident. Lauren was six months old. I had to put Dad in a full-care facility. And Roy convinced me to move back to his house. Shauna hated that, of course. I moved to Denton a couple of months later when I went back to work full-time. It made more sense to live closer to the hospital."

"You didn't see any signs?"

"As in signs of depression? No. I didn't see him as often after we moved. Roy seemed preoccupied. But Shauna made the town aware she'd been hiding his depression from everyone, especially me."

"But you don't think he committed suicide?"

"At the time? I didn't want to believe it could happen to someone so close to me, but it's what the authorities concluded. I didn't know to question their decision."

More than anything, she'd felt betrayed by the last person who'd given her emotional support. A very selfish thought to have. And then the guilt had hit her. She was a health-care professional, and several people had asked how she'd missed his depression. They'd almost accused her of being responsible.

"And what about now?" John asked.

"After Shauna and Patrick have kidnapped Lauren and killed Tory? I think Roy's *suicide* was very *convenient*." She wanted to confront them both and demand the truth. "It also makes me wonder if Dwayne actually had an accident. Roy questioned it all the time."

John shoved the car in gear, putting on a little too much gas, fishtailing a bit as the tires left gravel and connected with pavement. He hit the dashboard and then searched for the cell he'd tossed on the console.

"What's wrong?" She placed the phone in his hand so he could keep his eyes on the road. "I can help, if you let me."

"You should have said something." He tapped the breaks to slow down.

"Told you what, John? I don't understand."

"People are dropping around you like flies, woman. Haven't you noticed?"

"Noticed?" The shaky breath she managed to pull in barely stayed the tears of hurt from cascading down her cheeks. Hurt or fright? "I've done more than *notice* the ones I've loved leaving me. I've lived it. You can't possibly think Patrick and Shauna killed them both?"

John stared at her so long, she thought he might have forgotten he was driving the car. He got that look on his face. Troubled. Hurting. Haunted. The same things she felt deep down, especially when she was alone.

"I think there's something in that barn. Or there was. Something to make your father-in-law become preoccupied and stop seeing you and his grandchild. There's no other reason for Roy to hang out there like you said he was doing."

"Will knowing help get Lauren back?"

"We have to do more than get your daughter back, Alicia. Only the truth will get your and Brian's lives back. It's all connected. We just have to determine how and prove it."

"I can't believe I missed all this. You've been home less than a week and have uncovered so much. If I hadn't been caught up in my own little world of problems, I would have—"

"Stop beating yourself up. No one else noticed, either. No one had a reason to notice or suspect foul play. If there's one thing I've learned during twelve years of deployment around the world—" John paused, visibly swallowed hard "—evil has a habit of disguising itself to get whatever it wants."

The cold authority in his voice sent a chill down Alicia's spine.

Chapter Seventeen

It was a clear night, and the moon provided enough light to see through the open field and the overgrown path to Roy's barn. John cut the car's lights when he left the road. Each bumpy lurch of the small car felt like crossing a gully—lots of bumps as a result of nonuse. He wouldn't have cared if he hadn't spent the past two hours driving in circles, waiting for Alicia to fall into an exhausted slumber.

He pulled the rental slowly through the forgotten alfalfa and weeds on the far side of the run-down barn. Run-down, but he noticed a fairly new air-conditioning unit added crookedly in the middle of the wall. Odd, since units like that normally fit into windows. Whatever Roy had been doing out here either had been moved somewhere else, or no one felt it important, since it was obvious no one had kept this property maintained since his death.

The phone vibrated in his lap. He ignored it as he had the three times before. He hadn't answered it, fearing even his voice would wake Alicia. She'd been pushed to her limit. Everything had been taken from her and if she didn't get some rest, he wasn't sure how she'd react the next time something happened.

And the way his luck had been running, it—whatever *it* was—would definitely go wrong and happen. Military ops coordinated from halfway around the world seemed a lot easier than dealing with the unpredictable rationale of civilians.

Leaving the military would be a huge change. An idea that he was getting more comfortable accepting.

He parked the car and got out without jarring the vehicle too much. The inside bulb was still taped over, so no light shone on his sleeping beauty. He jogged out of earshot and answered the vibrating cell. "Yeah?"

"Where the hell have you been?" His brother sounded loud without raising his voice. Somehow he'd always been able to do that.

Then again, Brian's voice hadn't only come through the cell. He spun around and was face-to-face with his short-haired twin.

"When I texted where we were going, I didn't expect you to meet us here. You weren't followed?" Inadequacy reared its ugly head as John searched for the car he'd missed or additional cars on the horizon.

"I came on horseback." Brian threw a thumb toward the south end of the barn, indicating where he'd left the animal. "The deputy assigned to me is parked on the road, probably sound asleep by now. It's not my first time avoiding a tail."

Brian shoved saddlebags into his chest with an extra push that forced John back a step. His twin wasn't elaborating on "avoiding a tail," and as much as he wanted to ask about the past twelve years, he couldn't. He had other things to worry about.

"There was no way I was going to let Mabel get any more involved by bringing you food." Brian continued moving. He was always moving, never seeming to relax around him at all. "Which she insisted you'd need by now."

"Thanks. She was right, but you shouldn't be here." His words sounded as forced as they felt. Maybe he was as *unrelaxed* around Brian as it seemed his *big* brother was around him.

"Grow up." Brian threw his hands above his head and turned to walk to his tethered horse. "Did you expect Mabel to come?"

"I didn't ask for any food and I didn't ask for your help."

"But you got it anyway, didn't you?" He spun on his booted toe. "You're back three days and you manage to drag Dad and Mabel into a dangerous situation right along with you. We're all supposed to just chip in, follow your orders and lie through our teeth so you can play the big badass navy SEAL coming to the rescue."

"What does that mean?" He hadn't asked to become involved in the kidnapping. There wasn't any way to explain that to free his brother he'd had no choice but to get involved.

Brian threw his hands lamely in the air. "Forget it. We're all in this up to our necks now. You've got no right to keep us in the dark."

"Us? Meaning you. Why? How did *you* plan to rescue Alicia? I seem to remember you were in jail and she was headed there." The old Brian would never believe the deciding factor to leave Dad and jump into this fray was to clear Brian's name. It hadn't happened twelve years ago, so why would the selfish brother do it now? Right? At this exact moment he didn't really know the answer to that question, either.

"I don't know, but I wouldn't have put Dad and Mabel at risk of landing there, too." Brian scratched his freshly shorn head and pressed his lips together as if he wanted to say something, but he wouldn't. "Dammit, I probably would've done the same thing. It's not like you had much choice."

"I can tell it hurt to admit that." It had always been hard for him to admit Brian was right, and he hadn't enjoyed the experience. He should confess, too. One more minute to enjoy this moment. Involving them had been a tough

on-the-spot decision. It had been his only choice, but that
didn't make it the right one.

Brian paced liked a caged animal. The area was six
square feet. The same size as a jail cell. Something more
was bothering his brother. Bothered him, too. They needed
to talk. It just wasn't the right time.

Would it ever be? Not really.

"I didn't pick this fight," he admitted. It was the best
he could do.

"You're saying you aren't responsible for dragging us
into this mess?" Brian asked through clenched teeth, his
hands balled into fists.

"I couldn't let Alicia go to jail." *And can't admit that
wasn't the only reason you became involved.*

"But letting me go there was just fine. Of course, I
should be used to that by now. Right?"

"So we're back to the fire? Well, going to jail while they
investigated was your choice back then, since I didn't need
defending. I didn't do anything."

"Forget it. That subject is dead. Buried." Brian looked
around him, through him, but not *at* him. He didn't meet
his eyes, but he didn't walk away.

"Not quite buried. More like a zombie that rises at every
occasion. Sure doesn't seem dead."

"There's nothing left to talk about."

"How about the truth?" Maybe now was the right time
to talk about it after all? "I fought with Alicia. She caught a
ride before I could catch her. The party broke up. I looked
around and our truck was gone. I put the fire out and
walked to the old clubhouse."

"You must have done a half-ass job putting it out, since
the barn burned to the ground. I knew you were drunk,
and shouldn't have let Dwayne talk me out of dragging
you home."

His brother spoke with such venom and resentment.

Had he been feeling that way the entire twelve years or had the hatred been gaining ground with each year they'd been separated? Was it anger that had kept him from coming home to face Brian? Not recently. But a long time ago, he'd been pretty mad.

"That's the thing, Brian. I wasn't drunk. I saw you with Alicia. *You* were the one completely wasted that night. We argued after you made a play for my girl and I didn't believe Alicia when she said nothing happened."

"You're crazy. I wouldn't do that. Besides, Dwayne took me home." The pacing stopped. Brian stood, grinding a fist into his palm. Ready to fight. Maybe even subconsciously inviting a fight.

John's fist twitched, responding, until he forced his fingers open. He just shook his head. "That story's full of holes. I'm telling you, the truck was gone. I walked and wasn't drunk."

"If you didn't leave the fire going, then who went back? They had a witness who saw our truck there. Why lie about what happened, Johnny? You trying to convince Alicia you're worthy of her? Better wait until she's actually around."

His brother really believed the dribble he spouted. Even under moonlight, John could see the sincerity and confidence. Two minutes ago he'd been tired, worn-out and wanting to avoid another confrontation. The itch to fight and settle this once and for all was there, and no matter how exhausted he'd been, adrenaline kicked him into full gear.

Throughout their childhood and high school years they'd settled their differences with a fight. Rolling on the ground, punching kidneys, ripping shirts and jeans along the way. Why should now be any different? It had just taken twelve years to have it out about this one.

Without thinking too much about it, he rammed a sore

shoulder into Brian's gut and they tumbled to the ground. Brian landed a hard fist in his side. Already bruised from Gargantuan's punches, John yelled in pain.

"Admit that you left the fire burning," Brian shouted, throwing another punch that rattled John's teeth.

"Admit that you felt guilty about making a play for Alicia and never gave me the chance to tell you the truth." John threw his own fist to crack Brian's jaw, then clamped his mouth shut to stop the groan of pain he wanted to release. His knuckles and lots of other body parts were already raw due to his earlier brawl.

They rolled in a deadlock, equally matched and equally tired. Brian groaned after a flip to his back when John landed a knee close to his groin. Then they reversed and broke apart as he narrowly avoided a furious knee slamming onto his chest.

He locked his arm behind Brian's head but couldn't finish the defensive move without snapping his brother's neck. He needed a minute to catch his breath and decide where to go. In the past, the victor had won the argument. Problem solved. But winning wouldn't resolve this ongoing problem between them.

Finding out the truth would.

"Well, it's about time." A very feminine voice laughed.

John looked upside down into Alicia's gorgeous smile as she bent over them. She didn't appear mad at all.

They both relaxed their grips just like they'd been caught fighting by their mother all those years ago. They rolled off one another and scrambled to their feet. He expected Alicia to scold them for being stupid. Instead she stretched open her arms, running to them and pulling them into an embrace.

"How much did you hear?" John asked over her shoulder.

"Did you really expect me to stay asleep with the two of you yelling at each other?"

John's eyes connected with his twin's, reflecting the shock he felt. Alicia's face was buried between them but he thought she muttered something about waiting a long time for this fight to clear the air.

"Wait a minute," Brian said, pulling back from the awkward group hug. "I wouldn't say anything's been cleared up." He wiped the blood from his lip with the back of his hand.

"I agree." John set Alicia slightly away from him, half expecting her to stomp her foot in frustration.

John edged his tongue across his own lip, itching to wipe the wetness away, not ready to admit Brian had drawn blood.

"But you're finally fighting it out. If you'd done this that night, we could have avoided the strained relationships and years of hurt."

Brian backed farther away. "Nothing would have changed, Alicia. He was a jerk of a kid, always avoiding getting blamed for anything."

"Is that what you think? You've really believed I was guilty all these years? You think I was drunk and irresponsible. That I set the fire and couldn't face the truth?"

"I think I'll wait in the barn." Brian darted around the building.

"Oh, no, you don't, Brian Sloane." Alicia did stomp her foot and shout. Brian returned as far as the corner and leaned against the aging wall. "You two are going to get this over with, even if it requires a broken nose." She pointed her finger at him, then back around at Brian. "Or two. Now get on with it."

"There's nothing to argue about," his brother said, visibly clenching his jaw and swallowing hard. "He won't admit he was there."

Watching his twin, he realized just how much their gestures revealed. He was bone weary and emotionally done

and Brian didn't look much better. He was holding his right
ribs—not the left, where John's fist had connected several times. Somebody left-handed had taken some shots.

Alicia looked expectantly at him to start the reconciliation. He stuck his hand out in front of him and shrugged.
"What do you want me to say? I wasn't."

"Well, let's start with who drove the truck home that
night. It wasn't me. I rode home with Trina Kaufman. Or
I drove her home listening to her snores." Alicia put her
hands on her hips, forcing Brian not to turn away. She
flicked a finger and he responded like a little kid, shuf-
fling forward, back within arm's distance.

Do I look like that?

Was that a bit of courage straightening his own spine?
This slip of a woman, in spite of all the problems she'd
faced, would be the driving force behind resolving the
feud with his brother. She had courage and stamina worthy of any navy SEAL. He should be ashamed it had come
to this, but in a way, he was relieved.

For better or worse, the time had come to clear the air.

"It doesn't sound like either of us drove Granddad's
truck home," he said, drawing on the courage to see the
conversation through without throwing another punch. "I
was in the tree house."

"I stayed at Dwayne's," Brian mumbled.

Realization hit John about the same time as Brian. Neither of them was responsible for the fire. Twelve years of
anger could have been avoided.

"So neither of you drove the truck home. But there
were witnesses who saw the truck leaving Mrs. Cook's
after the fire started."

"Son of a bitch." Brian turned away from Alicia with a
string of curses and a fist slamming the rotten barn wall.
"Anyone could have taken the truck. We always left the

keys in it at those things since we shared it. Everybody knew that. I mean, we never thought anyone would steal it."

"Someone framed us good enough that even *we* bought the story." John wanted to punch something through the barn wall. He settled for slamming his fist into his palm.

"And since you never asked each other," Alicia continued, "you just assumed the other was responsible."

"Yeah. We were idiots and have paid the price for our stupidity," Brian admitted for them both.

"Twelve years." Alicia's body relaxed. Her arms went above her head and smoothed her curly hair, pulling it into a ponytail and twisting it into a knot. "Twelve frustrating years of silence when a two-minute conversation would have resolved everything. Men."

The soothing gesture hit him somewhere between his heart and lower regions. Sexy, natural, pleasing. It was all of the things he wanted but seemed far out of his reach.

He heard the cell vibrating in the dirt where he'd dropped it during the scuffle with Brian. His brother plopped easily on the ground to sit and answered it as he scooped it up. Speaker on, it was flat in his brother's palm before John could object.

"Sloane, cop scanner has them heading for this place. Somebody must have reported seeing you here. I'm taking a few essentials and packing out since you took my rental and your vehicle seems compromised." Devlin's stressed voice filled the awkward silence.

"Sorry, man."

"It'll take me a half hour to trek this stuff to another car. Where we meeting up?"

"That location I had you checking out. We're there now."

"Roger. Gotta run. Literally."

The line disconnected and Brian held out the phone. John grabbed it, shoving the thing in his back pocket.

He checked his lower back. No weapon—not in the dirt anywhere. Man, he'd left it in the car. What was wrong with him?

His brother stretched and yawned. Relaxed. Really relaxed and comfortable. He touched his forehead and then shoved his hand across the high and tight haircut. "Dammit, I hate short hair. Top of my head'll be sunburned for sure first time I feed the horses."

"Tell me about it." He scratched his own scruff, noticing they now had the same exact cut. "I've lost my cover a time or two in training. Sunburn up top is the worst."

Mabel would make a great military barber.

"Well, not the worst. I remember your mother talking about you two skinny-dipping one summer," Alicia dropped casually as she picked up the saddlebags. "Didn't you both fall asleep without any clothes?"

They all burst out laughing. That had been a miserable week spent sitting in alcohol and oatmeal baths. "At least when we fell asleep we were in the shade and not trying to lose our tan lines."

"Oh, my gosh, the burn I got that summer was horrible." Alicia protectively covered her breasts.

He remembered the miserable couple of days she'd walked around braless. Just as miserable for him and his imagination as for her and her sunburned flesh.

"Both of us were sicker than dogs," Brian said, still on the ground, one arm draped over a bent knee. "What now?"

He wished he knew. John was surprised his brother had asked the question instead of Alicia. But at a glance he knew she'd wanted to. It was in her eyes, along with the worry and fright concerning the unknown. Still there. She might smile and laugh, but it was still there.

"I, for one, am hoping there's food in those saddlebags." She headed for the hand-tooled leather.

Brian nodded. "Mabel sent something. I threw in a

change of clothes. My old boots are still on my saddle. Just in case you need to go into town impersonating me. Not many people look my direction or talk much to me, so you won't need to get up-to-date on my life or anything to keep up," he added with an unfamiliar smirk.

"I'll keep that in mind."

"And never smile. Brian never, ever smiles when he's in town," Alicia teased.

"Right."

What was the tension he was picking up between these two? Was it real? Or just a continuation of the night of the fire? She'd told him that what he'd seen had all been a joke. A simple dare from Brian's friends. He hadn't found it that funny, and they'd argued. Then they'd broken up afterward because of him not believing her.

At least he thought they had. They must have. Great. He felt like he was eighteen again. Confused emotions and a growing ache for Alicia that just wouldn't stop—no matter who was around or what danger they were in.

He wanted to pull her close to him. Her arms were still above her head, so they'd fall on his shoulders and her breasts would end up flush with his chest. The image of her next to him was so clear in his mind, he shook his head to get rid of it.

When he opened his eyes, she stood close in front of him, a perplexed wrinkle between her brows. But Brian... he had a knowing look. An "I told you so" laugh that turned into a short approving whistle.

"Where were you just now?" Alicia asked, still searching his face with questioning dark blue eyes.

"Yeah, brother dearest, where were you?"

Brian knew exactly where he'd been. No doubt about it. Behind Alicia's back he spotted his brother mouthing, *It's about damn time.* The momentary panic trying to creep up his spine was just confusion at his brother's perceptive grin. His twin seemed…almost happy at the prospect he was having thoughts about Alicia. Didn't his brother want her for himself?

Brian shook his head and muttered, "You're still an idiot."

"You're both idiots and we're wasting time," Alicia said, turning from John to face Brian, with a bit of apple between her lips. "You're no better than he is, you know. By the way, I'm sorry you went to jail because of me."

"No big deal."

"It's always a big deal." She dragged a finger across Brian's jaw. "That's not from your scuffle with John. Sure wish we had a frozen bag of peas to put on it. I really am sorry."

Brian's gaze connected with his and he took a quick couple of steps away from Alicia. If his brother could read him, he was definitely picking up on the instant jealousy that had taken over with an instant thought that had popped in his head.

Mine!

Her sympathy should be directed at him. John. *He* was the one who had the crap beat out of him by a giant while trying to unsuccessfully rescue her child.

Get past it. She isn't yours. She's with you because she has no other choice. Just move on and find her daughter. Then you can get the hell away from her and whatever this possessiveness is all about.

Right. Past her. Past the feeling of wanting someone who was much too good for him. He didn't deserve anyone as special as Alicia Adams. He knew it even if no one else did.

Chapter Eighteen

"What are we going to do now?" Shauna screeched as soon as the housekeeper had taken Lauren upstairs.

Break your neck so the endless screeching will stop. The situation was heartbreaking to only himself, but Patrick admitted he'd have to endure several weeks of screeching before it would ever stop. But he could dream.

The brat had screamed and cried for her mother every minute after the police escort to the station. She'd shut up as soon as he'd reminded her of what had happened to her babysitter. In fact, she hadn't uttered a word after he'd whispered in her ear. He wished the same could be said for Shauna.

Patrick watched his hysterical wife frantically twist a strand of the red frizz she took an hour to straighten every time she saw it in a mirror. He hated her hair. Almost as much as he hated her. The dyed color was purple in fluorescent light, nowhere near the red on the box. He knew only because she'd ranted for days and days that they should sue the hair-color company.

In his sad, wimpy way, he'd agreed with her until she'd moved on to the next threat of a lawsuit and rant.

Tory had had lovely hair.

He sat on the end of the couch and flipped up the built-in footrest. "You've got the kid, dear. Isn't that what you wanted?"

He yawned. As soon as his head hit the pillow, he'd sleep like a hibernating bear. He opened his mouth to suggest they head upstairs. Then reconsidered. He knew his partner in crime needed to spout her concerns out loud and he didn't want the housekeeper hearing her.

I wonder if I could slip a sleeping pill into her drink? Or two or three?

She'd pass out on the couch and he'd have the bed to himself, minus the stench of her night creams and moisturizers.

No. If he did, she would oversleep in the morning and the complaining would be worse. Tomorrow was an early one. Lots of bathroom prep for the camera attention she craved.

"The police suspect something. I know they do." Shauna poured herself a two-finger drink of his good scotch and shot it back easier than water.

"Keep your voice down. As long as you don't talk about it, they won't have any idea we're behind everything." *Same as you have no idea I've been pulling all the strings for years.* He sat forward, no longer relaxed, needing to be alert to keep her calm. "You heard them at the station. They issued a warrant for Alicia."

She slammed the glass down on the bar. "But not Brian. He was there. You saw him sitting under your girlfriend. That bitch, Mabel, is lying for him."

"Why does it matter so much? It's Alicia you want destroyed, right?"

She twisted more of her straw-like hair. Then pulled at the bottom of her shirt. She'd freak out when she realized that the kid had gotten dirt all over the frilly white thing Shauna had worn. His wife had wanted to be photographed in the see-through blouse after they'd "rescued" Lauren.

Everything was about appearances and the money. *Nothing wrong with money as long as you have plenty of it.* Even Tory had been all about the money. More of it. Every question had been about the money and how they were going to use it to get to Paris.

Well, he'd been to Paris and had no desire to go back. The money would last longer on a beach in Mexico, and that was where he was headed as soon as this crap was done. The kid would officially be in their custody and shipped off to a boarding school. God, how long would *that* take?

Shauna would come with him, of course. He already had her careful scrawling signature down pat. So he wouldn't have to put up with her too long while he transferred all the money to himself.

Once she's gone…heaven.

"Are you listening to me?"

"Of course I am, sweetheart." *Not really. My fantasies are much better company.*

He was lucky he didn't choke on the endearment. He'd transfer the money as fast as he could and would savor choking her scrawny neck. He had dreamed about it several times and would have all the details planned. He'd insist they rent a sailboat, small enough he could manage it on his own. Even now he could envision her tanned skin in one of those bright white string bikinis she liked to wear. He'd bring her a drink—something fruity so she'd sip it slowly. She'd sit up on her towel; he'd offer to put more lotion on her back to keep her from burning.

Then he'd slip his fingers gently across her larynx and tighten his grip. She starved herself all the time, so she'd be unable to fight back. Weak, she had no strength. Not like him.

Wait, that wouldn't do. If he was behind her, he couldn't see her eyes bulge and then go dead. Forget the drink. He'd untie the strings and make her think he wanted sex on the deck. Maybe he'd have her one last time before squeezing the breath from her and cracking her spine.

He'd always wanted to snap a spine. Had always been curious if you could really hear the pop like the sound effects they used in the movies and on television. Would it be as easy? Did it require practice? It wouldn't hurt to practice. Maybe he'd get a chance once or twice before the sailing excursion.

"What are you smiling at?"

Her whispered shout drug him back to reality.

"You, darling." He deliberately smiled bigger at her. If it irritated her, he just had to continue.

"There's nothing to smile about," she droned on. "It's obvious she's hired help. I have no idea where she got any money. Probably from that drug-dealer boyfriend of hers."

So they were still discussing how Brian Sloane could be sitting at the Aubrey Diner counter and not lying on the ground under Tory. He'd almost hated to pull the trigger and end that scene. She'd been clawing at him and he hadn't punched her once. The sheer strength in the man's hands was admirable. And deadly. A true killer in the making. *Or breaking.*

He'd never noticed that about Brian before. And the new haircut… Why had he shorn his head?

"You know there's another possibility of how Brian could be in two places at the same time." Why hadn't he reasoned it out before?

"What are you blathering about?" She crossed her arms under her tiny breasts.

Tory had a terrific stack up top. *Had. Past tense.* "John. He's back. He probably returned the day your private detective took the picture. Think about it. We've waited weeks for Alicia to do something with Brian. But remember, love, she was always *John's* girlfriend."

"Oh, my God. That explains everything. We have to call the police." She made a beeline to the phone.

"There's no rush, honey. You can have an epiphany during your interview tomorrow."

They'd already been contacted by the local news stations. Shauna had given her cell number to all of them. She'd answered the questions during their initial conversation with the county sheriff, which had frustrated the man to no end. It was definitely laughable.

Playing the silent incompetent had quickly grown tiring. But he'd sat there, letting Shauna do all the talking. Seeming in control. It wouldn't be long now. Just a matter of days and he could stop acting. They'd sell the rest of the Adams property, have the cash in the bank, control of the kid's trust fund, and all the ties to his small-town past working in stalls ankle deep in horse manure would be broken.

"What if they snatch Lauren back? Or decide to kill us in our sleep?"

"That's being slightly dramatic, dear. If Sloane—no matter which one—wanted to kill us, I imagine he could have accomplished that easily tonight. I'm sure both of them have had enough practice with a gun not to miss. And whoever was there had every opportunity. The man restrained himself from hitting Tory when they were squirming on the ground together." He remembered the power of pulling the trigger and watching the blood spread across her blond hair. The ground had darkened as it pooled beneath the yellow halo.

Knowing that he'd been in control of Tory's life excited him. His only regret was not moving closer. Had she known she was dying? Or was shooting her in the head as instantaneous as they claimed?

Then again, the surprise on Sloane's face had been priceless. That was where he'd really been watching. If it had been John, why was he so affected by the measly death of a day-care worker? Hadn't he seen death hundreds of times over while in the military?

Shauna was wringing her hands again and reaching for the phone. "They could find that girl's boyfriend and force him to admit that we hired him. He's still missing, you know."

He wrapped her skinny fingers within his fists. "I couldn't take care of him tonight. John or Brian—whoever was helping Alicia—was fighting him when I walked out with the money." He kissed her fingertips instead of squeezing to demand she stop. "I'm sure Tory's boyfriend is getting as far away from Aubrey, Texas, as possible. And if not, I can convince him to work for us a bit longer."

"Why didn't you take care of them all? You said you would. That was the plan. You said it wouldn't be a problem for you to shoot them and make it look like self-defense."

God, she was tiresome. "Shauna, neither of us could predict that Alicia would find the kid. I still don't know how they did."

"They probably followed you, you fool." She jerked her fingers from his and circled the room where not four hours ago they'd gone over the plan while having a glass of wine to soothe her nerves.

"Why don't you have another drink before we head to bed, sweetheart?" He poured another scotch, hating to part with any drop of it, but knowing she'd pass out sooner if he did. "You'll have to look your best for the local talk shows tomorrow. Remember, darling, you're a hero."

Before handing her the drink, he faked a passionate kiss, pretending it was Tory pressed against him. She sipped and he let his hands caress her skin, drawing his thumbs across her protruding collarbone.

It would be so easy to be rid of his annoying problem.

All he'd have to do was squeeze.

Chapter Nineteen

"I sure hope the air conditioner works in there. Especially if we're stuck inside all day. It's going to be another scorcher." Alicia wiped the sweat from under her neck, leaving the men gawking at each other.

Joking about the good old days might smooth things over between John and Brian, but it was so long ago.... What kind of memory would her daughter have of this? How would she ever let Lauren out of her sight again? Kids getting sunburned on the banks of the creek didn't compare to your day-care teacher being shot in front of you by a person who you thought of as a grandparent.

Keep a lid on it. Don't fall apart or John will check you into the psych ward for observation.

Alicia could only stare at her shaking hands. In fact, there was a tremor throughout her entire body that wouldn't stop. She couldn't control the fright that was bubbling somewhere close to the fear that she'd never see her daughter again. She broke into a trot, heading in the direction John had parked.

God above, please keep my legs steady enough so I don't fall flat on my face.

She needed to be alone for a few minutes before diving into whatever had kept her father-in-law inside that barn. There was so much to take in that her mind went blank.

Her only thought was to take one step at a time. Put her tennis shoe on the ground without turning her ankle and without tripping and falling. *One step. Another step.*

When she reached the car, she dropped her head against the cool metal of the roof, locked her knees in place and refused to cry.

"Don't lose it. You'll be okay." She'd chanted those words often enough in the past four years.

But she was far from okay. Tory was dead and her daughter had witnessed the woman's murder. Could she force herself to be in control? She'd done it before—she had to do it again. There wasn't a choice.

She turned around, leaning on the car and twisting her knotted hair into a tighter mess. It just took so much concentration to pretend. Constantly shoving the images of the night's events aside made her draw on a strength she hadn't used since Dwayne's funeral.

Her fingers were hot against her face as she scrubbed her eyes and held her breath for a moment. There was nothing there. Nothing left to draw from. After her husband's death, she'd replenished her empty heart by clinging to his daughter. And Roy had clung to them both.

What could she do? *Think of something else.*

The fight between Brian and John had taken her straight back to refereeing them in their teens. Even with all this stress, those happy days brought a smile. The brothers had bloody lips. She'd witnessed a restraint in John that had never been there in high school. He'd done his best to get the better of Brian back then.

Maybe he was as exhausted as she felt. Her short nap had only made her more tired. But it was more sleep than John had achieved. And she hadn't fought a giant of a man earlier or had an emotional encounter with her twin.

Nope, she'd just left her daughter in the hands of murderers. That was all she'd accomplished today. "Dear

Lord." Her eyes burned with the hint of tears. *Focus on something else. You can't do this each time you think of Lauren.*

"You okay?"

At first glance, she thought John had followed her. The voice was the same. But Brian was close to her elbow, then patting her shoulder. Brian, her longtime friend.

"John's taking a look around. Hop in, I'm moving the car into the barn." He walked around the hood, the moon shining on his new "high and tight" haircut.

That was what John had called it in high school when Mabel had shorn his head with the ancient hair clippers his dad owned. "High and tight, Miss Mabel. Not one of those jarhead trims," he'd said.

She took a deep breath, wiped her eyes again and stood straight, then asked Brian, "Did he tell you what happened out there tonight?"

"The bare basics." He leaned on the roof opposite her. "I'm sorry."

"I really wish things were different, you know?" She slapped the car hard enough to make her hand sting. "Ow, darn it."

They both laughed—kind of. *So he feels just as weird as I do.*

"I made a pass at you the night of the fire, didn't I?"

"Yes."

"I pretended to be my brother for some reason. Right?"

"Yes. The guys dared you to find out if you and Johnny kissed the same, since you were physically identical."

"We wore the same jeans, boots and jackets that night? That's the reason no one knew which one of us left when. But you didn't need a kiss to know I wasn't him. How did you always know?"

"I'm not sure. But I've been able to tell you apart since

the first day on the bus. You have two completely different attitudes about everything."

"I know. But that's not it. We can act like each other when we want to." He raised his brows, dipping his chin to his chest. The twins' longtime gesture to let her know that she was behind the curve.

"What do you think it is? Just tell me, please. Or do you really know?" Of course she was curious. She'd never been able to put her finger on the reason.

He tapped the hood with his finger a couple of times. Nothing dramatic, just a pause while he made up his mind. "I guess it's about time somebody set you two straight. Shoot. John looks at you differently. Always has."

"Like how?"

"Alicia, honey, my brother's been in love with you since he laid eyes on your skinny chicken legs in sixth grade." He got in the car. "If you need to hit someone, I recommend John."

She followed to the driver's side and bent to the open window. "I'm not going to hit you. I hardly believe a word out of your mouth." She laughed. On purpose, to cover her nervousness that Brian might actually be right. "Let him know I need a minute to think. That's why I came out here."

"I overheard Mom talking to Dad about it once. Way back in junior high, she told him you'd make a good daughter-in-law someday."

"There is no way on God's green earth that John Sloane has always been in love with me. We're friends. Same as you and me." She playfully gave a soft shove to his shoulder. "Stop foolin' around, Brian. He left, for gosh sakes. Just joined the navy and never looked back."

A sadness turned his playfulness into a death shroud.

"Alicia?" He caught her hand, stopping her from walking away.

She searched the stars for the strength to face him. She knew he wasn't John. He was right; somehow even their touch was different to her. But his voice, combined with the same haircut, made it hard to remember. And there was something in the way he'd said her name and held her hand that tugged at her heart.

"Yes?" She didn't bend down. She couldn't take him feeling sorry for her. She'd start crying for certain and lose it again.

"Give him a chance, will ya?"

Brian released her, started the car and pulled away.

Give him a chance?

"To do what?" she asked the retreating car.

She watched Brian pull into the barn and John shut the doors. Her legs wobbled under her, so she plopped to the hard, dry earth. *Give him a chance?* A chance to keep her out of jail? A chance to rescue Lauren? A chance to save her life? A chance to break her heart again?

Their time for chances had long passed. Twelve years ago the opportunity for *chances* had come and gone. Gone. Gone. Gone.

Chapter Twenty

Alicia had one objective, and that was to get her daughter back in her arms and keep her safe. Nothing else mattered. Nothing.

She leaned back and rested on her elbows, then lay down on the sun-shriveled stalks of Johnson grass, folding her arms under her head. She could tell herself over and over again that nothing else mattered. She could spell it with giant capital letters and try to believe she was telling herself the truth.

But she wasn't.

John mattered. The shock and hurt she'd seen in him. The way he'd held her. The way they'd kissed. Lord, was it just yesterday that they'd been at Roy's house and escaped the police chief by climbing into the tree?

"Good. Grief." So much had happened since John had come home. There was no way he loved her. No way. He couldn't. Could he?

"No way," she shouted to the stars. Brian had to be wrong. Either way, it didn't matter. Not now. They all had one objective, and that was to get Lauren back.

A soft breeze blew the treetops at the edge of the field, but it was the sound of feet crunching the dying grass that made her jerk to a sitting position.

"Did Brian upset you? Are you all right? I heard you cry

out and—" John said, out of breath. He must have sprinted from the barn door.

"Of course I am. I was just…just…" She couldn't tell him she'd been weighing what she valued and he'd come in the top two. She wasn't ready for that. "Were you watching me?"

The arch of his brows expressed an emphatic *duh* without uttering the word. Classic Sloane-twin look. Seeing it twice in ten minutes made her feel slightly inadequate to deal with him. He bent at the waist and leaned on his knees, clearly tired. Still dragging air into his lungs.

"Just how long has it been since you had sleep?"

"I don't need sleep."

"Nonsense. I bet Brian can handle things until Dev arrives. Whatever occupied Roy's attention can wait a couple of hours." She gathered her feet under her, but before she could push off the ground, John's hands spanned her waist and he lifted her skyward.

Her toes dangled, touching nothing except air. Instead of just letting her drop to the earth, he drew her chest to his and let her slide to a disappointing halt. She stayed there with her hands on his shoulders, his sneaking around to her back. "I go without sleep a lot in my line of work."

"I, um… But you… John?"

"What?" His lips were very close.

Too close. There was too much between them to just pick up where they'd left off before their argument at graduation. Darn Brian and his silly ideas about love. Did either of them even remember that horrible, public argument? Or remember that she'd loved and married another man?

Not if the way he's holding you is any indication.

"Did you want to ask me something?" he teased through a grin.

"You can let go of me now." She firmly tugged on his forearms. Nice, muscled with just the right amount of fuzz on them. As often as she'd been around the house with Brian, she'd never noticed that before.

It was basically the same body, and yet Brian walking around the house without his shirt made her feel like her brother was home. This one? Well, the body under her fingertips, the thighs snug to her thighs… The chest her breasts were flattened against caused every part of her to hum. And parts that had been asleep since Dwayne had gone began to stir awake.

John released her. Almost. At the last moment, he spun her around, keeping her back to his front, his arm circling her waist again.

"What are you doing?"

"There's no hurry," he whispered in her ear. "And I have something to say."

She tugged at the vise grip around her middle. It didn't hurt, but he wasn't budging. "You can't tell me while you're looking at me?"

"Exactly."

No more. Oh, goodness, not a confession. *I'm not ready.*

"So hurry up, then. Brian's waiting."

"Right." He shifted, taking her with him. Facing the edge of the field instead of the shaft of light peeking beneath the double barn door.

"We aren't kids anymore, Johnny. You can let me go. I won't run away. You're a grown man and should be able to say what you want. You do realize that we're both thirty. Adults, right? And that I'll listen to whatever you have to say?"

"The thing is, Alicia, I don't think I can honestly look at you when you answer. I need to know something before we go any further, and now's as good a time as later to finish the conversation." His hold on her relaxed and his hand trembled. "I understand if you thought I'd set the fire all those years. But can you believe me now? Do you believe me?"

He's afraid?

Looking at the treetops and the sinking moon was much easier than the temptation of his handsome face. So she stayed. Encircled by his arms, feeling safe. Filling her heart so she could go forward.

"At first, I didn't think either one of you could have done it. And thought it had been an accident even when Brian said he thought he'd put the fire out and other accusations flew around town. Life went on." Her voice didn't sound rattled any longer. "Until Dwayne died and Brian started coming around to help out, we never talked about it. When he told me that you'd been drunk and must have left the fire going, well, I didn't believe it but couldn't tell him why."

"Why?" His voice was soft and warm against her neck.

"It was your story to tell. I couldn't put a bandage on the wound you caused each other."

She suddenly wanted to kiss him and be kissed by him. Maybe it was better they weren't facing each other. Because if she started, she wouldn't want to stop. When he kissed her, she forgot the rest of the world and what was happening in it.

Lauren was too important. *Get her back, then worry about kissing Johnny Sloane!*

"Thing is, no one at the party would have left that fire going. Especially you and Brian. I've said that since the day you left."

JOHN'S BODY ACHED.

In training, he'd taken more brutal beatings than what Brian had dished out. For some reason this one had hit him hard. And then there was the fact that he was holding Alicia. He bent close enough that the hot summer breeze blew her hair against his cheek. He didn't want to move away, so he widened his stance, straining his already exhausted legs.

Alicia had never doubted his innocence. Nothing to worry about after all. Unlike his brother, who had jumped to a guilty verdict before ever talking to him. But he'd acted guilty by running off. He could admit that.

All his earlier resolve to blame his brother faded like a cloud covering the moon. He knew it was there, but couldn't see it clearly anymore. Believing John had been irresponsible, Brian had come rushing in to help again. Sure, he was full of blunder and guilt trips and better solutions, but bottom line? He knew his twin had his back.

They could trust each other again because of the woman in his arms. Probably a good thing they weren't face-to-face, since he wanted to kiss her till she couldn't think—among other things.

"Is that all you needed, John?"

"Needed?"

She rotated her body, negotiating the circle he'd created with his arms, letting his fingers drag around her waist. She lifted her left arm above him and skimmed just behind his ear with her finger. If she got much closer, she'd know exactly what he *needed*.

"Grass." She flicked something quickly away from them. "Must have been from the fight."

When her eyes tilted toward the heavens, they were nose to nose. Which also meant their mouths were just about on the same level, too. Alicia flicked her tongue across her bottom lip and rolled it between her teeth. He could feel his insides tightening at the thought of holding her even closer. It had been a long time, but he knew how soft her lips would become after he crushed them to his.

Not the spur-of-the-moment connections they'd achieved since he'd been home. He was remembering serious kissing. They'd both explored each other in a first kiss. He'd suffered through her years with braces. The scrapes on his lips had been worth it. In high school, they'd spent hours practicing everywhere. They'd joked about how kissing should be a game and kids could earn a high school letter jacket just like Brian had in every other sport.

How many times had he held her exactly the same way, not caring about the future? Dreaming of far-off places to explore—but only with her. That had changed after one argument and his stupid pride. Right here, right now, he just wanted her.

A future without her wasn't something he wanted to step into again.

His arms tightened, bringing her body flush with him. Sliding his fingers under her T-shirt, he connected with the flushed heat of her lower back. They were pretty much sharing the same space when his mouth devoured hers. Lips—slick and cool compared to the hot silkiness of her flesh under his fingertips. Soft and welcoming instead of contoured muscles, honed while working with patients.

Her body had changed, become more of everything good he remembered. He wanted her—it didn't matter if his brother was inside the barn or if Dev would be there any minute. He wanted to throw her over his shoulder and haul her to the far tree line so they wouldn't be found. They needed to be alone so she could cry out as much as she wanted. Or he could capture all her joy with his lips, savor it for the time they'd be apart.

The picture of her covered in perspiration as the moon shimmered over her naked flesh was vivid for him. He couldn't stop himself. He wanted more of her.

Their relationship had never been more than occasional young-love petting. Everyone thought they'd be the couple to get pregnant and forced to marry when they were sixteen, but it hadn't happened. Not that he hadn't wanted to, tried to, gotten elbowed in his gut a time or two.

"Johnny," Alicia said when he glided his lips along the V of her neck.

His thumbs skimmed the bottom curve of both breasts through the smooth satin of her bra. How many times had he fantasized about this moment? How many times had her face gotten him through a long night on a mission? Or through a long night rocking in his bunk, wondering what if they hadn't broken up?

"We have to…" Alicia sighed his name again and tipped her head back. "Oh, my."

He stopped thinking about teenage petting and dragged his thumb across the silky cup of lace. Her nipple immediately pebbled under the caress.

"We should… We can't."

"Why? Do you have a curfew?" he teased, stopping her questions with another long kiss. Tasting her unique combination of warm and cool and sweet.

His hand fully closed over her breast, and her hips surged into his. She knew exactly what he wanted. No doubt. He couldn't hide it. Her hand circled his wrist and gently tugged him away.

"No." Alicia's hands were planted firmly against his chest. Body contact lost.

John relaxed his hold, allowed her to step back. He should never have asked her a question or released her lips. They were adults, the only ones responsible for their actions.

"We can't do this—"

"You're right."

"You don't know what I'm about to say," she whispered, shaking her head.

"Yeah, I do."

She crossed her arms, tightly closed her mouth with a harrumph and shot him a look he couldn't really catalog.

If Texas hadn't been in the middle of a triple-digit heat wave, the air would have frosted up as she stomped past.

She marched toward the barn, then did an about-face, sticking her finger in his face so close he could see her fingernail polish chipping.

"You have a lot of nerve coming back after twelve years and trying to pick up like nothing ever happened after you left."

He opened his mouth to apologize, but—

"No. Don't interrupt me. I'm finally going to say this without the fear you won't help me find Lauren." She closed her eyes, inhaled deeply and slapped her jeans. "I get it. You're a naval officer who probably has a gal in every port. Well, Lieutenant Sloane, my little part of the world doesn't have a dock. It's centered around a four-year-old child who has never had a father. I'm it. Her whole world. And I don't take risks with it. I loved Dwayne very much. It was real and something I'll never forget."

"I get it."

"No, I don't think you do. I have responsibilities to Lauren and have no intention of jeopardizing that by dating. Let alone having sex in a dried-up field with a man I haven't seen or heard from in over a decade."

"Don't worry about Lauren. We'll get her back. I'll call for the rest of my SEAL team if I have to." He forced a grin. "I understand, Alicia. Don't think anything about it."

"I don't want you to hate me."

Her hands shook. He noticed the tremor when she stroked his cheek before she walked briskly away. A smooth stroke down his jawline, just like she'd given Brian after their fight.

"Never." He'd never hate her. He'd never stay in this part of Texas. He'd never stop wanting her with every part of his being. *Never.*

His phone vibrated with a text. Slick. It was Brian, watching from the barn. Lights at the gate.

Probably Dev, but they couldn't be certain, and he'd been completely distracted by the beauty in his arms. *Damn!* He had to get this desire crap under control. If he didn't, he'd get them all thrown in jail. Or worse…dead.

Chapter Twenty-One

John hid the car Dev had "borrowed" at the back of the property in the far grove of trees he'd wanted to drag Alicia to just a short time ago. When he entered the barn, said woman was silent in the only chair, her forehead crinkled in thought while his best friend and brother held a discussion loud enough to be heard over the air conditioner.

He'd been gone only a few minutes, but it seemed they were all deep in contemplation. The men had parked themselves on either side of the rattling AC unit.

They all stared at the wrecked car that had belonged to Dwayne. The same car he'd crashed over four years ago, dried bloodstains on the tan seat. Nothing more of importance was inside the barn, other than hay for horses waiting in another paddock, to be sold at auction tomorrow.

His brother's thumbs were hooked in his belt loops as casually as his ankles were crossed while leaning against the barn wall. A big change from the way he'd paced like a caged animal an hour earlier. Dev's hand rested against his chin, one finger tapping across his lips.

John knew that look. The team knew to prepare for an onslaught of random brainstorming ideas until a workable solution was obtained. If they could reach that point and come up with a plan, he'd endure any number of questions from Dev.

"We're assuming Roy Adams came to this barn, prob-ably turned on that clattering air conditioner, sat in that chair and what? Stared at the vehicle where his son died? Why?" Dev asked.

"And is answering that question worth our time before we figure out a plan to rescue Lauren?" Brian asked.

He didn't know.

"That's one mangled piece of junk." Dev half pointed with his tapping finger to the car they'd found. Hardly missing a beat, the tapping to his face resumed. "No drugs? No alcohol?"

"Toxicology screen was clean. Absolutely no alcohol in his system, man," Brian stated. "I'm telling you, he wasn't drunk. A friend of mine looked at the autopsy for me."

"You never mentioned you requested that, Brian," Alicia said softly. She looked straight ahead, through the missing driver's door of the car.

Brian shot John a plea for help, but there was no need. Dev's processing wouldn't be sidetracked.

"So they assumed he fell asleep," Dev mumbled, "but it wasn't late at night. Sort of a strange assumption, even for the cops."

"Shauna told everyone within earshot that he fell asleep at the wheel because he'd been up all night with Lauren."

"Had he?" Dev asked.

"Not more than usual. I worked all night and he was with her. He would have called if she hadn't been sleeping. She slept pretty soundly for a six-month-old. Still does."

There was a visible lack of emotion coming from Alicia. For a woman who had been so passionate less than twenty minutes before, her stare was disturbing.

"Did you think that he'd fallen asleep at the wheel?"

Alicia shrugged. John signaled to his best friend to cut the talk by making a slicing motion against his throat. He didn't want her to travel down the path of being responsible for the car accident.

"I don't get it. Why would Roy keep Dwayne's wrecked car? Do you think he was going to fix it up?" Brian asked. "That's the only reason I can think of. Or was he just sick with grief before—"

Both ideas turned his stomach. He could see how upset she was. A blank stare where he couldn't tell if she was aware he'd returned. He couldn't see inside the car, but it looked mangled.

"Did your father-in-law think he was responsible somehow? Is that why he killed himself?" Dev's question hung in the air.

John could only guess that Dev's research had turned up that information. He didn't know the answer. The man they'd known their entire lives would never have taken his own life. But none of the past mattered. People change after losing someone close to them. Only one person in the room could begin to understand what was in Roy's mind, but she remained silent. Not even a quick gasp of breath.

"We're missing something," Dev continued in his analytic mode. "Why wouldn't he get rid of the constant reminder of his son's accident?"

"Could he have thought there was a clue in the wreckage?" She looked hopeful and jumped to her feet, searching inside the car. "Could it still be here? Maybe you were right. Maybe that's why they killed him."

He quickly pulled her away to stop her. "If there had been, Roy would have turned it over to the cops."

"But—"

"I'm not following." Brian cut her off.

She turned to his brother, appearing ever hopeful for answers. "John thinks it's possible that Roy believed Dwayne was murdered. And then *he* was murdered to keep him from finding anything."

"Murdered? By who? Why?" Brian shouted.

No longer relaxed, his shoulders-back "fight me" stance called to John to respond in kind, but he held himself where he was. "I've got nothing but a gut feeling, that's all. Definitely not enough to base a plan on."

Brian hit the wall with his fist and the pacing began. "Son of a bitch, that's a giant place to leap for someone who hasn't been around for twelve years. Why are you doing this to her?"

"You weren't there tonight," Alicia said. "You didn't see Patrick and what he did. He killed Tory. Just shot her in cold blood right before the police pulled up. Yes, John's been gone. But maybe that's why he can consider what no one else has."

"You honestly think Roy Adams could commit suicide and leave Alicia here to fend for herself?" John asked his brother.

Brian drew a deep breath and turned into that mature son who helped their dad. "No one thinks it could happen to their family. I'm a paramedic. I see disbelief on people's faces all the time. Suicide, drugs, drunk driving. They all ask for proof. I'm sorry, Alicia. Guess I'm in the habit of not thinking much about it. I should have been there for you."

"You were," she answered softly, and returned to the chair.

"Did you say Weber shot someone named Tory?" Dev asked. "Could her real name be Victoria, um, Strayhorn?"

"I think so." Alicia shrugged, leaned back and slipped out of her shoes. "She worked at Lauren's day care, and I can't remember her last name."

"Let me look at something." Dev walked to his gear just inside the double doors.

"Did you find the money?" John asked.

"What money?" Brian asked, following Dev and lifting electronic cases.

"No. But Patrick and Shauna are converting all their assets into cash," Dev said casually.

"We knew about the sale of property and horses." He didn't find anything strange in Shauna's getting rid of things that didn't interest her.

"I mean, *everything.* Stocks at a loss. Dissolving business partnerships for any amount of cash that can be forked over. *That* kind of cashing out."

"What money?" Brian asked again.

"Mind catching him up to speed, Dev, while I...?" He nodded to Alicia, who stared zombielike into the car again.

Followed by Brian, Dev went to the rental. He opened his laptop on the hood and began assembling whatever portable equipment he'd managed to bring from the cabin. If John knew the SEAL who prepared for everything—which he did—he knew the guy had the capability to hack the White House from his cell phone.

Brian asked questions. Dev answered. Alicia stared. Their conversation faded into the background. Should John get her out of here? Or make her face the demon rusting in the jumbled metal? He laid a hand on her shoulder and she jumped.

"Sorry. I... You see, no one really told me much when the accident happened. All the details were shared with Roy. It didn't matter to me since... I mean, he was dead, so it just didn't matter."

"I get it. Closure is different for everyone." He did understand. He'd written letters when he'd lost a man and then received answers from a couple of parents. One man wanted every detail he could divulge about the fight, while his wife had sent a letter to John's commander, asking why he'd commended her son's performance in battle. He got it, all right.

"I remember that he crashed and they couldn't get him out of the car. That's probably why there's no door. They probably had to pull it off, right? He died at the scene." Her voice was barely a whisper. "Roy handled everything."

"It's all right." He lowered his voice and knelt beside her. "This isn't a good place for you to be. If I'd known the car was here, I wouldn't have brought you."

"You can't protect me from the fact that my husband died, John. Accidents happen. Life happens." She squeezed his hand and he realized he'd been patting her knee. "In your line of work, you've probably seen your own share of tragedy."

He couldn't talk about what he'd seen. It wasn't fair to burden her with his nightmares. She had enough of her own. Dev's low voice wafted through the background as he explained to his brother what he'd been searching for in cyberspace.

"Something happened to you, John. I can see it. Every once in a while, you drift, and your sadness makes me want to snatch you back. You can tell me about it. I'm still here for you."

"Maybe someday." *Or never.* He stood, but she didn't release his hand. "We should get started, and you should get some more sleep."

"You need it more than me. How are you going to think of a great rescue plan while you're running on empty?" She crossed her legs and tugged off her socks.

"I'll catch twenty after Brian leaves."

"Then we should get started on the plan to get Lauren back before he has to head home," she said, stronger.

"You're right. We need a plan."

"How do you figure to accomplish a rescue?" Brian asked. "She'll be watched 24/7. No matter where they go."

"And if you do accomplish your goal, I haven't proved Alicia didn't plan everything," Dev added.

Their options were limited. They couldn't just waltz up to the door and demand Alicia's daughter. Or could they?

"Exactly. That's why we're going to kidnap her during the auction today."

Chapter Twenty-Two

Once they'd worked most of the details out and the fine-tuning had come into play, Alicia had fallen into an emotional, exhausted sleep. She vaguely remembered John saying goodbye and maybe kissing her cheek.

With Brian's alibi established, the police couldn't connect him to Tory's shooting. So John planned to attend the auction using his brother's ID and be in position to orchestrate Lauren's kidnapping. Alicia had slept from dawn to about nine o'clock in the morning. Right until Dev had started his rental and driven off to purchase the rest of the gear they'd need.

A glance at her watch as she stretched awake for a second time told her it was nearly eleven. "I'm seriously hungry. Anything still in those saddlebags?"

"That's because you didn't eat before you fell asleep. Dev's almost back. Hope you like burgers for breakfast." Brian sat in the chair, looking so much like John it reminded her of when they'd all first met.

They were less gangly, had grown into handsome men and were good, helpful friends. As much as they tried to be different, they still had identical expressions and mannerisms.

"Anything will be much appreciated. Did he find the electronics he needed?"

"Yeah. That's a fairly big smile on your face, Miss Adams. Been a while since I've seen it where it belongs."

"You flirt. Am I smiling?" She laughed. "I'm happy this is almost over."

She was glad at the thought that Lauren would soon be back in her arms, protected, safe. The future after her rescue was still uncertain, but the most important thing was to get her daughter away from the murderers who had kidnapped her.

"Not all over. We still have to pull off a kidnapping and keep you guys out of sight until one of Dev's navy buds can track this money connection to Patrick. He passed it off to someone with a bigger computer."

"You don't sound too positive."

"Come on, Alicia. You think this chaotic plan of John's will work? Think he can act like a humble ranch hand again?" Brian pushed up from the chair, stretching and twisting as though he'd been stationary too long.

"To be honest, I can't *not* believe John and Dev know what they're doing. They rescue people in much more dangerous situations. Dev's not just some navy buddy, Brian. He's amazing with a computer."

Brian smiled once again. He might talk about her smiling, but he'd done more than his share since his fight with his brother. "And it hurt the guy to give in and call for help. Dev was in true pain. I guess you've had a bit more time to believe in John than I have. For twelve years I thought he was irresponsible—"

"And blamed him like the town blamed you."

"Uh," he began, and stopped himself. "Yeah, pretty much."

"Is that why you're so doom and gloom this morning?"

"I keep thinking of all the time I wasted." He rubbed his jaw. "The beatings I endured, the shunning of everyone except you and Mabel."

"Surely there's been a couple of others?"

"No one close. Hell, girl, I've never been on a serious date."

"You're kidding."

"I can't expose anyone to the treatment I live with just running to the grocery for a gallon of milk for Dad. And you know I can't move. I can't work more than three or four days in a row. Dad will work himself to death."

Alicia finger combed her hair and watched Brian shift uncomfortably on his feet. His confession must have been very difficult to make.

Instead of pacing around the barn like a caged lion, an action she'd seen often enough since his arrival, Brian stayed put. His eyes pleaded with her to understand. He was probably sharing thoughts he'd never told anyone. He was right. Who would he have explained to?

J.W. ate, worked, ate and went to bed. He had been a great friend to her father and Roy, but he wasn't from a generation of talkers. And unfortunately, Brian took after him more with every year that aged them all. John had been the one who always talked to her as they'd grown up. He, too, it seemed, had closed himself off. In two days, he hadn't said a word about his life over the past twelve years.

"I'm so sorry, Brian." She tried to imagine how lonely he'd been all these years. "But I think if you let someone fall in love with you, then they'd never doubt you were innocent."

"Is that why you've always believed in John?"

"What do you mean?"

"You believed that he didn't start the fire and wasn't there. You stood by him because you've always loved him." He stated it as matter-of-fact instead of really wanting to know the answer to a question. Just a little rise and fall of a firm shoulder. Acceptance that it was the way things had always been.

"I never believed you set the fire, either. Even after you confessed." She looked at him, wondering how the conversation had taken a turn to this place. "You know I love your whole family."

"Sweetheart, you do *not* love me and Dad like you do him." Brian laughed, completely at ease and relaxed. "And from the astonished look on your face, I think you're realizing that it's time to stop kidding yourself that you do."

"You're wrong. I don't. I can't. I loved Dwayne. I wouldn't have married him if I were still in love with Johnny. I'm just— Really, I can't possibly do that to Dwayne."

"Do what? Fall in love again?"

"Make people doubt our marriage. Or that I settled for him. Or that I was after his money. I couldn't." She dropped her head in her palms.

How could the world turn upside down in an instant yet again? She'd been so relieved that this ordeal would soon be over. So happy at the thought of seeing Lauren again and knowing she was safe. She'd actually been smiling, laughing. And now it was impossible.

No matter how much she cared about Johnny, she couldn't possibly be in love with him. It wasn't fair to Dwayne's memory. She felt a pat on her shoulder, then Brian's hand squeezed tight.

"No one will think you *settled* for either man. And there's not a single person in town who ever thought you married for money. I knew Dwayne. I was his best friend from the first peewee football team we were on. He'd be very happy for you both. I'm certain of that. You and Johnny are going to be good together."

One last squeeze and Brian walked outside, leaving her on her own.

Did she really love her high school sweetheart? Had she stopped only for the time she'd been with Dwayne? It might be true. Brian might be right about that, but he was certainly wrong about being good together.

John was a navy SEAL, for crying out loud. All he'd ever talked about in high school was joining the navy. He was a career man. He'd be leaving Aubrey and returning to his exciting world instead of living her day-to-day drama. After the dust settled from Shauna and Patrick's kidnapping, her world would be how to get a grape-jelly stain out of her favorite blouse. She'd patiently explained to him in the field that she'd never be with anyone again. So after all that straight talk, how could she change her story?

How could she possibly make him believe she loved him? And on top of all that…she hadn't known it until his brother had hit her over the head?

WEARING WESTERN BOOTS was a change that John welcomed. He would enjoy breaking in a new pair. If he had a reason to buy a pair again. Since Alicia had told him she'd never marry again—and he'd heard that underlying message of *especially him*—there wasn't much of a reason to think about moving back. He didn't have a reason to find a place to store boots in the barracks.

Brian hadn't been exaggerating about the number of people who avoided talking to him in town. There had been several women who were approaching and then had a sudden desire to stare into the hardware store window. The town truly had decided his brother's punishment.

And yet he was still here. Taking care of what was left of the ranch. Most definitely taking care of their dad. Always the responsible brother.

Brian had been right about the police officers, too. They weren't very good at tailing him. He gave them the slip long enough to meet Dev and receive the earbud and microphone. How and where his friend obtained his *toys* was beyond him. He was just grateful that he knew someone with that much talent.

He had to sit at the café lunch counter for a good ten minutes sipping coffee he didn't want or need before the cops showed up again. He needed them at the auction. Since Dev still hadn't located the money, if Patrick said or did anything, it was important to have reliable witnesses.

He was beginning to rethink the *reliable* about the time they pulled behind his granddad's truck to find him at the auction. Walking in a crowd of people who had shunned his brother brought back memories of the streets in Afghanistan. A foreigner in disguise on a rescue mission, praying no one knew his real identity.

Keep your cool, man. You'll get to tell these people off one day. Just not today.

"Everyone in place?" he asked just before he wouldn't be able to answer again without someone thinking it odd that he was talking to himself.

"Yes," Alicia answered hesitantly.

"Out of sight at the corral." Brian was in place for the distraction.

"Good to go, LT."

The line to register moved quickly and it was soon his turn. He filled out the information and returned the paper to the young woman. She smiled, clearly unaware of the treatment his brother normally received.

"What are you doing here, Sloane?" A man walked up to the registration desk. Dressed in a suit, obviously in charge. He knew Brian and each word showed his distaste at wasting his time on him.

"I thought it was an open auction." He couldn't wait to see this pompous ass eat his words.

"You're required to have a line of credit or cash to get inside. I already denied you that line of credit and I know no one else gave it to you. Unless you brought—"

John pulled the stack of bills from a bank envelope. "There's ten thousand. That enough to see if I want any of the Adamses' stock?"

"Where did you get that kind of money? You're broke."

"You don't really expect an answer, do you? Now, where's my bid number?" He put the cash away, looking around to see astonished faces everywhere. He could see the condemnation.

"I want this man thoroughly searched and if he has a weapon, hold him for the police."

John stepped to the side of the table and lifted his arms, forcing a smile to stretch from ear to ear, faking his ease at being frisked. He'd left his weapons behind for just this reason.

"They all believe I sell drugs," Brian said disgustedly, then laughed in his ear. "Now you just confirmed their suspicions and there will be worse rumors about why I haven't saved the ranch with the money before now."

"Don't distract him, man," Dev broke in. "Stay silent until you need to let us *all* know something."

Luckily Dev had intervened. John had been about to answer Brian himself. Go off on a rant right as he walked into the arena. His brother was the only person who could get a rise out him at this stage of an operation. He hadn't really been functioning at full SEAL capacity since he'd arrived in Texas.

Maybe he was losing his edge. Time to suck it up and focus. He knew he'd lost his heart for his chosen career months ago. He'd address his doubts after he secured Lauren. Walking from stall to stall of the animals for sale, he felt sick in his gut that Roy's life's work was about to disperse to parts unknown. These horses were Lauren's future. It was Alicia's decision to sell or keep them.

Avoiding a conversation with those around him wasn't hard. The locals kept their distance, and for the faces that tried to make eye contact, his angry expression should have put off a vibe that he wasn't too open for small talk. He didn't have to act interested in the stock—he genuinely was.

These were fine animals, good quarter-horse breeders his dad's ranch would be excited to own. He could hear the astonishment of the potential buyers as they chatted to each other. Some of the mares should never have gone to a public auction. They would go cheap because many of the bigger farms weren't represented. His fingers curled into fists. He had to grab the top rail of the corral to force his body to relax.

"Well, well, well. You never know what vermin will dare crawl out when there's food available."

"Hello, Shauna. It's been a while. Sorry to hear about everything your family's been going through."

"Right. Like I believe that." She parked herself in front of him, trapping him between a support beam and the stall of Roy's prize mare.

At least John had a view of the arena and could see Patrick chatting up the buyers.

"Making nice-nice with the enemy while I crawl through muck," Brian's voice was loud in John's ear.

"Come on, Brian. John's playing a part," Alicia said.

Just hearing her voice threw him out of step. "I'm, um, sorry, I didn't catch that."

"I said, we know your secret. We both know it's John who's helping Alicia." Shauna pretended to straighten his collar, lowering her voice so only he—and the rest of those on comm—could hear her. "I could have told the police, but Patrick convinced me to hold off. We don't know what you're trying to prove by attending the auction, but it's best if you turn around and leave."

John grabbed her wrists and pushed her away from him. Her little pout of hurt did nothing to him. He dealt with women acting like her in just about every bar he'd ever entered.

"If you believe that, Shauna, then call the cops over right now. I was eating pie at the diner last night when you claim I was in McKinney. The police have confirmed John is on a mission. He couldn't get home when Dad had his stroke and sure as hell doesn't care about any of our problems."

He made eye contact with Weber—still no sign of Lauren.

"Any possibility of me saying hello to Lauren today? You hiding her somewhere?"

"You're a horrible liar. Do you know that, John?" She tried to touch his head and he quickly pulled back. "Patrick and I think you're John."

"The auction's going to start soon and I've only seen half of the mares. I should be moving along." He tried to step around her. She moved into his path.

"Now, we both know you're really here to try to get our little angel." She laid on the Southern twang and put a finger over her heart while she glanced upward. "You can try to take her from us, but as you can see, she's being guarded very well today."

Shauna pointed to the security guards and then to…

Gargantuan.

He stood in the general direction Weber had been a few minutes before. Lauren was evidently holding his hand, but he couldn't see her through the crowd. The giant towered over everyone and it was easy to keep him in his peripheral vision. He seemed to be headed, along with most of the other attendees, to the midsection of risers in front of the center arena.

"You won't take her from me. I promise you that."

"Were you saying something, Shauna? Dang, I didn't hear a word of it. Guess I got lost thinking how well that mare will look with my stock. Pardon me." He'd heard every senseless word. With all the huffing and puffing she was doing, it was fairly obvious that not caring what she had to say sent her into a tizzy.

He looked over her shoulder, past most of the crowd and saw Patrick's hand slap the wall. *He* was the one listening. That was why Shauna was all over him. They were hoping he'd give something away.

Again he tried to move around her, but she grabbed his arm.

"You can pretend not to care all you want, but that guard doesn't earn a penny if Lauren leaves his side. I believe you've already discovered just how good of a fighter he is." She touched the side of his jaw where a darkening bruise had formed.

"That? I got whacked by a tree branch, tracking down a coyote that's been stalking my stock. One thing you should know—I protect what's mine." He placed his hands on her shoulders, keeping her in one spot as he passed.

Three voices burst loudly into his ear. He was afraid he winced in pain or, worse yet, it had been so loud that others near him would have heard. Everyone went about their business as usual. Shauna stomped back to Weber at the entrance, pushing people out of the way, then smiling sweetly as she said thank-you.

Whatever Alicia and Dev said was lost under Brian's distinctive, "What the heck was that all about?"

"She's wired," Dev suggested after they quieted. "Gotta be. No way they'd keep the info that you were here to themselves."

"Would have been easy for the cops to find out. My prints are on file and if you left any at that shindig last night—"

"Not a chance."

"Then they're either shooting in the dark or working

with the cops," Brian surmised. "Why the hell would she be playing footsie in the corner with you?"

"Can you see Lauren?"

"She's sitting next to the bodyguard. Same guy as at the house." He barely moved his lips to give his team the info.

"You need help?" Brian laughed. "Do we stick with the plan? Or call it quits?"

"We never quit, just adapt," Dev answered before John could.

"Affirmative. A diversion about now would be great."

John took the steps two at a time to the top of the risers. Gargantuan continued to look in Weber's direction, but behind him. The only part about this extraction he didn't like was that Lauren and her mom would be watching him succeed or fail.

He would *not* fail.

Chapter Twenty-Three

"Distraction number one, on its way."

John listened for signs that his brother might be in trouble. The sound of metal connecting with metal would be the vent cover being screwed back into place. The smoke bomb that Brian lit would be safe and nontoxic to breathe. It would irritate eyes more than anything else.

It didn't take long for someone to point to the gray smoke trickling, then pouring, from the air vents. The homemade smoke bomb should burn long enough to fill the arena. Long enough for authorities to be called.

If they accomplished nothing else, at least Roy's stock wouldn't be sold off today.

No one yelled *fire*. No one created panic. Several auction workers quietly moved through the crowd and gestured toward the exits. John took out his cell and attempted to search for an internet connection. If anyone asked why he was sitting in a smoke-filled room, he'd use it as an excuse to be unaware of his surroundings. Several people had already looked up in surprise after their heads had been bowed, praying to their smartphones.

Everyone exited quickly. It had gone as efficiently as they'd hoped. Alicia had asked all three of them to promise no one would get hurt. She was riddled with guilt over Tory's death. It didn't matter how many times they'd all assured her that Weber had been intent on killing the witnesses.

An option thrown around in their early-morning planning had been to just snatch Lauren and run with her. But it had been shot down, since the police would be all over them before they got to the main road. No, they had to create a situation where the Webers were separated from her. And to get that to happen, Gargantuan needed to take her outside.

A smoke-filled room and he didn't budge.

Workers argued with the giant, and Lauren sat unnaturally quietly at his side.

Had they drugged her? Threatened her? If the bastards had hurt Alicia's little girl, he wouldn't be able to restrain himself. *I swear I'll use every skill I've ever been taught as a SEAL. No holds barred.*

Lauren coughed and covered her face. *Leave. Get her out of here before I have to take matters into my own hands.*

"Sir, you really must go outside."

"What? Sorry, slow Wi-Fi." John was focused on Gargantuan and hadn't noticed the young man at his side. "Hey, is there a fire?" He searched for signs of Weber. Neither Patrick or Shauna were in sight. "Do you know where the people in charge are relocating?"

He didn't give a hill of beans where anyone running the auction was located. He wanted Weber in his sights. He'd never thought Weber would leave Lauren with someone else, but that scenario most definitely worked in their favor.

"I just know that we need to get out of here." The man sternly laid a hand on his shoulder, encouraging John to leave. Since the giant was leaving, too, John was ready.

"Lead the way. Don't let me slow you down."

"Assuming that was a disguised question for me," Dev said in his earpiece, "Mrs. Witch is in the car waiting with the engine running—probably cooling down. I still can't believe how freakin' hot it is here in Texas. My bad, no eyes on Weber."

"If they're acting like the concerned grandparents, then why did they both leave Lauren alone with that man?" Alicia asked. "And I agree with Dev that it's dang hot out here with all these layers of clothes on."

"Are you in place, Nurse Adams?"

"Yes, I am."

"Did you say something?" the guy escorting him outside asked.

"Just thanks, man." John ducked back to the registration area to watch for Gargantuan's exit. He'd heard the big man give in after the threat of calling security. And seconds later, he appeared, carrying Lauren on his hip.

"Ladies and gentlemen, there wasn't a fire." Someone shouted the announcement.

"She looks so scared," Alicia whispered.

Strange how he could hear her slightest whisper and pick her out instantly in the crowd. He assumed the rest of the announcement that he missed actually stated they'd begin the auction again soon, since people turned around and began talking instead of continuing to their cars.

"She stopped sucking her fingers months ago."

The giant headed to the car on the far side of the offices. John caught a glimpse of Lauren, fingers in her mouth, sad eyes watering not only from the smoke but also from constant tears.

"Focus on your job, Alicia. Don't look at anything else. Only your job, hon. That's it." John spoke into the cell phone so he wouldn't appear to be a crazy man just talking to himself. He should have obtained a wireless headset so his hands would be completely free.

He watched the woman he would give up everything for waddle toward him. A blond wig completely changed the way she looked. The padding making her look two hundred pounds helped a lot, too. Man, she must be boiling in all those extra clothes.

The police and fire truck arrived right on cue. Sirens blasted into the chaos and ceased just as fast. The men poured from their vehicles, quickly trying to assess what was wrong. The horses in the paddock nickered, getting more agitated as more smoke blew in their direction and the crowd got louder.

"You're almost up, Dev. Gargantuan's on his phone. He's headed to the car with Lauren." He stashed the cell in his pocket as Alicia pretended to trip and fall to the ground.

"Do you need some assistance, ma'am?" He was right there to help her. While he pulled her upright, she slipped his weapon inside his belt and covered it with his shirt. "Just remember, if everything goes off without a hitch, we'll have Lauren back before they know she's gone."

As hot as it was, he missed her when she'd stepped away from his hold.

"I certainly hope you're right."

"Piece of cake."

"I can't believe you said that, John," Dev whined.

"Why? What does Dev mean?" she asked, looking up at John with the same sad, worried eyes of her daughter. The tension and stress of the past few days had begun to show in the dark circles, but she was still the most beautiful woman around. Especially to him.

He had completely fallen for Alicia Adams—nurse, mother, friend. He could freely admit that he had it bad. But who would he tell? His best friend, who would try to talk him out of leaving the navy? His brother? Things were better, but he didn't feel like discussing a future with Alicia with him. Not yet.

"He just jinxed us. I'd elaborate, Alicia, but a cop is walking right toward me. Going off comm. Excuse me, Officer?"

"Dev's a superstitious old woman, that's all. He thinks it brings us bad luck to say an operation will be easy." He smiled, trying to reassure her. He didn't know if it worked. They had to separate before they drew more attention to themselves.

He also didn't want her to ask if Dev's superstitions were founded in truth. Unfortunately, they were. He hadn't been the person to say it back then, but he remembered how things had gone south real fast on ops that should have been easy ins and outs.

John stayed in the center of everything. Making eye contact with as many people as possible. Staying visible. Making certain Brian could not be accused of any part of this. If things went bad it would be on *his* head. Not Brian's.

He caught the silent version of his buddy's performance. It appeared convincing enough—at least from a hundred yards away.

Dev showed the Aubrey officer fake county Child Protection Services credentials and pointed to where Gargantuan had set Lauren on the back of Shauna's car. Where the man had obtained the necessities—earbuds, costumes, fake credentials—to pull this stunt off in such a short time, he had no idea. It definitely made him appreciate that his friend had come to watch his back and lend a hand. Or two. Or three.

The officer split the crowd, and Dev, dressed like a bent-over old man, followed. The officer showed the paper to Gargantuan, who immediately banged on the rear window of the car.

"Why are you still here?"

John spun in the direction his shoulder was being yanked. "Weber."

"You're behind all this smoke business, and when I find out how, you'll be in jail for good this time."

"Yes, it has been a long while, Patrick. Glad things are going so well for you."

"Why, I should—"

"Hit me? Go for it. Take your best shot, man." John wanted to throw the first punch. Wanted to make this piece of worthless scum bleed and beg for him to stop.

"Hey, John, hang on there, bro."

Brian interrupted his mental picture of tearing Weber to shreds. It would have been nice.

"Stick to the plan, Johnny," Alicia said. "Forget him. We need Lauren."

Today the objective was the rescue of an innocent four-year-old girl. One day it would be the arrest of the murderer in front of him. He hoped it would be his testimony that locked this rat away and sent him to death row in the Huntsville State Prison.

The *rat's* cell phone was buzzing like crazy. If he could keep Weber occupied for five more minutes, Dev might have everything wrapped up and be able to get to safety without any trouble at all. Let Shauna handle CPS taking Lauren into protective custody. Weber's involvement might slow Dev down. The more his friend was questioned, the more opportunity there was to mess up.

"What do you want from me, Weber? I just came to buy some horses."

Weber shoved at his shoulder. "I want you to leave. I've told everyone that your drug money's no good here. You'll never get your hands on Adams's stock. Your family's always been a second-rate quarter-horse farm and that's what you'll continue to be."

Weber removed his shades. His dead eyes stared while

one side of his mouth tilted into a smirk. "Or have you been gone too long to notice, John?"

Damn, his fingers itched to curl into a fist and lay this guy flat, teaching him a lesson or two along the way. Especially the lesson of the Sloane brothers. It didn't matter which one you were dealing with.

"Don't do it, John. They'll throw me in jail before you can blink. Remember, you're me right now."

"I got that," John answered his brother. Fortunately, the answer worked for Weber, too. If Weber drew him into a fight or acknowledging his identity, it would be more difficult to complete their mission.

"Then get out." Weber's cell buzzed again and he reached into his pocket.

Don't let him look at it. "There's one thing I don't get at all."

His opponent—even if only sparring with words—rolled his shoulders and angled his stance, ready to throw a punch. "I can't wait to hear. As if your opinion means anything to anyone around here."

Yeah, Weber was razzing up the crowd, upsetting them, reminding them of the past and another fire. John could hear their murmuring. He hated that Brian had fought this battle for so long on his own.

"I don't get how things work at your ranch, Weber. Remind me. With no horses or stock, we might have to call it something else, and there really isn't any word. But that doesn't matter. Who's in charge? Do you take orders from Shauna or her money? How does it feel selling off the horses you actually worked with in the stables?"

"Why, you…"

John prepared for the punch. He was going to roll on the ground right into the legs of the crowd gathering at their raised voices.

"Mr. Weber, there's an emergency at your car. They've been trying to get you on your phone." Weber's fist was raised and ready to strike, but he dropped it as soon as the messenger spoke his name.

"Dev has Lauren. The officer's escorting him to his car," Alicia said.

"See, piece of cake. No extra work involved," Brian quoted the mantra of the day.

"I may not be able to have you arrested, but I can do one thing." Weber dusted his hands off and gestured to one of his workers nearby. "Escort him off the property and see that he doesn't return."

John shrugged out of the hands of the man attempting to "escort" him to his truck. They needed Dev to have Lauren out of sight when Weber realized he'd lost her. John was certain he'd blow his top, and he wanted witnesses. But the unknown factor was that they didn't know if Weber had friends in the Aubrey police who might detain a CPS administrator until confirmation could be obtained from county.

So Dev had to be out of sight. He was only to his car, buckling Lauren into the child-safety seat.

"Tell me when they're out of here and completely clear."

"Huh?" the guy shoving him to the parking lot said.

Both Brian and Alicia confirmed and kept feeding him the details.

Another push between his shoulder blades and John had had enough. "Come on, man. I can walk faster if I'm not tripping every time you push. I'm leaving, so back off."

Most of the crowd had migrated toward the so-called emergency with Weber. The guy shoved again.

"Am I in the clear?" John asked.

"That's an affirmative," his brother answered, imitating Dev's voice. "Everyone's watching the show Shauna's putting on."

"Buddy, you ain't never going to be in the clear in Aubrey." The man—John thought he was the younger brother of someone they'd gone to school with—shoved again.

John didn't trip. Or budge.

But he did turn around.

Chapter Twenty-Four

Donny Ashcroft marched John to the parking lot just like Patrick had instructed. He hit John again in the middle of his back, but this time John didn't move. He pivoted and fired off a right cross that dropped Donny to the ground like a fly. Alicia watched from the corner of the building and tried not to giggle. Poor man, his jaw would really hurt for a while. It wasn't nice to hit someone when they weren't looking. But in all fairness, John had asked the guy to stop pushing.

"Dev's driving through the gate," Brian stated.

She waved to John so he'd know where to find her, but he followed after Patrick. There was a determined look on his face. The same one that had been there when he'd taken her away from Lauren last night.

"Let's get out of here." Brian's uneasiness was plain in his shaky voice.

"He needs to be down the street and around the corner. We can't risk anyone catching a glimpse of the license tags on the rental." John ran into the crowd.

"I've got another smoke grenade."

"Use it. We need the cops occupied here. Not pursuing Dev."

"But, John, Brian's in the paddock with the horses and they're already skittish." *Apprehensive* didn't begin to describe the level of nervousness thrumming throughout her body. For a couple of minutes there, it was almost over—right up to the word *pursuing*. When would everything be back to normal?

But did she want the return of her *normal?*

"Do it," John commanded, and ran in the direction Patrick had gone. "We don't have a choice."

Seconds later smoke billowed toward the sky on the far side of the corral. The horses neighed excitedly. They smelled the smoke and didn't know there wasn't a fire. She knew how they felt, scared to death by the unknown.

The makeshift fat suit she wore was cumbersome and stifling in this heat. And the wig was horrid and itchy. It was like having straw stuck into a woolen cap. They'd thrown her layer of fat together by stuffing clothing from the secondhand store into an outdated pantsuit. She couldn't wait to be out of this costume and back with Lauren. Before that could happen, they had to give Dev time to get away.

But she couldn't do anything except stand to the side and watch.

John's look after he'd punched Donny brought back more memories than of losing Lauren or Tory's death. Now she'd visually lost track of both brothers and was afraid of what John might do. She could hear noise and thought she caught bits of words through her ear microphone thingy, but they weren't clear enough to distinguish.

Dev was at his car, and the police officer had joined the firemen returning from the corral. She joined the back of the crowd and resorted to good old-fashioned face-to-face communication to find out what was happening.

"What's going on now?" She didn't ask anyone specifically and received a slew of answers.

"There's a fight."

"It's Sloane and that big man."

"Isn't that the Weber bodyguard?"

"I heard the police took Lauren Adams away."

"That must have crushed Shauna."

Once the people started gossiping, they wouldn't shut up. Some of them believed the media propaganda. Others didn't believe a word of what they saw on television. They all crowded together and wanted to see the fight between John and the man he referred to as Gargantuan.

A collective *oh* rang through the crowd as they witnessed a punch. All she saw were two arms soaring backward through the air.

Under her breath she added, "That looked like John flying backward." And then louder she asked, "Who's winning?" She was still unable to see over the heads in front of her. She had to get out of here before she passed out from heat and a lack of clear air.

"I can't say for sure, but I think John may be getting his butt kicked by this guy." Brian's voice shot inside her head like a DJ on the radio. It was a strange feeling, having someone chat in your ear. But also a comforting feeling, having them right beside you. She wanted to turn and glare at his words. In spite of their content, his friendly voice—so like John's—was comforting to hear and meant he was still close enough to help.

"What was he thinking?"

"I don't believe it was his idea. But it's just the distraction we needed while the fire department clears away my smoke. He'll be okay, Alicia. Don't worry."

"Is Dev gone?"

"Can't see any sign of the car, and the smoke seems to have gotten the police interested in real business instead of being ordered around by Patrick," Brian said.

"The police may want to get a handle on the crowd's rowdiness and not stand around watching the fight." Alicia pushed her way through to the corral fence where several men had climbed for a better view. The horses were crowding each other, and if one of these men fell under them—Well, she knew who would be blamed for their injuries.

"We have to stop this before someone gets hurt."

"Not so sure we can do that. John told me to get you out of here."

"Well, come and get me," she taunted, knowing he couldn't come to her. They'd all go to jail if he did. But even if he could, Brian would have to drag her, kicking and screaming. She couldn't run away and leave John. He'd never do that if she were in danger.

"It appears that two teams have formed—those for John and those against. If we're not careful, there's going to be a full-blown riot here." No one could hear her talking to herself over the crowd noise. Or no one seemed to pay attention.

"Is it nice to know that so many people care about you and Lauren?" Brian asked.

"I hear them talking about you, too."

"Humph." She could see that Sloane brow rising, questioning if it actually mattered at this point or not. It did; they just didn't have time to talk about it.

"How do we stop this fight?"

The auction had drawn ranchers from several cities, but there were still lots of Aubrey citizens around, egging on the beating of Brian Sloane. They wouldn't have cared if it had been John. Those people believed both brothers were guilty of the death of a beloved teacher. When several opened the corral and shoved the fight into the middle of the already panicked horses, she knew it wasn't going to end well.

If Gargantuan didn't kill John, the horses would. And two-thirds of those in this crowd would let it happen.

"We can't show our faces, Alicia. Think of Lauren's safety."

"But—"

"Stick to the plan. Your turn to leave."

Stick to the plan. It was exactly like John issuing an order. "And then what?"

"Huh?" Brian wasn't the only one paying attention. Those closest to her had given her an extra look or two to see if she was talking to them.

"And then what? We wait on him to be thrown in jail or worse?" She tapped the leg of the man sitting nearest her on the fence and recognized him. Dusty Phillips had bought several horses from Roy before. "Mr. Phillips, can't you please do something to stop this?"

"Why would I want to?" he said before glancing down at her. "Is that you, Alicia? I thought you... What in the world are you wearing?"

The men had rolled and become more visible. The crowd was chanting and she could see that Gargantuan had his forearm across John's larynx, choking him.

"Never mind me, can't you help him? If he passes out, the horses will trample him."

"Get out of there," Brian yelled in her ear. "That guy knows you. John will do a lot worse to me if you're caught."

Dusty shook his head and gripped the white steel rail tighter. "The cops are right there, why not ask them?"

"You know they won't help. Won't somebody stop this?"

"I will, Alicia," Dusty's wife said. "Anyone who's met you and seen you with your little girl knows there's no way you'd do what they're accusing you of. Good luck getting things straightened out. Come on, Dusty."

The couple threw their legs over the fence and dropped in with the horses. Alicia wasn't worried for them. Both Dusty and Carla had been around horses since birth. Carla was a champion barrel racer, and Dusty faced down bulls on a regular basis. Going through the pen was definitely quicker than through the crowd.

Alicia had no idea what Carla intended to do. John was a trained SEAL and hadn't managed to break free.

"Time for this to end, guys," Carla yelled at the police, then looked up at the onlookers. "Craig, David, Kerry, come on, this isn't right. You going to let him choke to death?"

The three men jumped down to the soft dirt and joined Dusty. It took all four of them to pull at the giant to get him to budge.

"Are you really going to just stand there?" Carla shamed the police officer and security guard into helping. Men hopped off the gate and opened it for the two men.

"Remember this, Brian. They think it's you out there."

John had been right. Gargantuan was unbelievably strong, but he was also very intent on not giving up. John twisted, kicked and finally gasped for air.

Alicia's insides seemed to bounce off her skin. Panic? She didn't seem to have any air, either.

The men pulled and pried at the thick hand clasped in place. Then John was free, gulping air. And she could breathe again with him. She was light-headed from just holding her breath. What did John feel like? But he didn't stop. He was on his feet, fists raised, waiting for a second round.

"Come on, Alicia. The cops can take care of the rest. We need to get out of here."

"I'm sort of stuck here."

Everyone wanted to see what was happening and kept pressing her closer and closer to the fencing. Four men could barely hold the giant who'd nearly killed John. She thought the police officer was trying to arrest the huge man.

As John backed up into the unsettled horses, he looked at her, pointed to his ear and shook his head. "I don't think John can hear us anymore."

"Do I need to come get you?" Brian asked.

Initially, she hadn't thought that a hundred people in an open area could trample a person. But confined as she was in her "fat suit," she was beginning to feel trapped. If she could take it off and squeeze through the fence rails, she could hide behind the horses and join John inside the building.

"Go. I'm okay, Brian. I'll meet you there."

Thank goodness she'd kept yoga pants and a tank on under the makeshift baggy clothes they'd filled with padding. Undressing took longer than she wanted, pressed where she was, but she managed. Even the hot metal of the railing touching her skin was cooler than being wrapped inside all those clothes had been. She could probably get out the way she'd come, but it would put her at greater risk than slipping in with the horses. The Phillipses had made such a quick trek through them.

Piece of cake, as Johnny said.

The lovely stock the Adamses had spent so many decades developing circled the paddock, still nervous, but calming as the smoke completely cleared.

Now was the perfect time. With all eyes on Gargantuan's removal to the police car, she slipped through the fence rails, pulled all her clothing through and bundled it in her arms. Then she was off. She bent as far as she could, trying not to be seen above the horses' backs.

She was close. She could see the door leading to the individual stalls. She'd almost made it when the horses stopped circling and all loped away toward the gate. Loud shouting she couldn't understand could be heard over the horses' frightened neighing and angry snorts. She was rooted to the ground, not knowing which way the horses would move next.

Gunshots. Two, then three pops.

The whinnying grew. The horses wanted away from

the danger and would stampede any second. The mare next to her reared. Alicia froze, staring at its underbelly and lashing forelegs.

Chapter Twenty-Five

John's voice was stuck somewhere other than his throat. Maybe Gargantuan had broken the cords, because they wouldn't work. No warning. No question. No nothing. Watching Alicia drop to the ground was the first time he'd ever frozen in fear.

He'd been in firefights in the middle of the Afghanistan desert and not been this frightened. Had the horse kicked her? Was she unconscious? Her arms covered her head while curled in a ball on the ground. She was covered with colorful sweaters and T-shirts and pajama bottoms. It didn't look real, and if he hadn't been paralyzed from the fright coursing through his veins, he might have wondered if it was a dream.

No, this was real. Dev and his dang jinx. Alicia hadn't moved. If he yelled to see if she was conscious, the horses would just spook again. It would have been easier if he hadn't lost the earbud in the fight.

A quick assessment of his surroundings showed the corral gate closed. Gargantuan was now secured inside the cop's car. They were hauling Shauna away for some reason and she was fighting them tooth and nail, screaming obscenities about Weber. Lauren was safe—Dev had texted. He'd heard gunshots. No signs of anyone down or in pursuit.

The mare still pawed at the ground. Folks on the other side of the rail began pointing to the pile of clothes. Then he saw her fingers wiggle. So did the horse.

"Don't move, sweetheart. I'm coming to you. Just stay calm."

The horses continued to dance around. Some guys on the other side of the paddock were trying their best to settle the herd. But they couldn't get to Alicia. He was her only chance.

His girl would move a little, but the colored clothing would move a lot. Then the horse would spook again. "Still, sweetie," he sung to both Alicia and the mare. "Just sit tight…almost there."

All the horses wore halters so they could be led easily in the arena. He just needed to grab… The mare reared her head and twisted out of his reach. "I'm close, hear me, hon? You okay?"

"Yes," she whispered.

"I'm reaching for her halter. Now, when I get it, you know she may buck, so be prepared. Can you see her hooves?"

"I'm ready."

"Great. One more step. And…got it."

The mare danced, hooves prancing in all directions, but he was able to back her hindquarters to the rail and contain most of the pawing away from Alicia. "You're clear. Stand up and let's get out of here. Lauren's safe. Time for her mom to be the same."

She sat, a bright yellow sweater fell to the dark dirt and applause burst out. John finally noticed everyone watching him. And he noticed the two horse wranglers who were calming and removing the horses back to their stalls. One came and took the frightened mare.

John stretched out his arms and pulled Alicia straight to connect her lips to his. A kiss that soothed his soul and hopefully hers. He didn't care if she was ready or not. He wouldn't lose her. She needed to know she was his.

"Don't ever scare me like that again." He wanted to shake her until she swore, but instead he kissed her some more. And she definitely kissed him back.

There was more applause.

"Wow."

"I agree. Maybe the crowd thinks I'm Brian, but I don't care. Dev sent a message as soon as he arrived at the location with Lauren. Hey, you're not putting any weight on your left foot."

"No, the mare stepped—"

He swung her into his arms, leaving the sweaters and pajama pants in the dirt. Her arms were locked tightly around his neck as he strode inside. "Can you tell me what possessed you to stroll into a herd of half-spooked horses?"

His lips couldn't resist touching her forehead, where a soft tendril of hair had escaped its bobby pin.

"I didn't stroll anywhere. I was trying to get out of that crowd and follow you."

"You're lucky they only stepped on your ankle and not your skull."

He continued to the side door of the stables, intent on getting them as far away as possible. Everyone at the auction knew Alicia had been there. And it wouldn't be too long before they confirmed that Lauren hadn't been taken by CPS.

"I think you can put me down now." She adjusted her head and cheek closer to the curve of his shoulder, giving every indication she was comfy resting in his arms.

Tired, physically exhausted, he was more than happy to hold her next to him. He ached to put her down and kiss her into oblivion and back again.

"Let's go. After all we've been through, I don't want you or *Brian* to be arrested. Or wait in a jail cell while the police sort everything out. After they connect his prints to the kidnapping house, Gargantuan will sing for a reduced sentence, connecting Weber to Tory's murder. Then Weber will—"

"Weber will what?" the man in question asked, stopping John in his tracks. He leaned against the side of the stables, an unconscious auction worker at his feet, a 9 mm Glock pointed straight at them. "Weber might just blow your brains out in self-defense right now. Or he could wait. Do you know which he'll choose, John?"

Weber was a killer who didn't fit a profile. You couldn't predict what he would do or when. He could pull the trigger without warning in the blink of an eye. It was the one type of profile that scared John more than those horses trying to stampede in the corral.

"What do you want, Patrick?" Alicia asked, tightening her grip around John's neck.

"Me? I don't want a thing. I'm here capturing the fugitives who've somehow fooled authorities, kidnapped my four-year-old step-granddaughter and caused my wife to shoot at the bodyguard."

"That's why they put her in handcuffs." Alicia had a little wonder in her voice. "She fired the shots and then was arrested. Oh, my, how awful."

John could tell she tried not to smile, but she was happy Shauna was in custody.

Weber rolled his eyes and casually waved his gun. "I can see you're all broken up. No escape for you this time. Having a getaway car hidden somewhere like last night won't help you today."

"My car is in the lot next to the rest, keys are under the mat. That is, if you need a getaway car. I'm sure you're worried about your giant cohort talking to the police." Alicia dropped her arm, sliding it down his back.

Switching her gaze to John, she mouthed, *Let me down.*

As he set her feet gently below her, her hand tugged at the tail of his shirt, slipped under it and lifted the SIG she'd brought to him earlier.

"Do you really think no one's going to catch you, Patrick?" she asked when she faced Weber, keeping the gun pressed against John's back. "There are an awful lot of people who know the truth now. You can't shut all of them up."

How were they going to get the SIG into his hand to defend them?

"You're such a bore, Alicia. Drop the gun that you're obviously trying to get and be done with it."

Alicia let the SIG hit the ground before John could deny it was there, bouncing between his feet.

"Kick it and let's get moving."

He kicked the gun about two feet in front of himself. Only two feet. He could dive and get off several rounds, but not before the psycho pointing his weapon at Alicia would squeeze the trigger.

"Where are we going?" she asked.

"Talking is such a tiresome strategy. It won't stop me from killing you."

"I should hope not."

"What?" John asked together with a surprised Weber.

"Well, um, it would indicate that we're stupid, for one thing. And I don't think any of us are stupid." She faced John and mouthed, *Play along,* then pointed to her ear. "Bullheaded and stubborn, maybe. But not stupid."

He didn't understand her sudden desire to communicate with Weber.

"You know what, Patrick? I'm pretty tired and hot. I'm going to sit right here on this tack box until you make up your mind where we're supposed to go. Aren't you tired, Brian?" She nodded her head and patted the wood next to her so dramatically John knew she was up to something.

She tugged him with her, keeping the gun on the ground just out of his reach.

Then he got it. Her microphone and receiver were still working. Brian must be in the wings giving her instructions.

"Get up. Hands where I can see them, John. It is John. Don't bother to deny it."

"Who's denying?" He shrugged and stayed put. "It feels good to sit and rest a minute. It's so dang hot out here and my feet hurt. They aren't used to the boots."

"Get up. Both of you. Now!"

"I don't think so, Patrick." Alicia stared at Weber but tapped John's leg, then pulled up on her black, stretchy tights. She pointed toward the ground. Stuck securely inside her socks, next to her anklebone, was a sweet snub-nosed pistol. She massaged her legs, coming up the last time palming the gun to where Patrick couldn't see it.

"I love you," he announced, not caring who heard—or threatened their lives. She smiled, looking confident that he'd handle the problem.

He slid his hand over hers and took the gun, pointing it at Weber as he spoke. "We'll wait right here for the cops. Or you pull the trigger and run from the cops, who are most likely on their way already. You go ahead and run in this heat. I'm with my gal here, we're sitting."

Weber looked stunned, totally thrown off while he tried to determine what game they were playing. Then something darkened in his eyes. The confusion cleared and the sinister soul from last night looked at him.

"Stubborn fools."

"Actually, Patrick, I told you we weren't stupid. Why would we ever make killing us easy for you?"

John saw the moment of decision. A microsecond where he knew Weber was tired of the game and would pull the trigger. He raised the snub-nose, pushed Alicia backward off the tack box and fell sideways on top of her.

As he fell, he heard Weber's gun fire and saw the kick-back in his forearm. Slow motion had nothing on waiting to find out where the bullet would hit. Low. Wood splintered. Weber stepped toward the stables for another shot at them both. John fired when he stepped into his sights.

The bullet caught Weber in the shoulder. His weapon fell to the ground as he dropped to his knees. But Weber didn't stop. He reached for the gun, raising it toward his head.

John pictured sitting on the stand, testifying, putting this deranged man behind bars and letting justice decide his punishment. "You're not getting off—" John fired "—that easy."

The weapon dropped to the ground a second time. A twice-shot, but very much alive, Weber fell the opposite direction.

"Is it over?" Alicia asked from under him.

"Sorry, honey." He crawled off her and returned to the tack box, helping her join him.

Brian ran around the corner, breathing hard.

"Where have you been?" John asked his brother.

Sheriff Coleman trotted behind him, didn't stop at the corner and kept trotting his large frame to Weber. He clicked the microphone on his shoulder. "He's alive. Where's that ambulance?"

"He'd better be alive. My team would have my marksmanship ribbon if I'd killed him without trying."

"He killed Tory Strayhorn and orchestrated Lauren's kidnapping," Alicia said. "He may have killed Roy. Shauna's just as guilty and wanted to kill us. She knew what was going on, Ralph. Everything. And—" she turned back to Brian, finally drawing a breath "—where's Lauren? When can I see her?"

"Whoa, slow down, Alicia. It's okay," Brian assured her. "Dev's on his way to the ranch. He'll be there before us."

"Thank goodness. But the police don't know what they did. Who do we need to explain things to? Can I see Lauren before they ask for our statements?"

"I have a feeling the police already know. Otherwise they'd be arresting us." Lauren was safe and John wanted Alicia alone. Now. Before they were required to give statements or explain why they'd avoided the police.

"Shauna and Gargantuan are claiming their innocence. Shouting that it was all Weber's idea from the start. Including Roy's supposed suicide." Brian gave him a sign that they should escape while they could. "Maybe you two should cut out before they realize they need to talk to you. I think there's a little girl at home that's missing her mommy."

"Yes, please? Will it be okay to leave?"

"I'll tell Ralph to come by after dinner. Looks like they have their hands full right now anyway." Brian stuck out his hand to bring John to his feet, pulling him into a quick bear hug.

It was a step toward reconciliation that John needed. But there was something else he had to find out first.

He swung Alicia into his arms again, remembering she couldn't walk. He preferred that she didn't walk, liking her just where she was. "Do you need a medic to look at your ankle?"

"It's just bruised and will be sore. I can walk."

"Not a chance. Still got that earbud?"

"Yes. It took you long enough to realize. Brian kept telling me to stall and then he'd shout at people or tell me not to be an idiot and tick Patrick off."

"Do me a favor."

"Anything." She snuggled closer and kissed his voice box with whisper-soft kisses.

"Hand the earpiece to Brian. Dev's going to have my hide for losing one. I have no idea what he'd do if I lost two."

"But I haven't lost mine."

Brian walked forward and took it from her anyway.

"No tellin' where it's going to end up in just a little while."

"Where are you taking me?" she asked sweetly, holding tighter to his neck.

"Does it matter?"

She smiled as an answer. She didn't make an excuse or try to convince him to stay for the sheriff or police. There was a car in the parking lot. He'd told her he loved her; now it was time to find out if that was enough.

"You may be ready…or not, Alicia. But here I come."

Chapter Twenty-Six

"Why, Johnny Sloane, are you trying to get me into the backseat of your car? Bringing me out to the middle of nowhere didn't even work in high school. I'm flattered, but I'd really like to see my little girl."

Alicia joked, but she had no idea where they were going. The air-conditioning felt wonderful on full blast, so they weren't melting in the heat.

"I only need a couple of minutes alone with you. Just a couple. Promise," he said, nibbling at her fingertips laced through his strong hand. "I don't think either of us will fit back there as comfortably as we did when we were teenagers."

He turned toward the ranch, but he'd given her the impression they weren't headed straight home. Maybe he'd changed his mind and was taking her to Lauren after all.

"I am ready. I was wrong last night, or this morning, whatever time it was out in the field."

He kissed the back of her hand. "I know."

"Where are we going?"

"There's something I need to do here."

"But this is…" *The fire.*

"Yeah, it's Mrs. Cook's place."

"Why do you need to come to where the fire happened?"

"Closure. Coming full circle. It just seems appropriate."

He stopped in the field where they'd parked as teens. The old barn had burned to the ground back then. Any remnants had been cleared away. But there was a familiar tree and stone wall that he led her to.

The last place they'd argued. He offered to pick her up, but she wanted to walk, to give herself time to think. She'd listened back then, wishing he'd just be satisfied to stay in Texas.

John lifted her to the top of the ancient rock wall. Most of it had broken away and lay at their feet. They could still sit like they had when he'd spoken about seeing all the far-away countries...about leaving.

"Twelve years ago, I left without a real goodbye. I thought we'd broken up and didn't really see any sense trying to apologize. I admit to being cocky and that the idea of having a girlfriend back home wasn't my first priority. Dang it, I was eighteen." He laughed at his embarrassment. "I didn't think I was coming back to Aubrey. For some reason, I never thought you'd leave."

"It's okay, I—"

"It's my turn, Alicia." He swallowed hard but didn't look away.

Whatever he had to say, it was important. Lauren was safe and John mattered to her. So she could hear him out before they went home.

"I was a hurt kid back then. I'm sorry. I've been around the world and back again, hon. And I know it'll seem odd, but I'm ready to come home. You can take as long as you need to 'get ready.' I'll be here when you are. I love you. I always have."

"My turn?"

He laughed and nodded, not releasing her hands.

"I sort of expected something like this when we pulled up. I mean, you said that you loved me back at the auction. Your actions, though—putting everything on the line for

Lauren and me like you have… Well, you've shown me that you love me many times over in the past couple of days."

"I'm glad I was doing something right."

"I didn't want to feel like this. But not for the reasons you think. I kept thinking it would be disloyal to my marriage. Then Brian said he'd known his best friend and that Dwayne would be glad we were together. He's right. Dwayne would want me to be happy. He'd want us all to be happy. I am so ready to love you, John."

He tugged her to her feet and kissed her. The moment his lips touched hers, guilt-free desire took over. No more anxiety and no more questions. Being with him was her future. She was certain of it.

"Are you staying around here for a while?" If he wasn't, she had every intention of staying wherever he was stationed. "You don't have to give up your career in the navy, unless that's what you really want."

"I'm home for good. We should head back. You need to introduce me to Lauren."

"She's going to love having a dad."

HOME. IT WAS full, cramped, and John loved it. The house smelled like fried chicken, white gravy and peanut-butter cookies—his mom's recipe. Mabel had started cooking chicken nuggets as soon as Dev had pulled in the driveway with Lauren. Now the little girl, soon to be his daughter, was asleep in his arms and still had a chocolate-milk mustache.

She was a resilient kid and had voluntarily crawled into his lap. It might help that he looked exactly like Brian, who she'd known all her life, but today, he'd accept all the trust and love she shared.

"You're lucky I'm not fighting you to hold my darling

girl." Alicia kissed Lauren's forehead and then John's as she perched next to him on the chair.

"I thought I'd give you a break." He leaned his head back and was rewarded with a long kiss. Something he'd never tire of. He lowered his voice so only Alicia could hear. "Brian spoke to me while you were bathing Lauren. He's determined to find out who framed us and really set the fire."

"It was such a long time ago. Does it even matter anymore?"

"It does to him. He said he needs to clear our name, but it's more than that. I don't know what. I tried to convince him it didn't matter. There's time to sort it out later."

Alicia laced her fingers with his. "I can understand, but it seems futile. Maybe he'll feel different when things settle down."

"You two can stop your smooching, now. Right, Dad?" Brian lowered his voice as soon as he noticed Lauren. He set his cell on the coffee table before sitting in the only other chair in the living room. "This thing's been ringing nonstop. I didn't know anyone had my number. The sheriff said Patrick ranted about his ruined plans all the way to the hospital. It appears he was leaving for Mexico so he could kill Shauna, too. Now they're all headed for prison."

"Did I hear you talking about the mare earlier?"

"Yeah, with Dusty Phillips. You'd think he'd give us a couple of days before attempting to finalize the deal on the mare I've been trying to sell to him for weeks."

His dad tapped where his watch should have been. Seems he'd made a lot of improvements in the past two days.

"Why now?" Brian said aloud for him. "No auction of the Adamses' stock, for one. National championships for Carla. If she's riding again this year, she needs a new horse."

"Do you want to sell her, Brian?" Alicia asked from the arm of John's chair.

"No question of want. We have to sell her or lose this place."

"As soon as—"

"We aren't taking your money, Alicia," Brian said firmly, and his dad nodded.

Thank God J.W. was going to recover. He wanted the relationship with his father that Brian took for granted. He also wanted to restore the relationship with his brother. "How about mine?"

"We need a lot more than you've got in the bank."

Dev laughed from the kitchen, where he'd been helping Mabel with KP duty.

"There's ten grand in my room. How much do you need?"

"Where did you get so much cash?"

"He's really good at poker," Dev answered for him. "He also has no life. No rent. No real car. No women."

"I like my truck."

"Chicks hate it."

"That's true. But I figure I've got enough to get this place back on its feet, hire a couple of hands. Give Dad time to recover and give you a much deserved vacation."

"Johnny, I do believe you've shocked your brother into silence." Mabel dried her hands on her ever-present apron. "With that, you should all go find a place to sleep. Key to my house is under the third flowerpot on the back porch. I'm staying here in case your dad needs something."

His dad's expression was different than it had been three days ago. There was no panic in his eyes, just acceptance.

"I'm driving back to my cabin and inventorying my gear. If one cable is missing, I'm tracking it down." Dev held a finger in the air for emphasis, but destroyed his tough demand with a grin.

"I have a nice comfy bed in the other room. That means you guys can have Mabel's guest room all to yourselves." Brian laughed. "Good luck with your new family, bro."

"No luck needed when love's involved," John told him.

Alicia kissed his lips, stroked Lauren's cheek with a tender finger and rested her head on the top of his. "Piece of cake."

* * * * *

The TEXAS FAMILY RECKONING *miniseries*
continues next month.
Look for THE RENEGADE RANCHER
by Angi Morgan

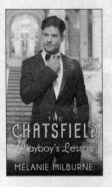

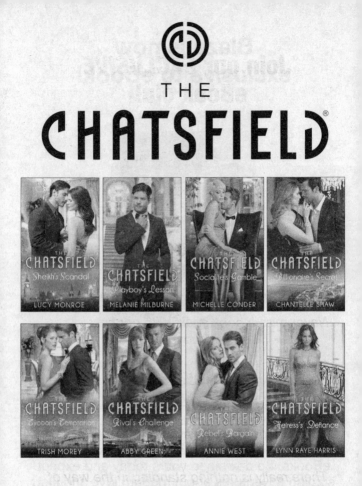

Which series will you try next?

HEARTWARMING

Wholesome, heartfelt relationships

4 new stories every month

Only available online

HISTORICAL

Awaken the romance of the past…

6 new stories every month

Medical Romance

The ultimate in romantic medical drama

6 new stories every month

MODERN™

Power, passion and irresistible temptation

8 new stories every month

MODERN tempted™

True love and temptation!

4 new stories every month

You can also buy Mills & Boon® eBooks at
www.millsandboon.co.uk

MILLS & BOON®
Book Club

Join the Mills & Boon Book Club

> Subscribe to **Intrigue** today for
> 3, 6 or 12 months and you could
> **save over £40!**

We'll also treat you to these fabulous extras:

 FREE L'Occitane gift set
worth £10

 FREE home delivery

🌹 **Rewards scheme, exclusive**
offers…and much more!

Subscribe now and save over £40
www.millsandboon.co.uk/subscribeme